# NOBILITAS

# NOBILITAS

*A Novel of Ancient Rome*

Neil Himsworth

Book Guild Publishing
Sussex, England

First published in Great Britain in 2009 by
The Book Guild
Pavilion View
19 New Road
Brighton, BN1 1UF

Typesetting in Baskerville by
Keyboard Services, Luton, Bedfordshire

Printed in Great Britain by
CPI Antony Rowe

A catalogue record for this book is available from
The British Library

ISBN 978 1 84624 355 4

*To Margo*

# Notes on Language, History and Names

The book is written in modern English with liberal use of the progressive tense. There may even be split infinitives. This is purely to make the book readable – and is due to my complete lack of Latin.

The path of descent for Roman Britain from prosperous province to a Saxon-dominated land subjected to the Dark Ages is not clear. Most sources I have read seem to point to a gradual, rather than catastrophic, decline.

What is certain is that Britain's fate was determined by events elsewhere in Europe. By AD 410 the western half of the Roman Empire under the leadership of Honorius was in disarray. In 402 troops had been withdrawn from Britain in large numbers to help fight on Rome's mainland borders. The effort was futile: Gaul fell and Britain was cut off from Rome.

Constantine III took an army from Britain and was successful in retaking large parts of Gaul by 409. This forced Honorius to recognise him as joint-leader. But the peace did not last. While Romans bickered, Visigoths sacked Rome in 410 and Constantine lost control of Britain.

At the same time, Roman Britain faced invasion from a coalition of Picts and Saxons. Civic leaders appealed to Emperor Honorius for assistance. But he could not help as Gaul, the route to Britain, was no longer completely under his control. Instead he sent them a letter stating that they were free of their obligations to the empire and that they should look to their own defences.


Coel Hen, Old King Coel, appears to have existed, though he may not have been the one referred to in the nursery rhyme. The Votadini tribe, based north of Hadrian's Wall, were long-standing allies of Roman Britain. As for everyone else in the book they are pure fiction.

The places referred to in the book are all authentic. A name that surprised me was the one for York. I have followed scholars' references to the city as Eburacum rather than the more common Eboracum, arguing whichever is correct will no doubt keep someone amused.

Malton, which is the location for the climactic battle, has been referred to by its Roman name of Derventio. The town's museum is worth a visit for its Roman section alone. Hadrian's Wall, of course, still exists and is an essential trip for any number of reasons – it might even spark your imagination. As a child I visited it many times and wondered what life would have been like for people living around it. This book is, in part, the product of those visits.

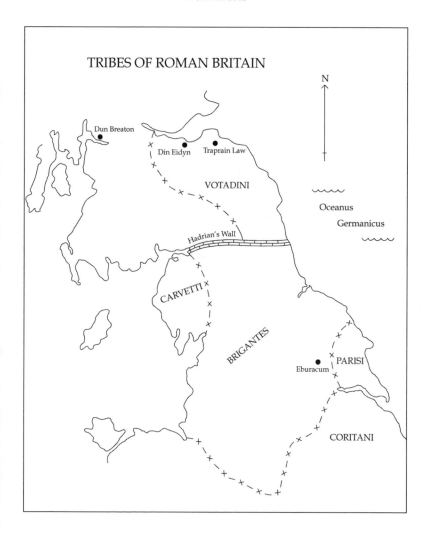

TRIBES OF ROMAN BRITAIN

N

Dun Breaton

Din Eidyn    Traprain Law

VOTADINI

Oceanus

Germanicus

Hadrian's Wall

CARVETTI

BRIGANTES

PARISI

Eburacum

CORITANI

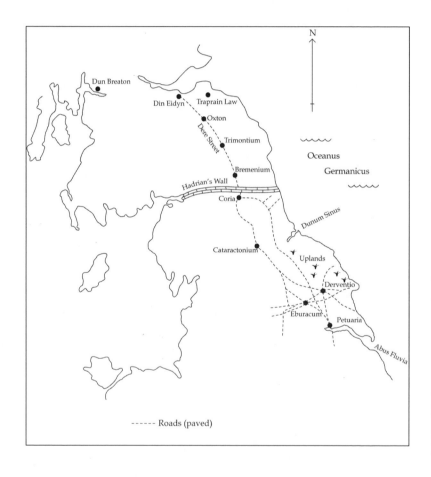

# *Prologue*

'Uncouth, ignorant and proud of it,' muttered the gnarled old senator as he tried to lift his frame out of a highly polished leather saddle to give a better vantage to his small, bulging eyes. 'You will have to travel far beyond the borders of our civilised world before you come across a more odious and repulsive people.' His words were lost before they left the confines of a narrow, muddy track that wound its way through dense pine trees. Ahead were the leading troopers of a cavalry escort, who had just left the dankness of the forest for more sparingly wooded meadows.

'Bloody good fighters though, Senator,' answered a battle-scarred officer riding just behind the old man. He gently nudged his horse around the senator's, expectorating spittle over a low bank of moss as he passed.

'D-Difficult times, Senator Antonius,' suggested Flavius, a young, clean-shaven man, desperate to make amends for the disrespect shown by the other rider. Flavius knew better than to risk the old man's temper. He and his family wielded enormous power and influence in the empire.

'Difficult!' replied Antonius, burying his face into the hood of his riding cloak to cough. Flavius noticed blood on the back of the senator's hand, which he quickly wiped away, not wanting to show weakness or illness to the enemy.

1

The effort had left the old man breathless. Flavius waited respectfully for him to carefully fold a piece of silk cloth, pedantically marrying corners, and continue. 'Desperate, I'd say, for us to have to meet with this scum.' The senator's horse snorted as though in agreement and two jets of steam added to the damp, dreary mist at the edge of the woods. 'Never forget, Flavius, that we are *nobilitas*, guardians of the greatest empire the world has ever seen. It is our duty to do everything in our power to ensure its survival so that it may continue to serve our needs.'

'But meeting these barbarians and offering Roman children as hostages, sir?' Flavius watched the cavalrymen stealthily testing their swords and tightening the arm straps of their shields. Some gazed ahead while others cast furtive glances to the sides.

'Sometimes small sacrifices have to be made for the greater good. That is the trait of a Roman and is the source of our strength.'

The old man should have been seeing out his last days in the comfort of Rome, cared for by the best physicians in the city and tended by his favourite house slaves, thought Flavius. Instead Antonius had eschewed such thoughts of peaceful rooms in his secluded apartment and ridden across Europe to help with these negotiations. Maybe he just didn't think Flavius was up to the task.

'Not that I don't trust you to do the right thing or make sacrifices should the need arise, Flavius,' Antonius continued, seemingly reading the younger man's mind. 'It's that we have to be strong and push ourselves harder for the greater good. You might have to see this through yourself. After I have seen the emperor I will be at my physical limit and may, at best, be a nuisance. Then the glory of Rome's survival will be yours alone.'

'What of the emperor, sir? He has approved the plan, I presume?'

'At last! They've decided to get things moving.'

'Sir?'

'You've missed out not being in the army. Listen,' whispered the old man.

Flavius pulled the hood of his riding cloak down but could hear nothing. 'To what, sir?'

'Exactly! There are no sounds, no birds or animals, which means that men are in the trees flanking us. There will be men on the track ahead but their real power will be spread out in the bushes to our sides.'

Flavius turned left and right, peering over thinning gorse, the barbs brittle and stems browning. Beyond the low bushes, the dark depths of the forest were guarded by occasional silvery beech trees. Yellow and orange splashes of curled leaves waited for a breeze to pluck and scatter them. Try as he might he could see no signs of the enemy and turned back, frustrated that an old man's perception was greater than his. He looked at Antonius, who suddenly seemed more energised.

'Emperors are merely cogs in the machinery of the empire. Some are strong while others are weak. But they are only men with limited lifespans and that makes them servants of the empire and, therefore, of the *nobilitas*. It has always been so.'

'But if the emperor hasn't approved this, it can't possibly work,' said Flavius in a hoarse whisper. The officer who had been riding with them was now at the head of the column, moving slowly towards an opening in the trees.

'Good! About time those Saxons got a move on – probably recovering from a hangover. Can't take their own weak ale, I'd wager,' replied Antonius, ignoring Flavius' plea for reassurance. 'Don't fret so. I told you we, the *nobilitas*, are the true authority of Rome. But, yes, the emperor will approve once I have explained the situation to him, rest assured.'

Flavius felt comforted by the senator's words. He'd heard enough not to argue the point and turned his attention down the track. Save for horses playing with their bridles and a distant metallic hammering, the forest around them was silent – just as Antonius had observed. Slowly, the officer walked his horse barely twenty paces beyond the head of the detail, swung himself off his mount and slid his feet onto the track. Facing him were six surly-looking Saxons. Each had their heads tonsured and long, plaited hair hung around their shoulders.

The officer with the leading troopers opened his cloak to show that he carried no sword and wore a tunic in the Saxon style. Then he raised his arm as a signal to more of his guards tending two wagons.

'A present for your king,' proclaimed the officer, in Germanic, as fifteen Saxon prisoners, each with their hands bound with leather thongs behind their backs, were led out of the wagons. 'To do with as your king sees fit,' finished the officer.

Mixed with the band of captured warriors were four women, all of an age to catch a man's eye. The Roman officer knew why the guards grinned greedily at the prisoners. If the king followed his normal custom, the prisoners would be the property of the men who had liberated them – those on escort duty. The warriors would be made to promise a ransom from future plunder and the women would be sold to the highest bidders, giving a fine profit, even after the king's dues were paid. Some of the guards looked as though they might bid for the women themselves.

With the guards distracted, tension lessened. Antonius, head buried deep in his riding cloak nudged his horse off the track and joined the officer, who held his horse. 'I am Cirius Antonius, you will take me to your king.'

The largest of the escort stood in the middle of the track

4

with a double-headed axe across his torso. He looked the old man up and down before he broke his silence. 'King Aelred accepts your offerings and awaits your company.'

The old man waved an arm and two more riders slowly joined him, each trailing a packhorse. Dismounting, the riders abandoned their mounts to a legionary but kept a tight hold on the reins of the packhorses.

There were no more pleasantries. The leader of the escort waved his axe as a signal for the group to follow. Hugging the hillside's contours, a deeply rutted track wound its way towards a village that gradually materialised out of dense fog that seemed to roll in huge banks off the nearby sea. Flavius noted that surrendering the most direct route for the road to the environment indicated a lack of engineering skill, but worse to Roman sensibilities was the bad odour that clung to the escort.

Ahead of them a rough wooden palisade surrounded countless thatched buildings, a quarter of a mile away. Even before they crossed a crude wooden bridge, over two hundred paces from a half-open gate the Roman could smell the source of the escort's distinctive aroma. Another engineering problem – poor sanitation.

The group, with the Saxon prisoners still bound, followed their escort across a defensive ditch and passed the heavy timbers of a gate. Inside the stench rose. Open sewers ran between primitive rectangular mud huts and mixed with outflows from animal pens. The big Saxon looked straight at Flavius. 'You no like smell of Roman wall?' he asked in staccato Latin.

'What?'

'You Romans like baths, yes? So we give legionaries who attack chance to swim through our shit and piss.' He swept his axe towards an inner ditch full of sewage. Even if your legions are stronger than Saxons we can still say that we pissed on you!' The big Saxon gave a deep roar of laughter, which was joined by the rest of the escort and the prisoners.

The silence of the forest had followed them, though this time they were the ones disturbing the normal occupants. Flavius could feel stares pricking him like sharpened arrowheads. Warriors, children, women and old men stopped and looked at them. A generation ago, thought Flavius, when his father was a tribune with the legions, men would have shirked from the Romans and children would have hidden themselves behind their mothers. Now they just gawped. Deference to Rome, its army, its engineering, its civilisation, had vanished. Something had changed and he would help the senator put that respect back into Rome's enemies.

Only a metallic hammering continued unchecked and soon its source was revealed. Between tightly packed huts young boys, presumably slaves, pulled on bellows that fed huge furnaces. Heavily muscled men punched great hammers against anvils, turning molten metal into axes, knives and swords. Occasionally one of them would plunge hot metal into a trough of water and steam would explode with a hiss. Taking account of the growing pile of weapons, Flavius judged that the men and boys had been busy for some time.

'They don't mind us seeing their defences and war preparations. That's confidence, sir,' whispered Flavius to the senator.

'Confident nothing! These barbarians are too stupid to think of blindfolds. Believe me, they're scum.'

The track turned sharply away from the furnaces and rose up an embankment. Below them mud was everywhere. Like a sea it lapped up to the stony track and wrapped itself around every wooden building. Maybe that was why the Saxons fought so hard to get into Gaul, thought Flavius. They wanted to escape to paved roads and solid, stone buildings so that they wouldn't drown in the chaos of such quagmires.

The stink lessened as they passed through an inner palisade and the track at last gave out onto a boot-sucking morass that passed as a high street. Antonius let Flavius hold his horse while he dismounted onto firmer ground. He pulled out a wooden staff that had been strapped to his horse and pushed back his riding cloak. As he intended he was immediately the centre of attention, for beneath he wore a far more finely tailored cloak, dyed purple – the colour of luxury – and stitched with golden thread.

Flavius could see men from the escort beckoning to them to walk along rough duckboards towards a large building, floating like a ship on a brown lake. Presumably it was the Great Hall and seat of power. Antonius held his ground, ignoring everyone around him, letting them see that he was in control. Flavius joined him in surveying the scene to the north of the village, away from their direction of approach. Crude wooden piers jutted out into an estuary, half-drained by an ebbing tide to reveal banks of mud and sand. But Flavius was stunned by the number of ships moored alongside the piers and countless more that were pulled high onto the estuary's banks.

'There must be dozens of boats, sir,' Flavius couldn't help himself. The sight was like nothing he'd witnessed before.

'Over three hundred and fifty, according to my information – but keep that to yourself for now, eh?' replied Antonius in a matter-of-fact tone, letting his gaze be seemingly distracted by sea birds flapping round the thatched roof of the Great Hall.

'They don't need to wait for the Rhine to freeze over,' went on Flavius, gushing with the knowledge of the danger he now saw. 'They can leap behind our lines any time they choose.'

Antonius smoothed his tightly shaven grey hair. 'I'm so glad you now perceive the seriousness of the situation.' His wrinkled face broke into a gentle smile as the birds settled on the roof's apex. 'Time to meet our host, I believe.'

Gulls circled overhead and screeched a mocking call as the men walked towards a flight of wide, wooden steps. 'That laugh of theirs makes me think that maybe they know something about this venture we don't,' said Antonius. 'Still, Rome wasn't built with faint hearts.' He marched up the stairs towards a heavy, wooden door weighed down with a myriad of ornate carvings.

When they entered, the Romans were searched then ushered to chairs. Slaves cleaned their boots and dabbed at flecks of mud on their cloaks, while others held basins of water and towels for each to refresh himself. At a nod from a guard the slaves bowed and slid backwards behind a curtained door.

'Come in Antonius, my Roman friend,' commanded a booming voice from the other end of the hall. 'At last we meet in person.' Flaming torches provided the only light and it took a few moments for the Romans' eyes to adjust. Flavius and the Roman officer followed Antonius as he moved nearer the voice. At the other end of the hall, Flavius began to make out the shape of the large Saxon who had led the escort, whispering to a man seated on a throne, presumably King Aelred. In front of the king were four large, wooden chests.

'You didn't need to deliver the hostages yourself. Perhaps you have come to check on our preparations, Antonius?' enquired the king as they seated themselves before him.

'I can see that you are well along with your side of the bargain,' replied Antonius. 'I have brought the men with me who will fulfil our side of the deal.'

'And if they don't?'

8

'Rome's families would not look too kindly on failure.' Antonius was seized by a bout of coughing and took a sip from a wooden goblet to sooth his convulsions. 'And some of Rome's finest families would weep for their lost children when the hostages we have brought with us, and who stand at the edge of the forest, become your property.'

Both men left a silence, thinking through their next moves. 'You are a calculating old devil, Senator, which is why your plan will work,' said the king jovially. He stood and walked towards Flavius and the Roman officer. He looked into the eyes of both men and held his gaze on the officer, examining his face. Even in the weak torchlight a wicked scar below his left eye was clearly visible. 'You have brought an administrator and a fighting officer. Saxon?' He pointed at his own right cheek.

'Battleaxe from a powerful Saxon warrior, your highness. Got through my shield,' replied the officer, recognising the reference to his scar. The king smiled. 'Just before he died on my sword.'

King Aelred checked his smile. 'This man will follow orders and this one,' turning to Flavius, 'no doubt has your cunning, but he'll be too scared not to follow orders. Yes, you both will do. Antonius, you have chosen well.'

Flavius felt belittled by the ridicule the barbarian king was pouring on him and burned with the desire to show his strength. 'We need to check the gold, sir,' he said to Antonius.

'As promised – your clerk can count it,' said King Aelred, nodding at Flavius and turning to the chests. 'Half now and the rest on completion. You know the best thing about this is that it's gold taken from Romans. And I'll be able to get it back, and more, next summer.'

'The children, my lord,' said the officer in a barely concealed snarl. The king whipped round as though the man had produced a dagger. 'What guarantees can you give that they will be well treated?'

Flavius shrivelled on the spot. The officer was unarmed and yet still challenged the king in his own hall. From the tone he may as well have told the Saxon that if any harm came to one of them he'd lose an arm or his head. There was only one person who seemed to be in danger of that. What madness!

King Aelred strode back to the officer and looked at him again, as though he'd missed something the first time round. 'You surprise me. A Roman soldier with a conscience. Very interesting.' The king nodded to a guard and eight young women were ushered into the hall. 'These women will look after the welfare of the children and answer to me alone in this matter.'

'Thank you, sir. I'll see you next year,' replied the officer.

# Chapter I

Mannius pulled back his blankets and felt the cold of a new day sweep across his face. In the fortified town of Coria – on the very edge of the Empire – close to Hadrian's Wall, mornings were always bracing. Late spring promised to delay its appearance yet again: the weather carried on with its cold, wet storms as though it had forgotten that winter had ended. An insistent pounding of a moment ago had been replaced by the drip-drip of water splashing into leather buckets around his room. Nothing worked any more: the hypocaust on the lower floors seemed to have suffered a terminal collapse; the hot room at his favourite bath house was habitually only capable of producing tepid temperatures and now not even the roof was weatherproof. No one wanted to spend money to repair things like roofs when they might have to flee in the face of an invading horde. But in any case there were too few skilled craftsmen to fix things these days. Everything seemed to be decaying. Only the adventurers, foolhardy or those too lazy to think of somewhere else to go ventured this far north.

Watching Eithne, his slave girl, take a flame to an oil lamp he wondered which category he fell into. A powerful glow flared, silhouetting her thighs – naked, smooth and shapely – beneath her light sleeping gown. Eithne turned towards him. More lamps soaked her in golden light and, through the thin material, he saw her firm breasts. There were of course other reasons to stay in Coria.

She placed his tunic on a chair next to his cot. Mannius

11

idly stretched out and ran a hand over the girl's thighs – feeling the warmth and firmness of her skin. Unusually she pulled away. 'Sir, we got visitors.'

'Tell them to wait until my surgery's open.'

'But sir, it's the governor's men – official like.'

'Tell them I know the governor.'

'Sir, it's the governor himself.'

Mannius brought himself up with a start. 'What's the panic? Is he ill?' As soon as he uttered the words he knew that the governor must have ridden through the night from Eburacum – a good test of fitness and health if ever one was needed.

Unannounced the wooden door opened and a soldier stepped in before being followed by an old, bearded man. 'Ill? Never been fitter in my life. But thank you for asking. Now child, get your master some wine and I'll have a drop while you're about it.'

Eithne nodded and conscious of the governor's gaze, covered her chest with her arms. While Mannius fumbled with his tunic the governor watched the slave girl leave to tend to her duties.

'She'd fetch a pretty price at the market.'

'She's too good to sell,' replied Mannius, sluicing water from a bowl over his head and dampening his hair. 'She's a first-rate nurse.'

'And helps you with your anatomical studies, I'd wager.'

Mannius felt himself redden slightly. The governor had spent most of his life in the army and was used to its coarseness, something Mannius had never fully come to terms with.

The governor sniffed disapprovingly at the buckets collecting rainwater and selected a chair by Mannius' writing desk. 'Sorry for the rude awakening.'

'Not at all, Governor.' Mannius always used formal titles rather than familiar names when others were present –

even if they were only soldiers or slaves. He tried to orientate himself to the day. Through the window he could see dark rain clouds that wrestled to strangle the early light of dawn into a feeble grey. For the governor to be up and about this early, something must be important.

Eithne returned with a tray. The governor looked on expectantly but the slave girl had replaced her sleeping robe with a working tunic and her hair was tied up. Disappointed, the governor turned his attention back to Mannius. The sharp eyes of the old man must have caught the questioning look on his face.

'These men,' said the governor waving an arm round the room. Mannius noticed that the guard at the door had been joined by another tough-looking officer. 'Are at your disposal. I suggest you take them as your bodyguard.' Eithne placed a plate of bread and cheese on a table and poured wine into two silver goblets. 'Now I need a moment with your master.' The slave girl bowed her head and left, followed by the soldiers.

'Time is precious for both of us so I'll get straight to it. I need someone I trust to deliver a message and then organise things until I can get back to help.'

'Of course, sir.' Without conscious thought Mannius slipped into respectful military tones. 'Happy to help.'

'You've met King Cathal.' Without waiting for so much as a nod the governor ploughed on. 'Putting guesswork onto what I know, I'd say we'll like as not have our defences tested on two or three fronts – at the same time – just like sixty-seven.'

'The Barbarian Conspiracy?' The governor stayed silent and sipped from his goblet. It was the nightmare used to quell troublesome children: less than fifty years previously Picts, Scotti and Saxons had coordinated their efforts and raided unchecked across much of Britain. 'A little before my time, I'm afraid.'

13

A silence hung between them. Presumably the governor was letting the message sink in. Then he stirred. 'There's plenty to be afraid of, mark my words. If you can get to Cathal and alert him to the danger he might be able to fend off any attack in his kingdom and keep our northern border secure. I need some time to sort things out down here before I can move to help him.'

'And if King Cathal can't hold out – we'll have to fight on two fronts at the same time?'

The governor nodded. 'We can't do that now. In the old days we'd have had enough men to hold them all while we destroyed them one by one.' The governor sighed. 'Since Constantine proclaimed himself emperor and decided to take the best of our legions to Gaul and assert his cause we've had no replacements – not one. It's even worse than your days in the army: we've recruited as many of the locals as we can but we rely too heavily on Saxon mercenaries, and who knows whether they'll fight if an organised Saxon fleet appears on our shoreline instead of the usual raiding parties.'

'You want King Cathal to hold in the north while you fight off Saxons to the south?'

'That's about the long and short of it. Mind, I can't spare any troops because I need every man I can get to meet this year's Saxons, now that the fighting season's nearly upon us, and I know they're coming – I'm certain of that. With a bit of warning he might be able to hold for a few weeks or move his people closer to the Wall – this side if necessary.'

'But – why me?'

'Because you're the son of my brother and I trust you. The king'll trust you. Both you and your father have treated him and his family – that's got to be worth something. And as you'll be acting as my representative you'll carry the rank of tribune – here's your commission.'

14

The governor handed over an ornate scroll stating that Mannius was *tribunus sexmestris* – normally a middle-ranking officer serving for six months but under present circumstances he would probably be the most senior officer for miles around. 'We've even brought you the uniform and armour. It'll help to show King Cathal that we still have respect for him and his people. You'll also get more respect round here to sort out any loose ends.'

Against his father's wishes, Mannius had entered the army. Unsponsored, he had risen quickly to the rank of optio – deputy to a centurion – primarily because he was one of the only ones who could read and write rather than as a direct result of his military prowess. Occasionally he'd acted as centurion during his commander's absences, but never in battle. Now the governor was suggesting that he take a position of command.

'Sir, I have a surgery – sick patients to tend.'

The governor slammed his goblet down on the table. He must be tired, thought Mannius, but there was a passion in him that left the young physician in no doubt that the old man was ready and willing to fight. 'These days everyone has at least two jobs. All I'm giving you is a temporary role in the army for a couple of weeks at most.'

Only the governor had just one job as far as Mannius knew – though he put in enough effort to cover five. He travelled the length and breadth of the country, pushing his tired old body on, trying to keep the remnants of the army happy, stopping mercenaries and their families defecting, and keeping the locals on his side. Taking this one burden from the old man would be a way of treating the stress he was under. Mannius consoled himself with the thought that at worst he would only be helping with a little organisation and at best all he might do would be to act as a messenger.

'When would you like me to go?'

Mannius saw the lines on the old man's brow lessen and his eyes shone with genuine warmth and gratitude. 'If it's not too much to ask, I suggest we have your slave provide some porridge, then we'll both be off on our business.'


Long years had passed since any Roman forces had been permanently based north of Hadrian's Wall. Yet stout, stone forts built centuries previously still stood, spaced periodically along the side of Dere Street, the main north-south road on the eastern side of the country. They had become eerily quiet, overgrown by moss and weeds. Some buildings had been pillaged for stone, though the locals had little ability with it, and a few forts had been taken over by extended families and turned into farmsteads. Most, though, were left empty. Bawling centurions and parading legionaries had been replaced by occasional visits from shepherds and their sheep.

In the growing gloom, Mannius counted off the old forts and fortlets, imagining what life must have been like inside. Such games kept him distracted from the rain that whipped against the three riders and prevented all attempts at conversation. Not that Mannius expected more than a grunt of acknowledgement to anything he said from either of his two bodyguards. As far as Mannius was concerned, the ride was now about getting to Fort Bremenium as quickly as possible without exhausting their horses. Buried in the hood of his leather riding cloak he hoped that the straps wouldn't come loose again. Alternating between trapping the thongs under his chin and biting on them passed another mile or so.

One of the bodyguards drew his horse alongside Mannius, grunted something unintelligible and waved towards the paved road on their right. After a moment's hesitation, Mannius guessed they had travelled farther than he realised. He slowed his horse, pulling on the reins to move it off the soft turf, across a ditch and onto the road. The hard surface was more of a strain for the horses so the riders reduced their speed. Changing pace meant he had to alter his riding position, which gave the rain a chance to find another way under his cloak.

The old, stone ruins of Fort Bremenium had become a regular forward position for Roman patrols. Situated twenty-five miles north of the Wall, its solid stone and clay walls, enclosed behind rings of ditches and perched on the side of a hill, provided reassurance to men in potentially hostile territory. Dere Street ran close to the north-east section of the fort. To the west, fields fell steeply away to a river that wound its way out of a pine forest that stretched for miles before giving way to moorland heather. Even as the last light of the day was squeezed out earlier than usual by dark clouds, the view from the entrance reminded Mannius of happy times riding across moorland fells with his father. Maybe it was time to move to less troubled parts of the empire and ride across some more tranquil lands, perhaps with a son of his own.

An optio in charge of the guards at a makeshift gate brought Mannius out of his musings. After declaring his identity and showing his papers, two old carts, barring the only useable entrance, were pulled aside. Across a cobbled quadrangle smoke curled out of old barrack rooms and was accompanied by a constant buzz of chatter that signalled men relaxing between duties. Shouted orders erupted from different parts of the ruins as officers moved round, checking sentries and organising tasks. Unseen, came a ubiquitous and comforting hammering sound. As long as Mannius could remember, throughout their waking hours, soldiers somewhere hammered stakes into the ground: for tent pegs, target practice, fence posts, palisades; the list was endless. At least some things hadn't changed with the passing of time.

Mannius dismounted by the officers' quarters, left his horse with his bodyguards and went in search of the commanding centurion. Two legionaries standing guard outside the low building came smartly to attention and saluted as he entered. Rainwater cascaded freely into the corridor and collected in large puddles. Trying to sound like an important officer, Mannius kept the crash of his hobnailed caligae as even as possible – all the time desperate not to slip on the broken, wet stone flags of the floor. Staying aloof he ignored laughter, curses and petty arguments in rooms either side of the corridor. Outside the commander's office another legionary stood guard. As Mannius approached, the guard gently tapped on the door.

'Good evening, Tribune,' said Centurion Curtius, rising. Somehow word of Mannius' new rank had gone ahead of him. Curtius saluted, then offered his hand, a friendly smile taking over his wrinkled and weather-beaten face. 'I've sent my orderly off for some food.'

'Seems a long time ago since I was with you.'

'Aye, must be seven years since you were a wet behind the ears optio, and now look at you. But I guess you didn't come here to reminisce with an old man.'

'Sadly not,' agreed Mannius. 'Yesterday the governor issued an edict: all military forces are to be withdrawn south of the Wall with immediate effect.'

Curtius dropped back onto his chair as though he'd been winded. 'But we always make a big demonstration this time of year. Reminds everyone in these parts we're still around before the raiding season proper gets going.'

'We both know it's much better to appear strong and

18

not have to fight than to have to clear up a mess afterwards,' said Mannius, trying to be sympathetic. 'But orders are orders – though I have a little discretion in the exact timing of your unit's move south.' The young tribune checked himself: this was the first test. The governor had impressed upon him the need to be careful with giving out too many details – even to those he would normally trust without a second thought.

'Aye, orders are always orders, no matter how daft. I've learnt that over the years. Do you reckon it's on account of some of the army down south deserting, and we're needed to plug the gaps?'

A sharp tap on the door signalled that two orderlies had arrived with trays of food. Both men fell silent and watched as the trays were carefully set down on a makeshift table – an old door held up by shortened beams that looked as though they'd been taken from the roof. No wonder it leaked. Curtius filled two leather cups with wine and offered one to Mannius.

'You might be right,' said Mannius, picking up the conversation. 'Like most of the army, I suspect that they probably haven't been paid in months.'

'And they haven't got the wit to make a little profit to keep everything sweet.'

'Being on the border probably gives you a few more trading opportunities, but you're right. I'd be surprised if the army holds together through the rest of the year if it doesn't get paid.'

'King Cathal won't like it,' said Curtius, breaking some bread. 'He'll be straight down to see the governor to tell him what he thinks. Oh, how I'd love to see that.' 'The king is my next call. I think we owe it to him to tell him that we can't support the Votadini in their southern lands. I'll take two squads of Seneca's cavalry and whatever can be spared from the auxiliaries.'

19

'You're right to make a show of it. Best to leave looking like we've still got some muscle.' The centurion still didn't look or sound as though he'd fully recovered from the news. 'Tell me, if you can of course, does the governor know of our little sidelines, how we pay the men and all?'

'I'm fairly certain that neither of the prefects have told him,' said Mannius, smiling into his cup. 'And every time someone comes from the governor's office, all they see are soldiers tending smallholdings, which they assume is for subsistence. They probably haven't got a clue how much profit you make.'

A smile reappeared on the centurion's face. 'Me and the lads owe you big for setting up our little enterprises. Here's to profit.' He raised his cup. 'Seneca has taken his men out to the old fort at Alauna. Said it was important to sweep along the coast but it's really so he can ride on the beaches. Big kid. He's due back the day after tomorrow, but I'll send a messenger to get him back sooner if you like.'

'No it'll be fine. I'll have a chance to meet some of your officers. What of Leofric?'

'His men are sweeping in a wide arc to the west, with the intention of camping at Trimontium for a few days before they march back down Dere Street to here. You'll probably catch up with them at the bridge.'

Darkness was finally taking a grip of the fort, prompting the centurion to yell an order for someone to bring a light. Mannius heard hurried footsteps outside and a slave quietly entered and put a smouldering wick to the oil lamps. Curtius refilled their cups and both men again paused in their conversation until the slave left.

'Have your patrols heard anything interesting?' asked Mannius, breaking the silence.

'Not a whisper. Seems to have been very quiet all over the place.'

'Maybe it's the weather that's delayed the start of the raiding season,' suggested Mannius.

'Don't normally stop them. This lot are used to bad weather – it's regular up here. Only thing I have heard,' said Curtius with a grin on his face, 'is that Ceretic's mightily pissed off with King Cathal. At the end of last year we intercepted a Pict raiding party trying to get back to their ships with loot and prisoners, which of course they didn't.' From the look on the centurion's face it had been a good fight. 'Well, we set the Votadini prisoners free and took the rest to King Cathal's soldiers. We took our finder's fee on the loot together with a share of the slave value of the raiders and left Ceretic's folks with them. They're never held as prisoners but Ceretic has to pay a fee for each adult returned.' Curtius slapped the table and had to hold back a growing laugh. 'Only there was the combined population of two villages. He couldn't pay straight off so he's had to owe the money. It's made him mad.'

'But King Cathal isn't the sort to insist on payment for the release of innocents.'

'No, but Ceretic hates owing favours or debts to anyone – especially his neighbour.'

'So there'll be trouble?'

'Reckon so. Ceretic'll need to get some gold to plug the gap in his treasury. It'd have been good to watch close up instead of from the Wall,' concluded the centurion in a more resigned tone.

'Thank you for your hospitality,' said Mannius, getting to his feet. 'I expect you've got preparations to make.'

'Aye, we'll have to see if we can sell the crops we've already put in the ground north of the Wall. I'd hate to think of someone making a profit out of us, even if it is the Votadini.'

*　　*　　*

21

Next morning Mannius was wakened by a frantic knocking on the doorjamb, which supported a sack as a curtain. He pushed himself out of bed and quickly pulled on a cloak before pulling the curtain aside. Two medical orderlies stood in the corridor.

'Begging pardon, Tribune, sir,' started the leader. 'We've got an emergency and I'd be grateful of your opinion, sir, if you please.'

Centurion Curtius came running along the corridor. 'What's the meaning of disturbing the Tribune?'

'Sorry, sir,' apologised the lead medic. 'We tried to find you but couldn't and we've got this emergency, sir.'

Mannius could see that Curtius was filling his lungs, readying himself to launch a verbal blast at the intruders to the officers' quarters. 'What's the emergency?' asked Mannius, holding back Curtius' verbal onslaught with a subtle wave of his hand.

'Please, sir, this local,' started the first medic.

'Rich and noble he is,' supported his colleague.

'So he's bribed you,' said Curtius menacingly.

'It's his son, sir,' said the first medic, not knowing who to address. 'He heard we was in the fort and brought his son. He's well sick, sir, and we wondered if you'd be good enough to give us your opinion.'

'So you think he'll die and you're afraid to tell the father – especially after you've taken his money. Is that it?' asked Curtius, still fuming.

'It's alright, Centurion,' said Mannius, picking up one of his saddlebags. 'I'll have a look and see if I can help.'

'At least have some breakfast first,' protested Curtius. However, from the desperate looks on the faces of the two medics at this suggestion, Mannius judged it best to perform the examination first.

The orderlies almost jogged back to a large room, lit by flickering torches. A boy in his early teens lay curled up on a stretcher. He clutched his arms over his stomach and moaned in obvious pain. Next to him squatted a large man in expensive-looking armour accompanied by four armed men.

'He has a fever, sir,' said the lead medic.

'Even a blind man could discern that,' retorted Mannius. 'Get me some bandages soaked in cold water and open those damn shutters to let some light and fresh air into this place. Even if we cure him, this damp will do for all of us.'

One of the medics ran to the shutters, then went for bandages. 'And you lot,' said Mannius, nodding at the warriors. 'Any of you medically trained?'

There was no audible reply, only mute shakes of the head. 'Then piss off and get some breakfast,' ordered Mannius. Before they left the guards looked to the boy's father, who nodded.

'Now then, young man,' said Mannius in a different, kinder voice. 'Let's have a look at you.'

The boy pulled his tunic up and pointed at his lower right abdomen, the action causing him to take short, quick breaths. Mannius gently ran his hands over the area the boy indicated, felt a swelling and noted when the boy winced. 'When did it start hurting?'

'Two days ago.' The boy's father spoke for the first time, a tremor in his voice indicating his concern. 'We thought it was something he'd eaten. He was sick, which we thought would take the pain away, but it got worse. Hasn't eaten a thing since.'

'Where did the pain start?' asked Mannius to the boy, who pointed to his belly button. 'Then it moved?'

The boy grunted in reply.

Mannius gently patted the boy on the shoulder and stood up. 'Any suggestions?' he asked the remaining medic.

'The fever seems to be caused by a stomach problem.

23

Probably poison of some sort.' He trailed off as Mannius started to shake his head at the diagnosis.

'It's his appendix. Needs to come out before it bursts,' pronounced Mannius.

'Can you perform such an operation?' asked the boy's father.

'Yes, I've done it before.'

'Will it hurt?' asked the boy, the effort making him grimace.

'A hundred years ago the pain would have been excruciating and could even kill you. But now we have this,' replied Mannius, fishing in his saddlebag and taking out a pouch containing a small vial. 'It's made from the seeds of a certain poppy. Worst you'll feel is like you're having a bad dream. Afterwards you'll be sore for a few days and you must keep the wound clean with a lavender solution that one of the medics will give you. A price worth paying, yes?'

The medic returned with cold bandages and applied them to the boy's head. When Mannius was satisfied he took out razor sharp surgical instruments and laid them on a cloth before calling out more orders. 'I want these boiled, I want fresh bandages boiled, and bring some warm water so that I can give our patient his painkiller.'

Two hours later, Mannius sat down with Curtius to a large breakfast, happy with his morning's efforts. 'From your light mood I presume the operation was a success?' enquired the centurion.

'No problems, and the boy is strong. He'll recover quickly.' Mannius patted the purse hidden inside his tunic. 'The boy's father is rich. Gave me five gold pieces, which I'll enter on your ledger. Helps keep the wheels of our army turning.'

'Why don't you leave this place and set yourself up in southern Gaul or even Rome, like your father? You'd make a fortune.'

'My father keeps sending me letters, asking when I'll join him,' replied Mannius, staring out of the window. 'He's got a fine villa in Gaul, lots of slaves, and travels between there and Rome treating ailments of the most noble families.'

'Then why don't you get yourself there? I could come along and run your household, keep your estate in order.' Curtius tapped a leather bucket set by his chair to collect rainwater from the leaking roof. 'Got to be better weather than this part of the empire.'

'This is where I belong, Curtius. I've lived here since I was born. My mother's buried here and all the friends I've ever had are here. So I'd rather stay and enjoy whatever weather comes my way.'

'Good on you,' said Curtius, raising his leather cup by way of a toast. 'And I don't want to retire just yet anyway.'

# Chapter II

'Thieves and murderers,' thundered King Cathal, undisputed leader of the Votadini, in thick Gaelic. His hard words echoed off the cold, stone walls of the Great Hall in Dun Breaton – the Fort of the Britons. A gnarled finger traced an accusing arc towards heavily tattooed men sitting at the edge of a large circle. 'I should rather find myself in a foetid pit of pus swarming with vipers than in an alliance with them. They and their kind have caused more pain and suffering than the worst pestilence.' At least the earlier buzz of excitement from the other kings and tribal leaders had subsided.

Perhaps fearing that the meeting was taking an ugly turn, one of the smaller Picts leapt to his feet. 'All north of the Wall are entitled to attend the Meeting of Equals. It is neutral ground.' He spat like a child reminding his opponents of a game's rules.

King Cathal ignored the interruption. 'We have all suffered attacks on our coastal villages and even lost brothers and sisters to their slavers. And now you say they come as our friends and allies.' Cathal paused to let the flickering torchlight play across the faces of those he accused. 'At least Romans can be trusted to keep their word.'

This time some men stamped their feet and murmured their approval. Whilst he was on his feet and had enough support he had to continue and try to make the most of the opportunity to talk sense into the gathering, there would be no second chances. 'The last few years have brought peace and prosperity. But you want it to end by us breaking our own pacts – for which we have all taken Roman gold – and attack them. I say our people will not thank us for a hopeless war and the gods will not look kindly on oaths so lightly broken.' Cathal remained in the circle waiting for a challenge to his words. He knew from where it would come.

King Ceretic sat half in shadow, watching the reactions of men around him. 'My dear King Cathal,' he said in smooth tones. 'I can assure you that very soon the Roman army will cease to exist.' The news was greeted with the interest he had no doubt anticipated and he paused to let it sink in before raising his voice, taking the men's excitement and amplifying it. 'Yes, it is true! The emperor himself has grown weary of their corruption and insubordination. None of you need worry about breaking oaths because the Romans will not be there to hold you to account.'

'Hah!' spat Cathal. 'The legions have controlled all land south of the Wall for centuries and I can't see an end to it in my lifetime.'

'There will be no grand army and in their impending absence it is our duty to take control of Britain for the benefit of our people.' Excited whispers raced round the hall. 'Before others do!'

'What of the Wall? Even without the legions it would take only a handful of Brigantes to organise themselves with weapons and ballistae to hold it.' Cathal peered at the faces in the torchlight and could see nods of agreement. 'Most of our bravest and best warriors would die trying to take that Wall and you know it!' He'd calmed the initial enthusiasm raised by Ceretic.

'If we merely throw ourselves headlong at it then you would be right.' Ceretic sounded too confident, as though someone had pointed out all possible objections he could face and shown him the replies. None of his men, not even his druid priests, were that skilful. It had to be outside help. 'But if we attack it from both sides whoever is on the Wall has to run, or die!'

'Excuse me, King Ceretic,' interrupted Ailean, a minor Irish king, 'but not even the Picts have a fleet large enough to carry sufficient warriors around the Wall.'

This interest in details of the plan seemed to be helping Ceretic. 'No my dear King Ailean, but the Saxons do.'

'So now not only do we fight alongside vermin like the Picts, we have to trust to the goodwill of Saxon sailors,' responded Cathal. Looking round the gathering he was worried. Too many minds seemed to have been set before the Meeting of Equals had even begun. How many had Ceretic bribed?

'No I do not ask you to step into Saxon boats. Those boats will be delivering an army south of the Wall. We move our men up to either end of the Wall and those on it will have to run or surely perish. Together we can take Britain!'

'And the Saxons have agreed to help us with your plan?'

'Indeed they have.' Ceretic smiled triumphantly. His chief druid cleared a path through the leaders and led three massive Saxon warriors into the circle. Ceretic rose from his chair and strode to greet the first Saxon with an embrace. 'Prince Wybert is here to reinforce our alliance with his father. They will land their army two months from now, so we must be ready.' This time Ceretic had to wave down the cheers to let himself be heard. 'Take note – if we don't move south soon, the Saxons will take everything!'

'I've heard enough,' said Cathal, turning to his two sons. 'It's time we left.' A path was made for the king. Before he left the gathering he turned to address them one last time and silence fell. 'This ungodly alliance is madness. If you are set to carry it through then so be it. I'll not stop you. But none of you will set foot on Votadini territory.' With that he spun on his heel, followed by Mo, his massive bodyguard, and joined his sons and their closest allies outside.

Cathal's party let their horses trot down a hill, away from the rocky promontory that overlooked the Clota Aest. 'Where's Taran?' demanded Cathal as soon as they were out of earshot of the fort's guards. 'I could have done with his support in the chamber.'

'He said he had an important errand,' Faolan, his youngest son, offered as a consolation.

Before the king could think of an oath sufficient to throw at his missing subject, a white stallion galloped along a side track, intent on joining the group. Instead of slowing, the animal and rider flashed in a white blur in front of, and rather too close to, the royal party before the horse was turned round, allowing horse and rider to trot alongside more sedately.

'I see your equestrian skills haven't improved, Taran,' said Maon, King Cathal's eldest son.

'I am always in control. A druid can tell animals to do what they wish,' retorted Taran haughtily, trying to regain control of his breathing.

'Perhaps you should try shouting to your animal next time – eh?' suggested the king.

'Thank you, my lord, I shall treasure your advice as always.'

'What of your errand?' prompted Faolan.

'Thank you, young prince, for taking the conversation to a far more important subject.'

'We're in trouble, Taran,' said Maon. 'It seems King Ceretic is intent on war and has some powerful allies. The only trouble is we seem to be in the way.'

'I've never seen such a gathering of nobles acting so,'

said Faolan. 'They seemed to have made up their minds before we got there.'

'They had,' replied the king in a resigned tone. 'Greed and fear had gripped them.'

'A powerful poison, amongst the weak,' sympathised Taran.

'Greed for gold, slaves and land south of the Wall and fear of losing out to each other,' said the king, almost to himself.

'And fear of Ceretic's spears and his new Saxon friends,' added Maon.

'I'm afraid the trouble is much worse than you think,' said Taran, pulling his horse to a slow walk and turning to the king.

'Is this some superstitious nonsense?' asked the king. 'If you were with some witch looking into cauldrons or shagging her assistant in the greater cause of druidism, I'm not interested. This is serious.'

'Such a lack of faith from non-believers is only to be expected – though she does have two very attractive and usefully experienced assistants,' said Taran, addressing his horse. 'No my royal friends, the trouble we face is much worse. We have been betrayed by our neighbours, Rome, and soon our allies will follow unless we do exactly what Ceretic requires of us.'

'Rome?' enquired the king.

'It seems that Ceretic has a Roman who has given him troop dispositions along the Wall and an up-to-date summary of discontent south of the Wall. But most of all he has told him that the island is to be abandoned by Rome and left to its own devices. The troops are to be disbanded and no more will be sent to help.'

'No one can know that,' protested Maon.

'Unless the emperor had told him to betray the island,' surmised the king.

30

'Betraying one's allies brings war,' pronounced Taran. 'But betraying one's own people brings anarchy and the darkest of times. Very dark times. I fear a cloud of misery is about to descend.'

'No,' protested Maon. 'Romans have been here for over four centuries, they won't let it end now.'

'Some things,' said the king, 'men can't stop. Like an incoming tide washes all before it, kingdoms get moved when the world around them changes.'

'The man I was told of carried a senatorial seal, spoke perfect Latin and had arranged the alliance with the Saxons,' said Taran.

'Why would a Roman tell Ceretic of such plans?' enquired Maon. 'I don't understand.'

'I'm afraid none of us do,' replied the king. 'But from Ceretic's confident tone, I suspect we'll find out soon enough.'

'Are we in danger?' asked Faolan.

'Not until we're back in Din Eidyn,' said Cathal. 'Even Ceretic wouldn't dare defy the oath of safe conduct for all who attend the meeting of equals.'

However, after witnessing the revelation of an unholy alliance, anything seemed possible. The king urged his horse on at a stiff canter. 'We can't get back tonight. But I want to be back at Din Eidyn early on the morrow to give Ceretic as little time as possible to make his next move. We need to be on our guard.'

# Chapter III

Din Eidyn might have been the administrative capital of the Votadini but its spiritual home was some twenty-five miles to the east on Traprain Law. A large, steep-sided mound over seven hundred feet high dominated the fertile plains for miles around. At its base was a collection of modest buildings housing peasant workers and slaves who toiled in the surrounding patchwork of fields. A track led from the village, over a wide ditch and through a guarded gate in a wooden palisade. From the entrance the track wound its way to another palisade and the grander buildings on the summit. Each was smartly thatched and connected to the other buildings by raised wooden walkways.

Wind gently pulled and rustled the thatch on the roof of a large, circular hut. It was an old sturdy building, built of heavy stone to the height of a man's shoulder with strong wooden beams taking the ceiling of dried twigs to twice the height of a man at the centre of the hut. Inside, the dirt floor had been swept clean; Borgach was particular about that. She liked her hut to be tidy. Smoke from an open fire curled upwards and lingered momentarily in the thatch ceiling before it disappeared.

'Tell me of the future, Borgach,' the tall, young woman commanded the old woman who sat on a stool close to the fire. She kept a careful eye on the girl who was bent over a simmering pot.

'The future will come soon enough,' answered the old woman, throwing some vegetables into a broth that the girl was stirring.

'But I need to know,' protested the woman, twiddling long red hair round her fingers. 'Who will I marry? What will become of my daughter? Please, Borgach.'

'Is the wind bending the pine trees on the old hill towards the village?'

The woman pushed a wooden board out from the doorway and ducked under a stone beam. 'Yes,' she said, having shot a look outside.

'Then it will rain soon,' pronounced Borgach. She went on as though she were giving a lesson. 'When the wind blows strong enough to bend the pine trees towards the village it will surely rain before the next meal is served. That is the future. To say that you're a widow, you really don't know much do you?'

Borgach was teasing her. She had been her tutor and mentor since she was a child. 'Borgach, you know that I'm not concerned with the weather. I need to know what will happen to me.'

'What would you do with such knowledge? It can be dangerous.'

'I will prepare myself all the better. When you told me who my husband was to be and that it would be a short marriage, I was able to be a good wife for the time we were together. His death was not the shock it would otherwise have been. Lots of things are changing around here and I need to prepare myself to meet them. Please, Borgach.'

'Your reasons for knowledge are true. Too many men come here and ask to know the future hoping that they can change it. Many of them talk with Taran about their death and hope to avoid it. We can do little to change the future but if we are properly prepared perhaps we can play a better part in that future when it becomes the present. Taran says that you can't change the future, at best you can only postpone it.'

33

'I heard it said in the village that people talk to Taran of death because he's so old that he's familiar with it.'

'Being close to something doesn't mean that you can talk about it. Can a child tell you anything of its time before birth? Of course it can't. It's born knowing certain things, like how to breathe and eat, without anybody in this world telling it. So who tells it, eh? By the time a child is old enough to say where they learnt that stuff they've forgotten where they heard it. Same as dying. When you're so close you can see into the next world it's too late to tell anyone in this. Stands to reason.'

Borgach looked into the pot and sniffed the steam coming off it. 'Such knowledge can be deadly. Some people have been driven mad knowing the future. Taran says Old Gibbons went mad with the knowledge. He killed a beaver, skinned it and cut it open only to find his future was in it. Been stupid ever since. Must have been a bad future to look forward to. He should have known better than to cut open a freshly killed beaver by moonlight.'

'How can you tell the future from cutting open a beaver?'

'They don't speak it to you; it's in their innards. You've got to know how to look at them of course. Gibbons must have just seen it straight off – happens sometimes. Taran says the best way to see the future is in the gut of a man. Cut open a man and he'll show you secrets. Just before you kill him you ask him what you want to know and as he dies he takes that question with him into the next world where he can see the past, present and future. His guts give you the answer. Can't lie. Doesn't have time to tell untruths.'

'Is that how Taran tells the future?'

'No, your father won't let him. Says it's barbaric. I think he'd rather trade prisoners for slave-profit than see them gutted anyway.'

'Why doesn't Taran cure him?'

'Who?'

'Gibbons, the man who went mad.'

'Doesn't want to. Says it'd be wrong to cure a man of the truth.'

'Why don't you cure him then?'

'It's beyond my power, dear. It needs the old power and I've only got a little of that.'

'You mean druid?'

'Aye.'

'Is Taran a druid then?'

'No, of course not. The Romans got rid of them a long time ago. Still, Taran says he was taught by the last druid alive after he came this way.'

'How long ago was that?'

'Too long to remember.'

'How old is Taran? I've heard it said that he's older than the trees.'

'Older than some, no doubt, and younger than others.'

'Taran says he's over two centuries old.'

'If you listen to him long enough he'll even tell you that he watched the Romans building that wall of theirs. Give him a mug or two of wine and he'll even claim that he told them where to dig the foundations for it.' The old woman let out a chuckle.

'Why do you laugh?'

'He's no different from any other man. Always bragging and boasting.'

'So how come he's lived so long? He told me that he could see death coming and every time it came his way he knew so he could be some place else. He said that he'll only die as a messenger.'

'Of course he will. That's hardly difficult to see. He's always telling people what to do with messages from this god or that. For someone as clever as you, you get taken in sometimes. You're cleverer than your brothers, I can see it in your eyes – always have done since you were a child. I can even hear it in some of your questions. You're almost as clever as your father.'

Borgach got to her feet with the aid of a short stick. 'Now bring that cloak back with you tomorrow night.'

Princess Caoimhe must have looked bemused and in need of explanation. 'You will need the cloak to keep the rain off or you'll not hear of the future because you'll be sneezing and coughing with cold too much. Now go, Una and I'll need some time to prepare.'

As Caoimhe picked up the cloak the first heavy thuds of rain hitting the roof could be heard. She left feeling as though she were a child again, having just listened to one of Borgach's lessons. Since her husband's death she had returned to her father's house and waited to be married off again. In her seventeenth year she'd been married to Arthur the Old, the eldest of four brothers. He hadn't been handsome but then again neither had he been ugly. He got drunk with the rest of the men but he never beat her and she had been thankful for that. Too often women, even princesses, would get beaten by their men. Sometimes she thought that men liked their hunting dogs more than the women they took to their beds.

After one drinking binge too many he had fallen from his horse while racing one of his brothers. His head struck a rock and he died instantly. The brothers protested that witchcraft had been afoot. They claimed that he was too good a rider to fall. Caoimhe's father would hear none of it. He knew that they were trying to squirm out of their allegiance and obligations to him. If witchcraft could be proved, Caoimhe would be executed and the marriage settlement forfeit. Her father sent some of his soldiers to stop any thought of trouble. She had thanked him but she was never sure whether he intended them to protect her or his interests. Perhaps she would ask Borgach which had been the more important.

That accident had been over a year ago and now that she was in her twentieth year she longed to settle with a new husband. Although she would be no virgin bride she had grown into a beautiful woman and had proved that she could produce offspring. Her father knew that he would get a good settlement for her. The price would be high. He would gain an allegiance, lands and more power.

In the lands between the old Antonine turf wall and Emperor Hadrian's stone monstrosity, her father, King Cathal, had become the most powerful lord. She was grateful for her father's wealth and influence but it meant she was bound by her obligations to him. Sometimes – maybe just once in a while – she wanted to be free; to show that she could be strong and noble like her father and brothers.


The next morning, Caoimhe awoke early, dressed and strolled to a small stone altar. Her father had ordered it built in memory of her mother, who had been the first of the Votadini's ruling family to become Christian. With a corner of her tunic she polished it then sat on a rock nearby, lingering in the morning sun, letting its welcome warmth soak in. She wondered what Borgach would tell her about her future.

Everything was calm after the rain during the night, even the wind was still asleep. She desperately wanted to wake Caitir, her daughter, to show her the flowers pushing through the ground, the blossom on the trees and the pockets of mist being held in the hollows. Already the early dew was beginning to disappear. In the fields below she could see boys at work, rounding up cows.

To the north, towards the estuary, the mist was thicker.

Perhaps a sea mist had drifted inland. Almost subconsciously she spotted something moving. A few moments of straining her eyes to look along the track and she made out the quickly growing form of a rider. He was moving fast towards the village. As he passed the cow field she could see him wave at the boys, who immediately started running towards the settlement.

The metallic clang of bronze on a hollow iron triangle in the village settled all doubt in her mind. Quickly the alarm was relayed by other clangs and trumpets. How bothersome to have such a beautiful day spoiled by an alarm. Maybe the steward wanted to get everyone outside, to enjoy the morning – if only. She ambled back to the Great Hall to be met by a maid sent scurrying to find her. She could see the rider urging his horse up the track to the inner palisade, where the steward waited. Running indoors, hiding from the news, however terrible, would serve no purpose. So she stopped and watched, pretending to make an adjustment to the small thong in her hair. After what she gauged to be a respectful time she slowly walked towards the men.

'Good morning, Princess Caoimhe,' said the steward, turning to her as she approached.

'Let us dispense with pleasantries this morning, Bran. Why the alarm?'

'Begging your pardon, ma'am,' said the rider. 'It's Picts moving up from the estuary. Must have landed during the night and come close under the mist this morning.'

'How many?'

'Three boats,' replied Bran. 'They probably heard about the Meeting of Equals and decided to treat themselves to a quick raid – perhaps they didn't get an invite.'

A fresh horse was brought for the rider. 'Best get going,' he said as he mounted the horse to take the news to Din Eidyn.

Caoimhe did the arithmetic. 'About seventy to ninety men?'

'That's the way I'd figure it. Less five or ten to guard the boats,' agreed Bran. 'I'll get everyone inside. We'll have at least a hundred fighting men so we'll be more than a match for them from inside. If they linger too long, I dare say your father'll be over to teach them a damn good lesson.'

Caoimhe thanked the steward for his time and went to find her breakfast. While her father, both her brothers and Taran were all absent, which was most of the time as they usually stayed at Din Eidyn, she was the highest ranking member of the family present on Traprain Law. Everyone would look to her to set an example. Let life carry on as near to normal as possible, her father had always advised. Keep calm: any hint of panic will quickly sweep through the village and destroy it as surely as the swords of the opposition.

Inside the Great Hall the servants and slaves were animated. Deliberately, Caoimhe took her place at the top table and ate a breakfast of porridge and cold meats. The nurse had just brought a sleepy Caitir to the top table when the steward beckoned to Caoimhe from the door.

'I'm sorry to be so rude, Princess Caoimhe,' apologised Bran, looking crestfallen. 'But I don't want anyone else to know.'

'Please,' said Caoimhe, not knowing where the conversation was heading.

'It's the Picts,' said Bran with barely concealed anger. 'Three more of our lookouts have reported in and it seems there's more than one lot of them. Looks like they landed in four or five separate groups. There must be four or five hundred of them.'

Caoimhe's heart stopped and she felt fear gnawing at her stomach. After a deep breath to help stop her voice trembling she said, 'So the first group were to get us to fall back on Traprain Law, then the rest appear to snare us. Clever for Picts.'

'There's still just enough time for you and Caitir to get out, if you hurry. I've got your horse ready.'

The mention of her daughter's name suddenly made her aware that it was not just she who faced danger. 'We will both stay,' she declared, holding up her hand to prevent any further debate.

'I'm sorry ma'am. I've let the both of you down, I know I have.'

'Nonsense, Bran,' said Caoimhe, giving the man her best smile. 'The Picts have taken advantage of us all. We must make sure they pay a heavy price so that my father and brothers will have an easy job of finishing them off later.'

Once Caitir had eaten her breakfast Caoimhe took her and the nursemaid to Borgach's round hut. It was the only round hut on the summit. A long time ago she'd guessed that Borgach must be a druid – despite what she said. The circle was the sign of perfect unity. Borgach stood in the doorway looking as if she expected her and probably a few others as well, seeking her wisdom, lucky charms and sanctuary.

'Take care of Caitir for me please, Borgach. And I'll have some of your best poison as well.' Caoimhe looked past the witch to the children huddled on the floor of the hut.

The witch took the toddler and reluctantly passed over a tiny earthen jar. Caoimhe tied a leather thong to it and fastened it around her neck. Borgach hugged the princess. 'I'll not let them take me and use me for ransom or their pleasure,' vowed the princess. 'I'll fight, but if they overrun us I'd rather take my own life than give it to those Picts.'

'Be strong, lassie.' For the first time that Caoimhe could

remember, Borgach looked as though she were crying. 'The wee one'll be fine with Una and me.' With that she turned and went back inside her hut.

Approaching the cliff fort of Din Eidyn, with its surrounding jumble of thatched huts, King Cathal could see that something was amiss. The gates to the fort were half-closed and two lines of people streamed out of the village. One line headed up the hill for the fort, the other away east. A rider galloped up to the royal party.

'My lord, a Saxon war band has been spotted higher up the estuary.'

'So Ceretic's Saxon friend wasn't alone,' said Maon.

'Easy lad,' replied King Cathal, holding up a hand and ignoring everyone else but the messenger. 'How many boats and where?'

'At least fifteen boats, no more than five miles away. They must have slipped past our lookouts in the night or the early mist. I'm so sorry, my lord.'

'How many men have we got ready inside the fort?'

'All of your guards and the local militia, and those near enough to get in. Around a hundred and fifty men, my lord. But...'

'Why so few?' queried Maon.

'Have messengers been sent to Traprain Law?' asked the king.

'Yes, but...'

King Cathal felt his heart sink. He sensed even worse news. 'Spit it out, lad.'

'Men from here were sent early this morning to help defend Traprain Law,' responded the messenger. He choked his words, barely able to speak. 'Picts were sighted close to the village, hundreds of them. The captains took the men to help bring the villagers here.'

41

'The Saxons could be marching to Ceretic,' suggested Faolan.

'No,' replied Taran. 'They would surely have sailed higher up the estuary. I fear that Ceretic will be marching to meet them.'

'My lord,' said the messenger, trying to be as tactful as he could. 'There is some good news. King Ceretic has sent some men. About four hundred have been spotted crossing the moors, no more than seven miles to the south.'

'A trap?' asked Maon.

'Then there is no choice,' pronounced the king. 'With so few we can't hold Din Eidyn and those in Traprain'll not get here fast enough. Maon and I will help evacuate the people here south along the paved road. We'll delay Ceretic and his Saxon friends as long as we can. Taran, you go with Faolan, find out the true strength of those damn Picts. If it really is hopeless get everyone south and hope that the Romans haven't left yet.'

'We will see you in Bremenium or the afterlife, my lord,' said Faolan leaning out of his saddle to embrace his father.

'The dark clouds are gathering,' volunteered Taran as much to himself as to the parting group.

# Chapter IV

Before dawn Mannius rode north with three squads of riders and their officer, Decurion Seneca. The son of a horse breeder, Seneca seemed to have been born on a saddle and had lived with and around horses ever since. Mannius considered himself to be a good rider, though he preferred to fight on foot. But next to Seneca, he felt barely competent.

Noise from the horses' hooves along the paved road together with the jangle of bridles and armour made conversation difficult and that suited Mannius. He enjoyed the sensation of cold, pre-dawn air chilling his face – a reminder of his first ride north to meet King Cathal four years previously. Then he had an escort of only four. Now it was over fifty, a number that would be swelled with some of Leofric's riders. Times had changed; there was more danger. Not that he wanted the Votadini to sense his caution. Fewer riders would have made the journey swifter but it would have lacked formal elegance, and Mannius knew that King Cathal would appreciate a show of Roman strength.

Riding through the lands of the Votadini was always a pleasure. Early morning mist lingered over fields and in hollows, close to the roadside. Rolling hills, thick pine forests and innumerable streams, swollen after the heavy rains of recent days, were around them all the time. The paved road kept to high ground, dipping down into woodlands only occasionally. Long ago Roman engineers had cleared great swathes of trees from both sides of the road to deny the chance of ambush; however, without proper maintenance the bushes and trees had started to grow close to the road again, adding sights and scents to Mannius' pleasure.

Before dawn proper, they had crested several tops of the Cheviot Hills and started descending towards a beautiful valley through which the Abo Flavia flowed. On the northern slopes, even in the grey half-light, Mannius could see small drifts of snow left by the winter in cold gullies. The promise of spring was welcome after the uncharacteristically brutal nature of the past season. It had been so bad that the governor had authorised Curtius to use some of the legion's own supplies to help feed many of the Votadini and their animals in the south of their lands. Expensive it had been, but useful in cementing relations with a key ally. However, both he and King Cathal knew that the governor would have provided the supplies anyway. It was the only human thing to do.

At the old bridge, over the dangerously swollen waters of the Abo Flavia, fifty of Leofric's riders waited to join them. The captain of the Saxon mercenaries rode up to Mannius and Seneca.

'Greetings Tribune! Captain Leofric sends his compliments and apologises. Our main force is a day's march behind in the hills. He says he will occupy the old fort here and wait for your return.'

Mannius was grateful for the additional show of force and ordered the officer and Seneca to sort out riding orders and scouting duties. After a brief rest by the river the group started ascending the road out of the valley over another set of hills.

Even this far north, old forts were still spread out along the road. Most had been pulled apart by the locals in search of good building material, though some survived as the centre for larger farms. Their destination was the old fort of Oxton, that had once served as a cavalry base. Now it was a farm, and an inn, much to the displeasure of Seneca. 'Such a waste,' he said, as much to himself as to Mannius who was riding next to him.

'Surely it's good that some of the old buildings are put to use.'

'Not sure about that, sir,' said Seneca, sniffing the air. 'It smells like a bloody farmyard. Those were quality stables. Should be used for breeding and rearing horses, not pigs and suchlike.'

'But it will do for a halt tonight eh, Decurion?' Mannius knew that the cavalryman lived to eat and through his carefully-routed patrols he seemed to be on good terms with all the innkeepers north of the Wall. The man's slightly growing girth and re-sewn tunic bore testament to his battles in the eateries.

'Yes, sir. We're right on schedule and the horses could do with some feed and rest.'

'So you won't mind making the arrangements?'

'Be a pleasure, sir,' smiled Seneca. 'And a good chance to get some intelligence.'

'Your horse will have to hope that you don't get much more intelligent,' said Mannius nodding towards Seneca's waist.

'Soon have that off, sir. A few hours in the saddle'll put paid to the damage of a good meal.'

Roman gold was always welcome and throughout their stay the matron hovered over slaves as they put together modest meals for the visitors. After a night's rest the matron had the slaves make porridge, soup, cheese, cold meats and fresh bread. Mannius took a bowl of porridge and some bread. Any more, he thought, would inhibit his riding abilities. Seneca, however, helped himself to everything and washed it all down with some weak, warm wine and a lot of attention from the matron.

During Seneca's second mug of wine a commotion started outside. A cavalry officer entered to report.

'Begging pardon, sir, but some farmhands just came in shouting like. Say that there's riders on the road coming our way, galloping fit to bust. Just sent four of the lads to check.'

'Well done. I'll be out shortly,' replied Seneca, seemingly upset at leaving the mug of wine. 'Tell the men to get ready to ride – no sense being caught napping – though it would be nice to have a quick nap after all that excellent food.' The matron beamed her appreciation.

Mannius had no time for pleasantries; he was trying to assess the situation. Both the innkeeper and his wife said that they hadn't heard of any raids for weeks. Perhaps the season had just started.

Outside, sheltered by old, moss-covered stone walls, the spring sun warmed them as they waited. Mannius decided to climb one of the dilapidated ramparts to get a better view. Soon the first rider appeared, quickly followed by another, then another. They were strung out. Mannius watched the scouts gallop alongside, then slow the riders. Next to the cavalrymen the riders appeared small – they were children. Nine children on seven horses were brought into the old fort.

The eldest boy, who looked about twelve years old, slid to the ground and had to be helped onto a bench. Mannius sat next to him and did not pull away when the boy grabbed his cloak and wept. He gave him time to compose himself before he started to question him.

'Who were you running from?'

'Picts, Saxons, Dumnoni, sir.'

'Which one?' asked Seneca slightly impatiently.

The boy pulled away from Mannius and looked at him, imploring him to believe him. 'All of them, sir. We was at Din Eidyn when King Cathal told us all to run to Bremenium. Said Saxons were coming.'

The matron brought mugs of water and hunks of bread for the children. No one interrupted. They waited for the boy to drink. 'Told us that Picts attacked Traprain and killed everyone. Our parents put us on these horses and told me not to let any of us stop 'til we was safe. Sir, is this Bremenium? Are we safe now?'

'Course you're safe, sunshine,' said the matron, taking the boy in her arms but casting a worried look at the Roman officers.

Unseen, the cavalrymen had been busy. 'Begging pardon, sir, but the lads have spotted more riders coming our way. Not military style, bit disordered like.'

'Bring the troop to ready,' ordered Seneca.

'I was going to suggest we check what the boy said,' offered Mannius, looking northwards along the road. 'But I think we've just had confirmation that something terrible has happened to King Cathal.' In an instant he had made up his mind. 'Decurion, send two riders back to inform Leofric. Ask him to bring some of his men north of the river to hold the hills and road to the crossing. Let's get every available man, cart and weapon to King Cathal as fast as we can.'

'Sir,' said the boy, 'please may I come – I can drive a cart for you.'

'Sorry, lad, but you're exhausted. I want you to help matron here move her things and the children to Bremenium. Can you do that for me?'

The boy nodded reluctantly. 'Please, sir. I won't be any trouble. I just want to help my parents.'

'Don't worry son, we'll get them for you.' And with that Mannius was fastening his helmet and looking for his horse.

Accompanied by Prince Wybert, Ceretic rode hard through the night. The Meeting of Equals had gone better than he dared imagine. 'Are your men in place, Wybert?'

'They are.' Wybert sounded surly and arrogant like the rest of his race. Ceretic ignored his tone. 'They will have slipped over from the north bank during the night.'

'This mist will help to increase the surprise on that old fool's face when he sees your men charging up to Din Eidyn.' Ceretic could hardly contain his enthusiasm.

'My men are happy to take Din Eidyn. We have suffered grievous losses along the coastline of the Votadini over the last few years. It is good that they do not join the alliance against Romans. Fighting alongside them would be difficult for my men.'

For the third time he checked with his captain, 'The men know not to attack until I'm there?'

'Yes, my Lord. The men are safely camped in the hills a short march from Din Eidyn. They know not to attack until you give the order.'

'Excellent! And the Picts? Please tell me that someone is controlling the Picts.'

'King Drostan is leading the attack on Traprain Law himself and his brother is landing the other force between the both of us.'

'Then the arrogant Cathal will find himself, for once, outmanoeuvred, with too little time to get all his men armed. I've waited for this for a long time.'

'With Votadini lands in our control it will be easy to move men south to the Wall, yes?' asked Wybert.

'Most definitely, my Saxon friend. Then, together we will outflank the Romans, force them off their precious Wall and open the gates to their lands. Yes, I think today will be sunny.'

# Chapter V

Caoimhe had dressed herself like the men, in trousers and boots. In place of heavy, metal armour she wore a thick, leather tunic under a short jacket of chain mail so that she could move more quickly. Fastened to her waist was a long dagger though her main weapon was a compact bow and a large quiver of arrows. She waited patiently on her horse next to Bran, near to the gate on the outer palisade, which she figured would be the site of the worst fighting.

The Picts looked to be in no hurry to storm the defences. All morning more and more of them arrived. Following lessons learned from the Romans, first they surrounded the mound, preventing anyone from escaping or reinforcing those already inside. Only when they were ready did they advance towards the outer ditch, though still over three hundred paces distant. Witnessing the ring of Picts closing around the mound felt to the defenders as though a noose was being tightened around their necks.

'Why don't they attack?' Caoimhe asked Bran quietly.

'They like to give us time to think about dying first. Weaken men's minds and their bodies'll follow sure enough. Be patient.'

Caoimhe slumped back onto her saddle. The initial surge of adrenaline, when she had felt she could fight and beat every Pict in sight, was wearing thin. Like Bran had said, she was beginning to feel mortal. Just as her mind started to wander and think of her daughter, the old steward brought her back to the present.

49

'Ah, service at last,' said Bran, looking towards the line of Picts.

Caoimhe followed his gaze and slotted an arrow in her bow. A lone horseman had come out of the shield wall and stopped just short of the bridge over the ditch.

'Easy now, Princess.'

'But I can hit him, I know I can.'

'There'll be plenty of time for that yet. This is only the verbal sparring you might say.'

Steward Bran!' called the man.

Bran looked a little startled to be addressed in person but recovered quickly. 'Greetings to ye. What'll ye be about this morning?'

'My compliments to you and your men on your preparations. We could use good men like you.'

'Having good men on your side would be unusual for Picts,' retorted Bran.

'Hah! You jest, Steward Bran, but we have serious business ahead of us.'

'And what exactly would be your use for good men?'

'We're on our way to take back our land from the Romans. Plenty of land for all of us.'

'So they want to travel down the Dere to the Wall,' muttered Bran to Caoimhe. 'Seems like we've just got in the way. Can't be helped.'

'But that's miles to the west. What do they want with us here?' protested the princess.

'They know we're friendly with the Romans. If the governor sends some of his men up here – maybe by boat like they did – the Picts'd have to watch their backs. A couple of hundred Romans'd soon put paid to that lot and any hope of plundering south of the Wall.' Then he bellowed back, 'The Romans are friends of ours. And by the by, they'll be along presently.'

'You should choose your friends more carefully. The

50

Romans are running home, leaving the Votadini to fight their battles for them alone. That is Roman gratitude.' The Pictish spokesman pushed himself as high as he could on his horse. 'There will be no Romans to rescue you. Men who come willingly now, can join us.'

'Men who join you will do so only as your slaves.'

'Those who stay will find our mercy in short supply.'

'Be gone with your threats, Pict. I fancy it'll be a hard day for ye.'

The rider shrugged and turned back to the shield wall.

The Picts still took their time. Caoimhe felt indignant at having to wait. She wanted the battle to start, the sooner the better, then it would be over. Close to midday the shield wall edged closer; the noose had begun to tighten. From behind the shields archers loosed arrows towards the defenders.

High on his horse Bran, like Caoimhe, could see what the Picts were doing. He ordered the defenders to keep low. 'Don't worry Princess, they're only meant to scare us into sending a few back. That way they'll know where our main strength is.' Below them, men pushed themselves hard into the thick timbers of the palisade and cursed the Picts as arrows whistled through the air.

Caoimhe had never been in so much as a skirmish, let alone a battle. She was terrified, and felt sick. Now she wished the Picts could have waited a little longer. She hoped that she wouldn't vomit – it would be so bad in front of the men. Thinking of that kept her mind away from the closing ring of Picts. Bran was now preoccupied with the defences, looking along the line and riding his horse around the mound to see where the attack would come.

Still the Picts came closer. Caoimhe could now see individual faces, snarling and contorted with hate. Jeers and taunts rose up from both sides. Suddenly she hated

51

the men on the other side of the ditch. She wanted to send her arrows at them, stab them, kick them. Caoimhe found herself joining in with the taunts. Then there was a loud cheer away to her left and the Picts attacked.

Bran waved a few men along the palisade towards the attack but kept most in position. There was only a thin line of defenders to meet the onrushing Picts. He saw Caoimhe's desperate look. 'Only the first attack,' he explained. 'Trying to get us to weaken the gate.'

Arrows started to hit the crowd of Picts. A lot fell on shields but others found flesh and as men fell the battle cries were joined by screams of pain. Picts started to jump into the swampy ditch when one of Bran's lieutenants gave an order, inaudible to Caoimhe, and a dozen spears joined the arrows. More men fell, turning the ditch from brown to red.

Another wave of Picts followed the first. Arrows and spears flew at the attackers. Gradually the Picts were getting closer to the palisade. The first clash of metal on metal indicated that the defenders were hacking at the attackers with swords and axes. In front of the gate a horn sounded and another cheer went up as a huge mass of men charged the gate. Bran gave out the orders and the attackers were greeted in the same way. Caoimhe joined the archers and shot arrows over the palisade, not knowing whether she was hitting anyone or not.

She could see the stockpile of spears, near the gate, was starting to run low. Closer to her two men took arrows. One was hit in the leg and limped a few paces back to tend to his wound while the other went wide-eyed as an arrow caught him in the throat. A scream erupted close by and she turned to see a man with a spear in his chest. Blood spurted from the wound and this time she could not stop herself from vomiting.

All around was carnage and chaos. Picts pressed onto

the bridge. Those at the sides were easy targets for spears and arrows from inside the palisade. Caoimhe could not believe that the Picts could force themselves through such wanton pain.

Bran waved a lighted torch and ordered the men back. Those at the gate were his best and steadiest men. Slowly they pulled themselves away, backing up the track, keeping their shields, swords and eyes facing their attackers. The Picts threw themselves over the gate and tore at its locks. Bran kicked his horse towards the gate and at the last moment wheeled away as he threw the torch at tar-soaked rags and kindling stacked against the gate. Immediately flames leapt up and the dozen Picts who had climbed over found themselves isolated from the main body of attackers. Horsemen charged into them and cut them down.

The action at the gate had given the men on foot time to climb higher up the mound. Seeing that the outer defences had been abandoned the Picts swarmed over the ditch at several different points and made for the track.

Caoimhe marvelled at Bran's expertise. He ordered men to form a shield wall where the track narrowed and steepened. Earlier he had had spears and arrows stockpiled at that very point. Now the weapons were deployed in the same manner as before. Arrows whipped towards the attackers, then spears joined the onslaught as the Picts closed. This time rocks rained down from above. They must have killed or injured hundreds, thought Caoimhe, and still the painted men came on. They had no regard for danger: like a pack of wolves they were only intent on killing their quarry.

Caoimhe could now see her arrows hit men below. There was no thinking, no guilt, only targets – animals – to be hit. So absorbed had she become that she nearly didn't hear the order to fall back to the inner palisade.

She kicked her horse up the hill and saw that a group of Picts had climbed behind the shield wall and threatened to outflank it. This time the retreat was not so disciplined and exhausted men fell as they backed away.

Bran had archers along the palisade to keep the throng of Picts at bay while the last living defenders escaped inside. Then the gates were shut and suddenly Caoimhe realised that there was nowhere else to run. The noose had tightened. Instinctively she touched the small jar around her neck for comfort.

The pattern was the same as before. Arrows and spears filled the air. Picts seemed to be all around. A shout went up from one of the men in the gate tower. He waved a spear to the west. Caoimhe followed the line of the spear and saw a cloud of dust and smoke. She knew the messenger had got through. Her father and brothers were on the way. Now they only had to hold on a short while longer. 'The king! The king's coming!' With a parched mouth her shout came out more as a squeak. It was enough. Men not on horseback looked to her, took up the call and found strength from the news. A flash of hope spread through the defenders and the Picts were thrown back.

But the Picts were too many, too determined, and their attacks well coordinated. The defenders started to tire and die. The last few moments of the battle were a haze to Caoimhe. The gate disintegrated and men were thrown back. Bran led a last-ditch charge into the throng. She watched the counter-attack break into a series of small fights as the defenders were overwhelmed. Bran was surrounded by six Picts. There were cries and the sound of metal and Bran lay on the ground with four of his attackers. Unthinking, Caoimhe charged and never saw the blow that unseated her.

# Chapter VI

As they rode north the stream of refugees grew into a torrent. A few faces looked to them as though they were saviours. Most trudged on, unseeing, in shock. Wherever men looked to have some fight left in them or a cart could be commandeered they were turned round and led towards King Cathal. No one had any news beyond that given by the boy. A few said that the king was fighting. That was only to be expected. Mannius knew that a brave man like Cathal would sacrifice himself in a rearguard action to give his people time to get to safety. For the first time he had a hollow feeling of guilt. If only he'd moved quicker to warn the king he might have been better prepared; he should not have stopped so long with Curtius.

Where the road rounded a small wood with budding hazel trees, the flow of people seemed to ebb, then ceased altogether. Scouts reported seeing fighting outside a small village a mile or so away. Mannius and Seneca moved to the crest of a hill, little more than six hundred paces from the village it overlooked. Houses burned unchecked and in the surrounding fields bodies lay in rows, indicating lines where fighting had taken place. A group of around three hundred men, in tight formation, offered a shield wall to a horde of screaming Picts. In the centre of the wall a weak breeze ruffled a tattered standard that swayed with the fight.

Turning away from the battle Mannius had little time to dwell on his feelings of guilt. Instead, the gaze of seasoned warriors bore in on him as they waited for orders. His heart pounded and his mouth was suddenly dry. He wasn't afraid of the fight – he'd fought in skirmishes in his time with the army. This time though he felt the full force of command. He was alone: if he ordered an attack some of his men would die (maybe they all would), but if he failed to act a king and a nation might be destroyed.

'I don't think they've seen us yet, sir,' said Seneca.

The words brought him out of his thoughts. Had he frozen? How long for? Mannius turned back to the village to gauge the time he'd taken. There was no discernible change. Fires still burnt as before, men still fought. Now Mannius had a sense of time slowing. Carefully and deliberately he ordered the Saxon auxiliaries to move through some silver birch trees on the right, to the rear of the village and wait for his signal to attack.

On the ride from Oxton he had seen the weapons that the innkeeper carried in his cart. There were a few useable blades but mostly the cart contained old spears and barely serviceable shields. Mannius galloped his horse to the innkeeper, a reluctant hero who had only been pressured and shamed into driving the cart after the exhausted boy had offered to take it.

'Time to be a centurion,' said Mannius to the overweight man who was trying to be invisible.

'I'm no soldier. I don't even look like a soldier.'

'You can shout. All innkeepers can shout, swear and wrestle with customers. It's part of your job, isn't it?'

'Yes, but –'

'Take those weapons to the far side of the track,' Mannius was spinning, shouting orders to those in earshot to put his plan into action quickly. 'Seneca, get the cloaks from your men. You men,' he shouted at the men they had taken out of the line of refugees and led back to the fighting, 'if anyone has a red cloak, borrow it, tell them

56

they can have it back. Take the cloaks to the centurion there.'

Mannius ordered the men to put on the red cloaks. Then he made each take an old shield and a spear. Seneca realised what he was about and sent two men to help organise the line of men just out of sight of the village.

'Centurion!' shouted Mannius to the innkeeper, who looked to be trembling at the prospect of battle. 'When we charge, order your men forward to the crest of the hill, no further!' Not that he thought the new centurion would be sprinting headlong down the slope to support them. As he rode back to Seneca's men, Mannius wondered who was the most frightened: the innkeeper or him. One was frightened for himself, the other for the men's lives he was about to risk.

The innkeeper nodded and seemed relieved at the prospect of delaying any fight by holding the line of men at the top of the hill. Seneca organised his own men in an arrow formation, waiting for the command to charge. Mannius checked that the Saxon auxiliaries were in position, then nodded to Seneca to order the advance, which he did with a wave of his arm.

Mannius, his two bodyguards and four cavalrymen detailed to stay close to him, followed the formation. At first they moved slowly, then, after they crested the hill, the speed picked up. Cavalrymen brought their horses close to each other, bumping one another at times. Mannius felt fear fade as adrenaline surged and could see that the route ahead was clear: a grassy embankment, gently sloping to the village and still no one in the fight, barely three hundred paces away, had spotted them. Seneca increased the pace, then a trumpet sounded: the charge began and the sound of pounding hooves filled the air.

In the village the defenders glanced round, thinking that they were about to be cut down from behind. As they realised that the line of charging horsemen was angled to the rear of the Picts a cheer went up and joined the war cries from the cavalrymen. Surprise was absolute. The Picts froze. Uncertainty then panic gripped them.

Caught in the open with no cavalry support the Picts were easy targets for the spears and long swords of the Roman horsemen. Their shield wall crumbled. Men scrambled to get out of the way of snarling beasts and mounted warriors pushing sharpened spears at them. Great holes were left in the Pict formation, which degenerated into small pockets of men trying to save themselves. The Votadini pushed forwards, hacking at the hapless attackers.

More Picts emerged from the village, running to the aid of their comrades. Before they could get to the fight they too were attacked from the rear by the auxiliaries. Two riders went down and Mannius pushed his horse to the front, hacking down with his sword onto exposed necks. Suddenly he was through and facing the Votadini shield wall. He'd become oblivious to danger and found himself disorientated. He reined in his horse, shaking and feeling a desperate thirst, then made for the standard-bearer.

A trumpet sounded the recall of the cavalrymen who gradually broke off their attack and regrouped on the flank of the Votadini away from the village. Picts still caught in the open threw down their weapons and tried to surrender. Men from the Votadini, hate and loathing etched on their faces, charged and cut them down.

Separated by burning buildings and a wide stream, both sides drew breath and waited. Some of the Votadini turned and saw a line of red cloaked men on the crest of the hill behind. Spears were pointed and another cheer went up.

Pockets of men, who had been fighting small battles around the village, appeared, moved passed the main group of defenders and climbed the hill to the Roman's position. They fell gratefully behind the wall of men only to be hauled to their feet by the innkeeper and bullied into the rear of his rapidly growing army.


Down in the village the ruse was complete. Through smoke the Pictish commander watched in shock as Roman horsemen charged into his men and cut them to pieces. Now those same men patrolled along tracks at the other side of the stream. On the hill above the village Roman infantry looked down, poised to strike. They had been joined by a line of auxiliaries, probably some Votadini warriors as well. Long shadows cast by the evening sun seemed to make the Roman infantry grow bigger and more powerful with every passing minute. Fatigue from a night then a day's fighting and chasing the Votadini set in.

The Pictish leader gathered his lieutenants together. 'We fall back to the other side of the wood and hold our position until Ceretic's men arrive.'

'We should wipe out the last of the Votadini while we have the chance, sir,' objected one of the officers.

'And the Romans?'

'What of the Romans? What can they do?'

'I'd say quite a lot by the look of them,' said a wizened, battle-hardened man, his face streaked with blood. 'Roman cavalry and heavy infantry means they've got at least two or three centuries up there with the same number of auxiliaries.'

'But the Romans...'

'My friend is right. You have obviously never witnessed the Roman army in action. Far different from a quick raid and one-on-one combat,' said the Pictish leader patiently. 'Even with fresh warriors, tackling such a shield wall is murderous work. Uphill and tired, our men would be gutted and filleted faster than a net full of trout. No, our men have done more than we could have hoped. Now we rest.'

'So why don't they come and attack us?' persisted the man.

'They may yet. Their scouts will be looking at us, assessing our strength, looking for weaknesses. Romans do everything deliberately, they know how to make war. When they're ready they'll strike and there'll be no mercy.'

'The interesting question to me,' went on the veteran warrior, 'is how come they're here in the first place. Why show up now in such force?'

'The question was forming in my head as well,' replied the Pictish leader. 'They had no business here. I will inform Prince Fidach. Someone must have betrayed us. Our king will need to hear what Ceretic has to say on this.'

# Chapter VII

When she came to, lying in an anteroom off the Great Hall, Caoimhe could hear men cheering and screams from women. The victors were enjoying their spoils. Her hands were bound in front of her and gently she explored her face. One side was swollen, bruised and extremely tender to the touch. Some of her teeth felt loose. She guessed that a spear handle had hit her or perhaps she had been dragged to the ground and kicked. Yes, her ribs ached as well. What had happened to her father? Surely the Picts must have seen the war band approaching. Why didn't they leave?

The door was thrown open and a drunken Pict staggered through. He grabbed Caoimhe's hair and pulled. Once on her feet she towered over the small man and spat her contempt at him. Instinctively he slapped her face with the back of his hand. Caoimhe felt the tenderness of her bruised face explode in pain. The man grinned but she merely smiled serenely back at her tormentor.

She was pushed into the main hall where drunken men were busy eating, drinking and fighting over trinkets. Torches blazed overhead. Through holes in the walls, presumably caused by the fighting, she could see that it was dark outside. Another warrior grabbed her wrists and pulled her to the top table.

'Ah, Princess Caoimhe,' said a Pict seated in the centre.

'Drostan! Scum like you shouldn't be allowed to crawl out of the cesspit!'

'Actually it's *King* Drostan now,' said the Pict, picking some meat out of his teeth and ignoring the insult.

'So you murdered your father as well as the innocent people here today.'

'He died honourably in battle.'

'Riding his favourite slave-whore, no doubt. Is that what you intend for me?'

'The thought had crossed my mind,' said Drostan casually. 'Though I think you need a little breaking in first before you aspire to such favours from me.'

'What have you done with the prisoners? The women and children?'

'We have no prisoners. Most of the men died well, they did your tribe credit,' said Drostan, emphasising the point by waving a chicken leg. 'A few squealed for mercy before they too died. As for the women, well they are being taught to respect their new masters before they become slaves. You too are our property now, Princess.'

Caoimhe reached for the small vessel of poison round her neck. To her horror she realised it had gone.

Drostan smiled. 'Perhaps you are looking for this?' he said, holding up the small jar. 'We tested it on two of your men. They died swiftly. A very high quality poison.'

'You are a barbaric murderer. My father will make you pay dearly for this.'

'I think not. If the Saxons didn't get him this morning then my brother will have finished him this afternoon.'

Was all hope lost? Maybe it was a bluff. The mention of Saxons brought a new factor to think about. She suddenly felt alone. Alone and desperate. Whatever had happened to her father she knew that she was now at the mercy of her attackers.

Outside she heard men's voices, quickly followed by screams of pain. Maybe some men still survived and were making the Picts pay. A man ran into the hall.

'A witch just burned two of our men!' The man looked terrified.

Immediately a young man next to Drostan stood up, a little unsteadily, and made as though to unsheathe his sword. The king put a gentle arm across him. 'Let the men take care of the witch. Better that you break in this bitch-princess a little.'

The man grinned and moved round the table to Caoimhe. He put both hands on her shoulders and belched into her face. She smiled back. 'Too pissed to stand up? Lean on me a little.'

The man slapped her hard across the face and she tasted blood. Why always pick on my face? I used to be pretty. Outside she could hear orders being given. The man pushed her back towards the broken wall. She felt the wall behind her and pushed back. He replaced his hands on her shoulders and ripped at her tunic until it hung round her waist. She tried her best to cover herself but with her hands bound decency was difficult. The man took out a knife and cut through her bonds, presumably so that he could move her arms out of the way and get to her breasts. She watched her attacker fumble with his knife, trying and failing to replace it in its sheath on his belt. Too drunk to care, he threw it onto the wooden boards. Caoimhe spat in his face and was rewarded with another slap that sent her sprawling to the floor. The man looked triumphant as he fell on top of her, pulling at the base of her tunic.

Outside there were shouts then a mighty roar. The Great Hall shook and screams pierced the night. Even drink could not mask the terror on the faces of those present. Men rushed outside. The man about to rape her looked uncertain. Only Caoimhe remained unmoved: there was no more terror that could come into her world. She was the first to react. The man's knife was close. She grabbed it, thrust it into his throat and felt warm blood gush onto her face. He pulled away, eyes gaping, but no one was looking at him. As fast as she could she slid through one of the gaps in the wall and found herself outside.

Borgach's house was burning fiercely. Bodies lay strewn around it and several men were staggering round, some on fire themselves. Well done Borgach! At least the Picts wouldn't get her daughter.

She kept low, running through the buildings. As she went she found a discarded cloak and helmet. Fastening the cloak with a belt and sword slowed her but it made her look more like a warrior. She ducked less and walked more. There was damage to the palisade and she slipped through and made towards the steepest, craggier part of the mound.

She could hear men talking excitedly about the fire on the summit. The Picts sounded as though they were on the bridge, near to the gate. She headed for the place where the initial attack had been made and found it deserted, except for corpses. She waded through the black ooze of the ditch and found herself free on the other side. Not daring to look back she ran along paths and hedgerows that she had known as a child. On and on she pushed herself until her lungs burned. Still she ran until her legs could go no more. Finally she collapsed under a bush, exhausted and trembling. She started to cry. Then an arm curled around her mouth and she felt herself sink again.

# Chapter VIII

The lengthening daylight hours of spring and a clear night illuminated by a half-moon aided the flight of the Votadini. Wounded men, exhausted children and those too weak to walk were loaded onto carts and taken the fifteen miles to Oxton.

King Cathal was taken to the crest of the hill on a cart strewn with thick rugs. A large black African slave from his bodyguard, arm in a sling and a bandage round his head, held the reins in his one good hand. At the top of the hill, behind the line of 'Romans', Mannius at last met the king.

'Easy, Mo,' said King Cathal to the slave, who had tensed on the approach of Mannius. 'Let my young friend come close. Master physician though he is, I doubt he can save me.'

'I'm sorry,' started Mannius, moving to examine the king's wounds.

'Nothing for you to be sorry about, my lad. Glad you came.' The king laughed.

'Easy now, my lord,' said Mo.

'Might as well go out with a laugh, eh?' You thought I was out of it but I heard you, moaning like an old woman, Mo, as we came up the hill.' The king convulsed in a fit of laughter and pain before he composed himself again. 'Fooled you didn't he, Mo? Our own men dressed as Romans!'

Mannius called for a hot iron.

'You've found the worst of it, physician, but it runs too

deep. I know I'm done for. Now listen the both of you.' Cathal's voice, like his life, was fading. 'You're a canny one, Tribune. My only regret is that I won't see you give them Picts a damn good hiding – as surely you will. I want you to promise me that you'll look after my family for me.'

Mannius nodded and smiled in his best bedside manner. 'Of course, you and your family have been faithful supporters of Rome.' Mannius applied the hot iron to cauterise an artery and the king jolted, more alert than before.

'Look at that smile. Delivers a hot poker with such a smile.' The king laughed weakly. 'It's important to remember to smile as much as to fight.' Both men nodded patiently, listening to the last ramblings of a dying man. 'For my last requests tradition needs me to tell a free man.'

Mo reluctantly lifted his spear and jumped to the ground. 'Wait there Mo! Physician, I need a witness and Mo needs a coin.' Mannius fished for and found one of the gold coins he'd taken in payment for the operation he'd performed on the boy. 'Give me the coin, Mo, to buy your freedom. You've been a good servant, bodyguard and the most loyal friend I ever had. Now take your reward, you're a free man.' The king's hand grasped Mo's hand and the coin in a tight grip. 'Now physician, if you'll excuse us.'

'Of course, my lord,' replied Mannius, stepping back respectfully out of earshot, where he watched as the old man spoke his last thoughts to the African.

'Physician!' shouted Mo.

Mannius jumped on the cart and felt for the old man's pulse. The king stirred. 'You fooled them. Those Picts ran from this lot.' His laughter was from the heart, loud enough to make men's heads turn. Then he fell back silent, dead, and with a contented smile across his face.

Mo was laughing with his king, tears streaming down his face.

'I hope my soul dies as merry as his when my time comes,' said Mannius, helping to close the king's eyes. Then it was to business again. 'Can you drive the cart to Oxton?'

Mo nodded.

'Good, then listen. The king isn't dead, understand?' Mo nodded. 'These people have had too much bad news today. We'll tell them tomorrow maybe. We'll wrap the king in these rugs and I'll have two of my men take the cart from Oxton as soon as you get there.'

Mo gently took the gold coin from the king's grasp and handed it to Mannius. 'That's yours,' said the Roman Tribune.

'Thank you, but I reckon it's King Cathal's now. Might be of use if he needs it to get across the river to the other side.'

The great warrior pushed the coin under the king's tongue.


Seneca supplemented his men with some Votadini riders and organised them into patrols to provide a screen between them and the Picts. Closer to the old fort Votadini warriors stood guard as pickets to prevent a surprise attack. Save for the moans of the wounded everything was quiet.

Inside the fort, the innkeeper-turned-centurion went round inspecting his troops, making sure they hadn't fallen asleep. Then he supervised a group of volunteer cooks in the kitchens. Everything had to be eaten or carried away. He was determined to leave nothing for the Picts.

Braziers burned in roofless buildings and on the old parade ground. Men stared at the flames, hypnotised like insects, looking for answers in the orange glow. Early in the evening some Pictish prisoners had been tortured, but their screams unsettled the children and they were quickly put to death. Now the only moans came from wounded warriors.

'I'm sorry for your loss,' said Mannius in a low whisper to Mo, who was warming himself by a fire of pine logs.

'Bloody treachery,' replied the big man. 'Ceretic told us to join him, said you Romans was going and that we could invade south with him.'

'But King Cathal said no?'

'Course he did – he wouldn't break an oath come what may. But Ceretic, his words are as hard to pin down as the wind and not nearly as useful.'

'Don't worry, Mo, we'll stand with our friends, the Votadini.'

'That's what the king said, sir. He trusted you and told me to do likewise.'

Mannius felt guilt turn his stomach. He had failed King Cathal and now the Votadini nation was in tatters, running before a powerful foe. If only he had sent for Seneca earlier and been able to help the king further north; maybe things would have been different.


All day Saxons and Ceretic's men had marched steadily eastwards. Wherever the terrain allowed, Votadini warriors had stood their ground. Then they'd broken off and let their horsemen act as skirmishers to allow enough time for the foot soldiers to escape to another defensible position. They had finally met up with men fighting for King Drostan's brother, Prince Fidach. Then fortune had gone with them and the Romans had saved them.

Now Drostan rode to join his brother in the village of King Cathal's last stand. They both waited for Ceretic and the Saxon leader to join them. As he entered, Ceretic noted that there was an air of hostility.

'Well done to the both of you,' said Ceretic. 'Your men fought bravely and the Votadini are vanquished. I hear that your men killed Prince Maon and gravely injured Cathal himself. The beacon on top of Traprain Law was an excellent idea – sends out a message, don't you think?'

'We would have taken him, finished his men off and had countless slaves if the Romans hadn't turned up,' answered Fidach.

'Romans?' spluttered Ceretic. He could sense accusing eyes boring in on him. Even the surly Saxon seemed to be looking at him with a greater degree of malevolence than usual.

'You know, those people meant to be leaving,' continued Fidach.

'Can't be. The nearest garrison must be over a hundred miles away,' protested Ceretic.

'Well they turned up here, large as life. Several centuries, auxiliaries and even some cavalry. Now what does your Roman know-it-all have to say about that?'

'He's gone south to help prepare the way for us all,' blustered Ceretic. 'I rather think that this was pure good fortune. Happened to be out on patrol.' He'd stretched it too far, he realised.

'A patrol by chance – I think not,' interjected Drostan. 'Too bloody many.'

'You say they turned up here, in this village?' asked Wybert.

'Yes!' replied Fidach. 'I was here. Saw it with my own eyes.'

The Saxon looked thoughtful. 'With such numbers of men why aren't they still in the village, dug into one of their marching camps? And I see no Roman shields or javelins.'

'They were on the crest of the hill,' protested Fidach.

'So how many men did you lose to the Romans?'

'Hundreds,' said Fidach awkwardly, presumably embarrassed that his lack of military cunning had led to such a loss. 'We was too tired after chasing those Votadini from the morning and the ones you two didn't deal with.'

'Patrolling Roman cavalry is one thing but infantry this far north I doubt,' said Wybert solemnly. 'And if they were here this afternoon they'd still be here, no doubt.'

Stalemate at last and it seemed like a good result for the time being. Ceretic tried to move the conversation on. 'Any interesting prisoners? I hear Princess Caoimhe took part in the defence of Traprain Law.'

Drostan was the one to look uncomfortable this time. 'Yes, I saw the princess. Very determined lady. Fought well.'

'So did she die or did you capture her?' persisted Ceretic.

'She was taken prisoner but escaped,' said Drostan sourly. After a nudge from his brother he carried on. 'It was witchcraft. That beacon earlier was an old witch's place. Went up with a roar fit to wake the dead. Killed seven of my men on the spot, started fires all over the place and the princess vanished.'

'Terrible thing, witchcraft,' sympathised Ceretic, sensing that it would do no good to pursue the matter. 'No fighting it. Still I suppose she can't have gone far. It'd be nice to get her back safe.' At last the meeting had something to agree on and after sorting out military objectives the two Picts took their leave.

'Can you believe those Picts,' said Ceretic turning to Wybert. 'I mean, witchcraft, a vanishing princess. More like Drostan was thinking with his bollocks and she got the better of him.'

'Perhaps,' said Wybert. 'And Romans appearing? Sounds like they was pissed or maybe they just pissed themselves when the Votadini started to put up a good fight.'

'Unless we've been betrayed by our Roman friend. We'll

have to keep a close eye on our Pictish allies. Very close.'
Ceretic made for a jug of wine and poured out two
mugfuls. 'Maybe we should send out more patrols to find
Princess Caoimhe.'

'She's nothing: a woman not a warrior, and soon her
people will no longer exist,' retorted the Saxon. 'If you
want her for your own pleasure we can send out patrols
but in the dark, with my men, your men and the Picts
all over the place, if they meet each other they'll probably
start fighting. We can start early tomorrow though.'

Mannius didn't get a chance to sleep. Everyone, himself
included, expected the Picts to chase them down Dere
Street. As each hour went by his anxiety increased as he
expected the enemy would soon deploy for an attack to
finish them off. During his wait he listened to Votadini
warriors and reports from Seneca's scouts. All he knew
was that the Votadini nation faced extinction. Only an
organised retreat would give them any chance to regroup
and save themselves. And if the Votadini collapsed then
Rome's enemies would be close enough to link their efforts
in attacking the eastern shores. He sent a coded summary
of events and a request for troops to be sent north
immediately to the camp prefect at Cilurnum, an old
cavalry fort, on Hadrian's Wall.

With his military duties done, Mannius helped treat the
injured. He removed arrow heads, stitched wounds and
set dozens of broken bones. His father was a master
physician and he had learned much from him. From his
mother he had acquired the rare skill of feeling a broken
bone and deciding the best way to set it. Now after years
of opportunity to practise on countless soldiers it was
second nature. By the time he'd finished, women were
preparing breakfast for their warriors. Most stirred pots

of porridge, though the occasional whiff of frying meat drifted over the crowded fort and its annexes.

In the lull of activity Mannius realised that he needed to plan: everyone would soon be looking to him to decide the order of marching. Who would act as rearguard? Should he stay or try to find reinforcements? When the governor had asked him to see King Cathal he couldn't have expected this to happen. He'd done enough: his uncle would surely send one of the prefects north with reinforcements and take charge – soon. The thought comforted Mannius: he felt he was sharing command. He busied himself with getting detailed reports from the officers around him so that he could properly brief the prefect when he arrived.

Surviving Votadini captains, who had volunteered to put together a rearguard, started assembling their men in the cold dark. Mannius went to inspect the defensive preparations and spotted Mo, who walked over to him.

'That arm of yours should still be in a sling, Mo.' Mannius had personally removed an arrowhead from the big man's left arm.

'I'll put it back there as soon as I can. I reckon I might need use of it over the next day or so.'

'You could leave the captains to lead the rearguard. I'm sure they'll cope without you for a while.'

'You're right Tribune, I'm not staying with them. Me and those guys are heading up to Traprain Law.' Four tough-looking warriors joined him. 'We're going to see if there's any survivors that need help. So far we've not heard from anyone near there.'

'There'll be lots of people need help, Mo. The trick will be staying out of the way of the opposition.'

'We know the tracks across the moors better than they do. And anyway,' said the big man, 'I owe it to the king to bring back as many of his people as possible.'

Mannius knew that it was no good arguing; the man was determined. Helping was a small way to repay any error that Mannius might have made in not getting to the Votadini sooner. 'Ask the captains for anything you need. We'll hold the crossing at Trimontium for the next two days, maybe three, and as many nights as well.'

'I appreciate that, Tribune.'

'And keep those bandages clean and tight, you hear? Now good luck to you!'

# Chapter IX

Under a bush barely two miles from Traprain Law, Caoimhe came to her senses. In her hand was a dagger that she'd picked up as she'd left the mound. She relaxed her body and pressure from the hand over her mouth lessened. There was enough room for her to manoeuvre and she did, spinning quickly. Another arm came up and stopped the dagger mid-flight and she was glad.

'Taran! Where on earth...' she started.

'Ssh!' he hissed back. 'There are Picts and Saxons all over the place. Not to mention some of Ceretic's men.'

The pair kept still. Caoimhe wanted to start running again then she too heard noises of men close by. 'Picts!' whispered Taran.

'I know. I can't understand what they're saying but I can smell them.'

'They're looking for you, my dear. Only they've got to be careful of accidentally bumping into Saxons.'

'Saxons?'

'Seems everyone's after us these days.'

They waited in silence for the men to pass, then Caoimhe hissed, 'What of Saxons?'

'It seems, my dear, that we were attacked on at least four fronts, maybe along the coast as well, who knows? Your father and Maon helped evacuate Din Eidyn in the face of Saxons and Ceretic's men while Faolan and I were sent to help you at Traprain Law.'

'So what happened?'

'By the time we met up with our men they were already

fighting. They were brave. Three hundred of our men against a Pict band more than four times its number. There wasn't much to be done except kill as many Picts as possible. I'm sorry, your brother fought bravely but there were too many Picts. The battle was chaotic. Everyone got separated.'

'But my brother might be...'

'I don't know what happened to him but I fear the worst. I'm sorry, truly I am.'

Caoimhe remembered how the fire at Borgach's hut had saved her. It seemed selfish to press him about her brother when his companion had blown herself up. After all, she was a royal and had to look after the welfare of her father's subjects before herself. 'Taran, I'm sorry too. I shouldn't have... And Borgach.'

'Yes?'

'Your house was destroyed by a terrible explosion. When Borgach set fire to it lots of Picts were killed too and in the chaos I slipped away. I'm sorry, Taran, truly I am. You weren't married but I know you had a soft spot for Borgach. And Caitir and Una were with her as well,' she gave a little sob.

'Nothing to be sorry about, my dear. I'm just glad it worked after what it cost me. Only downside is I ended up with that lot,' said Taran pointing into the darkness.

There were sounds of a quiet scuffle then nothing. 'Murderous bunch but very good. We've been clearing the patrols, making them frightened to come out and gathering folks together. Heard you running this way a while back and wandered over to see what the rush was. Come on.'

Caoimhe took the man's arm as he led them to the sound of the scuffle. Sure enough, eight Picts lay, lifeless, on the ground and another two were kneeling, their hands bound behind them. Beyond the group, in a hollow, more warriors stood guard and lower down around thirty women and children huddled together.

'Go on,' prompted Taran. 'Go and see them. They'll be glad to see someone from the king's family. It'll help them, you'll see.'

'And what's your plan?'

'We'll stay here 'til just before dawn. By then I should have been able to gather enough mist to hide us as we move up to the moors.'

'Hah!' spat Caoimhe, squeezing the man's arm. 'I could do that. Everyone knows that a clear night will bring a chill-mist.'

'There must be more druid in you than I knew.'

Self-consciously Caoimhe smoothed the rough cloak she wore, straightened herself and descended as confidently as she could into the hollow. In the darkness she was unable to see faces but those around her seemed to know who she was. A small woman with spindly arms took her in an embrace. 'Praise your god for preserving you, child. You fought well today, did your father and us all proud you did.'

'Borgach? How?'

'Yes, my dear. There are more ways to get in and out of a druid's house than simply through the door. Una! Una, where are you?' she hissed.

Una came forward, carrying a bundle that she handed to Caoimhe. 'Una carried her here all the way,' went on Borgach.

Caoimhe took the bundle, checked on the sleeping Caitir, and tried to thank Borgach. Words and any pretence at regal decorum failed her. Emotionally and physically exhausted she fell to the ground and cried. Borgach took hold of her in a tight embrace. She shook until finally she fell asleep cradling her daughter.


In the cold hours before dawn, with only the twinkling light of stars to guide them, a steady stream of carts, people and animals began moving south from the inn at Oxton down the paved road. The rearguard stood ready to cover the retreat, supervised by Mannius and the Votadini captains.

'It's risky staying here much longer,' said Seneca, earnestly.

'I know but so many more people keep coming this way.'

'It'll be that Mo telling them to pop over the moors and get stuck in to some grub.'

'Any movement reported?' asked Mannius, ignoring the decurion's glib remark.

'No, sir. Nothing as yet.'

'Good. And by the time we get reports of the enemy moving down the road we should have two to three hours warning?'

'Yes, sir.'

'So we should be able to get even the slowest movers six to ten miles away before the Picts get here. We'll go at noon, which should let us get everyone back to the crossing at Trimontium by nightfall.'

Well before noon a messenger arrived with an uncoded message from the prefect and bearing the governor's seal. 'Shit! Don't they realise what the situation is?' said Mannius to Seneca who looked at him quizzically. 'Orders for all our forces to be back behind the Wall by tomorrow night. What's the thinking behind that?'

'Probably knows that you'll stick your neck out too far to help these people.'

'But they've helped us plenty. We owe it to them.'

'If we don't get back we'll both be up on a charge. Though by the look of things it seems that you probably have a bigger command than the prefect now,' said Seneca, waving at the assembled Votadini warriors. 'And I've never had so many cavalry units. You could tell them to piss off, maybe that's what they're afraid of.'

Mannius, deep in thought, surveyed the soldiers before

him. The innkeeper appeared to have abandoned his earlier trade and have become a full-time centurion. 'Call the captains together. 'We've got enough troops to split them. They can take over from Leofric at Trimontium, then fall back to Bremenium.'

'At least they'll have plenty of room at the fort, sir.'

'Yes, and it'll give us some time to find somewhere for our new army south of the Wall.'

Mannius raced back to the fort at Bremenium, stopping just long enough at Trimontium to brief Leofric on the situation. The Saxon mercenary's men had been busy improving the defences at the crossing. A series of interconnected ditches and small towers guarded the approach to the old, stone bridge. On the other side more obstacles had been erected to slow the advance of attackers and give easy targets for mounted archers, which would allow the infantry time to withdraw from any fighting.

Approaching Bremenium, Mannius expected to find a scene of chaos. Instead Curtius had the place organised to his usual high standards. The old centurion greeted Mannius. 'Thanks for the new arrivals.'

'You don't seem to be doing too badly.'

'They're a stoic bunch, I'll give you that, sir. Not had any complaints from them.'

'Still in shock,' said Mannius.

'I think the prefect's got a shock in store for you,' said Curtius, pointing to two messengers. 'Keeps sending those types looking for you. Must be some big panic on down south. Oh and by the way, what shall I do with the old king?'

'Find a nice spot in our graveyard. Give him full ceremony. Only senior officers to attend. I still want to keep his demise quiet for the time being.'

'At least being buried here means he's on Votadini land, I suppose.'

A small child, clothed in mud-covered rags, stumbled and fell. Its mother seemed oblivious to its plight. Both senior officers watched a legionary pick up the child and place it on a wagon. Even soldiers hardened to the brutalities of war could have nothing but sympathy and compassion, thought Mannius. The wretched, beaten, homeless and hungry filed silently into the fort following sheep-like the person in front. He would do what he could for these people out of a sense of duty to King Cathal and because he hated to see good people suffer. As soon as fresh horses were ready Mannius with two squadrons of Seneca's cavalry and the messengers carried on south.

# Chapter X

Passing close to the town of Corstopitum, three miles inside the safety of the Wall, another exodus appeared to be under way. Roads south of the Wall seemed to be alive with even more activity than further north. Maybe it was just that the people were more alive: contemplating what might happen to them rather than reliving recent horrors. People and carts were on the move south towards Eburacum. The sight of an officer with a cavalry escort, galloping south, sent a jolt of panic through the eyes of those fleeing.

Well after dark and exhausted, Mannius finally found the prefect quartered at the fort of Vindomora, which was normally used as a supply base for troops along the Wall. If Mannius had been less tired he might have realised that it was an unusual place in which to find the prefect. But it was time to brief the man who would take over from him and push the Picts back north.

A legionary took his horse while another led him to the prefect's office.

'Ah! Come in, my boy,' said the old man, warming himself in front of a roaring brazier and nursing a goblet of diluted wine.

'Good evening, Prefect Leonius.'

'Though it might be spring outside, the slightest chill and my bones disagree.'

'It is a good remedy for stiff joints, I hear, sir,' replied Mannius.

'Of course! Your father was an excellent physician to

the army. Mended my arm after a horse I was riding decided to part company with me on manoeuvres. Hurt like hell when he put it right and I swore I'd kill him.' The prefect smiled into his goblet. 'But it mended like he said it would so I forgave him and sent him a barrel of wine for doubting him in the first place.'

A young man, not in uniform though smartly dressed, reclined on a sofa by a desk. Mannius had watched him eye the exchange, examining him.

'Pleased to meet you, physician.' The voice was silky smooth, perfect pronunciation – an aristocrat from Rome. Somehow Mannius registered an emphasis on his profession.

'This is Senator-elect Flavius,' said the prefect by way of introduction.

'Appointed by the Senate to help sort out the mess of this wretched province.' The young man spoke to a bottle of wine on the desk as though it was the only thing worthy of hearing his voice. 'Need to sort this scum out so we can return to Rome as soon as possible – eh?'

Mannius remained silent, gauging how the conversation was likely to develop. The prefect seemed unable to settle and hopped from foot to foot. He was nervous – was it the young man? 'I have no plans to travel to Rome at present,' answered Mannius.

'Talented physicians like you should be given a chance to practise their art in a more civilised and rewarding setting,' replied Flavius. 'I have many connections that can ensure you have the right introductions when you decide to set yourself up in our great capital.'

'And if I choose to stay here?'

'Surely you can't want to stay in this damp, infested land, not when the delights of Rome beckon?' The tone of the young man's voice remained smooth and confident – almost persuasive. It was too persuasive and triggered something deep inside Mannius' tired brain.

'You may be surprised that some of us enjoy this land and its people.'

The young man yawned and stretched his arms out wide, as though he was about to dive into a pool of water. 'That is a pity and to be regretted.' Slowly he got to his feet.

'And how does that involve me?' Mannius felt his fatigue clear as adrenaline started to pump round his body. Arrogance, decided Mannius, was making the young man provocative.

'Heard you had some success fighting off a war band,' replied Flavius, looking at him for the first time.

'Yes, yes, congratulations, well done,' added the prefect, presumably detecting the cold note of the conversation and trying to inject some enthusiasm into the proceedings. 'I read your report, first rate.'

The action had been part of a well coordinated, full-scale invasion that had swept away the Votadini nation – just as his uncle had feared. Mannius was about to correct the youngster. Instead his thoughts veered to the governor: he'd correct this whelp and send him back to Rome double-time. A warm feeling of smugness began to grow. Through the fatigue he had to concentrate hard not to smile, which could prompt more questions. Best to be straight-faced and soldierly.

'I also read your reports about the Votadini,' said Flavius. 'Excellent bluff with the ghost legionaries.' The young man was more skilful than Mannius expected. Squashing him then flattering him. He wished he could lie down, sleep then face the two men refreshed and ready.

'Still shows that those Picts have a healthy respect for the Legions,' added Leonius.

'Quite,' said Flavius, suddenly turning his attention to a map spread across a desk.

Leonius coughed, seemingly to indicate a change in

subject and joined Flavius. 'Your report was also rather disturbing. You mentioned Saxons fighting with the Picts. Difficult to believe that far north.'

'Yes, sir,' responded Mannius. 'I didn't believe it myself at first. I spoke with several of King Cathal's captains – all experienced soldiers – and they were adamant that Saxons had started the attack. As they fell back they met with Picts.'

Leonius whistled. 'Sounds like the conspiracy of sixty-seven all over again: Irish, Scotti, Picts all coming at us as one.'

'Never had much inclination for history, I'm afraid,' said Flavius, stifling a yawn.

'Surely we can get reinforcements from the south,' protested Mannius automatically. He went over the young man's words. There was certainty; he didn't doubt Mannius' report and neither did the prefect – that was unusual. Normally, someone in their position would look for corroboration.

'Ten years ago, maybe. Not any more,' said Leonius. 'Since Constantine went to Gaul with most of our best troops there haven't been any reinforcements. From the Saxon shore to here not one man can be spared. The only additions to the legions have come from locals or by hiring mercenaries as auxiliaries.'

'And if any fresh troops come from the south we will, of course, station them near Eburacum,' said Flavius confidently.

'How so?' asked Mannius.

'The governor's worried about the safety of Eburacum,' explained Leonius. 'He believes its defence should be the prime and only concern of the military.'

'We will strengthen our lookout positions along the coast and all other military personnel not on the Wall are to be withdrawn to Eburacum as soon as possible.

The Votadini are to be disarmed then repatriated,' added Flavius.

'Why? What have King Cathal's people done to deserve such treatment – except to be our greatest allies north of the Wall?'

Flavius looked and sounded bored. 'North of the Wall is where they should be; south of the Wall they may cause trouble and be a distraction.'

'Your orders are set out here,' said Leonius, interjecting to hand Mannius a scroll that carried a senatorial seal.

'But my orders, from the governor himself, were to help the Votadini then prepare our defences in the north, ready for him to lead a counter-attack against an expected invasion. Surely, Prefect, you are going to lead the counter-attack.'

Flavius held up his hand to interrupt. '*I* am the governor. I'm sorry, but yesterday, the former governor suffered a heart attack. Well – an attack on his heart with a dagger. It appears some Saxon mercenaries had a grievance about a lack of pay and attacked him. Senator Cirius Antonius, who I happen to be accompanying, nominated me to act as temporary governor. And of course I had the murderers executed and authorised troops to raze their village.'

The words hit Mannius hard. His uncle murdered! Something deep in his subconscious told Mannius that defeat was close. Troops stationed in lookout posts would be cut off and overwhelmed – just as he'd discussed with his uncle. Only if larger formations were created would they be able to mount an effective defence and that would require competent units near to possible landing sites. And they'd need the Votadini's help. Strategically the orders were a nonsense – surely the prefect at least could see that.

'We have recently received reports of a massive Saxon fleet moving up the coast and the governor is concerned that its target may be Eburacum. With that in mind he has requested that we send half our men to assist in its defence.'

Mannius put his grief to one side. He had to have one last try; maybe he could get the prefect to see sense. 'But there are enough men to hold them in the estuary until we could march there. And if they land in the marshes weight of numbers would be no good in the narrow causeways. It'd take them weeks to get out and we'd be ambushing them all the way.'

Flavius gave Mannius a sickly, arrogant, knowing smile. 'I am familiar with all the works of our best generals. My strategy is the only one that will work and is the only one that will be followed. Do I make myself clear?'

'You can put my orders on the brazier. At least they'll do some good there. Following such madness would be a dereliction of our stewardship of this province.'

'I realise that I can't compel anyone who bears the authority of the imperial seal to follow my military orders. However, as governor I am placing you under house arrest pending a full inquiry into your allegiance with the Votadini.'

Mannius knew the inquiry was spurious, dreamed up to keep him guessing. He was too tired to be concerned. 'I will go back to my surgery – at least I may still be able to do some good there.' With that he spun round and marched out, not waiting to be dismissed.


'He has friends in this province,' said Leonius quietly. Until Mannius left, the old prefect hadn't realised that he'd been sweating.

'Personally, I'd be happier to see him dead. But the senator thinks that he may still be of use to us. If he does nothing, then there is no further possibility of scandal.'

'And if he fights?'

'The senator feels that it would be useful for a few Romans to fight – to show that we still have some devotion to this land. And, of course, he'll lose. No question.'


'What do you mean your men haven't advanced down Dere Street?' snarled King Ceretic at the two Pictish leaders in front of his lunch table.

'Your men can go that way,' answered Fidach.

'But they're over a day away from here,' protested Ceretic. 'That'll give the whole Votadini nation time to escape. We need to pursue them, catch them. Think of the slaves you could have.'

'Fuck slaves!' hissed Drostan.

'I heard that's what you normally did before you sold them,' said Ceretic sarcastically.

'You're having a laugh at our expense, Ceretic,' Fidach bit back. 'First you said no one would fight at Traprain Law and we lose over two hundred good men. Then you say there'll be no Romans and, lo, a cohort appears by magic and we lose more of our brave brothers. I think you're trying to get us Picts killed.'

'Yeah!' added Drostan. 'You want us to clear your enemies away so that your men can march down Dere Street, all the way to Eburacum to help themselves and there'll be nothing left for us. Well let them or your Saxon friends go down Dere Street now and kick the Romans out of the way 'cos we ain't doing all the fighting.'

'And you'll need us when those other Saxon murderers turn up,' said Fidach. 'They'll not give you the time of day when they've got their men together.' With that the two Picts got up and marched out.

'Well thank you for getting that little misunderstanding off your chests, boys,' Ceretic said to his dog that was waiting patiently for scraps of food. 'Let's put the whole bloody campaign at risk just because of your paranoia. But I do take your point about the Saxons, thanks lads.'

# Chapter XI

Caoimhe was woken by Caitir tugging at her hair. When she'd seen Borgach with her daughter, the memories of the attack on Traprain Law started to fade. The adrenaline that had kept her going suddenly drained and all she could think of was sleep. With Caitir lying in her arms the pair had slept under a Pictish cloak. Now Caitir was hungry and demanded food.

Borgach seemed well prepared. 'Try some of this,' she said, passing over a handful of dried meat and nuts. 'Now Una'll make sure the wee lass gets some water and'll look after her. I dare say Taran'll need you more than Caitir here today.' Una looked as though she'd been up for ages. Surely not, thought Caoimhe, as first light was only just appearing and the dawn chorus had yet to get properly underway.

Around her the hollow seemed more crowded than she remembered. More people must have arrived during the night. Getting to her feet, she stretched and took stock of the slumbering bodies around her. 'Go on, he's over there,' said Borgach, pointing.

'How are you today, Princess?' Taran looked younger and more animated than usual.

'A little stiff and a lot bruised.'

'Good! Nothing that won't pass once we get going.'

'And where might that be?'

'We need to persuade some of your people to follow us out of here. They're not yet convinced of the danger they face.'

'Who and where are they?'

'Some families from fishing villages in the east. Pictish boats were spotted coming down the coast and their fleets took to sea, sailing south to protect the boats and nets. That left the rest of them to flee inland with everything they could carry.'

'They think that the danger will pass?'

'Seems that way.'

'How far are they?'

'Just under ten miles.' Taran smiled, anticipating her next objection and waved towards the undergrowth. There was the sound of a horse's whinny and a man appeared leading two horses towards them. 'Kind of the Picts to supply us with horses.'

Caoimhe did not resist being helped onto her mount and followed Taran out of the wood. 'What about...'

'Don't worry about Caitir and the rest. The men will escort them onto the moors and cut onto the paved road when they feel it's safe. So far we've not had any reports of the attackers moving south; a bit strange really but I'll not object.'

Trailed by two guards, they rode along old tracks and through ancient woods. Branches, disturbed by Taran, swayed and their new-grown leaves flicked morning dew across her face. Her brothers used to do the same trick and she objected bitterly. Not today. The sensation meant she was alive and free of her captors. At the edge of the forest Taran halted, looked around and sniffed the air. All Caoimhe could smell was the deep scent of tree blossom. Maybe that was all Taran could smell as well, she thought. Then there was a movement close by. She tightened her grip on the reins, then made sure her dagger was loose in its sheath. The undergrowth shuddered and a deer exploded across their track, steadied itself, took one look at them and trotted away into another dense area of trees.

Caoimhe relaxed and nudged her horse forward. Tree branches parted and six painted men burst onto the track, shouting their war cry. The two guards immediately charged at the attackers, taking two down and using the weight of their horses to hold the others back. Then four more men came from behind and ran at them. Taran turned his horse, shouted at the princess to ride on and charged the men. Using the momentum skilfully he held out his long sword and slashed open the head of the fastest man. Then his horse reared, its mighty hooves threatening the attackers. With their speed checked Taran took the opportunity to slice another man down with a fatal blow.

Caoimhe screamed as she saw more men on the track ahead of her. She looked back and saw Taran, having ridden through four attackers and killed two, turn his horse to run the others down. But he was too far away to help her. The guards were hacking at their attackers. Then one of them went rigid and fell, blood streaming from his chest. She felt alone and instinctively reached for her dagger. Five men came at her: she could see their faces twisted in hate; their teeth bared and their swords glinting in the sun. The leader was barely ten paces from her when his face changed. Hate turned to shock as a spear appeared in his chest. Another spear sailed into one of the other men, then another. Horses charged out of the trees and four men set about the attackers before doubling back to help Taran and the remaining guard.

'Am I glad to see you, Mo,' said Caoimhe, jumping off her horse to hug the big African bodyguard.

'And you, Princess.'

'You know, I thought I smelt you, Mo,' said Taran, wheeling his horse alongside. 'That's what confused me.'

'Saw this lot having their breakfast and leave it real fast,' replied Mo. 'Thought it must be some of our people using this track so we waited to see who came along.'

'Are you with my father and Maon?' asked Caoimhe. 'Has he come here?'

The look on Mo's face was enough to make her burst into tears. 'I'm sorry, Princess. Maon fell fighting Ceretic's men and your father died last night. Even a Roman surgeon couldn't save him, but he died laughing.' The bodyguard relived the king's last battle and how the Roman tribune had frightened the Picts with his bluff and told him to keep the king's death quiet. 'I promised your father that I would find you and look after you. It was his dying wish and it was easy to agree.'

After hiding the bodies in undergrowth and burying the Votadini guard in a shallow grave covered with stones, the group rode on in silence. Taran took them onto a fell side and finally down into a valley hidden from the plain below. He slowed his horse to little more than a walk until they reached a point where the track disappeared into darkness created by spring leaves and blossom of overhanging trees. Then he and the guards dismounted. One of the men took Taran's horse as well as his own while the other led Caoimhe's by the bridle. She too started to dismount. 'No, Princess,' said Taran. 'It looks better if a member of the royal household rides.'

The guards brought the horses to a halt and Taran went to a stream at the trackside. After soaking a cloth he presented it and a comb to Caoimhe. 'A chance to clean up before we meet your people,' he said. Then he disappeared down the track and into the darkness of the wood. Soon he was back with more warriors, who led them on. A little way off the track, above a stream and screened by thick bushes, a series of large caves housed dozens of families from the fishing villages.

Torches flickered in the darkness and several fires warmed the stones. Some of the faces Caoimhe recognised and she waved. More people seemed to recognise her and

91

quickly she was surrounded by people wanting to talk to her. One woman even thrust a baby, wrapped tightly in a torn cloak, into her arms. 'She'll be safer with you, m'lady.'

Caoimhe dutifully took the baby, gently kissed its forehead and smiled. The baby was quiet and smiled back to her. If the mother had witnessed what I've been through in the last day she might think differently, thought the princess.

Taran had a knack with wooing crowds, something he needed to teach his latest pupil. Now everyone was looking at her and in the orange light, protecting the baby in her arms, she shone as a symbol of hope. Her smooth, pale skin, even with cuts and bruises, looked waxy in the dim glow and her red hair seemed to be ablaze when she was silhouetted against one of the fires. Taran led her to a ledge in the cave where another fire burned and a small breakfast was laid out.

Time was short but Taran knew that everyone would be in a better frame of mind after some food. When all seemed to have finished, and only after more people had squeezed themselves into the cave, he stood to address the crowd. 'King Cathal has sent Princess Caoimhe to help guide you to the safety of his army.'

'We heard it was beat,' shouted a voice from the dark.

'If you mean pushed back then, yes,' said Taran. 'But if you mean have our men given up, then I say no!' His booming voice echoed off the walls and the druid sounded powerful. No one would argue with that voice, it had a tone of power about it, thought Caoimhe. A silence fell and Taran continued. 'Yesterday, our great nation was betrayed by cowards who joined together to attack us when our king and his princes were away. Saxons attacked Din Eidyn.' Taran had to wait a moment to let the murmurs fade at the mention of Saxons. 'Ceretic's men helped with the attack and our brave king fell back, protecting the women and children of Din Eidyn. He knew it was better to give ground yesterday so that we might fight tomorrow.'

Polite murmurs of approval rippled round the crowd. Taran let the news sink in. 'Picts attacked Traprain Law. Prince Faolan and I tried to assist in the defence but we were caught by a large war band a few miles from Din Eidyn. So, the defence of our holiest site fell to Princess Caoimhe, here, and Steward Bran, who died a hero.' Again a pause and she could hear oaths being cast in the direction of the Picts. 'Our defenders numbered less than eighty but none of them were cowed by the prospect of a thousand Picts. Believe me, we may have lost the mound but the attackers paid a heavy price. I counted over three hundred Pict bodies on the slopes of Traprain Law and thirty of them had the arrows of the Princess in them!' Murmurs of approval filled the cavern. She was glad of the darkness so that no one would know that she was blushing or did she look as though she was on the verge of weeping for her father and brothers? Taran thrashed his wooden staff against the wall for silence. Most people standing close by, herself included, jumped with each stroke. Caoimhe gently rocked the baby, using the motion to hide her own reactions. 'When the Picts had stormed the inner gates,' continued the old druid, 'Princess Caoimhe cut her way through the attackers and led as many women and children as she could to safety.' This time there was prolonged cheering.

Everything that had happened, thought Caoimhe, since they entered the darkness of the trees around the cave had been symbolic. The old druid knew his craft. 'Only together can we fight and go back to our villages. First we must join the king's forces. If you go back now the men will be killed and the women raped before they are sold into slavery. Follow us if you want to be free and your children to live in peace.'

As they walked outside, Taran let Caoimhe hand the baby back to its mother and in its stead a warrior gave her a bow with a quiver of arrows to sling over her shoulder. Mounted on horseback in the strengthening light of day, she felt like a warrior princess, which she suspected was exactly as Taran had planned.

# Chapter XII

After marching out of the meeting with Flavius and the prefect, Mannius had felt empty. King Cathal was dead, his uncle was dead and soon the land in which he had grown up would no longer be Roman: abandoned to foreign invaders. Fatigue consumed him; his bones ached and he felt ancient, as though his life force were being wrenched from him. Only a feeling of guilt kept pinching him and prevented him from falling asleep as he rode.

Following his two bodyguards, he let his horse carry him to Cilurnum, where he'd left Eithne. She had organised rooms in the fort's officers' quarters and had supervised their cleaning. Now she was asleep in a small chamber off the main office. Mannius removed his boots and riding armour as quietly as possible. Then he crept through the main room, passed the small chamber and fell, exhausted, into a cot.

Shortly after dawn he was woken by Eithne who was carefully laying out clothes for him on a chair. She wore a simple, white, three-quarter length tunic, pulled in tight at her slender waist by a thin leather belt. Mannius was glad that the warmer days of spring had come and she had stopped wearing the trousers that she'd used during the cold, winter days. He now had a clear view of her smooth, shapely calves that added to her air of elegance. Even when he'd first seen her, half-starved and grubby-faced, tied to a slaver's cart coming into the fort, he had spotted that same elegance. Her long neck, straight back

95

and graceful movement gave a seductive air to her character. And her blue eyes were full of fiery determination.

When Mannius' assistants had examined the slaves in accordance with the law to ensure that they brought no diseases into the city, they'd spotted that the grubby little girl was nursing a broken wrist. Mannius remembered remonstrating with the slaver who merely shrugged his shoulders and said he could have her cheap as she was more trouble than she was worth. Since then she'd shared his food and her figure had filled out into curves too tempting for him to resist, which he hadn't. But she never fought him. He'd trained her as a nurse, trusted her and rewarded her with freedom to shop, run errands and even tend his office when he was away.

'Did I wake you last night?' he enquired.

'No, sir,' replied Eithne in her quiet, Saxon lilt. 'I'm sorry I didn't wake to help you. Centurion Curtius sent one of the men to let me know that you were back so I could fix your breakfast. Though I think he was more concerned about him and the rest of the officers getting fed.'

'What?'

'Said that him and the men'd be needing orders and such. Did I do something wrong?'

'No, no. Not at all. It's just that I'm no longer in the army.'

'Well you said it was only for a short time. And there'll be lots of folks glad to see you back at your surgery, sir.'

'I'm afraid it's worse than that; the army's against me now.' He relayed some of the highlights of the previous evening's conversation and Flavius telling him that he was under house arrest. Somehow in the cold light of day he wondered why he hadn't just accepted the situation and moved to Rome with some fine introductions. But damn it: he wouldn't be pushed around.

'You shouldn't let them, sir.' He must have said more than he'd meant. 'They should be grateful for what you've done. It's always the same – no more gratitude left. Just take what they want then push you out when they're done. It ain't fair.' Eithne looked genuinely shocked. It gave him enough encouragement to meet the officers one last time to explain the situation to them. He'd visit the hospital to help with some of the casualties coming in from the north. Then, and only then, would he ride back to his apartments in Coria.

Sitting with Mannius and Curtius at a large, highly polished walnut table were three other senior centurions and Seneca. The men had eaten their way through porridge, bread, cheese, eggs, honey and some thickly sliced cold beef. It was a good feast for hungry men that Eithne had prepared. Now she stood quietly by a table in a recess, patiently waiting for any orders or a chance to refill a glass with milk or water. Nothing ever seemed to be too much trouble for her.

Mannius judged the moment was right to inform the officers of his news. Indignation and howls of protest greeted his short speech. It was heartening to hear support from such men. Each took it in turns to denounce the order of house arrest from the new governor.

'The young aristocratic pup'll never hold it together,' added Seneca. 'I heard a Votadini captain say that they thought the Romans had given away their lands and those of this province. So they won't want anything to do with a Roman they can't trust and that's probably restricted to us lot, as we fought to get them here safe.'

'Leofric and his men won't fight for Rome,' added Laurentius, a tall and powerful young soldier – as quick with his wit as his sword. Why had Laurentius stayed on so long? He came from a good family with wealth and influence. It must be the spirit of adventure, on the edge of the empire – or was he running away from something? Mannius dearly wanted to swap places and burdens; he would happily run away from this place if his guilt would permit it.

'You mean he'll only fight for money?' asked Mannius.

'I think,' said Curtius carefully, 'we all feel that Leofric will fight for someone he believes in and trusts.'

'And that isn't no wet-behind-the-ears, aristo pup,' concluded Laurentius.

'I heard that they'll only give us living rations,' said Seneca. Laughter went round the table at the thought of Seneca living on unsupplemented army rations. 'You'll be laughing when you find out that we've got to march to Gaul before they'll even consider giving us half pay. Bloody gratitude!'

'Don't forget the Brigantes. Without the old governor they'll go their own way,' warned another of the officers. 'I expect Prefect Artorius will take his cavalry and join his brother's estate down south. Can't see him wanting to stick his neck out if there's no one else supporting him.' Mannius knew that Artorius and his crack units were key to the defence of the uplands and coast to the north and east of Eburacum. They were well led and provided a formidable and very mobile force.

'So what you're saying is that no one will bother to fight the invaders. They'll just get the run of the place,' said Mannius.

'Aye, well it's not really for us to say, sir,' said Curtius, becoming unduly deferential. 'We'll get some new orders soon and follow those, leave the difficult stuff to people that know best.'

'Or care less,' concluded Laurentius.

# Chapter XIII

Caoimhe let her horse walk slowly up and onto the hill tracks that led south and west. Mo, the huge bodyguard, was at her side and four other mounted warriors protected the princess. Taran knew the influence of symbols on people's minds but even he could not have envisaged the power of the image of a slender princess, her red hair flowing in the breeze and glinting in the sunlight. To weary followers she was a beacon of hope and with her bow and quiver of arrows she was also a symbol of defiance. Instinctively the Votadini followed her.

Taran fretted to and fro. Messengers were sent to men guarding the paved road at Oxton. At last a rider returned with good news. Warriors were still in place, though reports indicated they were getting more nervous with every passing hour.

At the fort people flopped onto the ground thinking that safety was at hand. They were fed and then pushed and kicked on their way south. When the princess protested, Taran quietly told her that enemy scouts had been sighted barely two miles from where they stood. Some of the weakest were loaded onto carts and the group's speed increased slightly.

The princess insisted, to the frustration of her guards, that the royal group wait for the last person to leave the moor and be fed. Taran took Caoimhe to visit the officers holding the men in place. Another speech from the druid, made several times over as they passed down the line of men, brought cheers and renewed men's faith. Finally, to a sigh of relief, the Votadini infantry started to march south followed and flanked by a cavalry screen.

Caoimhe trotted her horse at the side of the column, encouraging everyone as she went. Occasionally, she would let one of the smaller children share her saddle for a short distance, anything to distract her people from their misery. After one such ride she caught Taran looking at her and smiling. Maybe she was learning.

At Trimontium she led her people across the bridge as though she were a conqueror. Leofric and his men greeted her with a guard of honour. This time she didn't wonder if Taran had organised the spectacle, she knew he had. For the first time in many hours and over thirty miles of walking the refugees were allowed to stop and rest. Some fell asleep on the ground, too tired and sore to worry about food.

In safety, provided by Roman auxiliaries, the Votadini warriors felt the tension of recent days drain and they too fell exhausted. Night came and the camp was still. Fires burned around the camp and across the river. Peace engulfed them but it was a false and shallow façade. To the north Ceretic's scouts clashed for the first time with Leofric's pickets and retreated with more stories of Roman infantry.

Overnight, in the safety of the improvised Roman camp, Caoimhe had cried for her father and her brothers. She hated the Picts, the Saxons and most especially she blamed Ceretic for causing their deaths. Taran had told her that to shed a tear was natural but sobbing was not a royal pastime. She hadn't cared. She'd told him that she was an ordinary person as well. Then he said that she was *extra*ordinary. People expected that in their leaders. It gave them hope: the most powerful weapon an army carried. And all the while the rain pounded down on the tent roof.

Una brought Caitir to the princess and dawn brought

an end to rain as well as tears. Caitir was playful, waking her sleep-deprived mother, forcing Caoimhe to play too. Then she was hungry and Caoimhe started to get annoyed because she had no idea where to get food. Unbidden, Una appeared and took the child away in search of food – no doubt on Taran's orders. Taran! He probably even brought the rain to mask the sound of her sobs.

Una returned without Caitir but with some food and a bundle of clothes. When Caoimhe was ready Una pulled the tent door aside and Taran stood waiting. He held out a fine, white cloak with purple and gold piping.

'The mark of wealth and power,' he said as he held it up for the princess.

'I am grateful for such fine clothes and the cloak clearly means you have in mind for us to impress?'

'Indeed Princess,' replied the druid. 'First impressions are so important and today you will lead our people through the Wall and meet the Roman commander who is to restore your people's lands.'

'Then for the sake of my people I will suffer the burden of these fabrics.' She saw Taran looking at her with his stern, probing gaze. 'And I will behave as someone extraordinary – a royal.'

Outside the world was damp. Everyone had found shelter of some sort in the old Roman fort to keep the worst of the rain off, yet most appeared soaked. But they were still alive. With that happy thought uppermost in her mind she set off to visit some of her wet subjects.

Without the urgency of being chased, the march to Hadrian's Wall was slower. Showers swept across them and dampened what little spirit the refugees had. Taran thought that the mass of people would barely make Bremenium by nightfall so he decided that the royal party would ride ahead to lead in refugees nearer to the Wall. A horse was found for Una so that she could carry Caitir.

Caoimhe noticed that Borgach was left to walk and suspected that Taran was merely leaving a watchful agent.

At Bremenium they changed horses. 'Where are the Romans?' asked Caoimhe.

'Gone, Princess,' replied Taran. 'They have started to withdraw their soldiers south. Somehow Ceretic and his friends got wind of it long ago. That knowledge gave them the confidence to attack your father.'

'So the Romans are to blame for our misfortune?'

'I think not, Princess. It was inevitable that they would go. I think the local commander did his best to inform your father but was too late. That means that someone higher up, who had knowledge of the withdrawal before the local officers, must have told Ceretic.'

'Still a Roman though.'

'Yes, you have the better of me there, Princess.'

All the way rain drenched them. Droplets seemed to get everywhere. At times it stung Caoimhe's face and made her narrow her eyes until they were nearly closed, but still Taran drove them on. Caoimhe discovered that she could keep the rain out of her eyes by turning her head towards the column of sodden Votadini that they overtook. She smiled to them as she rode and got an occasional cheer in return. Out of the corner of her leading eye she watched Taran, who was watching her.

Just over a mile from the Wall the line of refugees thinned and Taran called a halt.

'Why have we halted here, Taran? So that we can punish ourselves in the wet and cold?'

'The worst of this rain will pass presently, Princess,' replied the druid patiently. 'When it does, you will be able to lead your people ceremoniously through the Wall and on to the fort at Coria a few miles beyond.'

* * *

Inside the fort at Coria, Mannius was feeling angry: at the miserable weather, at the thought of Saxon invaders, at himself for failing King Cathal, at the death of his uncle. He was spoiling for a fight. From his office he could see a line of wounded filing towards the hospital. To alleviate his dark, brooding mood he toured the fort. He could see the first of the Votadini warriors exercising with some legionnaires and their efforts did not bode well. The latest recruits to the Roman army seemed to have wildly different ideas about tactics, wild being the proper adjective.

In the hospital he found numerous Votadini warriors being attended by the cohort's physicians. Instinctively he set to work to help. Most needed stitches for puncture wounds and a young man needed a broken arm resetting. Orderlies held the patient while Mannius felt along the arm, pulled, twisted then bound it in a splint. The man yelled, vomited, then passed out. Mannius was used to such reactions, avoided the vomit and left the orderlies to clean up.

Being preoccupied, Mannius missed the grand entrance of Princess Caoimhe. Officer of the day, Laurentius, watched the procession approach with the same fascination as the men around him. Below the rampart orders were shouted and men fell into line to provide a guard of honour. Laurentius wondered who had given the orders but instead of asking he straightened his cloak and strode down to meet the party.

The woman at the front of the procession was clearly a princess, accompanied by her own mounted guards. She smiled and waved at the parting line of refugees who acted as an informal honour guard outside the gates. Her long, red, curly hair sparkled as if the sun caught it yet there was no sun – strange. As she drew closer she stopped looking at the crowds and fixed a serious stare at the

Romans lined up ahead. Laurentius watched her move down the line of legionnaires, riding erect and looking in control of everything around her. As the party came closer he marvelled at her pale, smooth complexion, highlighted by some subtle paint on her lips and eyebrows. Bruises and cuts to her face showed she'd been close to the action – a fighting princess!

The princess drew her horse up in front of him. 'Are you in charge here?' she asked in perfect Latin.

'My dear lady, I am Centurion Laurentius, one of the senior officers here. And I am happy to be at your service.'

'Thank you, Centurion,' she replied. 'I should be grateful if you would get some of your men to look after our horses and take us to somewhere we might talk.'

'Certainly,' he replied, waving at some men close by. 'This way please.' He wanted to help her down to get a better sense of the scent she wore but her huge African bodyguard was quickly at her side. Instead he contented himself with watching the grace with which she landed and the slim lines of her figure. Laurentius led the royal party to Mannius' quarters, ordered Eithne to bring food and warmed wine, then went in search of Mannius.

'What do you mean they're in my quarters?' Mannius' voice echoed down the stone corridor. He wanted an outlet for his frustration and had at last found one.

'I thought it best if the royal party was allowed to stay in your –' Laurentius' earlier confidence was being cut down.

'You can kick their royal arses out and leave the thinking to me.' Mannius knew his guests would be able to hear him. He was past caring.

Votadini sentries outside the door to his quarters barred his way with crossed spears. 'You can put those toothpicks away or I'll shove them up your arses!' shouted Mannius, ready to explode.

'This is, I mean was, the commander,' explained Laurentius quickly, hoping to defuse the tension. But he could see that his fumbled introduction had just added to the confusion and made him look an idiot.

The door was ajar and Mannius pushed in. Taran was first off the mark. 'My dear Tribune Mannius.' His voice had a silky quality to it when he wanted, 'It is good of you to take such care of us under these trying circumstances. Might I introduce Princess Caoimhe, you met her father, King Cathal, a few times.'

The woman who had been seated at his desk with a toddler on her lap pushed the child away and stood, holding out her hand. 'I am very pleased to meet you, Tribune Mannius.' She was tall and had a figure worth going to war for. Her face looked as though it could be pretty, with high cheekbones, but it was difficult to tell with the bruising. Certainly her blue eyes looked sharp and engaging.

'Happy to help,' said Mannius, changing the tone in his voice. It was not often women of her quality were in his room. Pity that the others were in too. 'Mo! How's that arm of yours?' asked Mannius, gently slapping the big man's shoulder.

Mo winced. 'Suffering a little now but getting better thanks, Tribune.'

'Told you to keep it covered in fresh bandages and in a sling. I see and suspect neither. Best get you to the hospital to have it checked out.'

'Of course, I understand now,' said Caoimhe. 'Mo tells me that you took care of both him and my father at his end. I am grateful to you. Now, you said something about kicking royals?'

'I er, hum, do apologise, Princess, and I'm very sorry about your father. It was, er, a little tactical talk. We want to get rid of Ceretic and his men as quickly as possible.'

105

'I'm so glad that we agree on that,' said Caoimhe. 'And we must let you have your quarters back.'

'Not at all, Princess. Eithne will organise to get my things moved into the guest rooms and you're welcome to use my quarters as you see fit,' replied Mannius, trying to ingratiate himself. 'I've got some errands to run anyway. So, if you excuse me, I must be off.' As he left he caught a cold stare from Eithne. It was a look he'd never seen her use before.

Mannius stretched out and let a warm glow from burning pine logs chase away the evening's chill. Nearly summer and still they had to light fires to keep the cold at bay. Or was he trying to keep something else at bay: was it guilt or was it the truth that he should fight? Maybe it was time he left this place and followed his father to estates bathed in sunshine. The small fire thawed his anger and a smell of resin reminded him that the princess had also carried a powerful fragrance; far nicer than resin but just as potent.

Eithne entered, flustered and just ahead of a tall, elegant woman, dressed in an expensive stola tightly bound around her fine figure. He rose to meet her. She pulled back a hood covering her face – Felicita, his uncle's wife. 'I was so sorry to hear of the governor's murder.'

'Yes, well he had a habit of mixing with lowlife, vermin and such. Some of them didn't take kindly to it and bit him.' She seated herself in a high-backed chair, held her back erect and turned her gaze to Eithne. 'A stool if you please, child – for my feet sometime this year. By the gods: some slaves need a good beating every now and again, Mannius. Peps them up a bit. You do flog them regularly, don't you?'

'Not often, Aunt.'

'Happy to see it done for you, you know; gees them up; best tonic for work-shy slackers.'

'Thank you but that won't be necessary.'

'Yes, well you're the best judge of your own staff, I suppose. But don't be too soft on them, Mannius. Give a little and they'll take the Coliseum – mark my words.'

Eithne moved a stool and lifted Felicita's long, shapely legs onto a cushion. His uncle had had taste, there was no doubt in Mannius' mind. Even with forty years or so to carry her poise oozed beauty and class. Born on the fringes of the *nobilitas* she'd had the proper upbringing for a young lady but had suffered from being the youngest of four daughters. She'd married a decent man, on a good career path, and found that he was too decent, that he cared too much about the province he was responsible for. They'd stayed five years longer than intended – probably ten years longer than she'd hoped.

'Fix my hair would you,' ordered Felicita, sweeping her long black tresses through her fingers. Mannius enjoyed watching the sensuous movement that made her spine arch even more and threw her surprisingly firm breasts towards him. Surely it wasn't an invitation with her husband only just gone? He put the thought out of his mind.

'Excuse me for asking, Aunt Felicita, flattered as I am by your presence. But why have you given me the honour of this visit?'

'Oh don't bother, child,' said Felicita, waving Eithne away like an annoying fly. 'Ask my slave to attend me with my comb, she's far less clumsy.'

Eithne bowed and retreated to the corridor. 'And bring some more wood for the fire, it's perishing cold.'

'Would you like a blanket to keep the chill off?' asked Mannius helpfully.

'Blankets are for horses and soldiers, my dear. Ladies prefer a little chill in order to better show themselves.

107

The work of years of abstemious dieting, countless urns of expensive oils and thousands of massages has to be displayed to be properly enjoyed.'

'And I'm a very appreciative audience,' agreed Mannius.

'Especially now I'm single again.'

Mannius thought that maybe he'd flirted too far. Was this woman trying to seduce him? Some confusion must have shown on his face.

'Don't worry, my dear. I'm not planning on marrying you. I just need a safe household to be part of while I get myself sorted and you're the only family I have in this godforsaken land. So I place myself *under* your protection until other arrangements can be made.'

Of all the people in the province, Aunt Felicita seemed to be the least likely to need his protection. She radiated a confidence that was genuine and, therefore, all the more engaging. And her emphasis on the preposition 'under' seemed more like a proposition. Perhaps, he wondered. Before he finished his thought, Eithne returned carrying some logs.

'Time we got you wed as well. You can shag yourself witless with these local slaves all you like but you ought to take a bride from one of the better families. It is so important for your position and career. You can even keep your slave-whores if you've the appetite and energy. I'll use my contacts to get you the right introductions and –' She looked down at Eithne who was bent over the fire, '–don't worry, we'll find you something pretty.'

# Chapter XIV

Leofric stood erect, keeping his senses alert to anything out of place in the woods. He was a huge and powerful man. Like other Roman officers he wore a scabbard containing a sword to his left. Attached to the other side was a thick-bladed dagger. Brought up in Saxon villages, along the coast near the Wall, he had developed a healthy respect for a battle-axe in a mêlée and was glad that the Roman army had got rid of the short gladius decades since. Fighting in a shield wall the weight and length of his sword was a comfort. In his right hand, balanced on his shield, he held a heavy double-headed axe, which was his favourite weapon. When battles broke into smaller fights this was the ideal instrument to wreak havoc and put fear into his enemies.

'Are you sure this is the place?' he whispered.

'Yes, sir. They made it easy for us.' The captain was an experienced scout and sounded convincing. 'When they marched, during the day, there was over a hundred men either side of the ox carts so we figured it had to be something valuable. That's why we kept watch on them.'

'Where are they now?'

'Carts and guards are holed up in that old fort. They've got a few sentries and pickets but not much, sir.'

Leofric and his men had quietly abandoned the old fort at Bremenium when Ceretic advanced with several thousand of his men. Instead of going south, directly to the protection of the Wall, they had gone west, following the course of a lazy river along a narrow valley. Then, travelling under the cover of darkness, Leofric had led them north and east over heather-clad moors behind Ceretic's lines, close to Dere Street. From the cover of a silver birch wood he peered through the darkness at the old stone fort.

'I guess they feel safe in the fort,' suggested the captain.

Leofric snorted. The fort stood high on the hill in a commanding position, overlooking the moors below, but no one had maintained it. Tiles had been stripped from the roof and much of the stonework had been removed. Great holes in the masonry acted like a ladder for anyone with enough gumption to try it.

'The approaches?'

'We can work our way closer in the wood, then once we break cover it's less than two hundred paces to the ditches and they're full of gorse bushes, sir. Only obstacle is a set of pickets between the wood and the ditches.'

'Lead on then,' said Leofric, slapping the scout on the back.

At the edge of the wood, Leofric and the captain stopped. Hidden by thick hawthorn bushes and boulders, a dozen of his archers watched the pickets. To his right he could see men ready to storm past the pickets' position and into the ditches. To his left was another body of men held in reserve to protect the withdrawal.

Leofric nodded to the captain, who sent men crawling across the heather until he judged they could go no further without being spotted. Then he gave the order to the archers to loose their arrows at the men standing and sitting round a small fire. A hum of death filled the air and silhouettes fell. The men who had crawled close jumped up and stormed the pickets, quickly silencing the screams of those only wounded. Everyone tensed, waiting for a reaction from the sentries in the fort. None came, so Leofric joined his men jogging across the open ground to the ditches ringing the fort.

Dark figures scrambled up the broken wall and sentries on the ramparts were dispatched with ruthless efficiency. Then the attackers moved along the wall to the carts parked in the old stables. Several ropes were hung down and men silently dropped to the ground.

Astride broken stone flags on the parapet, Leofric peered down and watched his men investigate each cart. A man pulled a small chest from under a tarpaulin. The chest was attached to the middle of one of the ropes and hauled up, the man on the ground holding the other end of the rope to prevent the wooden box from scraping against the stonework. Another chest came up, then another, and soon there was a pile of them. Leofric shook one and heard the distinctive chink of metal coins. He dared not open it on the wall. Instead he motioned for men near him to start carrying the heavy boxes down the other side and away from the fort.

When the last of the chests had been lowered to the men in the ditches, Leofric nodded to the others. They had piled tinder around the wooden carts and now a man struck a flint, blew on an unseen ember and a small flame leapt from his hands. Soon tinder had turned to flame that was quickly caught by the carts. The men thrust their swords into the oxen, not out of mercy for the beasts but to prevent their use by Ceretic's men.

'Food, wine and arrows,' reported the captain, pointing to the other carts as they waited on the wall for their men.

'Well done, Captain,' replied Leofric in a hoarse whisper. 'Now the fun begins.'

The crackle of fire and the moans of the animals meant that the need for stealth was nearly over. Guards pushed at the stable doors, trying to force the barricades open. Shouts went up from inside the fort and suddenly torches were lit and men ran to the gate.

A group of Ceretic's men rushed out of the fort and saw the Saxon mercenaries retreating across the ditches they thought protected them. Without fear or thought they charged at the fleeing men. Leofric and his raiding party, hidden in gorse bushes, fell on their backs. The great Saxon whirled his axe overhead, tearing into exposed necks and hacking limbs. The noise of the skirmish alerted the rest of the defenders to the source of the trouble and more men were soon on their way. Leofric joined his own men, fleeing to the darkness and safety of the trees.

With fifty paces still to go, horsemen, closely followed by infantry, charged at them. Leofric's men kept going, willing themselves to go faster. A trumpet sounded to Leofric's right and the unmistakable hum of death filled the night air once more as arrows flew over him and into the horsemen behind. He looked around, noting that several of the raiding party had fallen in the skirmish.

Ceretic's men held their nerve and charged into the trees. Leofric smiled to himself. They'd assume it was a small raid and never think that all his troops were with him. All around him came the hammering of swords and axes on wooden shields, metal and men. More screams filled the night and quickly Ceretic's men were cut down or retreated to the now blazing fort.

Once the fighting had died away, Leofric and his captains toured the battlefield, checking their wounded. Casualties were reassuringly light but those with wounds that prevented them from being moved, even on horseback, were killed out of mercy by their officers. They knew that they would either die a lingering, painful death or would be captured and tortured. Neither prospect was appealing to proud warriors so they said their last and thanked the men who helped them on their way.

Leofric heard a moan and investigated, keeping his sword ready. In the dark it was difficult to tell if the wounded were his men or Ceretic's. He didn't want to be run through by a dying enemy. Getting closer he found a man with his stomach opened.

'I'm sorry, sir,' the man apologised. Why did they always apologise? It should be him taking the blame: he'd led them into battle and without that no one would have been wounded or killed. The voice sounded familiar. He knelt by the man and took his arm in a tight grip.

'Rest easy now.' It was the captain who'd organised the scouting of the mission.

'Got careless, waiting for my men to get past me, sir.' The man's breath came in short gasps. 'I'd appreciate your help and for one of my men just a short way over there if you please. And tell my sons to be brave.'

'I will, Captain.' Leofric stabbed quickly. The man's back arched in pain, then a smile spread across his face and he was gone from the clutches of his enemy. Leofric checked the other man and found he was already dead. This was the worst of any battle and he knew it would take time for him and his officers to let go of the memories of these mercy killings. No one ever spoke of this sordid part of their life as soldiers; the memories were endured but never shared.

# Chapter XV

Mannius woke with a crick in his neck. Had the cushions on the sofa been too hard or was there a draught that had caused the pain? As he was contemplating his discomfort, Eithne appeared with a mug of steaming mint and a face as dark as a thunder cloud. Clearly there would be no flirting today. She was dressed and looked as though she'd been awake for hours.

'Reduced to sleeping on a sofa in my own quarters. You know I'd be better under house arrest in Eburacum.' There was no softening in the girl's countenance. 'All right, what's the matter?'

'Nothing, sir.'

'Like a nothing that makes your face look like you're ready to fight on the front rank of a shield wall.'

'Lady Felicita's slave,' said Eithne. 'Said that as she's older she's in charge of the house now and that if I didn't do as I was told she'd have me whipped.'

'So what did you say to her?'

'Nothing. I, er, just slapped her.'

'Slapped?'

'Well it kind of took her by surprise like, and sent her across the floor. She went off to her lady.'

Mannius allowed himself a small smile. 'I suppose she knows who's the boss now?'

Eithne smiled and was about to say something when, unannounced, Taran appeared. 'If I might intrude on a moment of your time, Tribune?'

'I was just about to have breakfast.'

'Oh splendid – thank you for the invitation. I'm a little peckish myself.'

Between gulps of porridge and mouthfuls of cheese the old druid extolled the virtues of Roman medicine (though it still had limitations), the roads, the army. The list went on. Mannius knew he was being prepared for a request. As the praise grew so did Mannius' worries about the size of favour to be asked.

'So, tell me,' ordered Mannius when dishes were nearly empty. 'What exactly are you after?'

The druid stopped eating and stared at Mannius. It felt as though the man was looking deep into his soul, and he wondered what was really there. Did he have one left? Could the old man sense his feeling of guilt? 'A kingdom to be returned to its rightful owners so that a people can return in safety to their homes.'

'What makes you think I can help?'

'I hear that you now have no army to command. I am able, with the princess's permission, to give you an army. We need a man like you: a general other men will follow.'

'I'm flattered.'

'You're meant to be, but most of all you're trusted. King Cathal trusted you, the princess trusts you, and I trust you.'

'Thank you for the endorsements. But I was hoping to leave for pastures new – warmer, sunnier lands – maybe even take a wife and apartments in Rome itself. I even have offers of introductions.'

'Talk from those who would corrupt you. I know of plans to disarm our brave warriors and send us all back to our lands to become slaves of the Picts. Is that what your governor would have wanted?'

Guilt rose once more in his Mannius' heart. The old druid knew how to play on his emotional weaknesses. Mannius pushed the last of his porridge to one side. 'You have long ears, druid. Go on.'

'I hear that a Saxon fleet threatens the eastern coast even as we speak. It would seem best to strike north and secure a base that we can defend against the invaders.'

'I'm afraid not.' This time Mannius had the initiative; he could tell from the quizzical look on the druid's face. 'To go north without supplies would be dangerous and we'd have to fight all the way. If we won through we'd be exhausted and vulnerable to counter-attack.'

'You have a better way?'

Mannius picked up a warm hen's egg and a knife. 'My uncle had a strategy: don't try to fight them on two fronts. What's more, if the coastal units are left to protect our shores they will be overwhelmed: tough but thin and brittle.' Mannius hit the egg with the knife and soft, yellow yoke spilled out onto the plate. 'Then the invaders will be inside and able to choose which target to attack. A better strategy would be to pull back from the coast, gather all our forces together, then hit them hard – all of them.'

'A knockout blow.'

'Exactly.'

'You seem to have a lot of enthusiasm for this strategy. That will be worth a great deal when we gather our allies.'

Mannius stood quickly and knocked over a mug. 'Damn! Will no one leave me alone? Am I a toy to be tugged this way and that?' Without another word he marched into his office where one of his bodyguards stood ready.

Out of the main window a crowd had quietly gathered. 'Who are they?' asked Mannius.

'Some of 'em are Votadini, sir, and some of 'em are locals that's come here.'

'Why? Are they sick? Do they want me to open a surgery here?'

'No, sir. It's on account of they think you're going to lead us in a fight against the Picts and the Saxons.'

'Whoever gave them that idea?' As soon as he'd asked the question he thought of the druid at his breakfast table – or maybe some of the officers had put them up to it. 'And what's the panic?' Beyond the crowd Curtius was shouting orders to officers and men alike.

'Sir, I think it's Prince Leofric. Him and his men are overdue from action north of the Wall.'

Mannius felt another pang of guilt hit him. Leofric had willingly volunteered his men to act as a rearguard to protect the fleeing Votadini. Now the tribune, who had requested his men to risk their lives, was sulking around a miserable set of borrowed apartments doing nothing in particular, except trying not to get involved.

Mannius marched into the dining room, where Eithne was clearing the table. 'Do you know why those people are gathered outside?' Anger and guilt made his voice tremble.

'Yes, sir. They're hoping you'll help them.'

'Why me? What can I do for them?'

'Sir, they know that you help them when they're sick or get broken bones and such. Without the old governor you're the only one they know and trust to help them through this.'

Mannius felt humility soothing his guilt and sweeping away the anger. 'And what do you think?'

'You've never turned your back on no one as what needs your help. I think you've done your best to cure everyone that's come to you when they've been sick. Now the whole land's sick on account of the threat of invasion and they need someone to cure them and –'

'And?' he gently prompted.

Eithne stared into his eyes. Tears welled. 'And, sir, I think you will.'

Mannius stood for a long moment.

'Bring me my satchel of orders, get the house slaves to

fetch my armour and tell Centurion Curtius that I want to see him and the other senior officers as quickly as possible.'


'What sort of trap are we going to lure them into?' asked a young centurion. Strong and aggressive, what he lacked in intellect he made up for in brawn and his men respected him. 'Has the prefect got a couple of legions waiting to pounce?'

'We need to get them away from our lines of communication and into areas where their numbers can't be used in their favour,' replied Mannius for the fourth time.

'Get 'em in the marshes, just as they land,' suggested Amandus, another tough centurion again with more brawn than brain. In the old days Mannius doubted Amandus would have made optio, never mind centurion. But men were in short supply, especially those who could read and write. 'Best time to attack, before they get out of their boats. We can rig up some ballistae and give 'em hell.'

'My dear Amandus,' said Laurentius in a condescending tone, reserved for the most stubborn slave. 'All they need to do is turn their boats round, row them up or down the river and we'll not have time to catch up with them. We'll probably not even know where the fuck they've gone. So be a sport and think.'

Mannius sighed. 'Unfortunately, it seems we have to let them land. Next we need to find somewhere to give battle that suits us.'

Curtius had been quiet, watching, thinking. 'Seneca, you've spent a lot of time round here and at Derventio. You've had the luxury of covering more ground on horseback. Any ideas?'

'Terrain on the moors, north of Derventio's good for

snaring an army all right,' replied the cavalryman. 'Hardly any farms between where they'll land and Derventio. Desperate plateau in bad weather, full of bottomless marshes and wet peat bogs. Almost need a boat rather than a horse to get across it sometimes. If we can get them into one of the narrow valleys that criss-cross the place we'd have a chance.'

'But how,' asked Laurentius, 'do we get them to go there? Put a banquet on in their honour?'

'Any high value targets in one of those valleys?' asked Curtius hopefully.

Seneca shook his head. 'A few stone quarries with slaves and the odd iron mine but nothing to divert a Saxon horde.'

'A gold mine would've been nice,' suggested Amandus.

'Exactly!' Mannius seized the straw. Amandus beamed with satisfaction that he'd at last had a good idea. 'Let's make them believe there's a mine worth taking.'

'A silver mine's probably more plausible,' suggested Curtius.

'OK, a silver mine,' agreed Mannius. 'In one of those valleys. Take some of your men, Seneca. Find a good spot and then we'll have to make sure the Saxons find out about your secret mine, which we will of course race to protect so that you can get a big delivery away to safety.'

'Do you really think we can deceive experienced warriors with a ruse like that?' asked Laurentius. Mannius noticed that his tone was non-committal. There was no sarcasm, so he just had doubts, otherwise he would have ridiculed the plan out of existence.

'The Greeks had their wooden horse that they got the Trojans to collect and take inside their city,' replied Mannius, a note of enthusiasm growing in his voice. 'This time it's reversed. We've got the horse and they can't move it so they'll have to come and get it.'

'I hope that the outcome isn't reversed,' added Laurentius.

'Nothing is for certain so we have to try. I'll get some top-secret orders drawn up, which will mean that everyone will want to know what's in them. So it'll make it more convincing that an enemy spy will want to get his hands on them.'

'What happens if they go inland instead?' asked Laurentius.

'They'll over-extend their supply lines, run into our prepared defences and expose themselves to attacks along our roads,' answered Curtius confidently. Mannius too felt optimism beginning to bubble inside him – at least they had a plan to work with.

The officers filed out to attend to their duties. Mannius put a hand on Curtius' shoulder indicating that he wanted a private word. Eithne closed the door behind Seneca, who was the last to leave.

'Curtius, I need to know about Leofric,' said Mannius.

'Done a great job holding Ceretic's men back while the Votadini got away. Killed a load of Picts as well that tried to cross the river nearer the coast.'

'Kill any Saxons?' persisted Mannius.

'Ah, now I see what you mean. Saxon auxiliaries against Saxons.' Curtius nodded to Eithne who was busy clearing the table.

'Eithne is trusted, don't worry.'

'Probably best not to put them into that position, sir. And keep them away from the coast.'

'Will they desert?'

'Hard to say, sir. Men fighting their own kind's a bit difficult to judge. I'll keep a watch on them, sir.'

'I'd appreciate that, Curtius.'

Mannius sat on the stone window sill and looked out over the rooftops of the officers' quarters below. Without turning to the slave girl he spoke. 'What do you think, Eithne? Whose side will Leofric and his men fight on?'

'Warriors are not like women, sir.'

'But you're Saxon. You probably know them better than they know themselves.' He turned and caught her eye.

'If Prince Leofric gives his word he'll keep it. He's too proud not to.'

'And the rest?'

'Difficult to tell, sir.' Mannius kept his gaze on her, forcing her to reveal her insights. 'I'm Saxon but I was born in this country and this is where I belong. I can't even speak much of the language, in fact I probably know more Gaelic. So I'd rather things stay the way they is, sir.' Mannius watched her carefully. He could tell from the way she concentrated on polishing the table in order to avoid eye contact that there was more.

'What else, Eithne?'

She put her cloth down and turned to him. For once she looked uncertain. She pulled at the comb holding her long, blonde hair. 'Sir, you're a Roman soldier but you also live here, got friends here and the like. What if another Roman decided to attack us – like that Senator Flavius? Would you let him walk in here, organise things to his ways and get you confused – stop you helping the Votadini – or would you fight?'

'Thank you, Eithne. I doubt any of our great scholars could have explained it better. You really are a treasure!'

# *Chapter XVI*

Caoimhe had thought that she had risen early on her first morning in the fort but already there seemed to be a lot of activity. She stared out of the upper storey window of her borrowed apartment, ignoring the slave girl who placed a bowl of half-red apples from the winter store on a polished table. Beyond the officers' quarters a lot of movement could be seen.

'Eithne, isn't it?' asked Caoimhe pleasantly, still keeping her gaze out of the window.

'Yes, mistress.'

'Please come here and tell me who that is.'

Eithne joined the princess at the window and followed her finger. 'It's Centurion Curtius, mistress. He's the most senior centurion. Been in more battles and marched more miles than anyone else, so he says.'

'Tribune Mannius looks agitated today,' said Caoimhe, as offhandedly as she could, watching him pull tightly on the reins of his powerful grey warhorse to make it turn in tight circles while he talked to the centurion.

'Men are overdue, mistress, that's why he's worried.'

'Some men who helped my people escape?'

'Yes, mistress. They stayed behind to make sure it was safe and to pick up anyone that was slow.'

'Tell me please,' said Caoimhe, 'what's he like, your master? Is he as stern as he looks?'

'Mistress, please,' said Eithne, looking a little flustered. 'It's not my place to say.'

'You're right, of course. But how does someone as nice

122

as the tribune control so many tough men?'

For the first time Eithne smiled. 'On account of he's fair and everyone knows that. I've heard him bawl at men across the parade ground fit to shake the walls down when they've upset him. Then again he'll talk to them about their wives and children like he knows them proper.'

'Does he beat you?'

'No mistress!' Eithne looked genuinely shocked. 'Ever since I've been in his household he's treated me well and I've tried to do my best for him.'

'I can see that you're very loyal and that's good.'

'It's like I said mistress, everyone's loyal to him 'cause he's fair and listens to folks' opinions and –' Eithne trailed off, looking as though she were betraying a confidence.

'And?' prompted Caoimhe.

'Well, I've heard men say he's lucky. The men have been paid regular and fed good, which isn't to be taken for granted these days. Well, that's down to my master from when he was an officer up here: showed Centurion Curtius and his men how to run an estate; how to make a profit and keep it. And you know, like the time he was on his way to see your father and was able to help in the fight. They say he ain't never lost a fight he's been in.'

'That's reassuring to know.' Caoimhe left a gentle gap, hoping to move the conversation on.

'What do you think of him, Eithne? Is he a good man?'

'Mistress, of course he is. He's better than any man I ever met. I'd give my life for him.'

'That's high praise from a woman,' said Caoimhe, catching and holding eye contact with the slave girl. 'Men fight and give their lives for duty but women know that there are more important things than duty, like family and children. To give your life for a man means that he has to be special.'

'He is, mistress.' Eithne bowed her head slightly and Caoimhe could see tears starting to run down her face.

'You love him, don't you?' she enquired gently.

'It's not my place as a slave to love but I'd do anything he asked of me.'

'So it seems would most people in this fort,' whispered Caoimhe to herself.

# Chapter XVII

Mannius, his bodyguards and two squadrons of cavalry rode north as fast as they dared. A messenger from Leofric's band had relayed information to officers stationed at the Wall. After listening to the reports, Mannius took the riders east. Disobeying the governor's edict he then headed north, through an old gate and onto a minor track. The messenger had said that Leofric's men were making their way back. Something was amiss, otherwise why not retreat down Dere Street? He knew that nearly forty riders would deter casual interest from an enemy but if Leofric, with all his men, had run into serious trouble there was little Mannius would be able to do.

By noon they'd spotted scouts from Leofric's band. Another hour later and Mannius was riding with the Saxon leader, who had a grin spread across his face.

'Mostly silver but some gold in the haul,' said Leofric, proudly pointing at the chests strapped to his scouts' mounts that had become packhorses.

'You've done well, taking the fight to the enemy,' replied Mannius.

'Thought we'd not get the chance once we were south of the Wall so I figured a couple of raids might slow them down.'

'A couple of raids?'

'Two evenings ago we got behind a group of about two hundred Picts. We waited for them to start eating their grub and marched into their camp. As we'd come from the north they thought we were with them. One of them even waved to us to hurry ourselves over to the cooking pots. Soon as we were in the middle of them we let rip. Killed them all. *Then* we helped ourselves to some grub.'

Mannius laughed in appreciation.

'And my men wanted revenge for prisoners that Ceretic took and tortured last year. Don't think they were expecting us to get round the back of them, otherwise he wouldn't have moved his paychests up.'

'So you didn't follow the governor's orders to go south?'

'Messenger must have had trouble finding us, sir.'

'Me too! Have you taken your share out yet?'

'No, sir. We haven't touched it. Best that everything's done proper like, by the clerks back at headquarters with the situation as it is.'

'I wanted to ask you about that. How do your men feel about the likelihood of facing Saxons?'

'We've talked about it a lot recently and the men want to go back to their villages.'

Mannius felt his heart sink and his hopes faded. 'What, you're giving up?'

The big Saxon turned to face Mannius, who felt the only reason his head remained on his shoulders was out of respect for his rank. 'We don't give up, Tribune. We do our duty by our word. But I can't ask the men to fight their own kind.'

'I'm sorry. It was foolish of me.'

'Sir, it's complicated. I mean, most of us are from Inner-Saxony and Ceretic's friends are made up of Angles and barbarians from Outer-Saxony. They're not even Christians. But they're Saxons and my men reckon we should give them a chance.'

'What if they destroy your homes – enslave your families?'

'That's why they want to go home, to make sure their villages are safe.'

'But together we'd be stronger; spread across lots of villages your men will get picked off.'

'Aye it's a risk, but the men want to take it and I'd be a fool to ignore that.'

Suddenly Mannius felt a fool. He was alone. He'd assumed everyone would rally to the cause – his cause. Why had he let himself be pushed into such a hole? Was it as a favour to his uncle? Was it to help the beautiful Princess Caoimhe and her people? Or was it just his disquiet about how Rome had abandoned its duty to the people of the province?

The ride back to the fort was quiet and Mannius started to calculate the odds: around half a cohort of Roman-trained infantry, assorted cavalry units and a couple of thousand Votadini. Against them was an army five times the size, hungry to tear them apart and take over the land. Now he thought of it in those terms, they probably would.

Barely twenty miles from Mannius and Leofric, Ceretic was readying for his lunch with one of his generals. A guard pulled back the leather flap of his tent, admitting a messenger.

'Begging pardon, my lord, but a column was sighted to the north a while ago and I've just got back from speaking with them.'

The look of worry on the man's face betrayed bad news. Ceretic suddenly lost his appetite. 'Has the commander of the column deigned to grace us with his presence?'

'He's dead, my lord, and so are his two captains.'

'Is there no one from the column man enough to come and tell me in person what is going on or do they hide from my scrutiny behind a messenger?'

'The senior lieutenant is outside waiting your pleasure, my lord.'

'Then send him in!' roared Ceretic.

A wiry man shuffled into the tent, flanked by two guards. He kept shifting from foot to foot.

'What have you to say?' demanded Ceretic.

'My lord, they attacked us in the fort. We did what we could but they overwhelmed us.'

'Don't make me drag this out of you,' said Ceretic impatiently. 'Who overwhelmed you?'

'Roman auxiliaries, Saxons, my lord. They hit us, burnt everything, then ran. We chased them and inflicted casualties but they were too many.'

'Did they take the chests?'

'They burnt the food carts, wine carts and arrow carts, my lord. Set the stables ablaze and killed our oxen and mules.'

'The fucking chests, you moron!' exploded Ceretic, losing any pretence at dignity. 'Did they take the chests?'

'Yes, my lord. We searched through the ashes but there was no sign of them.'

'Fucking first bloody class! Some Saxon scum attack you in a fort and you let them take the chests.'

'The men fought hard and we lost many, my lord.'

'How many men did you lose?'

'Fifty, my lord, and many more wounded.'

'Fifty-one actually,' said Ceretic, control having returned to his voice. He nodded to the guards, who gripped the man's arms. With hate in his eyes, Ceretic pulled out his dagger and cut the man's throat. He turned to his guards. 'Get rid of this,' he said, gesturing at the lifeless man in front of him. 'Then get to the gate and take the first ten men from the column to come through and flog them. Now get out.'

'I fear the Romans know this area better than ourselves,'

commented the general. 'I think we will need to double our guard.'

'I want us to turn for the coast as soon as possible, general. There's no point making targets of ourselves this close to Roman lines.'

'Agreed, my lord.'

'Guards, send in that messenger again.'

The man shook and his face was pale as he was led in. 'Yes, my lord?' he said with a tremble in his voice.

Ceretic scribbled on a parchment and folded it before placing an imprint of his seal on a pool of cooling red wax. As he handed the parchment to the messenger with some coins he whispered the name of the recipient. The messenger's face went ashen, his hands shook violently, he bowed and then ran outside to vomit.

# Chapter XVIII

That night, in a smaller suite of rooms along the corridor from the apartment to which he was entitled, Mannius ate his meal alone, served by Eithne. The euphoric nature of his departure had been replaced by sullen looks from officers and men alike as he returned. Frightened eyes stared out from dark recesses and he knew he'd let them down. Everyone, himself included, thought that Leofric and his men would join their cause and help fight the invaders. It had been arrogant to think that his was the only just cause and that men should risk their lives without question. Now he wondered if he could even count on Leofric's mercenaries staying neutral.

The wine was strong, matching his dark mood. A mass of papers awaited his attention and orders needed signing. But as he drank more wine his inclination to look at any of them subsided. Apart from the changed room that he now occupied there was something else different and he struggled to identify it. Becoming bored, then frustrated, he banged his silver goblet down on the rough pine table and Eithne immediately stepped forward to fill it. A whiff of scent flowed over him. Looking carefully at the slave girl he saw that her full ripe lips glistened red in the light of the oil lamps. Maybe she'd also applied a hint of rouge to her cheeks, emphasising her high cheekbones.

Before he had a chance to enquire there was a smart knock on the door. Eithne opened it.

'I know how busy you must be but I wondered if I might impose on your time a little,' enquired Caoimhe.

'Of course, Princess. You're always welcome to stop by any time – even if you do bring guests with you.' Taran stepped into the room and Eithne escorted them both to chairs before filling silver goblets with wine. 'And I'm very glad of the distraction,' Mannius added, waving his arm over the pile of parchments.

'Taran was my father's counsellor and has agreed to continue in that role for me,' explained the princess. She sat upright, hands together on her lap, looking attentive and sincere. 'And I need a chaperone – you Romans have quite a reputation.'

'One I'm willing to uphold,' joked Mannius. But he knew it was no joke. With every bruise on her face that healed her beauty grew ever more impressive. It was like a spring thaw taking away the mask of winter.

'I wanted to say again that I'm very, very grateful for the help you gave my father and also my people. If there's anything we can do to help you, please ask.'

Out of the corner of his eye Mannius thought he saw Eithne uncharacteristically narrow her eyes disapprovingly at Caoimhe. He turned to Taran. 'I need every soldier I can get,' he said, sweeping away the parchments to reveal a map.

'So you're still going to fight?' asked Caoimhe, looking straight at him, clearly trying to sense his reaction. 'I heard that Leofric's men won't help us.'

Mannius saw Eithne blanch. Now he started to wonder whether the frightened faces outside had been due to the loss of Leofric or confusion and concern as to how he'd react. They were looking to him for answers. If he told them to fight they would get slaughtered; if they did nothing they would be enslaved. Running away would only bring poverty to most of them elsewhere. Deep within his conscious he knew that resisting the invaders was his duty because he was a Roman and Rome was committed to the defence of its provinces.

131

'You alone are worth fighting for, Princess,' he joked – that's all he could think of: black humour to ward off the evil that was about to descend on the land.

'I'm flattered and thank you for your kind words. But how do you think we can succeed?'

Mannius ignored the question and pressed on. 'The fort where we are now and those immediately north and south are reasonably secure but a few reinforcements – some of your older men and lightly injured – would be helpful. What I really need is as many of your fit men as possible to march to here,' he concluded, pointing at a blank section of moorland north of Derventio.

'But that's miles south of here,' protested Caoimhe. 'What about going north to push Ceretic, the Picts and Saxons out of Votadini territory?'

'Much as I'd like to I can't for two reasons – as I've already explained to Taran. Firstly, I'm not sure I could get all the army to go north, making the separate, small parts easier targets for the invaders, and secondly, if I did, our armies would be caught in a vice. Please keep this to yourselves but we have intelligence that a Saxon fleet is about to land somewhere close to the Wall, probably in one of the bays or rivers along the coast. They'll find somewhere that's easy for them to defend and I'm led to believe that there are plenty of such locations. With their forces north and south of the Wall we wouldn't stand a chance.'

'So your governor tells you to protect the silver mine on the moors,' Taran at last broke his silence and Mannius was pleased that he'd picked up on the rumour. He tried to look startled all the same.

'Actually he hasn't asked us to do that. I want men there because I think the enemy might go that way to Eburacum. They need a route that doesn't expose them to attacks on their flanks and it would give them a route to the Abus Flavia, a large estuary, from where their ships could re-supply them.'

'What of the people who live on the coast?' asked Caoimhe, a note of sincere concern in her voice that humbled Mannius: even with the fate of a whole people at stake she could still find time to consider the consequences for the meek and lowly.

'As we speak, my men are moving everyone and everything out of the coastal villages.'

'A scorched earth policy?' asked Taran.

'Almost: we're emptying all the food stores but the villagers will want to return and the crops in the ground are of little use to the Saxons.'

'Let the bastards fish!' said Caoimhe in a rare outburst. 'I am again grateful for you sharing this with us. I came here with the selfish aim of persuading you to march north. Now, though, I realise that we have to face a much bigger challenge. My captains stand ready to take your orders and will march to defeat our common enemy.'

'I am grateful for your trust, Princess.' For the first time since leaving Leofric, Mannius felt a little more optimistic – or, maybe it was that he just felt a little less pessimistic.

# Chapter XIX

Mannius returned to his office and the sofa that was his bed, to be confronted by Eithne, who sat quietly, glaring at Lady Felicita's slave. A confrontation, albeit silent, was the last thing he wanted before he turned in for the night. 'I'm glad to see that you two are getting along so well.'

Eithne huffed and stiffened.

'Please, sir, Lady Felicita hopes you've had a successful day and begs an audience,' said the slave.

Reluctantly Mannius climbed the stairs. The young slave girl skipped past him in the corridor, opened a door and motioned for him to enter. Mannius stepped into an outer chamber, followed by the slave who dimmed the lamps. Then she went to a table, gracefully lifted an ornate jug and filled two silver goblets with rich red wine. If he had to hear complaints at least the wine would help ease the pain. The girl left the room and Mannius gulped the red liquid. The door to the inner chamber opened and Felicita glided into the room in a low-cut nightrobe, pulled in round her waist with a thin, purple sash and generously slit up the middle to reveal her long, smooth legs.

Stylish, thought Mannius, as he watched her lower herself onto one of two sofas in the room. Every small gesture she made – even the way she caressed the silver goblet on the table – had a sensuous grace. He took another gulp and submissively she rose and offered him a refill, which he gladly accepted. The wine was hitting his mind and he started to feel mellow.

'I trust your day was not too disagreeable, Aunt.'

'Please, my dear Mannius, no more "Aunt".' She took the tiniest sip from her goblet, hardly enough to dampen the paint on her lips. 'The only disappointment was that barbarian princess and her entourage. I had the misfortune to meet her and I can say that I wasn't impressed. Dances in here like she owns the place, chirping away pleasantries and begs for charity – so unseemly.'

Mannius was trying to figure how her case was so different from that of the woman in front of him. 'She's lost her home, her family and her lands, she's bound to be a little down.'

'Why should her misery be our misery?'

'Because she's an ally and we owe her and her people our assistance because of that.'

'Now you're talking like my late husband; always on some idealistic endeavour to help these island monkeys and look what gratitude it got him.'

'She's offered to give me her soldiers to help fight any invasion.'

'Of course she would, she's got precious little else to give. And you'll have to feed them. By the look of her she'll probably enjoy fighting them as well – so coarse and lacking in class.'

The wine was letting his passions surface and he didn't like the way an ally was being denigrated. He wanted to emphasise her royal credentials. 'Princess Caoimhe is a brave woman.'

'Brave quite possibly, but so what? You really shouldn't trouble yourself fighting for these people, they're just not worth the effort.' Felicita seemed bored with the subject and moved the conversation on. 'Centurion Curtius was kind enough to provide me with a wonderfully exhilarating day's riding; gave me a good challenge.'

'I'm so glad you were able to find something worthy of your attention.'

'And now I'm afraid I must call on your professional expertise. I seem to have had a little mishap.'

Mannius relaxed. He'd heard the complaint about the princess, noted his other guest's advice and seemed to be through the lecture. Now he faced a situation he'd been in many times before.

'My left shoulder seems to have suffered a little.' Mannius automatically stepped across the room in order to better examine the injury. A little coquettishly Felicita turned away and slipped her shoulder out of her robe. Slowly she wriggled and let the robe fall off her other arm and down to her waist, exposing toned, firm skin.

Mannius slowed, wondering who was examining who. His professional eye looked at the injured shoulder. Felicita held her right arm across her chest to nurse her injured arm and just to keep her modesty. As he felt along the major bones, she rubbed her cheek against the back of his hand and Mannius saw her ample bosom heave as she sighed.

'You have a gentle touch for a soldier.'

'Does this cause any discomfort?' he asked, pressing on a tendon.

'No. It really seems difficult to raise it past here,' she answered, pushing her left arm high. She placed her other arm onto the sofa to support herself and Mannius saw the pose with the arched back that showed her breasts in their full glory. She appeared a magnificent spectacle and worthy of capture by one of the empire's leading sculptors. Slowly she rose and turned to face him. Her outstretched arm wrapped round his neck and her right hand tugged gently at her robe to cast it to the floor. Naked before him she pulled his face close to hers.

Through his tunic he felt the warmth of her firm body as she drew him ever closer. Her scent swirled around him, enticing him on. Instinct took his hands down her back and onto her smooth thighs. It was madness – a fly into a spider's web. If he succumbed he'd be her puppet with ever-increasing demands.

'It isn't right with your husband so recently taken from you,' he managed

She rested her head on his shoulder and kissed his neck. 'Nonsense. For years now he's paid me so little attention. Kept himself amused with at least two mistresses and a string of common slave girls. I knew it wasn't my place to complain so I pretended not to notice. But now that I'm single I feel so much more able to express myself.'

Mannius couldn't believe she'd ever allowed herself to be neglected. He took hold of her slim waist in a powerful grip, kissed her forehead and said, 'If I let myself become entwined with you it would be a pleasure I could not draw myself away from and I do have a war to fight. Goodnight, Lady Felicita.'

'Goodnight to you, kind Tribune. And I hope we have the chance of continuing this conversation soon.'

# Chapter XX

Even before the early spring dawn, muffled noises came from the corridors and kitchens of the Great Hall. Slaves were starting fires and preparing food for the royal family. King Aelred was gently woken before sunrise by his personal slave. He took the offered gold goblet of weak wine and strode, naked, to an open window. The slave silently followed with a brown bearskin that he hung over the still well-formed muscles of the old king.

In the first grey light of the new day Aelred looked down from the second floor on thatched, wooden buildings. Slaves ran with leather buckets of water from wells and as he expected a dozen warriors were already out, shining axes and polishing leather tunics. Usually they'd still be inside, letting the excesses of last night's feast leave their bodies before they ventured out. Today, though, was the day he had decreed the fleet would set sail. The wind was light, which would make rowing to the west easier. A day's rowing and they'd be able to pick up winds that wise sages said would strengthen and push them to Albion.

Aelred envied the young warriors below. They would be nervous, expectant, excited, hopeful: all the emotions he'd known on his first campaign. Now as their leader he had to wrestle with other thoughts. What of their allies – how far could they be trusted? Were they steady in battle? The reports he'd received from Prince Wybert were encouraging though hardly conclusive. He'd sent word that the Votadini had been routed and, as planned, the three armies were converging on the east end of the Wall virtually unopposed. Details of the campaign concerned him and gave him an acidic feeling in his stomach. What did the prince mean by *virtually*? How much trouble were they facing? Would they be able to seriously threaten the east end of the Wall? And what of Senator Antonius' men? It was time he was there to see for himself.

The king was brought out of his contemplation by a light rustle of the bed covers. His second wife, nearly fifteen years younger than himself, stirred. She had tried her best to satisfy him during the night, moving her lithe body around, presenting herself any way he chose and surrendering completely to his lustful needs. Then when he thought he was done she used her long, delicate fingers to raise his interest once more. Finally, they had become exhausted and for the first time in weeks he had had a deep and untroubled sleep, leaving him fresh for the day's challenges.

Idly he wondered where she had learnt so many ways to please him. Did she talk with the whores and slaves or had he shown her during some drunken session that he couldn't recall? She would not travel with him. Instead she would sail in the second wave in a few weeks' time. In the meantime he would make sure that he'd got two of the best slave girls to keep him occupied.

Contemplating his strategy gave him another itch so he turned away from the window and pulled up the bedcovers to gaze at his naked wife. Her long, golden hair lay strewn around her shoulders and across her smooth, pale back. She moved her legs slightly and the shapeliness of her thighs was emphasised. He knew that the pale, white body was firm and supple, and that her skin would be warm and smooth in his hands. Awakening, she wriggled slightly and the temptation was too much for him. He cast off the bearskin and took her in his arms one time more.

*   *   *

Aelred waited impatiently on the grassy bank of the estuary with his wife, three of his sons, the admiral and his generals. The priests had already slaughtered four bulls and now the sailors had to perform their own rituals. Whining horns accompanied a rhythmic drumbeat had begun to generate a headache he thought he'd got away with.

'Your men have more rituals than any I have ever known,' moaned the king to the admiral.

'That is because they not only have the enemy to be wary of but also the tides, currents, wind, fog, waves and storms,' whispered the admiral. 'And anyway the tide will not turn for at least another hour.'

He was right, of course. Supplies had been loaded, as had animals, slaves and weapons. Casting a glance at the assembled fleet, bobbing and swaying on the flooding tide, he saw that some of the ships already looked to be riding dangerously low in the water and that was without his men being on board. Still, like most of his warriors, he was no sailor and had to place his trust in others.

Finally the drums reached a crescendo and the horns seemed to squeak themselves to a strangulated death. The admiral looked to the priests who nodded their satisfaction. Well they might, thought the king. They'd feast on the slaughtered animals for the next week or two. Maybe he should order his slaves to get some prime cuts from the bulls but then, no doubt, some of the sailors would take it as a bad omen.

The king's mood didn't improve as he strode towards the royal ship. Foul-smelling estuary mud sucked at his boots. He was sure that Romans had built proper ports, where men could walk easily on and off ships. For once he envied them with their engineers. A wooden gangplank, set at a steep angle, at least permitted him to go on board in a dignified manner. Most of his men had to scramble up ropes and haul themselves over deck sides.

At a little over sixty feet, his was the largest and newest vessel in the fleet. Along each side of the ship his personal guards had fixed their shining, round, red shields. Each had a black bear at its centre – the royal symbol of power. At the top of the walkway he jumped down onto a strong oak crossbeam. From inside, the ship felt more solid and the stench of the estuary was partly masked by the tarred moss sealant, pressed between the overlapping oak planks. An order was shouted by the captain. Aelred turned to the thick mast and watched seamen unfurl a square, red sail with a snarling black bear at its centre. In the feeble estuary breeze the men tied the sail tight for everyone to see the royal ship in its full glory.

The king turned, saluted the priests, then waved to his wife and youngest son. Lining the banks, hundreds of children waved and wives cried. He wondered how many men were glad, like him, to be going to war at last. Some would sail in fear but most would welcome it like a brother. It was a chance to get away from domestic arguments, screaming children and the drudge of everyday life. An adventure beckoned.

When the captain was satisfied, he shouted his orders for the crew to push out their oars. More orders, and oars pulled in short, light strokes until the ship started to move. Then the men pulled harder and longer and King Aelred could feel the speed increase. He stood at the prow, saluting other crews, and was cheered along the estuary and out into the Oceanus Germanicus.

The euphoric departure was several hours behind them, land had become a thin line on a hazy horizon and the slow monotony of the sea journey had set in. King Aelred had not been rocked backwards and forwards since he was a baby. The seesaw sensation was unnerving and made him dizzy. He'd tried to rest under a small awning on deck and in his makeshift cabin below, but with no success. Next he tried to distract himself by counting the oak treenails in his cabin. Nothing seemed to help. After quiet minutes of gulping air and trying to control his throat muscles, pride finally came second. He pulled himself above the planking and puked for all he was worth. By the fifth retch he felt better, turned round and slumped down.

Close by a sailor lazily coiled a rope with a grin on his face.

'Something funny, sailor?' said the king menacingly. 'Never seen royal puke before?'

The sailor's expression froze and all he could do was shrug his shoulders. King Aelred drew his sword and rested the point on the man's throat. Everyone on board was suddenly silent. The only sounds were from creaking oars and the swish of seawater running along the clinkered planks.

'Now I'll show you something funny. Jump!' said the king, waving his sword at the blackness of the sea.

'My lord,' at last the man found his tongue. 'My lord, I, I can't swim.'

'Then you should have thought about that before you laughed at your king. Now jump and find another ship to have a laugh on before I have your balls removed from you as well.'

The man turned his head and saw two more swords being held by evil-looking warriors from the king's bodyguard. One of the warriors prodded the sailor, who dropped the coils and jumped into the cold water.

Aelred hummed an idle tune as he watched the man thrash around. Astern of the royal ship a line was thrown

out and the man pulled on board. Outwardly the king
was calm, untroubled, but inside he was angry with himself.
His short temper had got the better of him again. A small
nobody had made him explode with hate. No doubt when
the man recovered he would tell tales of cruelty about
the puking king. By landfall they'd be calling him King
Aelred the Puker! Well bollocks to them! If they did that
he'd take out a few tongues.

'I'm sorry about him, my lord,' said the captain of the
ship, standing easily on the swaying deck. 'He's got a bad
attitude about him. Had to flog some manners into him
a few times myself.'

'I'd forgotten your quaint sea customs. But tell me, why
do so few of your men swim?'

'It just puts off the drowning a little while, my lord.
Even fit men find themselves too cold to swim after only
a short time. Most reckon it's best to get the worst over
with and be onto the next world soon as possible.'

'Interesting.'

The incident had cured him of seasickness and so he
went to find the whore-slaves to help him with an itch
that was forming.

# Chapter XXI

Powerful oxen plodded along the paved road of Dere Street, dragging heavy ballistae and supplies. Even with an escort of Roman infantry to clear a path through the tide of civilians fleeing in hope of safety, moving the army south had been frustratingly slow. Mannius left Curtius in charge of the column and raced ahead in search of more information from his scouts.

In a villa close to the fort of Cataractonium, Mannius set up his temporary headquarters. Outside his door guards crashed their boots on stone flags as they came to attention, but they seemed unable to keep him safe from the stream of messengers that came with news of units delayed: by traffic or the poor state of side roads turned into quagmires by torrential rain and constant churning by thousands of feet. Then there were countless requests for orders; complaints about accommodation; problems with rations. After those, and above all else, preying on his mind was a constant worry about the Saxons and their allies. Had he done the right thing? And, in the quiet moments between those worries, there was still a pang of guilt. Worse: he'd heard nothing from units he'd dispatched to the coast to evacuate everyone and everything that could be moved inland.

Just when he thought that things couldn't get much bleaker he heard the guards come to attention and raised voices quelled by a woman's voice. Felicita strode into the room, fending off concerns from a protesting guard.

'My dear Mannius,' she said, gliding over to him, putting

144

her arms round his neck and letting her powerful scent waft over him. 'I'm so glad I've found you.' She pulled him close and embraced him, forcing her lips hard against his.

Instinctively he let his arms fall around her slim waist. Keeping him in a powerful grip she gently kissed his neck. Her attention was a welcome distraction from the stresses that faced him in the scrolls and wax tablets on his desk.

'Perhaps you want to carry on our earlier conversation.'

Her words brought him back to the reality of his situation. 'Please, Aunt,' he said, freeing himself. 'I'm sure you didn't ride all this way just to offer yourself to me.'

'Of course I would if it would ease the burden of your command. I am fully aware of the stress that such responsibility brings.' At last she'd taken a chair and Mannius felt more at ease. 'And anyway you're the most handsome and desirable man round here.'

'Tell me some news I don't know.'

'Ah, very witty.' She brought out a wax-sealed scroll from inside her stola. 'Despite you resisting my advances so far, I have arranged a present for you.' She handed over the scroll, a large smile on her face. 'I heard about your disagreement with Flavius so I went to see Antonius, who is a very nice man I've known since I was a child. He spoke with Flavius, who agreed to rescind his order for you to be placed under house arrest. That is confirmation.'

'I am grateful that you were able to make them see sense.'

'Of course I was, because you're such a nice person. And I organised a meeting between you and Flavius tomorrow to clear the air.'

'Very kind of you, Aunt.'

'I know. Now you can repay my kindness with a little wine while you update me on the state of our preparations.'

\* \* \*

'You seem pleased this morning,' said Mannius as his mount kept pace a dozen yards behind a cavalry escort.

Taran nodded. 'Fine morning to be riding: a breeze on our backs and a little drizzle on our faces. And I had a good result last night.'

'Result?'

'A game of dice. Some generous legionaries decided to help a poor refugee by giving him a few coins.'

'I wouldn't take too many coins if I were you. Best not to upset the men too much.'

'But the man I mostly played had a large bag of coins. Didn't seem able to keep them so I merely helped his need to rid himself of such a burden.'

'Does this sponsor of yours have a name?'

'Macro, a great bear of a man. Seemed to have muscles on his muscles.'

'Ah, one of Curtius' senior legionaries, a tough man.'

'Tough but stupid.'

'Where did he get such a haul in the first place?'

'I asked him the same question. Said he'd won it gambling, though the way he gambles I'd like to meet the people he took it off! Must have caught the most drunk and stupid man in the empire on an off day.'

The tribune smiled. If only the empire had men of energy, imagination and invention like Taran there would be no threats like the one they faced now.

'You realise, Tribune, it's a trap we're riding into.'

'Of course it is.'

'Then why accept the invitation?'

'To find out whose side they're on.'

'At least we'll die a little better informed,' concluded the druid, seemingly untroubled by the prospect of such a fate.

Away from the main road the riding was pleasant over soft turf. Mannius enjoyed the exercise and the chance

146

to leave the stresses of command with some of the centurions. Occasionally they joined an indistinct track where trees encroached, forcing them onto the regular route. The escort slowed as they neared a series of thatched, farmstead buildings. The track dropped at a shallow gradient through cultivated fields to a wide, slow moving stream, its dark surface pecked by droplets of rain. On the far bank, above a ford, was an escort of at least forty riders. At its centre was Flavius, resplendent in a purple cloak and armour that shone despite the grey, overcast sky.

Mannius dug his heels into the side of his horse and moved towards the ford by himself. His action was mirrored by Flavius who joined him in the middle of the stream.

'Good morning to you, physician.'

'And to you, Flavius.'

'Governor Flavius, actually but I'll let your oversight slip this time.'

'You wanted to meet, so speak your piece.'

The two men eyed each other before Flavius broke the silence. 'Much as I'd like to put you through the due process of law, the senator,' said Flavius, waving an arm towards the escort behind him, 'has requested that I be lenient.'

Mannius could see an old man with the escort, presumably Antonius. 'Then the law should be thankful that the senator has had the good sense to correct your childish outburst.'

'I don't need to take shit from you, physician.'

'It's Tribune, actually, but I'll let your oversight slip this time.'

Flavius' horse seemed to sense its rider's frustration and snorted in disgust before it circled round. 'This is your last chance to toe the line,' said Flavius, pointing a gloved finger at Mannius.

'Or what? Are you trying to threaten me?'

How long do you think an escort of four and an old man would last? I have fifty riders ready to cut you and your men down. It's time you began to see your reality for what it is,' sneered Flavius. 'The dungheap you command is occupied by nothing more than amateurish insects. If you surrender yourself to my command now, you and your men will be spared.'

'By the way, my scouts only counted thirty-eight riders plus an old man with you – so if you've managed to conceal another ten from us then I congratulate you.' Mannius could see confusion and concern breaking out over the young man's face. 'You read books about military campaigns yet you seem to have learnt little. This is a perfect place for an ambush, which is exactly what it is.'

Flavius turned his horse in a full circle, his eyes searching out for any threats. A flock of crows that had sat in the tops of a copse of horse chestnut trees suddenly cried out as one and took to their wings, seemingly disturbed by movement hidden from his view. 'In your desperation I find your jokes amusing.'

'If you make any movement for me, Votadini archers hidden in the trees will unleash a rain of death on your men and the four cavalrymen on the track will quickly be joined by sixty mounted auxiliaries.' At the edge of the copse the outlines of men could just be made out.

'Soon you won't have an army, physician.' Flavius pulled hard on his horse's reins, holding his mount in the river. 'It will disintegrate before your eyes and you'll come crawling to us for protection. Think about that but don't think long.' Flavius laughed, then kicked so that rider and horse exploded from the ford in a cloud of spray before galloping up the hill, back to the waiting escort.

\* \* \*

148

In Cataractonium, Mannius visited the officer commanding
the fort, an experienced centurion and an old friend.

'What will you do?' asked Mannius. 'Will you stay and
fight or move south?'

'I owe it to the men to give them a choice. For those
wanting to go into Gaul and beyond it's a way out.'

Mannius knew his friend was being fair but it felt as
though he'd been stabbed. The more men who left the
forts the more weakened the allies' defences became. His
disappointment must have shown.

'Don't worry,' said the officer, holding up a hand. 'I'm
staying and I'll tell the men why: that there's a good
reason and a bad reason for my decision. The bad reason
is that I don't trust our new governor – he's a liar and
a coward, who's unlikely to pay any men under his
command. The good reason is that you're leading the
only resistance to the invaders that has a chance and I
want to give it every opportunity to succeed for the sake
of my family and friends.'

'I am grateful,' said Mannius, taking his leave.

# Chapter XXII

Centurion Laurentius wondered how the men of the coastal forts endured such appalling weather. Rain seemed to come at his group of riders horizontally, straight from the sea. Clouds appeared to merge with the waves, reducing visibility to nothing in places. If Saxons landed here, both sides might struggle to find each other to have a fight. Just as he was wondering why anyone wanted to fight over this wretched piece of land he saw lights at the fort. Lights in the middle of the day – typical of this foggy island. Days like this one made him miss the warmth of Rome in the spring.

He sighed as he approached the fort at the eastern end of the Wall. He knew the man in charge, Centurion Tacitus, and had been dreading this confrontation. Tacitus was dedicated to stubbornness.

'Piss off!' said the old centurion seated across from Laurentius. 'I'll be damned if I'll give the order to pull back and leave the Wall and coast undefended. You may be well educated but you need to know the full situation. I have written orders from the prefect himself to defend this place.' The mention of the prefect irritated Laurentius, however, Mannius had stressed the need to appeal to Tacitus' better nature, so he persevered. If he tried to force him to obey the orders he carried they would be poorly executed, delays would abound and equipment damaged. Tacitus was a good soldier, strong on discipline.

150

However, he lacked what the prefects referred to as 'imagination' and hated taking orders from cleverer officers – especially those younger than himself, which was nearly everyone. 'I have orders to abandon this section. We must leave nothing that might be of assistance to the enemy.'

'But we've got over a thousand men guarding the Wall and coast in this sector,' objected Tacitus' optio, who had taken up a position flanking his commander.

'You might hold the Wall for a time until their numbers overwhelmed your position. Or you may find yourself fighting simultaneously on two fronts, north and south,' replied Laurentius.

'As the optio says,' said Tacitus, 'we have enough men. We've also recently commissioned over twenty new ballistae to add to our existing complement. Why should we be running before a few barbarians?'

'Those barbarians have got themselves together, killed and destroyed King Cathal and are heading this way to link up with a Saxon fleet a week or so away.'

'So why have we not heard of such a fleet?' asked Tacitus.

'Coastal signalling posts have been systematically destroyed and messengers intercepted.'

'Probably Saxon mercenaries playing both sides, sir,' offered the optio.

'Whoever is behind it has done a good job. It's too late to stop them but it isn't too late to fight back,' persisted Laurentius.

'Precisely, which is what I've been trying to tell you, my boy,' said Tacitus. 'We'll give them a good fight here.'

'You won't last long. We'd need two legions at least. Our information is that a mixed army of Picts, Saxons and Ceretic's men totalling six to ten thousand are coming from the north and a similar number from the south. As I said I doubt you'll last long.'

'Let's not be too hasty,' said Tacitus – a sense of

realisation finally seemed to be dawning as he slowly calculated the odds.

'How long ago were you and your men last paid?' asked Laurentius, thinking of another angle.

'Two months,' volunteered the optio without hesitating.

'There are more than enough funds at Coria to pay you and your men everything that's owed.' The centurion eyed him suspiciously. 'I will get the tribune to inform the clerks to pay your men as soon as they report to the fort.' A widening of the old man's eyes betrayed him. Laurentius knew he'd got him hooked.

Tacitus leant back and sighed. 'What's the plan?'

'Fall back to Coria and secure the Wall and our communications at that point. The tribune thinks your experience will be vital in securing the town and fort.'

'Very well,' said Tacitus, quietly. The sweetener, more than the pay for Tacitus, was command of Coria, the key position in the north-east of the province and thus the most northerly outpost of Rome's empire. He wouldn't fail to respond to that.

'Start the evacuation of civilians immediately.' Laurentius saw both men exchange a knowing glance. 'Burn everything that may be of use to the enemy. Destroy any animals or food stores that you don't have time to move.' Laurentius waited for confirmation that the orders had been understood. 'And get every man you can spare to report to the tribune at Cataractonium in two days' time.'

At this last request there was a whistle from both men. 'We'll see what we can do,' said Tacitus. 'But while I organise things here perhaps you could spare the time to accompany my optio to the village to start the evacuation of civilians?'

Laurentius nodded. It seemed an amicable trade and would add no more than an hour to his mission.

*   *   *

'I'm glad of your help, sir,' said the optio. 'Especially with our recent local trouble.' Laurentius cocked his head to one side, indicating that he wanted to hear more.

'The villagers round here have become quite belligerent in their attitude towards us, sir. And it's nothing we've done.'

'Go on.'

'Just over two months ago a missionary appeared with his followers and started preaching. We thought nothing of it, Christianity being official like. But he twisted it, made out that the villagers had nothing to lose by kicking us out. Said that they'd be rewarded in this life or the next.'

'Sounds like some malcontent Bacaudae,' said Laurentius, referring to violent opposition to Roman rule in Gaul. 'Any recent sightings of this preacher?'

'Yes, sir. Came back here three days ago. Since then we've had a few of our signal stations damaged, but nothing we can pin on anybody. That's why we might have some trouble getting them to leave.' The optio's confidence seemed to drain. 'If you could spare the time, sir, I'd appreciate you talking to some of the elders, help them see sense.'

'No time like the present, eh? Let's get straight down there.'

Laurentius noticed that the worst of the weather seemed to have blown out to sea. He could see cliffs and beaches being assailed by a gentle swell. A short walk from the fort, protected by a fold in the land, stood an ancient fishing village. As the Roman officers accompanied by Laurentius' men and two squads of legionaries approached the village centre, men stopped mending nets and eyed the visitors. Laurentius was used to doors closing and people vanishing from streets as soldiers approached, but these people came out. Were they looking for conflict, he wondered?

'Looks like they don't want us to have a quiet chat with the elders, eh?' remarked Laurentius to the optio.

'No, sir. Might spoil their chances of a fight.'

The Romans halted on an area of flattened grass close to the village centre. Laurentius was surprised by how many people lived in the village. 'Over there, sir,' said the optio, pointing to a group of four men in black cloaks. 'That's the preacher, the big one, and his men.'

'My friends,' began Laurentius, projecting his voice, drawing on his lessons in oratory and shouting practice from parade ground duties. 'I am glad to see that the fishing is going well.' He looked in the direction of a portly man with a rope around his waist, struggling to hold his tunic in place. There were a few smirks in the crowd and almost a bubble of laughter.

'I'll be brief.'

'That'll be a change for a Roman windbag,' came a voice from near the preacher.

'This windbag is here to save you and your families.'

'We don't need Romans to save us, we need saving from the bloody Romans!' came another voice. This time Laurentius nodded to the optio, who sent a squad of his men towards the hecklers. Two were grabbed by legionaries.

'Look! See what I mean?' shouted one. 'I ain't done nothing so why're you arresting me?'

'On account of you're ugly,' shouted Laurentius, who got a ripple of laughter. 'And your face might frighten little children. Talking of children, a few days ago an army of Picts and Saxons attacked Votadini villagers, your peaceful neighbours. We sent men to rescue all we could yet still many perished at the hands of their attackers. They put children in front of their shields, hoping that we wouldn't attack them. Any child that wouldn't obey was killed, instantly. I saw many Saxons riding with the heads of children stuck to the ends of their spears.'

The villagers had fallen silent. 'That same army is headed this way with more coming by sea so we want to save you and your children by getting everyone inland to the safety of Coria, where there's plenty of food for everyone.'

'We'd be better off with the Saxons,' shouted one of the preacher's men, struggling to free himself. 'At least they won't tax us as much as the Romans.'

'Believe me,' replied Laurentius. 'The Saxons won't tax you, they'll kill you. The only thing they want is your land for themselves. Any of you who survive will be sold as slaves. If you want that, stay, otherwise do as the optio and his men say.'

The preacher and two of his other men had been moving round the crowd, just out of snatching distance of the soldiers. Obviously deciding they were beaten, they started to run. Three of the squad chased them down the high street. Uncluttered by armour and weapons, the hecklers seemed to be getting away when another squad of men stepped into the street from behind a hedge and blocked their path.

# Chapter XXIII

'You've got no right to hold me!' bellowed the preacher, who was seated on a low wooden stool in the optio's office.

Close-to, with his hood pulled down, Laurentius could see a deep scar below the man's left eye. His manacled wrists exposed a tattoo. 'Did much fighting with the legions?' asked Laurentius, nodding at the mark.

'I don't have to answer your questions. I'm a Roman citizen.'

The man's Latin was perfect and his accent reminded Laurentius of home. There was no doubt as to the legitimacy of his claim to Roman citizenship. 'I can and I am asking the questions here, preacher. If you don't like it there are others who can no doubt ask you in less subtle ways.'

Not a tremor or a flinch in his eyes. He was either stupid or brave, and Laurentius guessed the latter as the man looked to be in good physical shape.

'OK preacher, why are you here, at the edge of the known world?'

'Spreading the word and helping the Lord.'

'Even when it involves turning people against Rome?'

'I only help people see the world in a different light. There's nothing wrong in that.'

'Unless some of your audience start to demolish signal stations.'

'I don't know anything about signal stations,' protested the preacher.

'Didn't say you did. All I suggested was that you know how to demolish them, you being ex-army.'

'You haven't a scrap of evidence to connect me or my associates with such activities.'

'I thought a quicker way to find out about you and your team was to question some of the locals you've met,' said Laurentius, leaning back in his chair. 'I find a good flogging, followed by a kick in the balls and some minor dentistry is usually sufficient to loosen the tongues of casual acquaintances. In the meantime let's talk about you. Who authorised your work?'

'I have a letter from the Bishop of Rome himself but it is a little difficult for me to reach it right now,' said the preacher, raising his manacles.

'How is the old bishop?'

'Very well,' replied the preacher. For the first time Laurentius thought he detected a note of uncertainty. 'He was in the rudest of health when he signed my paper. Said the lands in the north need enlightenment.'

'We've saved you a trip,' said Laurentius. 'We have a lot of people from the north who're staying at Coria. I think you should come with us and enlighten them and my commander.'

'I have no time to run errands. God's work waits for no man.'

'What's the difference between doing it here, where there soon won't be anyone anyway, or in Coria where there are lots of pagans?' Laurentius paused, sensing the man was impatient. 'You might even be able to cure some more acute arthritis, you know, the same ailment that used to afflict the Bishop of Rome. Never used to be able to sign anything, even struggled with a spoon last time I saw him.'

'You're a clever man, Centurion,' said the preacher. His tone seemed more resigned. 'Unfortunate that I had to meet someone from one of Rome's finer families.'

'Thank you.'

'No problem,' said the preacher, rising to his feet from the stool. With a flick of his wrists the manacles fell to the floor and he leapt at Laurentius, smashing a fist into his jaw. 'Now piss off, old boy.' In a haze of concussion, Laurentius watched the man leap out of the window, climb a wall and disappear.

# Chapter XXIV

'I'm sorry, real sorry,' said Laurentius, nursing his jaw, in part because it was sore and also for sympathy, which was in short supply. 'He caught me by surprise. I'd just nailed his story as a complete fabrication, then he took his manacles off like they were gloves and suddenly it was his turn to nail me.'

'Great!' said Mannius sarcastically. 'Have any of his associates talked?'

'Same sort of toughs as the man himself. Look and sound like they'd rather die than talk,' answered Laurentius, wincing as he rubbed a tender spot on his jaw in case Mannius forgot that he'd suffered. 'Except one, who seems to be the real article, a proper preacher. Says he was hired to write sermons and answer any awkward questions from religious know-it-alls. Unfortunately, the rest of the group hardly spoke in front of him.'

'Shit! Anything from the locals?'

'Not much, though they couldn't have been more helpful if they'd tried. The preachers turned up a few weeks ago and lectured them on the oppressive ways of us Romans. Why pay taxes so that fat Romans can live in luxury? That sort of thing.'

'Tallies with reports from villages nearby.'

Laurentius shifted uneasily in his chair.

'Something else?' enquired Mannius.

'Er, yes, sir,' said Laurentius, who looked pale. 'My document pouch with the secret orders. He, er, must have taken it.'

'So they'll have secret orders showing that you've been ordered to protect a silver mine.'

'Yes, sir, and my tablet notes that it was a ruse which mustn't be divulged to anyone.'

'For fuck's sake! Why did you write it down *and* carry it round with you? Oh, we're done for now.'

'I'm sorry, sir, truly I am. I thought your plan was brilliant and I was hoping to keep a diary record of it, you know, to write it up afterwards.' Laurentius got up to leave. 'I'll get my things together, write you a letter of apology, resign and leave you in peace.'

'Not so fast!' exploded Mannius. 'You've got us into the shit, you can damn well get us out of it. There'll be no caving in at the first setback, we've got to fight as best we can and I still want you out there. Keep the loss of your notes to yourself. We've got ourselves an excuse to bring all our warriors together, which is exactly what we'll do.' Mannius paused to recover his composure. 'Go to your men, check them, and make sure you're ready to march first thing tomorrow.'

'Excuse me, Tribune,' said Taran, hardly waiting for a reply to his knock and not requiring a reply. 'The guards don't seem to have made much progress with the interrogation.'

'They know what to do and how to do it,' said Mannius, irritated by the intrusion.

'I'm sure they do, but time is of the essence. The prisoners appear to have intimidated the guards, so there's not much of an interrogation taking place.'

'What?'

'Despite several good beatings, the prisoners have kept very quiet. The guards are superstitious, they think that the men really are God's messengers and that He's protecting them.'

'How do you know all this?'

'I've seen it with my own eyes.'

'Why were you down there, with the prisoners? No one is allowed to interfere with prisoner interrogation.'

'Oh, I didn't interfere. Oh no, I only went to see if they had anything to tell us. Something that might help us track their leader.'

'What do you know of him?'

'That he gave Laurentius the slip and sneaked off with his pouch of secret orders.'

'And what,' said Mannius, an undisguised tremor of anger in his voice, 'do you know about those?'

'Only that they confirm the rumour that there's a silver mine to be guarded against Saxon invasion, somewhere on the moors above Derventio.'

'You have doubts?'

'I know of a few sites where iron, lead and even copper are produced down there. But I've never heard of anyone finding silver. Still, even a druid doesn't know everything.'

'You seem to know most things. Now apart from depressing me with news that you know our plans, what did you come in here for?'

'Permission to interrogate the prisoners.'

'And you think that you can succeed where experienced gaolers have failed?'

'I have other ideas to free their tongues and a unique opportunity has just presented itself.'

'Whether I let you or not, you'll find out somehow. Very well, but I want them alive and I want you to report to me as soon as you have anything.'

# Chapter XXV

Surrounded by thick stone walls, in Fort Cataractonium's secure dungeon, Taran and Una worked fast by light from flickering oil lamps. One of the young guards had assisted by screaming and moaning; another guard vomited spontaneously when he saw what they were doing. Taran was overjoyed as the stench added to the atmosphere. Then the old druid pronounced himself satisfied, nodded to the guard to stop screaming and stood back to admire his work. A body, barely recognisable as a man, was swinging gently, upside-down from a hook in the ceiling. Leather thongs bound the man's ankles and held him in place.

There was no skin left in place, giving the cadaver the appearance of butchered meat. Taran extinguished some of the torches, then finished by taking a bucket of animal blood and tipping it out under the body.

'Bring the prisoner in now, please,' said Taran authoritatively. This was his show and he needed a good performance from everyone.

Pushed by three guards one of the prisoners was forced into the room. He wore the same surly face that Taran had witnessed a few hours earlier. Their eyes met and for the first time Taran saw a flash of panic as the man took in the scene.

'Put him onto the hook, please,' said Taran, casually pointing to the man's bound wrists. 'And secure his legs.' While the guards worked the druid drained a goblet, feeling wine warm his throat. Once the man was properly

162

bound, the guards retreated to the edge of the room. 'Strip him, please, Una.'

Una emerged from a dark recess with a sharpened dagger and silently cut into the man's clothing. Soon he was naked and sweating. His eyes had become wild, like a hunted animal. Una sneered at his manhood and put the dagger between his legs. 'Where would you like me to start?'

'In Latin, my dear,' replied Taran, sounding like a physician with a patient. 'It is the language of science.' She repeated her question in Latin and Taran looked absently around as though he had misplaced a treasure. 'Ah, here we are,' he said, picking up a thick piece of leather and shoving it into the man's mouth. 'I am not insensitive to your needs. Best to bite on it when you feel the pain.' He looked at Una. 'Not so fast this time, my dear.' He looked at the prisoner. 'I'm afraid we had a little misunderstanding. I told her to take his heart out, and she removed it completely, killed him.'

'Sorry, my lord,' said Una, bowing her head.

'I have heard of men lasting five days of agony before they die. My best is barely a day and a half,' continued Taran modestly. 'However, looking at how fit and strong you are I will be disappointed if I don't have a new record soon.'

Una ran the butt of the dagger over some dark bruises from the man's earlier interrogation. Taran saw the man's eyes register pain. 'I'd like to see what a bruise looks like, my lord, from the other side.'

'So you shall, my dear. And those boils on his face. Fascinating. I always thought they went right through but I think you'll see otherwise.'

Taran and Una moved to the back of the man. The prisoner's breathing increased. He tried to wriggle himself free but he was bound and stretched too tight. Una scraped

163

her knife against a sharpening stone while Taran took a piece of ice and ran it down the man's back. The man spat out the leather and screamed.

'OK druid,' gasped the prisoner. 'What do you want to know?'

Taran continued as though no one had spoken. 'Careful on the buttocks now. If you get it wrong they can bleed something terrible. Where's that sand? Guard!'

Una applied the ice and the man screamed again. 'Get me the gaoler! I don't want to be skinned. I want an honourable death.'


There was a light tap on the door. 'Yes!' snapped Mannius.

Princess Caoimhe was accompanied by Caitir. 'I'm sorry, is it a bad time? I can come back later if you wish.'

'I should be the one who's sorry,' apologised Mannius. 'I'm afraid there doesn't seem to be a good time for me right now, but please come in and sit down. Let me get you some of this wine.'

'Only a small measure, thank you,' said Caoimhe, taking an offered goblet. 'It's Caitir. I'm afraid she's had a little fall and grazed her knee. Una is on an errand with Taran and Borgach is away, and I know you're a good physician and I wondered if...'

'Of course I'll have a look,' replied Mannius. 'I'm only hurt that I wasn't first on your list. Now let's see what the damage is.'

Caitir sat still and let her knee be examined. 'Ah yes, painful. I've got just the thing.' Mannius went to a bag and produced a large bottle. He poured a small measure of liquid into an empty goblet, diluted it with some water and then dabbed it onto the wound.

'Smells familiar,' remarked Caoimhe. 'May I?'

The physician held out the bottle. Instead of taking it,

Caoimhe wrapped both her hands around his and pulled him closer. Mannius felt a tingle of uncertainty as her soft palms enclosed his and as she lowered her head to the bottle her tunic fell open to give him a tantalising glimpse of her cleavage. She lowered her nose and gently inhaled. Mannius felt his hands tremble – but was it him or was it the princess?

Mannius thought about reaching out and pulling her into his embrace. But if she refused – as surely a princess would – then she may be offended and he might lose thousands of men from his new army. He chose caution. 'Camomile juice. Very good for wounds, cuts and grazes. Stops them going septic and eases the pain.' Caitir seemed to agree and smiled as Mannius tied a bandage round her knee.

'Thank you,' started Caoimhe, almost apologetically. 'I find myself even deeper in your debt. One day I will have to find a way to repay you.'

'Please, it is a pleasure to help you and as for your people they are our allies.' An awkward silence fell as though neither knew which way the conversation should head. 'When I returned I noticed your men were training much better today.'

'Taran told me to go and watch them. He said it would help to concentrate their minds. It was tedious being a spectator as they marched and charged but the captains were very pleased.'

'It's often like that,' said Mannius. 'Show the men that something's important by being there, they understand and try harder.'

'I've learnt a lot recently,' said Caoimhe. 'Fighting on Traprain Law was easy. There was only an enemy and us. Afterwards, though, I found it difficult to know how to lead people when the way ahead is less clear. I just wanted to ride off with Caitir and find a quiet spot, a hut, deep

165

in the woods, untroubled by wars. I wish I was as clever and confident as you.'

'We're not so different: I wanted to leave for southern Gaul or Rome to practise medicine. Leave the stress and uncertainty of war for others better qualified.'

'So what kept you here?'

'Maybe I wanted to help a beautiful princess and her people.'

Caoimhe smiled in appreciation: her eyes lit up and dimples formed on her cheeks. 'I'd like to believe that but you Romans are driven by greater forces of duty and honour that give you a strength so terrible that it can change the world.'

'Then it must be a duty to your people and honour to your beauty that drives me.'

A long silence fell on them. Neither dared risk eye contact. Caoimhe gathered Caitir, who looked tired.

'How have you coped?' asked Mannius gently.

'I've had a good teacher. Taran is clever, very experienced in matters of men. He has shown me ways to help others. If you wanted I'm sure he would help you.'

'Taran seems to know everything that's going on round here and a good deal more besides.'

'I'm sorry. I didn't want to impose him on you. He means well and he won't betray you.'

Mannius heard the sympathetic tone in her voice but his mind was distracted. Fatigue seemed to be his constant companion and listening to the princess' voice was a welcome tonic.

'So tell me, please Tribune, how does a tribune become an expert physician?'

'Ah, I'm slightly irregular you might say – and it's more the other way round. My father was an expert physician with the army and now tends to the ailments of some of Rome's finest families when he can be bothered to leave his estate. Against the wishes of my father I joined the army, trained and became an optio under Centurion Curtius. When Constantine declared himself emperor he took most of the seasoned legionaries with him to Gaul. My contract with the army was at an end and I was about to leave to join my father – but I stayed to practise medicine here.'

'So why haven't you joined him?'

'I pretended that I had duties here, but really, well, I suppose I just wanted to make my own life.'

'A rare luxury, being able to choose how to spend one's own life, and one I am envious of.'

Surprised that a princess could be jealous of anything in his life Mannius looked into her eyes and saw only sincerity. 'My father's brother, my uncle, was the governor until a few days ago. He came to me and asked me to take a message to your father and then organise our defences until he returned. It was he who gave me the temporary rank of tribune. I guess there wasn't anyone else suitable.'

'I think you're very suitable.'

'Thank you.' Praise was rare. Mostly he only heard problems and complaints. He was trying to work out whether there was a deeper implication in the princess's words.

'But you could go any time you like?'

'I, er, suppose,' Mannius stuttered, wondering whether he should say that if she asked him he would stay. His deliberations were cut short. Outside there were excited voices. Next moment after a brief knock, Taran walked into the room. 'I er, Princess, Tribune.' He looked awkward for a moment. 'Our guests decided to rethink their silence.'

'How did you manage that?'

'One of our warriors died from his wounds in the hospital and I, er, used the body to demonstrate what might become of the prisoners. Fortunately they had sufficient imagination to see sense.'

'I feel that you will want to talk about unpleasant deeds,' said Caoimhe, rising. 'Please make sure that our fallen warrior is treated with respect and given a decent burial. Caitir, time for bed.'

Mannius stood while the princess made her exit.

'Threatened to skin him alive and he didn't like the prospect of it one bit. Said he'd seen it a couple of times because he's a soldier. Imperial staff no less. Come all the way from Rome,' said Taran, excitement in his voice.

'So who sent them? What's their mission?'

'Couldn't say, which means someone clever's behind all this. An officer, called Galerius, the one who gave Laurentius the slip, recruited them all in Rome. Said the Bishop of Rome had commissioned them to help repressed Christians in Britannia. He'd noted that the upper classes hadn't converted as fast as they should.' Taran helped himself to a goblet of wine. 'Only they didn't restrict themselves to helping Christians here. They went north, above the Wall. Must have nearly met them myself at Clota Aest, when their boss gave them a full heads up on your troop numbers and dispositions – across the whole island mind, not just along the Wall. Since when did the bishop have access to that sort of knowledge, or does his god give it to him?'

'Anyone can get that type of information by just noting down the units stationed around the country.'

'Yes, but not up-to-date figures, the desperate lack of officers and that they hadn't been paid for over three months,' responded Taran almost triumphantly. 'Recently they got a bit squeamish about taking down some of the signal stations along the coast. But Galerius said it was a small diversion to focus the military on potential Saxon saboteurs and away from the rural Christians. Do you believe that?'

'Seems a good tactic, though it could backfire and put the heat on the locals.'

'And they told Ceretic and his mob that you'd be ordered to withdraw from north of the Wall a full week before the meeting at Clota Aest.'

'Shit!'

'I bet that's before you found out.'

'I can't believe that anyone from Rome would help our enemies. It would be a complete betrayal.'

'That is your privilege, Tribune. I can only go on what I see and hear. I know they're a malevolent force doing us harm.' Taran took a gulp of wine. 'They were on their way south, causing a few disturbances. Presumably to meet up with King Aelred and his Saxon fleet.'

'How do you know about him?'

'It is of little consequence and a small piece of deduction. The only problem is that none of them were told where the fleet is to land. Only Galerius knows that, and he's already on his way.'

'Anything else?'

'They knew that you didn't have orders to withdraw from that part of the coast and were surprised when your men started forcing people inland. Up till then they'd been trying to create diversions to keep you thinking that the fleet might land near the Wall.'

Everything seemed to fit. Someone in Rome, perhaps an agent, was helping the Saxons. Why was not important to Mannius, only how.

'I think we need to redouble our efforts to find Galerius. I'll get Seneca.'

'Your plan to trap the Saxons on the moors is our only hope,' cut in Taran. 'If the Saxons land in force then there'll be no way back for Princess Caoimhe and the Votadini. There'll be anarchy and an unceremonious land grab.' Taran played with his empty goblet, looking at reflections for inspiration. 'We need to stop Galerius telling the Saxons that the mine is only a ruse.'

Mannius shook his head. Caoimhe was right, the druid was clever. 'It's not only that,' he said almost dejectedly. 'He could stir up trouble for us in some of the coastal communities further south. There are a lot of Saxons in them and if they rise up against us we'll be fighting on more fronts than we can count.'

After a long silence Taran said, 'If you send more men they'll search in the Roman manner that Galerius knows only too well. But he's never been tracked by a druid. I'll take only Una and a few Votadini riders, find him and bring him to you.'

'I'll have papers drawn up for you, otherwise you might be the ones arrested. If you see the patrols looking for Galerius tell them who he is and that I want him alive if possible.'

'I will see you and the princess at your *silver mine*.'


'What's the matter, Eithne?' asked Mannius after he heard his slave slam down a third goblet on her tray.

'Sir?'

'Something not right?' he said, turning to face her, but she held her gaze low, focusing on the tray in front of her.

'Sir, I know it's wrong of me. I've always known and the other slaves have told me time and again but I can't help myself,' she said, her shoulders shaking a little. 'When the time comes for you to take a wife, please sell me on. I couldn't bear being around you when you're some other woman's husband.'

'Eithne, look at me.' Her face rose, covered in tears. 'Why are you so upset tonight?'

'I don't know.'

'Come on now,' ordered Mannius.

'The princess, sir.'

'What?'

'She's got a soft spot for you. Only...'

'Yes?' He'd hoped that he might have a chance but thought that such a royal beauty would never have time for him. It was good to hear such encouraging news from Eithne, who always seemed so good at reading people.

'She shouldn't have dressed as she was today. She was far too tarty for you, sir. She should have the proper respect.'

'Ah, so you think that I might be after the princess?'

'She's after you, sir. Plainest thing I've seen and she was nearly naked under her tunic. You've got enough distractions as it is without her coming at you and trying to get you to do what she wants.'

'Never thought I'd be attractive to a princess.'

'Of course you are, sir. Any woman round here'd have you, princess just the same. You're young, clever and powerful.'

'I wish I had the power to stop all this fighting before it gets any worse,' Mannius said in a resigned tone.

# Chapter XXVI

Surrounded by four slaves, Flavius reclined on a red sofa opposite Senator Antonius and waited while the steward passed a parchment over and whispered to the old man. Antonius nodded, silently weighing up the situation. On an unseen instruction, the steward waved the slaves out and two guards led in a dirty and unshaven Celt, who grovelled on the floor.

'You are a brave man to bring this message to me and I thank you,' said the senator. 'How is King Ceretic?'

'Please, your worship, he's in fine mood and spoiling to fight,' replied the man, not daring to look up.

'The Votadini put up a good fight, yes?'

'Sir, they did an' all. The old king and his sons went down glorious but they still got done for dead by us spears.'

'But Princess Caoimhe escaped?'

'Sir, I's sorry but believe it, so I do. They say she perplexed the Pict prince with witchcraft and disappeared. Powerful magic it was, they say.'

'Difficult thing, witchcraft. Hard to fight with swords and spears,' said Antonius sympathetically. Flavius nodded his agreement. 'Look at me now.' The senator waited until the man's gaze lifted and he had eye contact. 'What of your king's men? Are they ready for the fight? Don't lie to me now.'

'Sir, please, I don't want to speak ill of no one.'

'Come on now, speak the truth or I'll have it beaten out of you.'

'When the Picts took Traprain Law, sir, they lost a lot of men – good ones they was. Then chasing King Cathal and his men they got mauled some more by your regular Roman legionaries. That made 'em mad so they says to King Ceretic for him to lead the way down Dere Street and fight the Romans.'

'Go on.'

'Sir, since then it's been them auxiliaries of yours, them Saxons. They've been fixing ambushes with some Votadini that escaped. There's not much food and that's grating on the men like.'

'Thank you, messenger. Here's something for your efforts,' said the senator, tossing him a golden coin. 'See that the man and his horse are properly fed, then get him travel papers to take him north.' He turned, once more to the messenger. 'Tell King Ceretic that nothing has changed. Now go.'

Antonius held his counsel until the guards had left with the messenger. 'I always thought Ceretic would wobble a little. Not really a military giant and not got the respect of his men. Still, it all seems to be working out nicely, even if Ceretic gets cold feet.'

'Will Princess Caoimhe be a danger to Ceretic?'

'No, she's no Boudicca,' said Antonius, draining his wine goblet. 'She'll not trouble us.'

'What of our units?'

'They'll be ineffective soon enough. None of them have been paid for months and they certainly haven't been re-supplied. I'm surprised more desertions and examples of ill-discipline haven't broken out already. Perhaps it's time you went and had a look at what's holding them together.'

'What about Mannius, sir?'

'I have greater concerns regarding the Brigantes, so no need to worry about Mannius. I had thought of sending an assassin after him but, on balance, I think our friends will be pleased with his efforts – therefore I see no reason to distract him. That is, if he can take his eyes off Princess Caoimhe.'

# Chapter XXVII

After three days on board, King Aelred had found his sea legs. He stood on deck, letting his leg muscles absorb the vessel's pitch and roll. The captain had steered the warship round to the north, taking advantage of a southerly wind instead of sailing across it. Running with a strong southerly wind that filled the red sail, the craft planed through surf, giving the king a sense of power.

'How much longer before we make landfall?' he asked the captain.

'Probably two or three days for us. We're one of the faster ships in the fleet, my lord.'

The king grunted an acknowledgement but seemed preoccupied, hypnotised by the easy rise and fall of the waves. 'How did you know when to turn?'

'The admiral has a few scout ships ahead of us, my lord. They've sighted land and signalled to the ship astern of them, passing the message back to the Admiral and us.'

'So we're going up the side of their country?'

'Yes, my lord.'

'My word, I fancy going up some of their women when we land. Might take a raiding party to one of the local villages myself. Got quite an appetite for it now, I have.'

'Do you think there'll be much fighting, my lord?'

'I doubt it. I hear Britons are mainly sheep-shaggers these days. Their women will probably welcome a bit of Saxon iron. They've gone soft, my friend,' said the king, emphasising his point with a hearty slap on the captain's back.

'What of the Romans?'

'All those that could fight were withdrawn to Gaul years ago. The ones that are left are old, stupid and weak. I doubt they'll even bother to trouble us. In fact they probably won't.'

'My lord?'

'Remember we have hostages and they want more gold, so we should get lots of slaves without much of a fight.' The wind increased and the ropes hummed. King Aelred tried to copy the note that the sails made, happy that he would soon have a new kingdom.

On land, progress seemed to be painfully slow for King Ceretic. First he had to wait for his men to join him in force, then his men had to wait for supplies to be brought by cart from their homeland. Every day there were ambushes from Votadini warriors who had stayed behind. He hated the men for attacking his army but also admired them. They were proving to be a harder proposition to subdue than he'd thought possible. But worst of all was finding food for the armies. Everyone had carried what they could and anticipated plundering Votadini stores along the way.

Inside his leather tent a small feast by the standards recently endured was set out. Across a battered table the Pictish prince, Drostan, chewed noisily on a slice of mutton, then washed it down with some of Ceretic's best wine. Next to him Fidach pushed cheese into his mouth while he chewed on a thick hunk of bread.

'You have a rare appetite, gents,' said Ceretic. 'Perhaps I should open an inn.'

'Mighty generous of you, Ceretic,' said Drostan.

'Yes, very good,' agreed Fidach. 'But it's not appetites we've got, it's hunger. Wybert won't share anything and he's got plenty, smelt and seen what they feed themselves.'

'Gets his supplies mostly by boat, I've heard,' said Ceretic, not wanting to waste an opportunity to put a little needle into the Picts' relationship with the Saxons. Any fallout would leave him nicely in the middle, able to choose which side he favoured.

'Yeah, go fishing and such,' said Drostan. 'That's why he won't go inland with his men.'

'According to our agreement they're supposed to do their share of the fighting,' protested Fidach. 'But they don't. Leave it to us to face the Romans and it's our men dying.'

'Don't trust them an inch,' continued Drostan. 'All they've been fighting is boredom while we do the dangerous stuff – especially like your men, having to face ambushes.'

'They've broken the deal we had with them so it's only fair and proper that we do likewise,' carried on Fidach.

'What do you have in mind?' enquired Ceretic, curious as to how the Picts thought they might take on Saxons as well as the remaining Romans.

'Let Wybert and his father fight any Romans. They can kill each other as much as they like – they both seem to be good at it,' said Drostan.

'Yeah, we don't want to get in the way of them enjoying themselves, do we?' added Fidach.

'Then when the Saxons are done for we'll move on them. With your men and ours against tired fighters it'll be easy. If there's too many we'll do a deal with some of the Brigantes and share the land out,' said Drostan.

'Sounds an interesting plan,' said Ceretic, not sure if his lunch guests grasped just how big the Saxon army was likely to be. 'When do I sign up?'

'Just keep on the lookout. If we don't get them first, they'll turn on us all, soon as the Romans is out of the way,' finished Drostan.

# Chapter XXVIII

Mannius' men made short work of the journey south from Cataractonium. Paved roads made marching easy and enabled their support carts to keep pace. Only standing orders to use a screen of cavalry or infantry, along the sides of their column, slowed them. Recent years had seen an increase in attacks, though not usually on army columns. But bureaucrats ran the legionary machine and dictated that they must not take any chances, even when moving in their own territory.

As the column moved south, villas along the way grew in size and grandeur. Roman architecture had been followed to the letter. It seemed that the further people were from Rome the more they wanted to be reminded of the great city. Using local stone, villas the size of forts had been constructed to control vast estates. However, something looked wrong to Mannius. There were changes that he found difficult to nail in his mind. Riding next to Mannius, Curtius seemed to be having similar thoughts.

'Fields look a bit empty, sir. Some don't look like they've even got any crops planted in them.'

'Yes, of course,' replied Mannius. 'I was trying to figure what looked different. Not many people working in the fields.'

'Do you suppose they've taken fright and gone south, sir?'

'Doubt it. It looks more like they've been losing slaves and we haven't found enough to put into the markets. That's what the governor's men are always complaining about.'

'Maybe we'll be able to get some Pict and Saxon slaves, make a profit and pass them on to these estates.'

'It'd be good to see the old order of things restored,' said Mannius. Survival for him and his men was the priority. Prisoners to be sold as slaves would be a welcome bonus but he'd just take getting through the next few weeks as his reward.

Once the plan had started to be put into action a weight seemed to have lifted from Mannius. At the outset of the march he worried that one of the units would miss a rendezvous or Taran and the scouts would fail to find Galerius, the traitor. Gradually he realised that he could do nothing for them and that knowledge helped him relax for the first time in a week of sleepless nights. He and his men had their task: it was that simple.

Two long marches had put them close to the untamed uplands, north-east of Eburacum, the regional capital. At the end of the second day the men had established themselves in a marching camp by the side of the road. Lines of tents were set up with their sides parallel to the camp's earthen ramparts. Cooking fires were evenly spaced along the lines and officers' tents faced those of the men. Like the villas, there was reassurance for a soldier to be had from the order of things.

Shortly after their arrival, a dozen ballistae with an escort of three centuries of men had arrived, courtesy of the prefect in charge of the western end of the Wall. Though the war engines would slow them a little they were a welcome addition. Mannius went to meet the men and their officers as they paraded inside the ramparts.

The commanding centurion saluted Mannius. 'Centurion I am pleased, if a little surprised, at your presence.'

'The prefect thought it best that we join up with you as soon as possible, sir,' replied the man, who looked and sounded as though he had run with his men all the way from their base. 'Heard you was getting ready to put up a fight and we volunteered to help, sir.'

'How about some grub?' shouted an anonymous voice from the ranks on parade.

The centurion spun round to face his men. 'I'll have that man's name!' Then more quietly to his optio standing alongside, 'A flogging please.'

The man made to go to select some unfortunate as an example from the vicinity where the comment originated. Mannius leaned across and motioned for the man to stay. 'Where are my manners?' he said loud enough for everyone on parade to hear. 'Once your officers are satisfied that your equipment is properly sorted and stored there will be enough food for all. We have brought plenty with us.' There was a murmur of approval. 'But don't think that I won't be right with your officers, kicking arses, if you're not out of your miserable pits by first light tomorrow!'

'Thank you, sir,' barked the centurion, and gave the order for the men to be dismissed. 'I'm afraid we've suffered for lack of rations and discipline has gone down a little, but at least the prefect has made sure we've been paid.'

'Interesting,' replied Mannius. 'I didn't realise that any units had been paid recently. It sounds like your prefect's done a good job.'

The newly-arrived centurion joined Mannius in his tent for an evening meal, served by Eithne. The time allowed Mannius to brief the officer on the situation they faced and his plan. Far from reeling at the prospect of taking on an enemy that vastly outnumbered them, he seemed thrilled.

'Good to have a chance to get stuck into a proper fight,' he said. 'Too often we're obliged to help local tax gatherers – they're mean men, sir.' Like everyone else Mannius had heard stories about the men who bought concessions to collect taxes. 'A lot of the estates can't afford taxes as they're not being worked properly and the tax gatherers can't squeeze them 'cause they've mostly got connections to someone or other. So the city plebs and villagers have to stump up extra taxes to pay for the upkeep of the province.'

'Which seems to be an irony as the taxes that your soldiers collect are mostly used to pay for the army as precious little else seems to have had money spent on it in the last few years.' Mannius began to wonder what was happening to the taxes that were being collected – especially as at least some of the army didn't seem to be getting paid.

'Yes, and it's a recipe for disaster. Revolts keep breaking out, with people desperate to feed themselves. Terrible job to go tax collecting. Cuts the lads up real bad.'

Mannius watched him eyeing Eithne. 'I guess you're right. Can't remember much unrest over taxes near the Wall, but then again there was a lot else besides to worry about.'

'With cooking like this from a girl looking like that, I wouldn't have thought there'd be much to worry about, sir.'

Mannius smiled. The centurion was trying to be comradely but the addition of *sir* still gave respect. The man had obviously been a soldier for a long time.

'It helps to have a good meal to look forward to,' replied Mannius. Then almost hiding his eyes behind a goblet he drained he added, 'And is a useful distraction from soldiering at other times.'

'Don't blame you, sir. Wish I had the money.'

'Maybe we all will after we get ourselves some prisoners, eh?'

'I'll drink to that, sir.'

Hardly had they finished their toast than they could hear a challenge being issued at the gate. Shortly afterwards there was a commotion outside the tent and the insistent tones of a familiar, female voice. The speed of their arrival spelt trouble, but why had Aunt Felicita sought to get involved? More trouble. Surely the Saxons weren't already closing? Ceretic was miles north of the Wall, according to the latest reports Mannius had received. He sighed: that was the trouble with war, it was difficult to be certain of anything. Steeling himself, he waited.

A guard held back the tent flap to allow a centurion to enter. 'Tribune Mannius?' asked the man.

'Yes?' Mannius stood.

'May I announce Prefect Leonius.' Felicita strode into the tent, quickly followed by the prefect. To Mannius it seemed as if Leonius followed her like a dog. He watched and waited for her to be seated before he removed an ornately decorated pair of riding gloves and idly cast them adrift on the table that Eithne was hurriedly clearing.

'Isn't this splendid?' said Felicita. 'I was strolling round the tents before I turned in, when I saw Leo and his men arrive.'

Mannius ignored his aunt and concentrated on the prefect.

'Heard that you and Flavius had settled your differences,' said Leonius, not waiting for any further formal introductions. 'Good to see that you've gathered together a sizable fighting force. You'll be able to support the new governor's defences around Eburacum.'

Manius noted the order of the prefect's words, 'new governor's defences' not 'governor's new defences'. Leonius was always precise – a lifetime in the army had ingrained a pathological hatred of ambiguity.

'We have other plans, Prefect Leonius,' replied Mannius. The man would notice that he hadn't used 'sir'.

'Might one enquire as to what they might be?'

Mannius paused, eyeing the man in front of him,

wondering how far he could trust someone who hadn't wanted to take the fight to the enemy.

Rarely quiet for longer than she had to be, Felicita was the first to speak. 'We're going to intercept a Saxon army, Leo. Something the new governor doesn't want to do.'

'On whose orders?' asked Leonius.

'The standing orders of the former governor, backed by the imperial seal,' replied Mannius before Felicita could say more.

'Governor Flavius is the proper authority in the province now,' objected Leonius.

'Flavius has no authority over us since only an order from the emperor can negate our standing orders.'

A quiet descended on the tent. Eithne stopped working and retreated to the shadows – even the sound of hammering had ceased as though everyone in the camp was straining to hear the exchange. Mannius eyed the man who had become such a source of disappointment to him. Before he could reply, Felicita again took over.

'Tell him your news, Leo, about my late husband's murderers.'

'Yes, I was on my way to join the new governor with some of my men when I received word that the leaders of the men who targeted Lady Felicita's husband are not far from here.' Mannius saw that the old man seemed to be avoiding eye contact, constantly looking around the tent – anywhere but at another person.

The prefect settled back into his chair, placed his hands on his lap and kept his eyes focused on his interlocked fingers. 'My men found that your husband's assassins worked for a man who is quartered close by. A local noble who goes by the name of Coel – set himself up as something of a king in this area.'

'Go on,' prompted Felicita. Mannius could feel his heart sink as he suspected more trouble was coming his way.

'It seems likely that he knew something of the murder and it could be useful to question him.'

'At the very least!' said Felicita, becoming animated and slapping the table. 'He must be held responsible for his own people. We need to teach these people a lesson – king indeed! Where is this wretched man? He needs to be shown who his betters are!'

'A few miles from here. I was on my way to demand he explain his part in the cowardly act when I received word that Tribune Mannius was here with an even larger force.'

'Then it's settled,' concluded Felicita. 'First thing tomorrow we shall meet with this King Coel and demand an explanation.'

'But the Saxon army...' objected Mannius.

'No buts, please Mannius,' said Felicita, waving away his objection. 'Your uncle deserves some justice and we haven't even found any Saxons to fight as yet, have we dear?'

'Good!' said the prefect. 'Then while you're looking for them perhaps you'd be so good as to help me.'

Alarm bells started to sound in Mannius' head. Now the simplicity of march and fight seemed to be becoming a little more complicated.

'Might I enquire as to your requirements for us, Prefect?' asked Mannius, trying to find a way to regain control of the army from his aunt.

'At first light we can march to a villa a little over fifteen miles south and east from here,' said Leonius, his eyes on Eithne, who had started to work again now that the earlier tension had subsided. 'We will be joined by three more centuries from the militia at Eburacum, then assault the villa, taking as many prisoners as possible. We need to make examples of these people. They must be made to do their duty for Rome! But first, if you can spare some hospitality I'll have some food.'

'Of course,' said Felicita, clapping her hands for attention.

'Girl, some food and more wine for Prefect Leonius.' As Eithne walked passed, Felicita grabbed the slave-girl's tunic at the arm and with a thoughtful look on her face said to Leonius, 'Perhaps, you'd like to be entertained by the slave girl.' To emphasise her offer, Felicita lifted Eithne's tunic well above her knees to reveal firm, sleek legs.

Eithne, shocked, looked ready to fight. 'We will be happy to get you some food,' said Mannius quickly. 'I'm afraid the girl is no slave. She's a freedwoman in my employ. I promised her father that she'd be well treated.'

Perhaps Leonius was cleverer than he looked or maybe more of a coward, thought Mannius. The old soldier looked visibly relieved. Whatever the reason he shied away from confrontation. 'No matter,' he said airily. 'We must respect law and order, eh? It is the girl's loss. But I could do with a tent for the night – sorry for the imposition.'

'Not at all, please use mine.' Honours even, thought Mannius.

Mannius sent other slaves to serve food to the prefect and caught up with Eithne in a smaller tent he had managed to get from one of the centurions. 'I'm sorry about Lady Felicita and Prefect Leonius.'

'No matter, sir,' replied the girl, helping him undress. 'It wasn't your doing. I'm just a slave and can't complain, sir. Thanks for lying for me, lots of folk wouldn't have bothered or had the guts.'

Mannius sighed. 'I didn't exactly lie,' he said, handing a parchment to Eithne. 'I wrote this out and had it witnessed before we set off. I was going to give it to you before we catch up with the Saxons.'

Eithne took it as though it might explode in her hand. 'It says you're free,' said Mannius. 'Everything's changing in our world. I don't know what tomorrow or next week will bring, but I want you to have it. You deserve it after what we've been through. Please take it.'

185

'Thank you, sir,' Eithne sobbed. 'I never thought I'd ever be free. Thought my children'd be taken soon as they was grown enough and sold.' She dropped the parchment, then pulled at the brooch securing her tunic, letting it fall about her feet. Naked before him she pushed him onto his cot.

'You don't need to...'

'I always wanted to from the first, sir. It was never a chore, like what it would have been with that fat, old man.'

Sitting astride him she gently rubbed oil into his aching back, releasing days of stress. Then she took a sharp knife and scraped the oil away, cleaning his shoulders and back. When Mannius felt the last scrapes and heard the knife drop to the ground he turned over. Gently teasing him, she slowly smeared oil over her breasts and onto her legs. Then she rubbed some oil onto his chest and leaned close to him. His hands ran along the oily smoothness of her thighs and to the small of her back. Pulling her towards him he felt the last of his tensions being eased away.

# Chapter XXIX

The villa was one of the largest Mannius had seen. Stone walls over twenty feet high surrounded the main compound and enclosed a parapet. Around the wall, watchtowers controlled the approaches. Thick wooden gates made of seasoned timbers barred the two entrances, and they were behind a ring of ditches. This was no easy villa to assault. No simple house call. Noises coming from behind the walls indicated that there was a significant body of men readying themselves for a fight. Judging from the archers on the parapet they were not about to give up easily. Storming the place would take time and cost valuable lives. Of course he could send for the ballistae he'd ordered south. They would destroy the walls and gates, which should make an assault easier, but that would take precious time – at least a day. Mannius wanted to waste neither men nor time.

He ordered a table and two chairs to be brought to the front and spoke to Eithne, who disappeared. She returned quickly, having changed into a brilliant white tunic. Together they accompanied two legionaries up the track towards the villa's main gate. Leonius realised what was about to happen and tried to intervene.

'It's no good talking to those rebels. They won't listen,' he insisted.

'Worth a try. Always better to win without a fight than to have casualties – some of them will be our own,' said Mannius.

'Tell those cowardly murderers to surrender immediately

and hand themselves over to Roman justice,' added Felicita in loud, shrill tones that left no one around her in any doubt as to the nature of the day's mission.

Prefect Leonius was not mollified. 'I care nothing about casualties, Tribune Mannius, I want those rebels dead!'

'That's not the Roman way and you know it. We always give our enemies a chance to surrender. That way there's more prisoners, which means more slaves.'

'I don't think you heard me. I'm not interested in prisoners. Kill them. Kill them all!' Leonius suddenly sounded desperate and looked to the centurion accompanying him, who merely shrugged his shoulders as if in agreement with Mannius, but unwilling to acknowledge the fact openly. 'You there,' shouted Leonius to a centurion. 'Order your men to move forwards ready to storm the villa on my signal.'

'Won't happen, sir,' said the centurion in a matter-of-fact manner.

'What did you say?' responded Leonius becoming apoplectic with rage.

'Can't be done, sir. Defences too strong and too many of them. We could try but we would surely perish.' The centurion spat on the ground to show his contempt for the order 'Best talk to them, get them out and wait for the extra troops that are on the way. Give the lads a chance to get some grub inside them. Then things'll be different. And anyway, sir, the new governor don't control this army, Tribune Mannius gives the orders. Sorry sir.'

On one of the watchtowers that overlooked the approach to the main gate the leader of the rebel force chewed the end of a clay pipe as he watched Roman preparations. Earlier panic had gripped his men when they witnessed the arrival of several centuries of soldiers, accompanied by cavalry. Thankfully, that had died away to be replaced by curiosity. Now the action of the officer, little more than a hundred and fifty paces in front of him, was causing confusion. He watched as the officer propped his shield against the leg of a table and then removed his helmet. Next to him a young woman, dressed in a white tunic, stood ready to pour something from a silver jug.

'Got balls, sir,' suggested one of the rebel captains standing next to him. 'Having a picnic in range of our archers ain't what you'd call a healthy breakfast.'

'Permission to storm the table and take her prisoner, sir,' said another officer.

'Don't mind helping out myself,' added the captain. 'Ooh, she's worth chancing your luck for, eh?' The woman's tunic tightened as the breeze caught it and pressed the material against the curved contours of her body.

'It's an invitation,' replied the leader as much to himself as the officers around him. 'A chance to talk. Open the gate! Let's see what this man has in mind, eh?' He thought about taking his wife with him. She was a rare Irish beauty and sure to distract. But knowing soldiers, it would only serve to increase their efforts to get her as booty. Instead he settled on a travelling priest and the two set off to the picnic.

'Greetings! We come to you under truce,' said the priest as he approached the table. 'I am pleased to announce Coel Hen.'

Shit! Mannius felt like a pickled egg, waiting to be eaten. Roman administrators controlled the cities, the army controlled lands around Hadrian's Wall and tribal nobles held sway over much of the countryside. Coel Hen and his family led the Brigantes, who held most of the north. Coel Hen wasn't just a king, he was the king of the Brigantes. 'Lord Coel, it is a pleasure to meet you,' replied

189

Mannius, raising himself slightly. 'Please take a chair and have some wine.'

'I wish I could say the same.' Smooth, educated Latin suggested that the priest wasn't lying.

'Let me introduce myself,' said Mannius.

Coel held his palm up. 'No need, Tribune. You have been recognised by a good friend of mine. Seems you saved his boy a week or so ago. I'm grateful for that and now I'll take that drink.' Coel sat, took the offered goblet and passed it to the priest. With an anxious look the man tasted it before he pronounced it as wine.

'I do not wish to poison you,' said Mannius, desperately rethinking his strategy. He'd hoped to frighten and bully the defenders into submission. Somehow he didn't think the man in front of him would give way so easily. The strongly fortified villa made sense now as it was, no doubt, his family home. 'In fact I'd rather not hurt anyone here today.'

'I don't have a problem with that,' replied Coel. 'So you might as well be on your way.'

'I'm afraid it's not as simple as that. You see I've got an old man over there who's pecking for trouble and clucking about murderous rebels in your villa who won't do their duty to Rome.'

'Hah!' spat Coel. 'Rome is not doing its duty for those people. Last year they lost their houses, possessions and some even had members of their families taken in Saxon raids along the coast. That season is upon us once more and they fear the same.' Coel tested the wine. 'Your army is weaker than last year, morale is lower and the enemy bolder. What hope can you offer those people, my people?'

It was a challenge. 'There are no guarantees in war but I'll guarantee you one thing, and that is I'll try my damnedest.'

'And the other Roman guarantee is that we'll be taxed

for the privilege. My people lose everything then they're told to pay taxes for soldiers. Surprise, surprise, they can't pay because those soldiers didn't stop their enemy from taking everything they had. So the tax gatherer's men say that they'll lose their freedom and threaten to make them slaves to work in the fields.'

'My men haven't been paid for months, the centurions included.' Some information, Mannius knew, is best held back, but he couldn't help himself. He'd been needled.

A look of uncertainty swept across Coel's face. 'Truly?' Mannius merely nodded in reply. 'Then why stay? Why not go back to Rome?'

'Most of my men are Britons themselves. They have families here, they speak the local language, eat the local food. If they went to Rome they'd be foreigners. Even our Saxon auxiliaries are mostly second, third and sometimes fourth generation Britons.'

'So you will fight for Briton, to keep it as it is?' Coel smiled at Mannius' frustration. 'Then you are no different to us. There is no need for us to fight. The only man who wants a fight is that clucking hen.'

Both men turned to look at Leonius playing with the reins of his horse. 'Prefect Leonius is using the pretext of hunting the former governor's murderers to use you and your men to storm the villa and kill everyone, yes?'

'It seems reason enough in today's world. Has he another reason?'

'Two months ago a young man, who works for a Roman senator, sent a messenger, an errand boy, to my house, asking me to help him. He wanted an escort of six men and two men to drive carts from north of the Wall to near Eburacum.'

'Flavius, I presume?'

Coel nodded. 'I asked why he didn't use the militia or

191

regular troops and he replied that he wanted to keep it low profile. There were to be no regular imperial connections.'

'So what was on the carts?'

'Difficult to say,' admitted Coel, taking a mouthful of wine to help him with the story. 'We heard rumours from staff employed in the governor's household that it was gold. A few of us saw chests on the carts but no one could check their contents. The men I sent never came back. Flavius said they'd been sent on another mission so I requested payment for both and he told me to piss off. He'd only pay them when they returned.'

'Sounds like good business, so far.'

'Until three days ago when a field slave on an estate just north of here found a body in a shallow grave. We searched around and found four other bodies, all decomposed but having the clothes and equipment that identified them as part of the special duty escort, and all killed in the same way – hands bound behind their backs and throats sliced open.'

A burst of intuition hit Mannius. 'May I indulge you a little further? Last night I was supplied with the descriptions of men responsible for the assassination of the former governor. Would you be so good as to cast your eyes over them?'

Coel nodded and Mannius slipped a hand inside his tunic. The priest looked on nervously until a parchment was produced.

After a few moments reading Coel shook his head then laughed, a deep thundering roar that rumbled across the table. 'These are the dead men we found in the field.'

'Why the humour?' asked Mannius.

'Because those men had been dead for over two weeks when we found them – I know because I saw them with my own eyes. And the governor was murdered about a week ago. Someone's trying to cover their tracks and they're doing it badly.'

Mannius pondered. 'I am short on men and time. I cannot permit myself to be distracted into trying to solve a murder mystery. A horde of Saxons are begging for my attention and if I don't oblige, then in a few weeks no one round here will be left to care.'

'Then the solution to your dilemma is easy,' said Coel, raising his goblet. 'We offer ourselves to fight alongside our Roman, sorry, our British allies. It is our Roman duty. Afterwards we can sort out any trifling differences.'

Mannius held his goblet aloft. 'I'll drink to that! And I'll need some liquid encouragement to face the pecking I'm about to get.'

'I have something that may be of assistance to you,' said Coel in a quieter, conspiratorial tone. 'Last year I travelled to Gaul and was privileged to have an audience with Emperor Honorius. He listened sympathetically to my request to send troops and apologised – can you believe it? He said that he had no men to spare but would do his best to help. So he gave me a letter, with his seal on it, saying that he understood our situation, recognised our devotion and welcomed our support.'

'May I see the letter?'

'Of course,' replied Coel, slowly reaching into his tunic and withdrawing a parchment.

Mannius read the document. Times were changing: a Roman emperor openly admitting that he couldn't control a province. When he'd finished he pushed the parchment back to Coel. 'I guess this makes us allies.'

Coel gave another, even deeper laugh that could be heard in the villa. 'I'm glad you said that, Roman. I have faith in you. Your eyes have honesty and determination. I will accompany you to see this clucking hen.'

'As you wish. Eithne, please stay here with the priest to show our goodwill to Coel's friends on the ramparts.'

The two men walked down the track to the Roman lines as though they were old friends returning from a night's drinking. Leonius pulled hard on his horse's reins to turn it towards the back of a group of officers edging forward.

'Centurion!' Leonius pointed at Coel and bellowed at the man in charge of his escort 'Arrest that man!'

'Easy, Centurion,' said Mannius, holding up a calming hand. 'Lord Coel is here under truce and enjoys my protection. I think all senior officers present should hear that our emperor has faith in this man to support the Roman cause.'

'Lies of a desperate man!' shouted Leonius, circling on his horse. 'He and his men must be executed as examples.'

'Shut up, will you?' shouted Mannius, losing his temper. 'If you bothered to look you'd see that this letter carries the imperial seal. That's a higher authority than your governor.'

Leonius, sword in hand, urged his horse towards Coel. Mannius drew his own sword and stepped between them. Before the horse reached Mannius, Leonius was dumped on the floor by Centurion Laurentius, who pulled at the man's boot. Other swords scraped their way out of scabbards. The only one without a sword was Leonius who was winded on the ground.

Mannius replaced his sword and turned to the leader of Leonius' escort. 'I suggest you take your charge out of harm's way.'

The centurion nodded, sheathed his sword and helped Leonius to his feet. Too winded to speak he walked between his horse and the centurion for support until he felt able to be raised into the saddle once more.

'I think we've got another enemy there,' said Coel.

'When we face thousands already I don't mind one more like that,' replied Laurentius.

Mannius preferred to hold his counsel, guessing that the old Roman had worse to throw at them.

# Chapter XXX

Taran marshalled the Roman escort that Mannius insisted he take with him. He at least had a chance to follow Galerius in the same manner that his quarry travelled. After running from the village, Taran guessed that there had been a fallback position. There were probably one or two men with horses, hiding in case of an emergency. Laurentius' men had failed to find the escapee and none of the locals reported horses or supplies missing, which fitted his theory.

After a full day of searching, Taran found a small camp near the edge of the moors. A grassy clearing, hidden by a copse of budding silver birch trees, had been home to five horses and two people. Taran read the signs like a parchment: old leaves and soil had been hastily used to camouflage a scorched patch of earth; numerous prints from horses and people; discarded animal bones from a number of meals; and bark worn away on two trees that had been used to tie off a line to tether horses. He began to get into the skin of the man he was tracking, thinking like a fugitive.

The group had gone south, along the coast. Galerius would know that the army was moving people inland and that would make it easier to move unobserved, close to abandoned villages. As predicted by Mannius, Taran came across mounted patrols looking for Galerius. Each time Taran would order his escort to stay behind the other group for a while to see if Galerius broke cover after the passing of the first patrol. But all they caught were a few startled deer.

Clear skies and crisp spring air added to the pleasure of hunting, a good distraction from the horrors of the very recent flight from his homeland. Then, after two days, rain clouds started to drift over and greying skies mirrored the group's mood as they failed to find any further clues as to Galerius' whereabouts. Even Taran was starting to feel the elation of the chase waning. Sheltering from a heavy shower under the boughs of an ancient oak tree everyone was depressed. The troopers cursed the rain and their damp clothes. Everyone – save Una, who remained quiet on such matters – yearned for a warm hearth in a friendly inn. Reminiscences of popular drinking haunts and stories of good times started to be traded. That was when Taran dismissed the escort. The soldiers looked startled as the druid told them that he would head inland to the paved road. Without waiting for the rain to lessen he nudged his horse into the grey world of the fields beyond.

'Why are we going inland?' asked Una.

'Because that is where the best inns are, is it not?' answered Taran.

'So we've given up on Galerius. A little rain and we quit?'

Taran laughed. 'Galerius won't be out here, will he? He might let his men camp in the hills but if he's the man I think he is he'll be drinking wine in the best inns available and shagging the tastiest crumpet he can get his hands on.'

'But surely he'd want to hide,' protested Una.

'And the best place to hide is where you can blend in. He's a Roman. Likes his baths and good living. I've no doubt he could survive out here but what's the point? And he'll have the use of the best roads in the world to take him wherever he wants to go.'

Late afternoon brought them to a paved road that ran

parallel to Dere Street. Taran decided to head as far north as possible before nightfall, then find the first decent inn as the start point for the search. Ten miles south of the Fort of Concangis they found a suitable inn and took a room. Una was loaned to the innkeeper, who put her to work in the kitchen, while Taran went to work, drinking and gambling with the other occupants.

At the end of the evening they pooled their discoveries, which Una found disappointingly few. 'How many more nights will I have to work in kitchens with drunks leering every time I serve them at their table?'

'We are indeed fortunate that so many people have decided to move south. It's created a demand for good kitchen service that the usual slaves seem unable to cope with,' said Taran, relaxing on the only cot in the room.

'So I cook, clean and serve, while you have a fine time. Then I get the rug as my bed. Well just bloody thanks!'

'You could be outside with the other poor unfortunates who can't even afford a room, if you wish. And even after the innkeeper's exorbitant charges for his modest offerings I calculate that we've made a small profit on the evening.'

'Well that's just bloody terrific.'

'Yes, I'd knew you'd like it. And while you're here I'll have that leftover beef cold for breakfast in the morning.'

'Piss off! You're not the one, who –' But he was already snoring.


The next day Taran and Una journeyed south at a leisurely pace. The old druid stopped to befriend anyone travelling north. He talked with them about the weather, crops, Saxon raids, troop movements, taxes and strangers in their midst. Twice he got lucky with the same story. A fierce-looking priest was staying at an inn barely twenty miles south.

At the inn, Taran made the arrangements. Once again, Una was loaned to the innkeeper to work in the kitchens, tend tables and clean rooms.

'I thought it would be busier,' Taran commented to the innkeeper.

'It'll get busier,' replied the small, round man as he used a rag to clean an ancient oak table. 'In afternoons folks are walking, trying to get places. Come evening they get thirsty, hungry, and want a roof over their heads for the night.'

'Many regulars?'

'Why d'ya ask?'

'Just wondered if you knew whether any of them liked to gamble a little, just socially.'

'There's a merchant comes by every week, he likes his dice. Apart from him none of the other regulars gamble much. Most just sup themselves stupid.'

'A worthy pastime at an inn that serves ale with such fine flavours,' said Taran, taking a gulp from a pewter goblet. 'And rewarding for you, no doubt.'

'Aye, even the preacher likes his ale.'

'Preacher?'

'Aye, proper Christian preacher he is with his assistants, an' all. Goes out preaching during the day and comes back at night. Keeps himself to himself but likes his ale.'


Everything was as Una had expected. Reluctantly, she volunteered to serve ale and food to increasingly drunk men at battered wooden tables in the hope of getting near the preacher and his men. She'd had her backside groped too many times to count, already fought off two determined advances and darkness had fallen over two hours previously. Still the preacher and his men failed to appear.

Just as Una was thinking that she'd allowed herself to be groped by every drunk in the inn for nothing, the door opened and a lean-looking man in a riding cloak put his head in to the room. Satisfied, he stepped in, followed by a bigger and tougher man. Immediately Una's gaze was drawn to a wicked scar below his left eye. Unsmiling he followed the first man across the room and to the rooms above, not to reappear. Nor did he or his assistant ask for anything to be taken to their rooms.

'Did you see them?' Una asked Taran once they were in their room at the end of the night.

'Yes, my dear, clear as day.' Taran eased himself onto the only cot in the small room.

'I thought it was my turn to sleep in the cot,' protested Una.

'Tomorrow I have a long ride to get a message to the tribune that we have found the spy, while you keep watch here. I'm sure you won't begrudge an old man his sleep.'

Una rinsed her hands and face in a bowl of water, perched on a tiny table. She'd thought of a good reply and turned to deliver it. Then she heard his first snore and knew debate was useless. Once again she found herself making the best of the blankets on the floor.

True to his word, Taran left before dawn and returned in the early evening, winking at Una as he entered the main room. She worked hard, serving tables, getting groped and fondled by countless, laughing drunks. Some even offered a few miserable coins for her to dance naked. But she ignored them all, waiting for the man they were tracking to appear. Again it was late in the evening when he entered the inn but this time he and his assistant took a table.

Una put down the empty jugs she was carrying on the bar and went to meet the new arrivals. 'Evening sirs. Can I get you anything to eat or drink?' She expected a lewd comment or a grope but none came.

'You're new here,' the scarred man said, almost accusingly, as he removed his cloak. Una saw his arms were well muscled and also carried scars.

'Yes, sir. My master loaned me to the innkeeper. It helps to pay our way.'

'Who's your master?'

'The tall man, near the bar with the other gambling gentlemen, sir.'

'Ah, yes,' said the scarred man, picking out Taran. 'Your accent is Gaelic, yes?'

'Yes, sir. From just north of the Wall. My master thought it'd be best for us to head south for a while until the trouble up there dies down a touch. It's a bit too exciting for folks like me up there just now, sir. Now can I get you something?'

Una took their orders and returned with two full mugs of ale, a loaf of bread and bowls full of steaming vegetable soup. After a slight pause she took out more ale and plates piled high with chicken and vegetables. From a distance Una kept a careful watch on the two men, occasionally going close to their table to check their mugs weren't empty. Towards the end of the evening, as some of the poorer guests were getting ready to sleep on the stone flags of the floor or tables – if they were lucky – another man joined the two she was watching. She was sure that they seemed surprised to see him and walked over with a mug of ale and took his order. When he'd gulped his food down Una went back to clear the plates away. 'You must have worked hard today to be this hungry,' said Una.

'The Lord's work can be trying on the body,' said one of the assistants.

'You're preachers. I thought you was army types.'

'What d'ya say?' snapped the largest of the man's assistants.

'It's them tattoos on your arms. They're like ones I've

seen soldiers having done near the Wall. Look real impressive, bet they cost a pretty purse of coins.'

'We are soldiers of the Lord now, spreading his word among a heathen population,' replied the scarred man in an unruffled tone.

'Well, you must have been doing a lot of spreading to be this hungry. The cook'll be right pleased to know that you enjoyed this lot. I'll get him to make some extra come breakfast, that ways you'll be able to take some food with you and you won't come back half-starving like.'

'Very considerate of you. Tell me, what's your name?'

'Una, sir.'

'Now then Una, tell your master there's three silver coins waiting for you in my room tonight and an extra bronze one when you send two of the kitchen girls to each of my assistants – but they'll only pay the girls four bronze pieces each.'

Una cleared the empty plates away, stopped by Taran's table and bent to whisper to him as casually as she could. 'He's offered me three silver pieces to sleep with him. Do you think I should, I mean –'

'Absolutely not, my dear,' replied Taran, keeping his eyes firmly fixed on the die in front of the players round the rickety table. 'You know what to do. With your training you're worth at least four pieces, tell him.'

'Are you happy about me going with him?' she persisted.

'Of course. It'll be easier to keep a watch on him and your snoring won't keep me awake. Good luck!'


On hearing a light tap, Galerius opened the door. Being one of the larger rooms it had a table and chairs. Beyond the table, in a recess overlooked by a shuttered window, was a large bed, draped with rugs and lit by two flickering oil lamps.

'Come in, Una,' he said. She'd taken care with her preparations he noted. Her long hair was neatly combed and tied up. There was even a hint of paint on her lips. He held his hands out to her and drew her into his room, taking in a refreshing scent.

'Lavender?' he asked.

'Yes, sir,' replied Una, keeping her eyes away from his. 'I make my own lotion and like to wash my hair with a little – as well as sprinkle it on the rest of me.'

'The scent suits you.' Una pushed him towards a chair. Slightly surprised but not wanting to resist, he sat down.

'I want you to be sure you're spending your money well,' she said, facing him and slowly loosening the belt that held a woollen tunic tight to her small waist. She cast the belt to one side and pulled at the fabric fastenings at her shoulder. First one shoulder appeared then the other. She held the garment to her body and turned to his right, bowing her head as though shy. He wanted to tear the tunic away, like a child desperate to remove a cloth concealing the secrets of an unknown present. She was teasing him with anticipation of as yet unseen rewards. At last the tunic fell to the floor and delicately she stepped out of its ring. Naked before him she drew up her right knee, preserving some mystery for a while longer. She threw her head back and arched her spine. Galerius took in the rounded figure of a girl, just matured into a sensuous woman. Long slim legs gave way to the curves of her smooth thighs. The small waist and flat, firm stomach finished in the shadow of her large, firm breasts. Una unfastened the thong holding her hair in place. Keeping her pose, she shook out her hair and ran her fingers through it.

'You like what you see?' she asked, her eyes fixed on some indistinct part of the ceiling.

Galerius was aware that for him and his men having

women could be seen as an extravagance. But they were soldiers about to go into battle. They needed a distraction, a treat, and the woman in front of him was certainly worth his money. He knew it would be a long night but his interest had been raised and he was ready for the challenge. Without a word he answered the young woman by walking to her, put his left arm round her tiny waist, his right arm between her legs and lifted her onto his bed, anxious to delve into her promised mystery.

# Chapter XXXI

'So Mannius has teamed up with Coel's bunch of louts?' asked the senator.

'I'm sorry, sir,' gasped Prefect Leonius, nerves rendering him breathless. 'I tried my best but the centurion was too cowardly to carry out my orders. I've broken him to the ranks.'

'It's probably just as well he didn't intervene,' said Antonius, strolling over to an open window that gave a view across the inner courtyard of the governor's house. 'Otherwise you'd all be dead now. There's no real harm done. Just means that King Aelred will have to wipe them all out when he arrives if he wants to take over this place.'

'Sir, it's worse,' went on Leonius, taking a gulp of wine to fortify himself sufficiently to pass on more bad news. 'Some of the retired veterans are joining Mannius' army. It's even rumoured he's paying them.'

'A few old men won't help him much.'

'Sir, it's said that there are hundreds.'

'Well Flavius'll just have to keep an eye on things, won't you?' said Antonius, turning to the young man who was reclined on a sofa, enjoying the old prefect's discomfort. 'If it looks like they're getting too strong we'll have to take care of them.'

'Have them assassinated, sir?' asked Flavius, his earlier smugness quickly vanishing.

'Best for everyone really,' replied Antonius, sounding almost bored with the conversation.

'Get them to make it look like they killed each other,'

added Flavius anxiously – seemingly desperate to add something of value to the planning. 'They could have had a fall-out over that princess that's with them. Everyone'll believe something like that and by the time they think of anything different the idea will be of no use to them.'

'You have a vivid imagination that does you credit, Flavius. But for the time being keep it to yourself. I have agents in place to take care of the situation should the need arise.'

An attractive household slave entered the room carrying a tray with a jug and three silver goblets. All three men watched the girl in silence as she poured out wine before retreating. 'What will you do with the slaves?'

'You can have her if the fancy takes you, Flavius,' said Antonius.

'I, er,' started the younger man, slightly embarrassed that he was so transparent, 'I was wondering about all of them.'

'An admirable appetite you have,' teased Antonius.

'But will you take them with you, back to Rome?'

'The good ones yes, the others will be sold.' The senator sighed. 'Though with an invasion in progress prices will be depressed. I suspect the only buyers will be the galleys and the whorehouses. So, like I said, if you want one, take one.'

'Thank you, sir.'

'Before you get busy on that front though,' said the senator, spinning to face Flavius with an edge to his voice that hadn't been present a moment before, 'I suggest you visit the Gauls we brought with us and take them to visit the village of the Brigantes who took part in the murder of the former governor.'

'Yes, sir,' replied Flavius, a hint of uncertainty in his voice. 'Do we know which village they were from?'

'Really, Flavius!' exploded the senator, 'it doesn't matter

which village, does it? Just make it public, gruesome, and bring back some prisoners who'll give us confessions to confirm the legitimacy of our actions – Romans against Brigantes. Now can you fill in the details yourself or shall I draw you a picture?'


In a large tent, outside the fortified town of Derventio, Mannius and his senior commanders entertained local representatives of the Parisi – a people who had settled in the area long before Romans came to the province. Over a makeshift meal and with several goblets of wine inside them, they solemnly assured him of their support: men of the village would stand on the walls alongside his soldiers, the women would help treat the wounded in hospitals and throughout the area they would support the Romans and their allies.

Annoyingly his aunt had invited herself to the proceedings. She knew most of the Parisi elders and they her – at least by sight. Holding Mannius' arm she took it upon herself to make introductions before making sure she was seated at his side. The only plus point for Mannius was watching Princess Caoimhe glare at his aunt every time she laughed at a witty comment and squeezed his arm. Then, while he was thinking about the princess, his aunt took the evening over. On her signal several torches were extinguished, music started and a troupe of half-naked dancing girls skipped in to the tent. They stretched lithely across tables, gyrated exposed thighs that glistened in torchlight and mesmerised the men in the audience with their uncovered breasts. The obvious pleasure of Mannius' guests was heightened when five bare-chested male slaves entered, their muscular torsos greased. Each took hold of a dancer and thrust themselves suggestively at their partner while other girls draped themselves around the men.

Mannius had a war to fight and such distractions would only prolong the visit of the Parisi. For a moment he wondered whether, if the party degenerated into an orgy, it might give him an excuse to get closer to Caoimhe. He looked over to her and saw her hiding behind a raised goblet, eyes on him. She eased the goblet lower and he saw a smile. His face flushed. A commotion near the entrance broke the trance and took his gaze to guards who had appeared. It was a welcome opportunity to take back control of the evening. Dismissed, the dancers bowed and gracefully strode to a side entrance where they waited, looking to his aunt for a signal to leave – none came. Mannius rose and spoke quietly with a guard, then nodded to a centurion standing in the entrance, before turning to the diners.

'I am sorry to have to leave the evening's entertainment, I and my commanders have urgent business along the coast. Gentlemen, if you would.' No further explanation was necessary. Outside the general alarm rang out: weapons clanged and boots pounded as officers and men ran to their posts. Mannius went to Caoimhe and bent to impart the news in a whisper. She nodded her understanding and out of sight of the drunken diners, gently squeezed his hand.

'Princess Caoimhe has kindly agreed to supervise the conclusion to the evening's entertainment,' announced Mannius. Slaves appeared with small, golden goblets and honeyed pastries. It was a signal for everyone to leave. Eithne arrived with three slaves, who carried the tribune's armour and weapons. As he left the tent he saw three of the local elders each take a dancer in the same manner that other guests took the proffered desserts. His aunt encouraged them. Was she being socially proactive, beguiling them with Roman hospitality? Another thought began to surface but he was too occupied with dispatching troops to think further.

# Chapter XXXII

Before dawn's light came through the open window, Una heard slaves starting fires in the kitchen below. Gently she lifted Galerius' powerful arm from around her waist and quietly stepped onto a thin rug. Silently she pulled on her tunic and tidied the preacher's clothes, carefully laying them out on a table for him. When she was satisfied with her efforts she collected the silver pieces he'd left out for her and went back to the large bed. Despite his size and strength he'd been considerate and not hurt her. She kissed him lightly on his forehead and watched him stir a little before she left to find Taran.

Creeping in to their room she heard Taran move in the cot. 'It's me,' she hissed at him. 'Time to get going.'

'Not yet, darling,' came a woman's voice, stifling a yawn.

'Taran?' quizzed Una, checking she was in the right room. In the grey light of the new day she could see him grinning at her.

'Be a treasure, Una, and make sure the slaves are behaving themselves. Don't want breakfast burnt now, do we?' said the woman's voice.

'The preachers are leaving,' persisted Una. 'I thought you wanted to ride with them a while.'

'Don't worry, darling,' answered the woman. 'They always ride south then east. The stable slaves see them off every day. You'll catch them up if you want to. Your master's got another bit of riding to do first!'

'But Taran that's –'

'The innkeeper's wife,' answered the woman. 'Don't fret

209

so. My husband's more interested in young boys these days. Doesn't appreciate what a real woman's got to offer. Now, druid man, let's be having some more of your magic.'

Una quickly gathered her few possessions and left. As she closed the door she wondered how both of them managed to get into the small cot. Another druid trick that Taran had yet to show her, she presumed.

Una dutifully went to the kitchen and looked in, but everything seemed well in hand so she took her bags out to the stables. Slaves were leading horses across a small, cobbled courtyard and making them ready for guests with too much money to be bothered to tend to the animals themselves. Taran didn't pay for their horses to be groomed so it was another chore for her as the apprentice druid. At least the beasts were kinder to her than the men in the bar.

From an upper storey window Taran had watched Galerius and his two assistants head south, driving three heavy, single-axle carts with their regular horses tethered behind. Unusually, the carts were pulled by heavy horses instead of oxen, suggesting that Galerius was aiming for speed rather than power. Just before they were lost over the horizon, the group turned east and into an area of thick forest.

In the warming summer morning the trail was easy to follow. With such heavy carts the men had to keep on established roads and tracks, the recent rains having left heavy mud in the fields, preventing any deviations. Even on good routes, the wooden cartwheels cut new shadowed, furrows. On several downhill sections with sharp corners, skid marks were clearly visible, indicating that the men were in a hurry to get through the thinning forests and open meadows towards flatter lands that led to the coast.

Careful not to ride too fast and risk catching up with

the carts, the two trackers moved unhurriedly and in silence. Whenever possible they rode parallel to the track, always looking ahead to see if the men had stopped. Unexpectedly, as Taran and Una emerged from a small beech wood into a meadow, they could see the track off to their right, snaking down through fields of oat shoots to a small hamlet. A gentle, easterly breeze brought the harsh smell of burnt wood.

Slowly and carefully, Taran signalled Una to follow him. He pulled his horse towards the edge of the meadow and circled around the hamlet, splashing through a stream that fed water to the buildings. On the other side, under cover of a large bramble bush, rich with green fruit, they looked down into the hamlet. Walls stood with no roofs and all the animal pens were empty. Not even a chicken pecked its way round the buildings.

'Saxons?' asked Una.

'Soldiers, but not Saxons,' Taran whispered. 'Work of the tribune's men. Clearing everyone and everything so that nothing's left for the Saxons. He's right to make sure they don't have a chance of getting food or having shelter.'

'Seems hard on the folks that lived there.'

'Aye, but it'd be harder still if the invaders took over their land.'

They waited to make sure that Galerius' men weren't concealed in one of the buildings. Then Taran moved close enough to see that fresh, deep tracks indicated that carts had recently crossed a wide ford close to the hamlet and taken a track alongside the slow, wide stream. Instead of following, Taran and Una rode their horses up a steeper track, away from the buildings. Near a grassy knoll they dismounted and slowly walked around the summit, making sure that their outlines were not easily visible to anyone below. From their vantage point they could see across acres of purple heather, all the way to the reeds and numerous watery inlets that indicated marshland. They were close to an uncertain boundary between the Tesa Flavia and the rough meadows around it. Taran knew that the men would struggle to take the carts much further into the marshes and strained to hear telltale sounds of animals and carts.

The pursuers walked their horses parallel to the main track. From the shadows of leafy birch, sycamore and the occasional oak tree they would examine the way through the next meadow, wait, and only when they were certain no one was watching, make their way slowly across open spaces. Two miles beyond the smouldering hamlet their options started to narrow. Slow-moving streams and deep, brown pools barred progress, forcing them onto the only available route. The dirt track wound its way along firm embankments and causeways, occasionally fording widening streams.

Across a wide, muddy river an old wooden bridge led to a small island and another bridge. Taran dismounted and slowly led his horse across. At the other side of the bridge he heard a horse snort and waited for Una to catch up with him so that she could hold his horse's reins. Knee-high in foul-smelling mud and hidden by high reeds he circled towards the noise.

Una unslung a bow and slotted an arrow onto the sinew. She judged the distance to the far side of the second bridge at around fifty paces – close to her maximum killing range. At least if Taran ran into trouble she would be able to give him a little support.

Approaching the building, Taran could see that the main track petered out at a rough, wooden barn. Thick poles driven into the mud indicated mooring points for small fishing boats, though he noted that none were visible – presumably hidden by villagers or sunk by Mannius' soldiers if they'd got this far.

Taran kept himself hidden in the reeds and circled to a small path that led further east, deeper into the marshes along the estuary. Clearly visible were the tracks of three horses, disappearing into the mud and sand of the path. Dragging himself out of deep sludge he whistled and Una led the horses across.

Inside the barn were three carts. The heavy horses that had pulled them chewed on fresh straw, hardly noticing the entrance of Taran and Una. Slowly their eyes adjusted to the dimness and they could see sacks on two of the carts.

Una climbed onto a cart and looked into the sacks. 'Salted beef,' she whispered as she opened the first sack. 'Apples, bread loaves and again.' She moved down the neat piles cataloguing the contents for benefit of Taran. At the end of the row of sacks were several skins. Carefully she opened two and tested them. 'Water!' she announced. 'They've got enough here for an army and they didn't even mention it when I went to the trouble of making cook fix them pies and meat to stop them getting hungry!'

Taran climbed onto the other cart that held packages covered with a large, heavy oiled cloth. He whistled softly as he uncovered them. 'You were right about the army. Look at this.'

Una skipped across the carts to where Taran stared. 'Aren't those Roman uniforms?' she asked.

'Roman uniforms and armour,' replied Taran. 'And the peculiar thing is I don't recognise them. Whoever this lot's for it's not just ordinary legionaries I'd say. At least one of them looks important.'

'A picnic for important Roman soldiers in the middle of marshland. I don't understand. What's going on?' asked Una.

Taran let the cloth fall back into place. In silence he examined each cart and noted that they were all in excellent condition. Outside he sat down and looked along the path that the horsemen had taken.

'The tribune's men cleared the coastland and now soldiers come into it,' said Una, taking pieces of cold chicken out of a leather saddlebag and handing a leg to Taran. 'I don't understand. Is there a trick that someone's pulling on us all?'

The old druid remained silent, deep in thought for several minutes. Reeds rustled in the breeze. A noisy gull wheeled overhead and seemed to bring Taran out of his trance. 'Someone's expecting to collect something along here and move it out on those wagons, escorted by Roman soldiers. The supplies could be for a lot of people.'

'Or they could be for a few people for a long time,' suggested Una.

'No, I doubt that,' said Taran. 'They've brought bread that'll go stale and mouldy in a few days at most. Why the soldiers have come here I can't say.' The old druid waved a drumstick at the path ahead. 'Any ideas?'

'Could they be like, just trying to pretend to be Romans?'

'I doubt that. If they wanted to impersonate Romans they'd be best to get uniforms of units nearby – and they're easy enough to get hold of.'

'Maybe the uniforms aren't genuine,' suggested Una.

'Are you now contemplating that Galerius is attempting to emerge out of the marshes with three cartloads of men pretending to be Roman legionaries to cause mayhem? If that was the case he wouldn't have brought three carts. Any infantry would march.'

'I suppose he is a real soldier,' conceded Una sulkily. 'More likely than him being a preacher. He's too tough and he's got army tattoos.'

Taran fell silent again. He felt confused and more than a little unsettled. Unless he'd witnessed the evidence himself he would not have believed any report of high-ranking Roman officers undertaking a secret mission along the coast. Everything seemed so out of place. The uniforms were not in use locally so that meant the prefects probably weren't aware of the men. Someone else – very high ranking – had given them orders and when he realised that, his spirits fell. And how, he wondered, did such a mission call for causing trouble along the coast? Maybe Una was right, Galerius was going to bring men out of the marshes to wreak havoc.

The day had worn on through the afternoon without either of them noticing the lateness of the hour. Shadows lengthened as the sun began to sink below the low hills to the west. Like the passing of day into dusk, Taran saw Una's pale expression and knew her mind was being drawn to darkness. Lying against one of the building's supporting poles, he chewed away the last meat from a chicken leg then turned to her. 'Why do you fret so?'

'I'm wondering what's down that path yonder and why we're here by ourselves.'

'Those questions I am able to answer readily enough,' replied Taran, energy and enthusiasm creeping back into his words. 'Galerius and his mission are down that path and we are by ourselves because it is easier to conceal two people than two hundred.'

'But if we're found, no one will be any the wiser.'

'Please,' said Taran, getting to his feet. 'I have sent a report – in code – to the tribune as to where we are and what's happening. When we get back I hope to fill in a few more details.'

'Where are we going now?' asked Una.

'I find myself in the unusual and uncomfortable position of not knowing something that I feel I should. So the only way I am going to resolve the situation is by finding out. Are you coming or are you going to witter on about endless possibilities that may or may not be true?'

215

# Chapter XXXIII

A night and a morning's ride with their mounted troops brought Mannius and Coel to a series of low, rolling hills, eight miles inland from Abus Fluvia, a wide estuary that was the main route for ships navigating from the Oceanus Germanicus to Eburacum. From a high point they could see miles across thickly forested land. Looking south, towards the wide, silt-brown estuary in the far distance, a green, leafy canopy thinned and gave out to wetlands: a thick barrier of marshes scored with streams and dark pools feeding slow-moving rivers that lazily meandered towards tidal flows beyond. In the middle distance smoke curled into the sky.

'The smoke's coming from the Saxon village.' One of the Parisi elders, a veteran of fighting alongside the legions judging from his bent nose and scarred face, had ridden with them to supply knowledge of the area. 'Our village is three miles closer in the next valley.'

Mannius followed the man's outstretched arm and looked again. But no smoke came from the Parisi village. They had passed most of its inhabitants in the last three hours of riding. Like other refugees near the Wall, their faces had a vacant look of shock and confusion. Quietly, they were trudging west in search of safety. What safety could he offer them other than a desperate fight with a vastly numerically superior invader? But something didn't feel right.

'Who's attacked the Saxon village?' asked Coel, voicing Mannius' own thoughts.

'Not the Parisi,' answered the elder, shocked that his peace-loving people might be implicated.

Both men ignored him and stared ahead. Through a break in a copse of old beech trees two scouts were riding towards them at speed, urging their mounts to even greater efforts. 'Begging pardon, sir,' said the older and more senior of the two as they reined in, 'Saxons in the village, sir, about three hundred, give or take.'

'Thank you, trooper,' said Mannius, calculating the odds. There were two hundred of Coel's men, three centuries of mounted Roman infantry, twenty scouts and sixty Votadini archers: over five hundred and with surprise an easy fight.

'Sir?' the trooper had not finished.

'Yes, trooper?'

'More Saxons in the tree line yonder, at least a hundred, sir.'

Panic rose inside Mannius. His mouth was dry. They must be good or he'd have spotted them himself at this range. Suddenly the odds were less certain and maybe surprise was with the Saxons. An all too familiar sense of guilt gripped him: the men had trusted him, followed him here, were ready to fight on his command and he'd been outwitted. Carefully controlling his voice he called his officers to him and laid out the order for battle: Romans on the right, Coel's men on the left, archers behind the centre and scouts in two groups to patrol the flanks.

Quickly the men moved into position, horses were taken to the rear and men made ready to advance. Mannius joined his men, keeping his gaze on the far side of the meadow. Bushes moved and two riders trotted out. Orders were relayed up and down the lines to make ready. Men on the front ranks hoisted shields in front of their faces, others further back held javelins and archers slotted arrows

217

into their bows. Everyone waited. Adrenaline-fuelled perspiration beaded on foreheads and hearts pounded. Officers looked around, expecting an ambush. The riders came closer and finally Mannius gave the order, 'Hold fast!' He'd recognised the man.

'A parade?' asked the Saxon prince mockingly as he approached Mannius.

'In your honour,' replied Mannius.

'Then I accept,' said Leofric, jumping down to join Mannius.

'The smoke?' asked Mannius, nodding in the direction of the Saxon village.

'I'm sad to say that it seems you were right to suggest that we join you,' said Leofric, a little crestfallen. 'From the accounts that I've heard, it seems that yesterday seven boatloads of Saxons escorted a dozen of their supply ships into the estuary and up the river to the village over the ridge. At first everyone got along but it didn't last. An argument erupted that escalated into a pitched battle. The villagers were outnumbered and ran. Many were cut down but a few survived and sent word to me of the outrage.'

'What started it?'

'What?'

'The argument,' prompted Mannius.

'Religion, slaves, women, the colour of the night sky. It doesn't really matter. Fuelled by drink, differences between the two groups no doubt surfaced. But they showed no restraint: men, women and children cut down. They only wanted to wipe my people out.' Tears welled in the great man's eyes. 'We were about to launch a counter-attack when we spotted you. With your support it'd be easier.'

'Of course. For what it's worth, I'm sorry we weren't in time to save the village.'

'No matter, we've time enough to stop the disease

spreading. Is this the start of the invasion, do you think?' asked Leofric earnestly.

'No,' replied Mannius. 'I already have word of where the main fleet landed a few days ago, in Dunum Sinus. This is an attempt to create a supply base and test the will of your Saxons to join them.'

'The only place my people will join that scum is in the next world and even then we'll still fight them.'

Dismounted, the combined units moved together to surround the village. Archers went ahead, close to smouldering remains of houses. With arrows and knives they silently killed pickets stationed to give early warning of an attack. Mannius waited until the attackers were close to their quarry – near enough to see lines on defenders' faces tighten into tortured grimaces of horror. Only then did he signal the trumpeters to sound out the shrill notes of the attack.

Surprise was absolute. Men woke from drunken stupors to be immediately dispatched to a longer sleep. Against a ferocity of vengeance unleashed by Leofric's men the defenders never stood a chance. Uncoordinated and separated they quickly became mere target practice. Cowed by the visible tide of hate coming at them, men tried in vain to surrender. The attackers looked at dead villagers strewn across the streets, bodies nailed to doors, children with crimson stains on their tunics, men hung upside down with throats gouged, women naked and covered in blood – and gave no quarter. Mercy and the chance for slaves were forgotten.

Mannius had positioned himself in the centre of the front rank. His men were more disciplined than Leofric's but no less effective in their attack. Spread out in two ranks, supported by a third, they moved swiftly and menacingly through the village. On the flanks, men with slings hurled lethal pieces of shaped lead and stones that whistled through the air to break bones and open heads. In the centre, shields blocked blows, cracked jaws and pinned victims ready for a killing thrust from a legionary's sword.

Mechanically and unquestioningly the men bore down on their victims. Where a man fell injured, his place was quickly taken by another from the next rank. Occasional javelins flew overhead unerringly skewering the rough-clad invaders.

The trap was completed by Coel's men. They waited for the attacks to get underway before they broke cover. Any men trying to flee the panic and slaughter were cut down. Some invaders ran for their boats. Coel's men were on them quickly, hacking and stabbing, but sheer weight of numbers meant many got through. Beached at a previous high tide and unable to set sail, groups of men barricaded themselves on the ships. Rather than waste time and risk casualties, Coel ordered the ships torched. Soon men screamed in agony or ran out trying to fight, but arrows and spears took them.

In the village, Mannius' men had run out of targets. Saxon bodies littered the route they had traversed but as suddenly as the killing had started so did it end. Mannius, sword bloodied, felt himself breathing hard. They'd had surprise and discipline on their side but it had still been a fight. As adrenaline subsided he waited for telltale signs of pain. Nothing hurt. For the first time he heard screams of other men in desperate pain. The stench of death enveloped him and he moved towards Leofric's men who were handling the final remnants of the invaders.

A woman, holding rags for clothes around her body and hair bedraggled, staggered out of a low doorway, shaking as she moved to her freedom. Mannius stepped forward to help her. Unseeing she kept walking. At one of the fallen Saxons she bent down and drew out his dagger, then she spat onto his upturned, lifeless face. She turned, put both hands onto the dagger's hilt and thrust it into her heart. For a moment she grimaced as iron tore through her flesh. Then her body went limp and Mannius saw a look of contentment wipe away the pain. She was free of a horror that had made her take her own life. To Mannius it gave a measure of the struggle they faced: it was to the death. He knelt, gently lifted her and carried her away from the bodies of her former tormentors.

Mannius turned back to Leofric's men from where whimpers had turned into sobs. A dozen boys, most not even in their teens, hands bound behind their backs, knelt in the mud. It was too much: the executions had to stop.

'Who are they?' asked Mannius, approaching Leofric and waving his sword at three bloodied but unbowed men.

'The swine who led this herd of pigs here.' Leofric's tone sounded bored, almost resigned to the killing that must happen.

'Then we'll take them for questioning.'

Leofric and his men turned to Mannius, their faces contorted by hatred. The wave of loathing was uncomfortably close and now in his direction.

'Take them to the druid,' announced Mannius. 'He'll loosen their tongues.'

Leofric smiled. 'Taran will make them pay.'

A chant of 'Taran' started around the prisoners. The Saxon leaders had anticipated death with stoicism but now it seemed a worse fate awaited them.

'Leofric, I'll not see children murdered – no matter where they're from,' said Mannius, pointing at the group of boys.

'Thank you, general,' said a man in Latin, standing close to the boys.

Mannius marched over to the man. 'For what?'

'I will die easier knowing that the lads have been spared this ordeal.'

'You are father to one of them?'

'No, sir. They're all dead. That one there is my brother's son.'

'Why have you come here?'

'King Aelred promised good farming land for any man that fought with him. My family's too poor to have land so I have to fight for it.'

'You will go with the boys to look after them.'

The man looked more shocked than if Mannius had drawn his dagger. He bowed and ran to join the boys.

'What of the rest?' asked Leofric, nodding towards another thirty or so dispirited-looking men.

'Get them to clean this mess up. If they do a good job then we might keep them as slaves. Otherwise, they'll have to dig their own graves.'

Casualties from the assault were remarkably and mercifully light: twelve dead and twenty wounded, though six would be lucky to survive. Mannius realised the assault demonstrated that the allies could work together effectively and lethally. But almost as important was the knowledge that with surprise and resolve they might yet overcome their larger foe.

Carts were loaded with wounded and filled with supplies from the seemingly pitifully provisioned transport ships; then flame was put to the remaining vessels.

# *Chapter XXXIV*

Along the sandy, well-defined path, widely spaced hoof-prints suggested that the men had travelled quickly, so the two pursuers allowed their horses to move at a brisk walk. Taran felt in better spirits now that they were once again on the chase. Even Una's apprehensiveness seemed to have disappeared. Always good to be doing something instead of brooding, he thought.

Behind them the setting sun occasionally found a gap in gathering clouds. Taran looked around and decided that the light would be good enough to continue tracking for another hour or two. Any longer and they'd risk bumping into their quarry. He guessed they'd covered over four miles from the barn with the carts and thought the men wouldn't go much farther. Just when he thought that they must soon be in the sea, the land rose slightly, becoming firmer, and the path ended. The men and their horses had clearly continued straight ahead but Taran had a sense that they were near to the destination. Without a word, they dismounted and strained their ears, listening for clues.

Beyond the rustle of grasses and reeds there was a rhythmic wash of waves over stones. Taran led his horse towards the noise and tied the animal's reins round a large rock. Una followed and together they slid down a small embankment onto a shingle beach.

'Are we at the ocean?' asked Una in a hoarse whisper.

'Probably only a bay, just before the estuary meets the sea proper, I think,' replied Taran.

They followed the beach in the direction of the open sea. Ahead of them the beach curved round into another inlet. Brown, foamy water drained out over the mud as the tide ebbed. At the other side the ground looked firm. A few low birch trees and sea buckthorn bushes clung to the grass. Suddenly Taran dropped into a squat and rolled into the embankment, quickly followed by Una.

'Did you see them?' asked Taran, heart pounding. 'The masts?'

'At least ten,' replied Una, a trace of panic in her voice. 'Saxons?'

'Definitely not the right sort of masts for coastal patrol ships. And no one else has that many ships.' Taran checked around, looking for sentries. When he was satisfied he started to move quietly away. 'They'll have men out guarding the approaches. We need to be careful.'

'Where are we going?' hissed Una.

'Back to the horses. I'm starving.'

On a shingle beach, further up the inlet, Taran strained his eyes in the fading light. Nothing stirred on the opposite bank. Finally, when he was satisfied, he stripped off his tunic. Carrying a wickedly sharp dagger in one hand and his sandals in the other he delicately stepped over sharp pebbles to the water's edge. Looking to his right he stopped and saw Una, already naked. Even in the gloom her white skin glistened and the curves of her blossoming body were silhouetted against the dark water. Taran told himself that it was time he paid her another visit – soon.

They made their way across the flooded inlet, through a surprisingly strong and cold current, to emerge in the mud on other side. Both of them kept low, rubbed mud over their skin and listened.

Without discussion, Taran led them up a grassy

embankment. At the top he took his time before moving again. Carefully they tied the leather thongs of their sandals and moved silently inland. Gorse and thorns scratched their bodies but adrenaline kept their minds away from pain. Cresting a small, grassy knoll they heard murmurs and laughter. Crawling closer they peered towards fires lit in front of at least forty ships.

Small fires, away from the main source of noise, marked the position of sentries. Taran lay in a hollow, letting his eyes adjust and taking time to establish a route closer to the centre of activity. Experienced as he was, sweat poured down his face and his heart pounded so much he thought the Saxon sentries must hear it. Una was shaking. She lay half on top of him. Her warmth and the firmness of her body next to his was a pleasant sensation and made him linger a little longer in the hollow.

Heavy footsteps came towards them. Taran gripped his dagger, ready to strike. He felt Una's limbs tense next to his. Then the sentry stopped. A light pitter-patter of a small waterfall on gorse leaves came over the night air. The man grunted in satisfaction and moved off to his position, out of Taran's sight to his right – the way he'd thought of moving. Una's presence had saved him. She felt even warmer against him. Maybe he should reward her by taking her in this hollow. He put the thought quickly out of his head and slithered to his left, through a small gap in the barbs and under prickly gorse. Una followed.

The earlier breeze had stiffened into a wind and flames from fires bent into the night. In front of a small village of roughly constructed tents, Taran could see chairs set between two large fires. Galerius sat in one with his assistants either side of him. They faced a large Saxon flanked by four enormous guards. Each carried a heavy, double-bladed axe.

The wind carried the conversation away from Taran and though he dearly wanted to hear he knew that they could get no closer. With Romans in the camp all sentries would be alert.

Both men waved their arms and a heated discussion seemed to be taking place. Four saddlebags were tossed onto the ground in front of Galerius and his assistants retrieved them. Una pointed urgently away to their left. Taran saw a line of children, hands bound in front of them and each tied, like slaves, to one long rope fastened around their necks. Some of them looked to be in their teens but others seemed smaller. Encouraged by Saxon guards the children were led towards Galerius. The large Saxon man rose from his chair, palms held up to Galerius, and stormed away to a tent. The meeting seemed to be over.

With the first spits of rain hitting the gorse above them, Taran decided he'd seen enough and that it was time to leave. He tapped Una's legs and pointed away from the Saxon camp. They followed their earlier route and were shocked to find an incoming tide had turned the inlet into a cold, dark sea of gurgling currents.

'The current's too strong,' whispered Taran. 'If we try to swim we'll end up near the crossing Galerius and his men used.'

'Shall we wait?' asked Una.

'We can't afford to, I'm sorry my dear,' Taran said apologetically. 'Best we check the crossing.'

Keeping to the water's edge they moved towards the ford, hoping that it was unguarded. Taran knew in his heart that the Saxons would have secured such a strategic point. Still, they had to see if they could escape the island before morning when they'd be found for certain.

Another small fire illuminated three guards close to the bank and, unfortunately, lit the inlet as well. None of the Saxons looked interested in sentry duty. Each man lounged against small boulders, staring into the fire. Taran knew that if he led Una into the water they'd be seen. Taran whispered to Una, who looked at him wide-eyed then nodded her agreement. He hoped the young woman could keep her head and follow his instructions. Silently he whispered a prayer, hoping that his god might still be awake at this late hour, then moved in a loop around the sentries.

The old druid was now close to two of the sentries, dagger in hand. A gust of wind fanned the flames and he saw the man farthest from the inlet sit up in surprise. He stared hard into the darkness and pointed, urging his companions to look. The other men laughed but the one closest to Taran got up and followed the first to the edge of the bank.

Taran knew he had to move quickly. He slipped his hand over the guard's mouth and reached round his chest, thrusting his dagger into soft flesh. Twisting his knife in the sentry's throat, he felt the man's panic as he tried to fight. Unhurriedly, Taran whispered a druid death curse and cut across the windpipe.

The other men had left the firelight but now Taran could hear them shouting and whooping. Without thinking, he picked up an axe and ran towards Una.


Una lay as flat as she could, then when she was sure she'd given Taran enough time to get into position she quietly stepped into the edge of firelight, just long enough for a sentry at the other side of the fire to see her. She swept her hair back, pushed her breasts towards him, then looked as though she'd been startled and skipped off along the bank. Terrified she crouched behind a low gorse bush. For the first time that night she noticed its powerful scent.

She heard noises and knew that the men would be on their way. They looked tough – could she cope? Would Taran get to them or would they be killed? She'd not considered that. If he was dead she would die, but only after a protracted and brutal gang rape. She'd have to kill herself. She waited, shaking with fear and cold. A huge monster of a man stood silhouetted by the fire. He peered into the darkness, no doubt trying to accustom his eyes to the blackness of night.

Una waited and waited, trying to time her next move. She took a deep breath, thought of the scent of the gorse and rose up close to the man. He whooped, then grunted like an animal as he jumped straight towards her. She froze, letting him come close, letting him share the gorse scent. He dropped an axe and reached out with huge hands, taking her breasts like trophies. She smelt foul ale on his breath. Faster than the man could blink she brought her right arm from behind her back and pushed her dagger into his chest. The man groaned. She twisted the blade, pulled it out and plunged it in again. This time the man collapsed onto her, pushing her backwards. She fell heavily, losing her dagger, and was trapped.

For the first time Una saw a second man close behind. She pushed at the man lying on top of her but the brute was too heavy for her to lift. His blood oozed over her and she felt sick. She wanted to vomit. Wriggling her legs she tried to escape and gasped as air was slowly squeezed out of her lungs. The second man stood over her and laughed, giving encouragement to his friend. She realised that he hadn't seen he was dead. In the dark he couldn't see his friend's blood spilling onto her and the coarse grass. He was waiting his turn.

Una heard footsteps crunching quickly through small pebbles behind the second man. She saw him turn, raise his battle-axe. Then the man fell away with an axe lodged in his chest and Taran was beside her, gasping. Together they rolled Una's attacker away. She knelt on the pebbles, desperately sucking in air. Both of them knew that other men could have heard the struggle so they had to make their escape quickly. Taran took her hand and dragged her to the fire where he let her sit while he worked the corpse. He searched the man, taking coins out of his tunic and spreading some of them around the fire. Next he poured out the contents of two wine skins, then put the dagger of the man Una had killed into the man's chest.

'Just trying to make the issue confused,' said Taran, his voice coming in gasps. 'They'll think they fell out and fought each other – with a slice of luck.'

Tired and exhausted, Taran and Una walked to the water's edge. Footsteps pounded on the bank behind them then the man that Taran had downed with an axe screamed at them. He slashed at Taran and caught him in the side. The effort had been too much for the man: he slumped to his knees. Una grabbed the shaft of the man's axe and Taran, his energy draining quickly, pushed his dagger deep into the man's neck. The man fell forwards and Una helped Taran through the dark water of the inlet in silence.

Around them the dark sea water exploded with thousands of raindrops. Cold water round their bodies, rain on their faces and a chilling wind took their last reserves of energy. When they got back to their tunics Una, shaking violently, could contain herself no longer and vomited. Both struggled to dress themselves, then Una noticed Taran was bleeding. She touched his side and saw him wince.

'It seems I was a little careless,' said Taran. 'That sentry nearly managed to skewer me on the point of his bloody axe.'

'Hold still,' said Una as she tore off a strip of cloth from her tunic.

229

'Ah, good girl. That's right, bind it tight. We don't want to leave a trail of blood.'

Sodden and exhausted they retrieved their horses, ate some food and rode as fast as possible through the increasingly wet night.

Waiting until first light, which coincided with low tide, Galerius led his group across the inlet and to the main path at the other side. Two young children bobbed up and down in silence on the back of his horse. A child with a broken leg was on another horse and at the rear of the column was a teenager with a light fever.

At the barn the children, exhausted and most still disorientated from their experience, fell onto the carts. Galerius' men shook them awake and forced them to eat a little and drink some water before they were allowed to curl up under thick blankets.

Outside the barn, Galerius pulled on his uniform and strapped his armour in place.

'Feels good to be back in uniform, eh?' he said to the two men with him, breaking the long silence that had settled on the whole group.

'Yes, sir,' snapped the centurion.

'When we move, let some of the older boys drive two of the carts, the track is easy enough. Titus, you lead on horseback, Primus you take the first cart to show them where to drive and I'll follow at the rear.'

'What did you make of the Saxons, sir?'

'I'd rather dig latrines than do business with them. Listen you men, you need to know these things in case we don't all get to Eburacum. The saddlebags are only a quarter of the gold promised by King Aelred, but worst of all he only handed over fifteen children.' He tested his sword to make sure it hadn't rusted in its scabbard.

'That means he's got another twenty-five somewhere else. They may be on other ships yet to arrive but I don't trust him. We'll get these kids out of here and come back for the rest. I told him we'd see him again soon.' Galerius bit into a loaf of bread one of his men offered him.

'Sir, what did you make of those sentries fighting each other?' asked Primus.

'They'd definitely drunk too much, could smell it a mile off,' said Titus.

'I'm not sure, Primus. They could have fallen out over some gambling game or – '

'Surely it couldn't have been a set-up, sir,' objected Primus.

'Maybe, but not by Saxons,' said Galerius. 'Yesterday I thought someone was tracking us when we got into the marshes. Someone good mind – I never saw anyone.'

'Why didn't you let us ambush them, sir?' asked Titus, always spoiling for a fight.

'Because I guessed they were most likely Saxons on patrol and it wouldn't have helped us if we'd got into a scrape with them. Now I'm not so sure.'

'Sir?' asked Primus, looking confused.

'The rain in the night obscured most of the tracks on the path back to the barn but I'm sure there were more horses' hoof-prints than we left.'

'Saxons, sir?' suggested Titus.

'Maybe, Titus, though I don't think the Saxons have yet got sufficient numbers to patrol far. Keep your eyes open at the front, lads, now let's get moving.'

# Chapter XXXV

From the top of a large, grassy mound King Aelred had a splendid panorama over gorse bushes, marsh reeds and across the bay that provided his fleet with a large, natural harbour. Sitting on a polished wooden chair with two of his senior officers he chewed noisily on a mouthful of salted pork and waved a dagger at the increasing number of ships.

'Admiral, tell me, where are the food transports? Have you hidden them in the reeds with the rest of our ships?'

'My lord, they are the heaviest and slowest of our vessels. My captains report that they should be no more than two days behind the rest of the fleet.'

'Two more miserable days of this salted, beetle-infested muck to endure before we can have something fresh to get our teeth into. Any good news from your scouting parties, Horsa?'

'Nothing, my lord,' said a massive, one-eyed veteran. 'Under cover of darkness, my men have gone nearly to the paved road. Only in the last mile or so did they encounter any Romans and withdrew without being spotted as ordered.'

'What of food in the villages?'

'My lord, both on that route and to the north the villages have been destroyed. Not a roof has been left on a building and all animals have been taken inland. In fact, I haven't even seen so much as a boar or even deer tracks.'

'Maybe you should get someone else to look in your stead. A man with two eyes – eh, Horsa?' The king laughed and saw his officers relax. 'With a ditch dug and sentries on all the approaches I'm sure we have a secure base to unload the rest of the fleet. And the advance will be easy, even if we have to move without being able to get supplies from villages. But the thing that troubles me is that someone told the Romans we were on our way. That's what gave them time to clear the villages.'

'My lord, it could mean that Galerius is helping both sides and the Romans are preparing to fight us further inland,' said Horsa.

'Or it may be that they've decided to run home to Rome, my lord,' suggested the admiral.

'What of our sentries at the crossing?' asked Horsa. 'They could have been killed by Roman spies.'

King Aelred laughed. 'Perhaps, but most likely my friend, they were bored – look!' Aelred held out his dagger. On cue below him sand flew as four men threw punches and wrestled each other. 'The men are restless and spoiling for a fight. We need those ships and quickly, Admiral, before we all start fighting each other. I can't start the campaign proper until I have those supplies.'

'Yes, my lord.'

A lookout ran to the admiral and waited until the man bent his head to him. After a brief exchange the admiral turned to the king. 'My lord, it seems that two vessels are approaching from the north.'

'Are they ours?' asked Aelred.

'Too far to tell as yet, my lord. I'll have six of our warships stand by as close to the bay's entrance as they can in case they're hostile.'

'Tell them to row out and see what they're about. If they're ours they can help them in. If they're not they can help them in anyway.'

'My lord, the wind and tide are against sailing any of our ships into the ocean at the moment.'

'Don't give 'em excuses, Admiral. Flog the men then the captains if they don't get out of the bay. A bit of leather at their backs and we'll soon see that Saxons are stronger than your wind and tide.'

'You bloody moron!' exploded Senator Antonius. 'You bungle an attack on a village defended only by women and children. Instead of getting the Brigantes to hate Romans you've given them over a hundred armed men.'

'Sir, it seemed that some of the militia knew the villagers,' protested Flavius.

'Of course they would.'

'How was I to know?' sulked Flavius.

'Did it never occur to your feeble mind that given the proximity of Eburacum to the village some would know each other?'

'Sorry, sir,' said Flavius, keeping his eyes on the mosaic floor tiles at the old man's feet. 'But we killed a dozen or so of them.'

'I presume you're referring to villagers and the militia rather than cows grazing in meadows?'

'Yes, sir.'

'Then I find that not only are you stupid but you can't even follow orders. Now how are we to extract confessions, have a trial to prove the guilt of the Brigantes and demonstrate our power with a series of executions?'

'Sorry, sir.'

'Sorry doesn't come close. This was a golden opportunity. I promised Aelred that we'd stir up trouble. Now we'll have to find another way or he'll use it as an excuse not to pay us our due.'

# Chapter XXXVI

Taran and Una rode as fast as they could to the hamlet. In fresh, cool water by the ford, Una helped Taran strip and bathe. While he was drying in the warm breeze, Una galloped her horse to the edge of a meadow, dismounted and returned quickly. Unbidden she crushed some wild garlic and sprinkled it onto the druid's wound. Next she took several stems of marsh woundwort with its spikes of dark pink leaves, crushed them in her hands and squeezed the juice into the gaping hole that refused to stop bleeding.

'Borgach has trained you well, Una. I thank you for your attention. I'd hoped to reward you with some of my own attention but I feel my strength is deserting me.'

'Lie still for a moment. You need to eat and drink to replace the energy you're losing through the wound before you can give any woman your attention, leastways a druid apprentice.'

Taran laughed and winced at the pain it caused him. 'It's deep, my dear. The wound has warmth,' he pronounced.

'That is a good sign, yes?' asked Una, looking into Taran's eyes, desperation in her voice.

'Ah, Una, you are a good nurse,' responded Taran, his voice starting to grow weak. 'It means, my dear druid apprentice, that it is infected.'

'What can I do to cure it?' she asked. 'It can be cured – can't it?'

'Boil some water so that we can make a poultice to draw out as much of the infection as possible. But I must find one of the Roman surgeons to remove the source of the infection.'

'I'll make a poultice, then take you to the road where we'll find one of the army units. They'll fetch the tribune – he's a good physician.'

'One of the best, I hear. But I'm afraid he's a little busy and I need you to be busy keeping an eye on Galerius.'

'But –'

'But nothing,' said Taran, smiling. 'We must all do our duty and yours is to watch the enemy. I'm sorry I can't help you, my dear.'

'Don't talk so stupid.' Tears welled in the young woman's eyes. 'Shall I get Borgach?'

'I'm not done for yet. I'll find a doctor to seal the wound properly. As for Borgach, she can do no more than the tribune and she's on an errand for me anyway.'

Una sniffed back more tears as she applied a fresh bandage. 'I'll stay here, careful and silent – like you've showed me – to keep watch on them. Then I'll let you and the tribune know where they've gone.'

Una boiled water and added some herbs and grain before binding the mixture into a poultice. 'You are a rare treasure, Una,' said Taran. 'Take care of yourself and don't trust anyone.'

Una helped the old druid onto his horse and watched him ride across the ford. Near to the top of the hill, at the other side of the valley, she saw him slump forward against the neck of his horse and realised he was more badly injured than he'd admitted. She stood crying for a while before she washed away the dirt and salt of the last day, and finally tended to her own grazes.

Titus led the convoy up the track, scanning left and right

for potential threats. Behind him the carts creaked and jolted their way towards the burnt-out hamlet. Despite thick grey clouds overhead and a chill wind the children's mood started to lighten. Maybe it was the sight of familiar Roman uniforms or perhaps just not having their hands tied that helped to bring them out of their stupor. They relaxed and took energy from the food that was regularly passed round. Gradually a quiet chatter started and Galerius thought he heard a giggle and a laugh. He dearly wanted silence to listen for threats but he knew that the children needed to start adjusting to their freedom.

By the time they reached the ford by the hamlet, the clouds had disappeared and sun warmed them all. Primus encouraged the children to use some soap and clean themselves. The shock of cold water wiped away the last reminiscences of their captivity. Soon they were jumping and wading in the clear, gurgling stream. Ahead, Titus sat on his horse guarding the route, continually scanning for threats. Galerius stood by a cart with the two sick children. The fevered boy looked pale and he dabbed his forehead with a damp cloth, but the boy with the broken leg gave him most concern. He seemed to have become delirious. Galerius knew that he needed to get them to a physician as soon as possible so ordered the children back to the carts.

Galerius saw Titus lift his arm as a signal to halt. Thinking that he must have spotted some unusual travellers on the road he trotted his horse past the carts to join him.

'That hill to our right, sir,' said Titus, looking to his left. 'I saw some movement and reflected light, like off a sword.'

Galerius scanned the hill. 'Can't see anything but could be our friends from yesterday. Take the convoy round the next bend, then leave them and loop back around the hill. I'll make to relieve myself and amble up to the summit using that line of trees as cover.'

Both men pushed their horses hard, knowing that the other would do the same, and reached the top of the knoll nearly together. After days of sneaking through woods and marshes Galerius began to sense that there was a chance of real soldiering action. A feeling of danger close by and a chance to engage an enemy sent adrenaline coursing through his body. His mouth was dry. Quickly he checked that his sword was free in its scabbard. He saw a lone horse chewing grass with a polished brass bit that caught the sunlight as it searched through grass shoots. Fearing a trap of some kind, Galerius reined his mount in, as did Titus. Fifty paces apart they silently moved down the hill. Pushing through some dense undergrowth they found a grassy hollow and saw someone curled up under a riding cloak.

Galerius dismounted and drew his sword. He signalled to Titus to stay on his horse, knowing the man was sufficiently experienced not to have to be told to watch for a possible ambush. Slowly Galerius approached the bundle. 'On yer feet, lad!' he said, kicking the cloak.

A sound between a scream and a squeak answered. She had been desperately tired. Watching the track, with a warming sun, waiting for the convoy and listening to the birds chatter in the trees, she had been lulled to sleep. Now she was done for. She wanted to see her fate, not merely feel it kick her, so she slowly pushed aside her cloak, blinking as her eyes were hit by the dappled light of the sun filtering through spring leaves into the clearing. A sword was pointing at her, then it was gone. She heard her name.

'Una? Una?' A man in a Roman uniform was calling her name. 'It's Una, isn't it?' he asked again.

'Yes, yes, sir,' she said, scrambling to her feet. The face looked instantly familiar. She was pleased and terrified at the same time.

'What might you be doing here?' asked her inquisitor. 'Practising to be a wood nymph?'

'Sir, I –' She searched for words that wouldn't betray her. 'I hope the pies were to your liking, sir.'

'I wouldn't have expected to find a servant girl up here, waiting to ask about the food she supplied, would you Titus?'

'But you're soldiers, sir,' protested Una, playing for time, trying to think.

'We're full of surprises, just like you. Now tell me what you're about.'

'Sir, it's been dreadful. I didn't sleep a wink with my master and me being chased like.'

'Go on,' said Galerius, suspicion evident in his voice.

'Sir, you know my master likes gambling,' Una saw a nod. 'Well he was gambling with the innkeeper and winning big time. But the man's too mean to easily part with money if there's another way, if you know what I mean?'

'I know innkeepers all right,' said Galerius, letting himself be drawn deeper into the story.

'So he offered my master the pick of his women for the night to cancel his debt and he decided on the man's wife. He had to honour the debt and I think his wife was quite pleased to get the attention, truth be told.'

Galerius laughed and was joined by a guffaw from Titus. 'He shagged the man's wife?'

'Yes, sir. Then in the morning – yesterday I think, unless I've got really stupid with my days – he chased us out. Claimed that my master had cheated his way on top of his wife. He got a dagger and tried to kill my master.' Una shook her head as though she were remembering a terrible fight. 'I was gathering our things, then my master

239

got stabbed in the side with the innkeeper's dagger and staggered out. The man's wife was half-naked, swinging a bread pan round her head trying to stop her husband committing murder and it was all terrible. When we got out we rode our horses down the road and I saw that my master'd been badly wounded.'

'So why are you here now?' asked Galerius, the amused look on his face indicating he'd enjoyed the story so far.

'We rode south for a while, then rested so that I could put a stop to my master's bleeding, sir. Then we heard that some Votadini warriors were a little farther south so my master set off to join them and find an army physician to treat him. Meanwhile I came back here 'cause I'd spotted a good piece of old woodland and knew that I could get some healing plants.' Una raised a small pouch that she passed to Galerius to examine. 'I started to pick some, then I just got tired and fell asleep.'

Galerius finally sheathed his sword. 'You have a skill for healing?'

'A little, sir. My master is good with all sorts of mixtures, some of them for healing. He even sells a few to Romans.'

'In that case we may be able to help each other. I want you to help us look after some children that we're taking to a city not far from here. You'll need to take special care of two of them and when we're at the city I'll make sure you're properly rewarded for your effort. How's that sound?'

'Sir, but my master needs me.'

'By now he'll be with a good physician so don't worry about him. You'll be able to see him soon enough and take him some coins that'll pay for any medicine he needs.'

'Sir, you know best and I ain't going to argue with two such grand looking soldiers.'

Titus retrieved Una's horse and she joined the convoy.

# Chapter XXXVII

Still visible in deepening twilight, a tented city dwarfed the buildings of the village that surrounded the grey, stone fortress of Derventio. Mannius followed his escort through the camp, stumbled into his tent, and fell exhausted into a chair. Eithne appeared, unbidden, holding out a goblet of weak wine. Without a word he gulped down the offered liquid and his servant refilled the silver vessel. This time he drank more slowly and let the girl remove his sandals. Then she tried to help him remove his tunic. Instead he pulled himself up on her shoulders before dropping onto the blankets of his cot, instantly falling into a deep sleep.

Mannius turned over, sensing a commotion somewhere deep in a troubled dream. The noise came closer and Eithne was shaking his shoulder, rousing him. So unfair after so little sleep. Then he realised that the sun was already high, warming his tent. He ran a hand over his face, feeling two days' untended stubble, and swung his legs onto a rug. Princess Caoimhe pushed past a protesting Eithne and sat in a chair facing the cot.

'Sir, I –'

'It's all right, Eithne,' said Mannius, holding his hands up to prevent further conflict. 'Some of your dandelion water for both of us, please. Oh, and while you're about it I'll have some porridge.' He looked at the princess questioningly and got a swift shake of her head in reply.

241

Eithne huffed her disapproval, cast a dark glance towards Caoimhe and strutted out.

'You have me at a disadvantage, Princess,' said Mannius, rising and taking a chair to face his guest.

'I'm sorry to barge in on you unannounced but a messenger said that Taran was wounded. How is he? Will he live? Is he dead? I couldn't bear to lose him.'

Mannius felt his head spin. 'What messenger?' Just as he asked the question, a centurion entered with a leather satchel bound tightly with a thong.

'Arrived before dawn, sir. Messenger said it was from, er, Lord Taran, if you please.'

'Thank you, Centurion,' said Mannius, unravelling the package. 'Any news of Lord Taran?'

'Messenger said he was being treated by an army physician for a wound. Lost a lot of blood but still able to cuss and swear like a good 'un at the man he gave the package to, sir.' The man saluted and left the tent.

Mannius pulled a blanket tight around his shoulders. 'You know I've been cold ever since I left my apartment to help the governor.'

'It's been unseasonably chilly and wet,' said Caoimhe, humouring him. 'But Taran?'

'No, it's inside where I feel cold. Like no matter how long the sun shines I'll still be cold. I mean this war's changing us all.'

'Not you,' said Caoimhe smiling and taking his arm. 'I heard how you stopped the killing; saved the lives of those Saxon boys. You're better than all of us for that.'

'Depends how much blood's been lost.'

'From the Saxons?' said Caoimhe, trying to piece together the tribune's thoughts.

'No, from Taran. If he's been wounded and got to a physician it usually depends on making it through a day

242

or so to be sure of recovering. As I said it's a matter of how much blood he's lost.'

Caoimhe could contain her emotions no longer. She leant on his shoulder and clung to him, sobbing quietly. Mannius stood up, pulling her with him and felt her shake as they hugged one another. Eithne returned, carrying a tray with two goblets, a jug and a bowl of steaming oat porridge. When she saw the two embracing she slammed the tray down on a rosewood camp table and smartly walked out.

'I'm sorry, I don't know what's got into her today,' said Mannius.

'She's only jealous, and rightly so I hope,' replied Caoimhe, looking directly into the tribune's eyes. Then she pulled away. 'Shall I pour for us?' she continued, taking charge of the jug. The fresh fragrance of roasted dandelion roots finally brought Mannius out of any lingering stupor.

While Mannius read the message contained in the satchel, Caoimhe passed him his breakfast. 'Are Una and Borgach with him?'

'They're fine,' lied Mannius, knowing that the thin walls of the tent would not prevent their conversation being overheard. The truth was for another time.


When Mannius had served as a junior officer in the army, most of his time had been spent drilling, marching, training and waiting. There was always so much time to wait. Nothing seemed to happen for long periods. Men would get bored and cause trouble until orders were received to march somewhere else, guard a bridge or patrol a road. But most of the time they waited. Now he found himself at the centre of things and nothing waited, everyone wanted a piece of him and events that required his attention seemed to come along all too frequently. A rising babble of voices, exchanged salutes and a pounding of feet signalled that something else was about to come his way.

Felicita burst into the tent. 'There you are! Come quickly, Centurion Curtius has at least a hundred deserters under arrest. Come and order their execution.'

Mannius felt the cold grip him again as he anticipated more needless deaths. He got to his feet, straightened his tunic and strode outside to be met by Coel.

'These men are heroes!' shouted Coel, waving a finger at a column of men, four abreast, standing on parade. 'Two days ago, mercenaries from Gaul attacked one of my villages, these men fought to help my people escape.'

Mannius beckoned for the senior officer in the column to come over. 'Militia?'

The man snapped to attention. 'Eburacum, sir.'

'Explain yourself.'

'Sir, we was ordered to help some Gaulish mercenaries, working for Governor Flavius. We marched with them to this village, thinking we was getting ready to fight Saxons and such.' The man cast an anxious look towards Coel. 'But all the governor says is to kill everyone in the village on account of they're traitors. Sir, they was only Brigantes, women and children going about their business.'

'So you refused his orders?'

The officer shuffled and this time looked anxiously towards Felicita. 'We did, sir. And there was a disagreement like and we ended up fighting.'

'And you brought my people here,' said Coel, sweeping an arm towards a crowd of civilians behind the column.

'Those people are murdering scum, who killed my husband,' interjected Felicita.

Coel's deep rumbling laugh started. 'If they're murderers then I can play a flute with my arse, which I can't.'

Felicita sniffed, as though she'd just caught a bad odour

from where Coel stood. 'He's a barbarian, just like that lot over there.'

Mannius looked at Curtius, ever the disciplinarian. Worryingly he seemed to be in agreement with Mannius' aunt. The column of men was being disarmed and Curtius' legionaries stood ready in full battledress. He needed time to think. 'Even barbarians tell the truth sometimes, Aunt.'

'Hah,' replied Felicita. 'They wouldn't know it if it bit their flute-playing arses! They're not coming in this camp.'

It seemed to Mannius that Curtius and his men agreed with her on that. 'Centurion, please take your men into the fort and take orders from the senior officer there – and tell your men to collect their weapons before they leave.'

'You can't be serious,' protested Felicita.

'You said they shouldn't stay here and we're a little cramped as it is.'

'But I'm staying in the fort.'

'Then you'll be able to rest easier, knowing that you've got another century and a half of men to guard you.' Mannius saw a look beyond hatred; of pure contempt in his aunt's eyes. Then he heard a low rumble that indicated Coel was about to launch another round of laughter. 'And Lord Coel, we have business to attend to.'

# Chapter XXXVIII

At first Una travelled by cart, with the sick children. With all the blankets she could find, she cushioned her patients from the worst shocks of the wooden floor as they trundled along. She held their hands and quietly spoke to them, trying to give reassurance. The young boy with a broken leg slipped in and out of consciousness. All she could do was pour wild garlic juice over the exposed wound to prevent further infection and hope they found a physician quickly. The other sick boy had a fever and diarrhoea. Spasmodically he retched without bringing anything up. When the convoy passed close to a pond she jumped off, took her horse and picked some water mint. Galerius held back with her and made a fire so that she could boil water. From the plant's hairy stems and pink flowers she made an infusion. They quickly caught the convoy and Una administered the liquid to the fevered boy and put freshly-boiled bandages round the other boy's wound.

Then she turned her attention to the healthy children, making sure they were eating and drinking. She combed and plaited the hair of some young girls. Her work done she stayed in the carts, feeling every jolt and bump from the rough, wooden wagons. Ignoring her discomfort, she pulled faces every time the carts rolled and kicked: a curious look, a smile then a giggle. Eventually it became a game and laughter rose. Occasionally she glanced at Galerius and the other two soldiers. She could tell from their expressions that they had become more relaxed.

Maybe the children playing a little helped or perhaps it was that they were getting further away from Saxons.

Galerius pushed them on through the afternoon, stopping only occasionally for natural breaks that seemed to test his patience more each time one was necessary. Just when Una thought they'd been lucky to keep the warmth of the sun on them she felt a cooler breeze. Dark clouds blotted out the sun and she felt the first spots of rain. Still Galerius pushed them on. Una made the children pull rough canvas sheets over them and another game began.

Twilight came and threatened to turn to the dark of night before the carts were finally halted in the courtyard of a large villa. Una helped the children down and saw them inside before picking an armful of the daisy-like camomile flowers she'd spotted on the way in. Returning to the children she saw that slaves were pushing food in front of them. Una strode into the kitchen and ordered hot water. She supervised the preparation of a weak, sweet-smelling mixture. Then slaves passed out mugs of the steaming liquid to the children before they helped them to mats, covered them with blankets and were amazed at how quickly they were all sound asleep.

Over centuries of Roman occupation Eburacum had grown from a legionary fortress to a prosperous, walled town. Paved roads from across the north of the province converged as though the settlement was at the centre of a spider's web. Seagoing ships travelled along the river that connected with the Oceanus Germanicus and brought goods from every part of the empire, reinforcing the location's importance as a trading and military centre.

Like every other town and village along the eastern side of the country, Eburacum's population had been swollen several times over by refugees streaming south and inland. At each of the double gates guarded by legionaries people queued to be permitted entrance to the town. Even merchants with essential supplies of wood for fires, animals for market, grain and other foodstuffs had to wait their turn. Anyone remotely resembling a Saxon was unceremoniously pushed, and sometimes kicked, away.

Inside the walls, lining paved streets that ran in grids across the settlement, beggars held out their hands for coins or scraps of food. Their numbers had also increased. Destitute villagers and their families joined those looking for charity, trying to extend the meagre rations they'd brought with them. An old woman dressed in black rags moved among them. Somehow she managed to find more food than anyone else. Every morning and afternoon she was near the gate, watching the world pass by as the other beggars did. But, after the great oak gates were swung shut and the guards left she brought out food. Occasionally she gave out medicines for sick children. Quickly word spread of the woman and she had a growing audience. All she asked in return was that people talked with her. She was skilful at talking and made everyone feel at ease as they told her what and who they'd seen during the day or imparted secret rumours they'd overheard.

None of the beggars missed the entrance of the Roman soldiers on horseback, accompanied by a teenager and a young woman who drove two of the wagons. Legionaries at the gate shouted and bawled as the carts were driven straight to the gate, ignoring the queue along the road. The officer at the front rode his horse to the sentries, seemingly oblivious of the crowd around him. A junior officer stepped out to witness the commotion and immediately called for the duty centurion.

'That's far enough,' shouted the centurion, raising a

hand to the approaching mud-covered horseman, who reined in his mount and looked down.

'Centurion, we need a squad of men as an escort for our wagons,' said the rider.

'All non-garrison, military personnel have to report to the east gate. Join the queue there,' replied the centurion.

The rearmost rider walked his horse to the front of the queue and pulled back his riding cloak to reveal his uniform. 'I am General Galerius of the Jovian Guard. Now are you able to help Centurion Titus or do I have to mention to the governor the slipshod manner in which this queue is being administered?' There were mumblings of agreement from the crowd.

Una suddenly registered the title and watched in amusement as the centurion did a verbal about face and toadied to Galerius. Ten men ran out to be led by the centurion himself. Through the gates the carts rolled and Una thought she saw some familiar faces in the crowd inside the walls. Instead of waving to them she focused on following the soldiers ahead, who cleared a way through crowded streets.

Progress was slow along streets choked with people and animals. Una had never visited Eburacum before and was glad they had to dawdle and occasionally stop while soldiers cleared another cart out of their way or made a merchant move his stall. The place was a seething mass of activity. People moved to and fro, sometimes stopping to examine their convoy but mostly going about their own business: looking at goods for sale in shops and on stalls that decorated the streets. There was so much choice. The convoy turned a corner and started up an easy angled slope to a large villa. Higher up the shops seemed to have greater selections: there were even jewellers. While they halted for yet another delay, she watched slaves carefully working precious metals at the rear of one shop.

On the breeze she caught the scent of spices and marvelled at the sweetness they promised.

The convoy moved again and she heard shouts in front. Heavy gates swung open and more soldiers directed them to a courtyard at the side of a grand villa. She knew this place must be the governor's residence as all the soldiers were immaculately dressed and even the numerous slaves wore good clothes. Only when the carts were inside and the gates had been closed, preventing prying eyes from seeing in, were the sheets removed and the children helped down. Suddenly there was calm and quiet. Una found her ears buzzing, realising that the streets had been full of noise.

Slaves emerged from the villa and organised everyone. Galerius and his men bathed and slept before they were served a small meal. Una joined them, exhausted.

'My dear, you look tired,' said Galerius.

'I am, General, sir. It is *general* – isn't it?' she replied, feeling as though she was in a dream. 'The children were a little unsettled.'

'But you helped them with your medicine?'

'Yes, sir. To tell you the truth, I think I could do with a little myself. I'm not used to such excitement.'

The soldiers laughed good-naturedly and she smiled appreciatively, nibbling at some bread and cheese.

'We're due to meet a senator, with the children, in an hour. I'd like you to be there.'

'Sir, I'll be there but the little ones are tired rotten. It'd be wrong to –'

Galerius cut her off. 'They are from noble, Roman families and will be reminded of their duty.' His tone had finality about it.

'What about those that's ill, sir?'

'They may be excused. The house slaves will bathe you and find a decent palla for you to wear.'

250

She'd never worn a palla – the robe used by ladies from noble classes – and bathing inside would be a new experience for her. 'Thank you, sir. I can't say I've ever had slaves bathe me before. In fact I can't rightly remember being in one of your Roman bathhouses. My word, wait till I tell my master, he won't believe me.' Except for the royal family, she hadn't heard of anyone from her village bathing, and most struggled to wash themselves properly.

King Cathal's palace at its best had never been as grand as the governor's house. Everything was a wonder and a surprise – like the underfloor heating. When they lined up to meet the senator in a high-ceilinged hall Una marvelled at fine silk curtains, busts of men – presumably former governors or emperors – and statues of nymphs dancing round a fountain. All the pieces were exquisite, made by craftsmen. The fountain gurgled and a vague scent of incense lulled her into a dreamy state. She imagined the polished mosaic on which she stood coming alive. Her feet were on the prow of a boat and she began to feel the rise and fall of the sea. With power to make such beautiful things she wondered why the Romans needed someone of her modest abilities and surely they'd be able to defeat the Saxons.

Everyone, even Una and the children, stood to attention, waiting for the senator. A full hour after the designated time there was a crunch of nailed sandals and grounding of javelins in the corridor. The soldiers in the room stiffened, knowing that the guards outside were giving a formal salute to someone of importance. When she saw him, Una was surprised at how short he was for a man who wielded such power. Bright torchlight gleamed off his bald pate and forced her to look at his small, dark eyes. She was sure his round cheeks were unnaturally white – did he have anaemia or was he wearing cosmetic paint? A shine suggested paint.

The short man straightened his toga and took time to deliberately centre a shiny buckle on a belt, directly in line with his small chin. 'General Galerius, how good it is to see you again.'

'And likewise yourself, Senator,' replied the general.

'Flavius is now governor of this province – eh, Flavius?' said the senator, gesturing to a man who walked into the room behind him. Una thought he looked like a weasel, definitely not a soldier from the stoop that had attached itself to him.

'Congratulations,' offered the general. From the curt, flat tone Una quickly took an inference of hostility between Galerius and the weasel but was unsure about his feelings towards the old senator. She knew that Taran would want all these observations and more.

'Glad to see you've got the children safe and sound, Galerius,' said Antonius, taking charge.

'Not all of them, sir. And, though we pressed him, he didn't give us all the gold either,' said Galerius, passing a heavy saddlebag to the senator. 'Said that they were on another ship that had been delayed.'

'Very convenient, eh?'

'Too convenient for my liking, Senator,' said the weasel. 'Maybe they need a little more pushing?'

'My thoughts exactly, Flavius,' said the senator.

'Sir, we promised King Aelred that we'd return in a few days' time when more of his ships have reached the bay. Perhaps Governor Flavius would care to accompany us?'

Una saw the weasel's face flush red for a moment. Funny, she thought, never seen a red weasel before. She must be tired, not concentrating.

'I would dearly like to give Aelred a piece of my mind

but I find it necessary to work on the other side of our deal, General,' said Flavius.

The senator stepped towards the children and went down the line as though they were soldiers on parade. 'They seem healthy enough,' he pronounced. 'And who is this one, she's not Roman – speak.'

'Please your Senatorship, sir, I was just taken on to help with the children and look after the sick ones,' responded Una, keeping her head bowed so as not to have eye contact with the man. Slaves had washed her hair, removed the journey's dirt and rubbed creams into her skin until it was silky smooth. She looked better than she ever remembered. She'd let them splash scent on her, tie her hair up and tightly wrap her in a light blue stola before they draped a brand new palla over her shoulders. When they'd held mirrors for her she'd felt as though she were a princess. Tight curls bounced down either side of her face and made her smile with sensuous pleasure. She hoped the senator appreciated the effect, though with the other fine ornaments on display she felt second best.

'Sick?'

'Sir, two of the boys are ill,' responded Galerius. 'One has a fever that the girl was able to treat and the other has a broken leg.'

'Damn Saxons, can't take care of anything. This province'll soon be ruined. This girl of yours any good then, Galerius?'

Una noticed the way Romans talked about people, especially slaves and women, as though they were animals and couldn't understand what was being said about them – usually right in front of their faces. 'Yes, sir. Very good at calming the little ones.'

'Excellent, then she will accompany you when you retrieve the rest of the children.' That was the senator's final word. He walked down the line of children and out of the room.

Galerius nodded to Una and she understood it was her signal to usher her charges out to the slave girls waiting to take them to beds. At the door she waited for the last of the children. Flavius ambled over to her, looked her up and down and pressed his right hand against her left breast. Immediately Una slapped him hard across the face, making him turn away.

The weasel pulled his arm back and clenched his fist ready to deliver retribution. Una ducked behind one of the legionaries guarding the doorway before she looked back at her molester. Galerius had the man's arm in a vice-like grip, making the skin go white. Pain was obvious on the weasel's face.

'You touch that lady again or disrespect her in any way and I'll gut you faster than you can order bread to go with the soup that'll come out of your yellow stomach. Understand?' The general delivered his question with a rotation of his hand that pushed Flavius' arm high and wrenched his shoulder, forcing him onto the floor. Una watched him nod and, with some satisfaction, saw blood oozing from a split lip.

# Chapter XXXIX

Taking Coel into his tent helped prevent any further confrontation with Mannius' indignant aunt. He dearly wished he was a simple optio again – sending men to scrounge for food to cook on one of the communal fires scattered throughout the camp. But now he had to scrounge for favours. And the more he received, the more he owed. It was a trap and he was well and truly snared.

Mannius waved Coel to a table on which lay a large map. 'Taran has sent word that Aelred has landed with his force here,' said Mannius, pointing to the north bank of an estuary, high up the east coast.

'For sure?' said Coel, interest clearly in his voice.

'No doubt,' replied Mannius.

'Ah, he'll be with his main body of men.' Coel stroked his beard, taking in the information. 'How long?' asked the Brigantes king, not lifting his eyes from the map.

'Difficult to say but certainly more than a few days, judging from the state of his camp and the number of ships hidden in the bay.'

'So why hasn't he moved?' asked Coel as much to himself as to Mannius.

'Can't be certain but something's keeping him there,' answered Mannius. 'Something that's important to his campaign – supplies, men, it doesn't really matter. What matters is that he's stuck there until it arrives. If he's waiting for men from the north then he'll have to wait another few days as they seem to be making slow progress.

If it's ships then the foul weather we've had might be hampering his fleet.'

'So we know where he is. Let's get up there and smash him before he lays waste to our lands.' Coel emphasised his point by smashing his fist on the map table.

'Can't be easily accomplished with the men we've got. He's got us outnumbered and he's got ships to move his forces around to outflank us – something with which we can't compete.'

'Surely we don't just wait for him to turn up in the valley?' asked Coel, looking straight into Mannius' eyes. 'Or do I see another thought in your mind?'

'I thought we'd put a little needle into his preparations,' said Mannius, watching Coel's anticipation grow. 'He's hidden his ships close into the north shore, behind bushes and trees. I think a few fire ships on a windy night could give him a nice warm welcome to our shores.'

A twinkle flashed in the big man's eyes. 'I like it. We owe it to him – don't we? Even if he's unloaded them it'll let him know we mean business. When do we leave?'

'I've found three captains, Brigantes, who've hidden their boats higher up the estuary. So we need to take a force to man the vessels and hold the south bank in case of trouble,' concluded Mannius.

No sooner had Coel left his tent than Mannius' day exploded out of control – not that he felt he had had much control since he'd been woken. A steady stream of clerks brought papers for him to sign, punishments to countersign, requests for stores, requests for javelins – the list was endless. Between signing sessions, officers sought audiences. Usually it was a request to move up to the old mine where defences were being prepared; anything to get their men and themselves away from the increasingly cramped village of tents. With men and officers restless for action it was no wonder that squabbles and fights were breaking out.

It was already mid-morning and the pile of parchments that a team of clerks ferried to and from his desk seemed to have hardly reduced. Mannius heard a salute and gruff retort from Curtius. He remembered he'd asked to see him. A disproportionate number of the punishments that crossed his desk seemed to be from his century, the best and most seasoned legionaries. Something seemed amiss but Mannius had to be tactful – he still needed the man's wholehearted support. Instead of inviting him in for a formal interview, Mannius stepped outside and gestured for the grizzled warrior to share a walk.

'An impressive sight, all these warriors together,' said Mannius, stopping to survey rows and rows of tents.

'Never thought I'd see an army of ours gathered here in this province ever again. Not after Constantine took the last of our hardened regulars. And it'll probably be the last for a long while.'

'Makes a man proud to be a part of it, eh?'

'Aye, I'll have a part of that, sir. Still it's a pity we've got to rely on others,' said Curtius, casting a glance towards one of the camps that contained Brigantes.

'Rome's always relied on allies to help its cause and sometimes it's not easy keeping all those men and officers satisfied.'

'Fighting's the only thing that'll bring 'em together, sir. Good shield wall and a victory'll put them at ease now.'

Mannius started to walk the short distance to the tent used by the clerks. Centurion Laurentius stood outside handing a small leather bag to Eithne. There was a sound of chinking metal.

'Another man looking after his life savings,' said Curtius, watching Eithne disappear into the tent, no doubt to lock away the man's savings in the cohort's safe box. If a man was killed the money would be sent to his family or disposed of according to his wishes – after deductions for any outstanding debts.

'You seem to have more than your fair share of fighting to deal with in your century, Curtius.'

'Like I said, sir. Fighting's the only thing that's good for soldiers.'

'Go easy on the lads, Curtius. It's hard for those that haven't been through a big battle – hell I should know. We all want reassurance from veterans like you.' Mannius saw the centurion's eyes drop towards the ground – unusual. Normally he met any and every challenge face on. 'Just do me one favour, Curtius. Bring them together and get them ready for me. And while I'm away with Lord Coel you'll have to keep an eye on the camp.'

'Yes, sir. I suppose we could do with some more drilling maybe. That'll keep them occupied.'

'Thank you, Curtius. I know I'll appreciate your efforts.'

# Chapter XL

Before dawn, Una woke in a cot – her own cot – in her own tiny room, next to two rooms shared by some of the children. She could hear slaves moving around, starting fires and putting pots down. The door to her room opened and a slave girl, roughly her age, brought warm water so that she could wash in private. Una leapt out of bed and asked the girl to stay. Hurriedly, she washed and then got the girl to help wrap her in the stola that she'd hung on the back of the door. Una sat on the cot and held a small mirror, admiring herself. The cloth felt light, cool and smooth. When she put her face into it she could smell the odour of new dye and everything felt fresh. Then she quickly looked in on the children, making sure that the slaves were waking and dressing them. Lastly she visited the two sick boys. The boy with the fever seemed almost recovered and sat up, talking with her. With the other boy she took her time to make sure that her lotions were properly applied by the slaves and fresh dressings bound on.

After a lonely breakfast in the servants' quarters, Una decided she wanted to visit some of the shops she'd seen the day before. She found Galerius and asked if it was all right for her to go. He insisted on two of the villa's guards accompanying her, which she thought was excellent as she had no idea how to find her way round the town.

Walking down the main street with two armed bodyguards made her feel like an aristocrat. She wondered if this was how Princess Caoimhe felt when she went out. Una pointed down the street and the guards nodded, seemingly bored with their assignment barely fifty paces outside the villa's gates. Already she could hear the sound of crowds and caught a whiff of spices. Smells of frying eggs, grilled beef and fresh bread drifted to her. The noise grew, the smells became more powerful and suddenly she was swept up in the hustle and bustle of people pushing their way round stalls in front of shops. Merchants fought for space and shouted for customers. Una wanted to visit them all, see everything. Her bodyguards were close and it gave her room to look and touch fine fabrics, smell unusual fruits and admire fabulous jewels.

Between the shops beggars held out open hands, looking for charity. An old woman with a short stick to support her tugged on Una's sleeve and one of her guards raised a club, ready to strike.

'That ain't necessary,' said Una, stopping the blow with an outstretched arm. The woman mumbled her thanks. 'You're Votadini, yes?' said Una, loud enough for her guards to hear. The woman nodded and Una launched into broad, colloquial Gaelic and received fast, quiet replies. Around them the crowds thinned, drawn to an overturned cart and its load of soil-covered carrots. The guards backed away, more interested in the commotion caused by the cart than Una. Before she parted, Una held out two silver coins to the woman and wished her luck in Latin.

# Chapter XLI

After a night and day of riding, the column of soldiers slowed as it neared flatlands close to a hidden inlet in a bay of the Dunum Sinus. Scouts reported seeing no one on the southern shore, yet still the horsemen moved carefully with a squadron of cavalry protecting each flank. Firm turf was replaced by tall, reed-like grass that parted easily under a horse's hoof to reveal black, wet mud. Overhead, leafed branches of great hornbeam trees tried to cut out the last of the sun's rays. Under the canopy fluted, grey bark reflected some light, lessening the gloom.

Ahead of the column, scouts lay sprawled at the top of a heather-clad hillock. Mannius and Coel dismounted and joined them, straining their eyes across the bay. At first Mannius saw nothing, but as his eyes adjusted, he spotted an orange glow from several large campfires. Then he picked out ship masts, swaying with the swell.

Behind them, Laurentius ordered legionaries to dismount and spread out along the shore and the main line of approach. Fishermen who'd volunteered to crew four small boats prepared a light meal and ate with twelve Votadini archers who had also asked to help. Concealed by high-growing brambles, teams of engineers raced to build twelve rafts. Each carried six barrels of flammable oil and would be towed across the bay to their targets.

'We're in luck,' announced Coel. 'The fishermen say that by the time the light fades completely they should have the benefit of an ebbing tide to help them across the bay.'

'I still think it's lucky that there aren't any Saxons on this side,' replied Mannius.

'Maybe they don't realise we know they're here or they think we haven't the gumption to attack them.'

'Doesn't really matter, I suppose.' Mannius tested his sword. 'I think I'll take some javelins instead of a bow with me.'

'No, you don't,' said Coel. 'Your place is here, Tribune. We can't afford to lose the man who's brought this little alliance together. Who knows what sort of commander the Romans would send our way if you weren't around?' The deep laughter started. 'You never know, I suppose, I might even like him.'

'Sorry, but I'm going,' insisted Mannius, determination rising in his voice. 'There's no way I'm sending men across there to do anything I wouldn't be prepared to do.' The issue wasn't for debate.

'Then my friend, I will go as well,' answered Coel. 'We all know that Romans make poor sailors.'


With daylight all but gone, the fishermen pulled their boats out of hiding places they'd used to conceal their craft when they'd had to abandon their villages. From under tangles of brambles that overhung a small tributary, four boats emerged.

Mannius waded out to a boat, second in line, and clambered over the side, landing in an ungainly heap on board. A legionary waited patiently for the tribune to settle himself, then passed in six javelins. Other men pulled on ropes, connected to rafts that were then secured to each fishing boat.

Using long wooden poles the fishermen pushed their vessels silently out into the estuary. At first the sailors pushed and rowed further inland, away from what looked like two submerged trees.

262

'What are those?' asked Mannius, pointing to the trees.

'Markers,' replied the old captain. 'Around them trees water's a mite shallow. We'd probably get over in these boats but with you lot and all we're carrying it could be a close thing. So, best not to risk bottoming the boats.'

Once they had cleared the obstacles, the sailors unfurled small, black, square sails that flapped in a stiffening breeze. Behind each vessel was a rope connected to a convoy of small rafts. Even with sails tied down the sailors still rowed while their captains used large steering oars to point them towards the Saxon encampment.

Mannius tried to stand, like the captain, to get a better view of events, but as soon as the craft were out of the protection of the land, waves rose, bouncing and rolling them. Spray fumed over the sides and made the deck slippery. Suddenly Mannius remembered he hated sailing: there was no control.

In the Saxon encampment, Una stood alongside Galerius and his two officers, in front of Aelred. The man drained a mug of ale, spilling much of his last two mouthfuls down his bushy beard that seemed to hide most of his face. For all his powerful build he looked overweight and Una pitied the man's horse. She watched his eyes. They darted this way and that. She knew the man behind the eyes was cleverer than his oafishness made out.

'Senator Antonius would like to conclude the transaction as soon as possible,' said Galerius.

'That lily-livered senator of yours is so frightened he daren't even leave his house to pick his own whores. Has to send his slaves out to get them for him, when he isn't shagging them that is.' The king held his mug out for more ale. 'You see, General, I know what is happening in your lands and your people are scared. They want to get out as fast as possible before my friends pay them a visit.'

'I trust both your Persian slave girls are keeping you sufficiently occupied at nights,' retorted Galerius. Una noticed the line was delivered in such an offhand manner that the general could have been swapping notes on livestock. The effect was palpable. King Aelred stopped laughing at his own jokes, checked over his shoulder as though someone was spying on him and narrowed his eyes. He leaned forward.

'I also know that a tribune has taken a force of a thousand legionaries to guard a Trojan Horse of a silver mine in the hills to the south. And that he has got two thousand seven hundred Votadini infantry and cavalry with him together with around three thousand Brigantes.'

'It is of little consequence,' said Galerius, careful not to give anything away. 'As you say, your friends will soon be paying them a visit. Now if we may continue with our business. I am anxious to be on my way before the tide turns and delays us further.'

'Perhaps you don't want to spend a night with my friends, General,' said Aelred with a mischievous grin on his face that showed gaps in his yellowed teeth. That was exactly what the general wanted to avoid. He had told Una, when they walked through the camp, that he sensed a heightened tension among the warriors. Men held his gaze, staring, measuring potential enemies, guessing their strength from the gait of their walk. Every camp with soldiers before a campaign or battle was the same. The Saxons, he said, were getting ready to move and take the country by force.

'I would not presume to impose myself on your hospitality, King Aelred.' Honours even, thought Una.

Aelred sat back and waved for a line of children to be herded forward. Again their hands were bound by leather thongs that had cut into some of the children's skin and drawn blood. The whole line was held together by sections of rope tied around their necks. They looked like slaves going to market, which Una presumed was the impression that the Saxon king wanted to portray: that he had the power to enslave Romans.

Titus and Primus stepped forward and cut the children free. Una beckoned them towards her, putting protective arms around the two smallest boys. She felt them tremble and instinctively pulled them closer. In front of her was a line of frightened faces. Quickly she counted and came up short. Resentment and indignation welled up in her. 'General, sir, there's still plenty missing.'

Galerius turned to her and counted for himself before he turned back to Aelred.

The king shrugged his shoulders and spread his palms. 'The girl speaks like a witch.'

'There is no need for magic, Aelred,' spat Galerius. 'I can count.'

A Saxon officer whispered to Aelred. 'Delayed at sea,' said the king without ever contemplating an apology. 'The transports carrying them should be here within a day if you care to stay.'

'Thank you, King Aelred,' said Galerius. 'I shall see you for the remainder of the children in a few days' time.'

Una was relieved that the general hadn't made them stay. She followed Galerius out of the camp, across the tidal inlet and along the small path to the fishermen's barn, where they'd left the carts. Una quickly cooked them soup then applied ointments and dressings to those with cuts. Even before she'd finished, Galerius was urging them to leave. She sensed, like the soldiers, that Saxon scouts were close.

* * *

265

Crossing the bay, even with a steady, following breeze was difficult at first: the tide still flooded in from the open sea and, with wind acting against it, large waves formed that broke over the sides. Mannius swore every time the boat crashed down. When he judged their position from the land he realised that they hardly seemed to be moving. They would be in the estuary longer than he had estimated and that thought gnawed at his stomach.

The archers looked nervously about, clearly discomfited by the rise and fall of the wood beneath them. Tension coupled with the seesaw motion forced most of them to vomit over the low sides to the accompaniment of smug laughs from seasoned sailors. Mannius hoped he wouldn't give the captain of the vessel the satisfaction of puking. Then as if by magic the waves lessened as the tide turned and their speed increased.

Ahead of them the Saxon camp was clearly visible. All the way from the entrance to the bay to the encampment, large fires shot up into the air and lit up the beaches, helping ships that had used the earlier flooding tide to enter the bay and navigate to the camp. They were close enough to see individual warriors but the wind carried their shouts away. The fishermen pushed their steering oars to port, let the sails pivot on the masts and forced their boats to starboard, across the wind. Slowly the convoy spread out, ready to attack. The archers unwrapped their bows from leather coats and refitted strings that had been kept dry inside their tunics. All thought of seasickness had vanished.

On a long beach ahead of them Saxon warriors turned and moved to the water's edge. Unnerved, the fishermen looked around and saw a large transport with two lanterns strung on its cross-mast making for the shore. As one, the captains on the fishing boats ordered masts to be lowered and everyone waited for the ship to pass. The lead fishing boat was closest and archers made ready, but every sailor on the Saxon ship appeared to be looking towards the beach. Once it had passed the sails were hastily re-rigged and the convoy continued towards its targets. Suddenly another large Saxon vessel loomed into view, this time between Mannius' boat and the lead vessel. There was no time for the fishermen to manoeuvre; the transport was close and had too much speed. Hurriedly, the archers in the lead boat pulled on the rope, trying to bring the fire rafts clear of the transport. Their efforts were futile. The connecting rope snagged on the transport's prow. The captain held an axe, ready to cut the rope. There were two unmistakable thuds as the timbers of the rafts crashed into either side of the transport.

Sailors on the transport started to look down at the obstacles they had hit. In the depths of the leading fishing boat a smouldering cord was put to fire arrows and archers made ready. The tow rope came tight and pulled the small boat towards the transport. Hearts pounding, the fishermen watched and waited for the captain to give the order. At less than fifty paces he brought the axe down on the rope and the archers sent their arrows into the two rafts they could see.

Two arrows landed inside the raft alongside the transport and another lodged in the transport's hull. Three more fire arrows arced through the night sky, this time towards the billowing sail of the transport. Men on the ship ran to beat out flames growing on the sail. Unseen, the final raft was set alight and allowed to drift into the side of the transport, closer aft.

The transport turned sharply to port. Saxon sailors, who had been running to fight fires, froze in fear and uncertainty. Oil on the first raft caught fire. Great flames leapt up and soon oil on the second raft was ablaze.

The joy of the Saxon sailors at seeing their destination turned to panic. They became too occupied fighting fires to pay any attention to steering the ship and left the transport to drift with the wind and tide. Heat from the flames was forcing men back. They ran to the sides of the ship, waving to other ships to come to their aid. Then they started to jump overboard to save themselves.

Mannius could see horror on men's faces as the night's dangers became clear. The large, blazing transport was drifting towards several moored ships. Men ran into the surf with poles, readying themselves to fend off the burning vessel. One of the rafts exploded, ripping a hole in the side of the transport and making men cower. Burning oil and timbers were strewn across the sea. Immediately the large vessel listed towards the gap in its burning side and slowed. But burning timbers, although not moving as quickly as the ship had been, were spread out.

Further out in the bay other rafts had been set ablaze. Satisfied that no more could be done, the Brigantes captains gave the order to turn into the wind and row out into the bay. Another Saxon ship appeared but this time the fishermen were lit up and silhouetted by the fires they had started. Above them men were ready with spears and arrows. Without warning an archer screamed and fell overboard, a spear in his chest. Then the air fizzed with more arrows that quickly took an oarsman and wounded two more archers.

Mannius and the remaining archers replied in kind. An unnatural calm seemed to descend for a moment as both sides took stock. It was then that Mannius noticed the captain slumped over the steering oar, an arrow in his neck. He pushed the dead man aside and took charge of the oar. Above him he could see men giving orders, waving at an unseen helmsman, directing the ship towards them. The Saxons were closing rapidly. He guessed they intended to ram them. With the tide and wind against the small boat there seemed little chance of escape.

Rather than try to back away, Mannius turned the boat to run with the wind and ordered the sail unfurled. Wind caught and the vessel slowly began to accelerate towards land. He glanced at his pursuers and saw Coel's boat pulling alongside the Saxon transport. Men hacked at the timbers and threw fire into the hold before they pushed away. Distracted by a growing inferno in their hold the chase was ended and Mannius swung the steering oar once more and his men rowed desperately towards safety.

Out in the main estuary the lead fishing vessel bobbed up and down, waiting to help. An arrow hit the captain's shoulder and men fell about him in a rain of death. Two remaining Votadini archers sent arrows up at another Saxon transport and men fell away, but the captain knew they were doomed: they had no momentum and were easy prey for the larger vessel. With only moments left he ordered ropes to be tied to axes and spears, then the small barrels of oil that they had on board were opened and set on fire. Seeing the danger the Saxons hurled everything they could find at the burning boat. The prow of the Saxon ship hit the aft of the small boat with a sickening crash. Timbers buckled and then snapped. The last act of the captain, helped by two of his men, was to hammer the axes and spears into the hull of the transport. Flames leapt up the side of the ship and then another explosion ripped into the large vessel and fires started in its hold. The Saxon crew ran out an anchor to hold the ship. But the anchor rope quickly caught fire and the wind pushed the vessel towards the beach. Released once more, the ship took its flames into a mass of moored vessels.

Mannius watched helplessly as survivors from the first fishing boat flailed desperately in the water. Some sank quickly but two tried to swim towards the other boats. Cold and fatigue overcame their strength. Without a scream or shout of complaint both men quietly slipped under the dark water. Was that to be their fate, wondered Mannius: to be mercilessly cut down and sink without trace to leave the land for Aelred's Saxons?

There was still too much to do to have time to think of the future. Like the other captains, Mannius ordered his men to row out into the bay. When they began to tire he changed sailors for archers. Finally he ordered the sail to be hauled up and the small boat ran slightly into but mostly across the wind, away from the growing conflagration. He took them towards the estuary's mouth and the open sea. Then oars were used again to pull the boats close to the southern shore. In the lee of the shore and with the outflow of the tide slackening, the men wearily rowed in the direction of their start point.


King Aelred was woken by shouts. Heavy footsteps pounded near his tent. He heard sentries outside draw their swords. A slave entered and helped him dress, strapping on his armour as fast as possible. Outside he was momentarily blinded by the brilliant light from a huge fire. He heard its hungry roar and, even though he was a long way from the beach, he felt its warmth. Nearby, horses whinnied in panic.

Followed by four sentries the king drew his sword and strode towards an unfolding disaster. One of his captains ran up to him, bowing so low that he fell to his knees.

What is it, man?' bellowed the king. 'Are we under attack?'

'My lord, the Romans attacked three of our in-coming transports and sent fire ships into the bay.'

'So this is the way the bastard Galerius rewards my

good faith. It's probably a diversion. Sound the alarm and get the men up ready to fight.'

Aelred marched towards the beach and took in the scene. A breeze carried flames from ship to ship along the row. The next vessel in line had started to smoke. Two men used their shields to protect themselves from the heat and dragged a charred man up the beach.

'Leave him,' ordered Aelred. 'He's as good as dead, which is exactly what Galerius will be when I catch him. Go help the admiral.'

Near the water's edge the admiral had organised teams of men to push three ships into the water in order to create a firebreak. Further along the beach to his left men were jumping onto ships moored close to the shore. The king saw that they were trying to row the ships out into the bay, again to create a natural barrier to halt the flames.

The ships on the beach moved. When the admiral was satisfied he ran to the king. 'My Lord, transports were using the tide to make their way into the bay when the Romans attacked.'

'Why were no picket ships posted to protect our fleet?' asked the king, waving his sword at the fires along the beach.

'We had warships at the entrance. They must have come from the bay itself. I understood that the Romans wouldn't attack,' the admiral flinched as pots of oil exploded. 'They have no effective fleet, my lord.'

'So you keep saying. Does this look fucking ineffective to you?' Aelred cut down at the exposed neck of the man in front of him. The admiral's scream was lost in the braying of cattle fleeing a hurriedly unloaded transport. Their stampede took them through the king's camp. Tents were trampled and dragged across fires, starting another round of panic. 'You men throw his body onto that ship,' said Aelred pointing to a beached ship that had started to burn. 'He might as well enjoy the mess he's responsible for. Then find the man responsible for those cattle and have him flogged.'

The breeze that had brought chaos and destruction to the wooden ships at last brought relief. First drizzle hissed on hot timbers then sustained, heavy rain stopped fires from spreading and finally extinguished them. But not until much damage had been wrought.

On the south bank of the bay, Laurentius and his men watched the Saxon fleet burn. 'I didn't think it was possible,' confided the centurion to his optio in hushed tones.

'Me neither, sir.'

'Begging pardon, sirs,' said a legionary. 'Scouts report some of our ships are on the way back.'

'Excellent!' replied Laurentius, jumping up.

'Sir, they're being followed by at least two Saxon ships.'

Laurentius and his optio galloped their horses onto a small finger of land that jutted out into the bay to watch the unfolding race. Three small boats were being chased by three larger ships and the gap was closing quickly.

'Get archers here quickly,' shouted Laurentius.

The leading boat rounded the spit of land, then the second drew close. A long time seemed to pass before a Saxon ship caught up with the trailing fishing boat. On board the men stopped rowing and picked up weapons ready to fight. From the shore Laurentius witnessed a frustratingly one-sided battle as the Saxons overwhelmed the defenders with arrows and spears before they boarded and butchered them.

The other two Saxon ships chased the second fishing

boat that was slowing alarmingly. The Saxons closed almost within range of their own archers.

Mannius could see that his men were exhausted – he'd even done a stint on an oar himself. Barely ten paces behind him he saw three small plumes of water left by arrows. He wanted to push the boat. He thought of veering to shore but guessed that the larger vessel would have time to cut them off. Then in the first light of dawn he saw the marker trees. He ordered everything other than weapons over the side – the dead included – and pushed the steering oar to take the ship close in to land.

With the last effort they could muster, the crew pulled hard. Beneath their feet they heard and felt the keel scrape over mud and rocks. Mannius gripped the steering oar and felt it vibrate as it scraped over the bottom. A cheer went up from the sailors and they pulled again on their oars.

Laurentius had his men ready on the spit of land near Mannius' boat. Before he could order an attack, a loud crack came across the water followed by the sound of wood splintering. The Saxon ship came to an abrupt halt. The second, chasing ship pressed on after the small boats and this time Laurentius gave the order to loose arrows. Over twenty fire arrows lit the night sky, tracing a path towards the Saxons. Men screamed as they were hit and fires started across the ship.

A third Saxon ship backed oars and turned out into the bay, not wanting to risk taking fire arrows. Men jumped from the first Saxon ship as it began to sink. On the second ship, flames started to take hold as men fell to arrows and were unable to fight the fires.

It was the laugh that Mannius recognised first, growing from a low rumble as Mannius' ship escaped, before exploding into a full boom as the chasing Saxon ship crashed onto rocks. He knew that Coel had survived. Unbidden, the two remaining fishing vessels returned to the stricken Saxon ship, intent on finishing it, circling like sharks, waiting for the moment to move in for the kill.

Laurentius spread his men along the shore ready to attack any Saxons that made it to land. A few survivors drew knives and tried vainly to fight but were swiftly cut down. Most who made shore simply collapsed, exhausted, and accepted that they had become prisoners, too tired to care.

Among the survivors were seven bedraggled Roman children who had been hauled out of the bay by the fishermen and wrapped in blankets. Mannius gave orders for the children to be taken away from the shore, then the Saxon prisoners were executed and their heads impaled on poles by the water's edge. Rain that had been threatening for a while finally came down in sheets that washed Saxon blood off the land and into the sea. A fitting conclusion to the night.

Even half a mile away, at the top of the low hill that overlooked the Saxon camp, King Aelred could smell the charred embers that still smouldered. From his vantage point the full extent of the devastation caused by the fire ships could be seen. Around the edges of the beach were black, skeletal hulks where ships had been beached. The thick timbers of their hulls, charred by flames, stood like whale ribs that had been chewed by a monstrous ogre. Nearer to the centre of the fire there were only heaps of ashes. In the shallow waters of the bay a few ships had sunk with their cargo, leaving their masts as the only marks of their existence. Floating in the gentle swell of the tidal water was a mass of wood together with assorted cargo, animal carcasses and bodies of men.

Aelred chewed disconsolately on a hunk of cold mutton. 'The attack was good,' he said to a group of senior officers gathered around him. 'The admiral was probably right: the Romans are not great sailors so it could well have been others.'

'But who could mount such an attack, my lord?' asked Hengist, one of Aelred's trusted generals.

'From what I saw it took little to cause such damage. Perhaps a few displaced Votadini fishermen or locals fearing our presence. What were our losses, Hengist?'

'Thirty-one ships destroyed, another ten badly damaged, three hundred and fifty men killed with forty more likely to die today from their wounds.'

'So it is not so bad. Merely a pinprick. Look how many warriors we still have ready and eager to fight,' said Aelred, sweeping his arm towards the mass of men and tents below.

'My Lord, among the transports we lost a lot of food and horses.'

'That is of little consequence. We can take what we need soon enough.'

'But my Lord, some of the hostages were on the transport that ran onto rocks.'

'So what? The Romans are more interested in gold than people. Anyway, after this I was going to send their heads to Galerius.' Aelred's depression passed and he found a new energy and a sense of urgency. 'Today we march inland to meet with Prince Wybert, then we will set about these people.' He knew that as long as his men remained in the bay they would have stark reminders of the attack. 'Hengist, take three thousand of our best warriors across the estuary and move inland. That way, if the Romans try to ambush us they'll be caught between both of us. We'll keep in contact via the ships.'

'My Lord, some of the transports have not yet been unloaded.'

'Then send them along the estuary to meet us inland.'

# Chapter XLII

'What did he say?' asked the senator, the veins on his neck pulsing visibly.

'That he'd deliver the rest of the gold to us personally in Eburacum when his forces are in control,' replied Galerius.

'And you accepted that?' prompted Flavius. Neither the senator nor Galerius acknowledged the young man's existence, so he shut up.

'The impudence of the barbarian,' fumed Antonius.

'Sir, he said that the other children were still at sea.'

'They could easily be delayed by bad weather or a poor crew,' said the senator, dismissing the detail. 'But not to have the gold is inexcusable. I think you should tell him so.'

'I don't think he'll take too kindly to that after what happened to his fleet, sir.'

'And?'

'It was attacked by fire ships from across the bay. Looked like they found their target. All we saw was a huge ball of fire on the horizon.'

'Ye gods! If he thinks we're behind it we can kiss goodbye to the gold.' Antonius turned to a small chest on the floor and opened it with a key he had on a chain round his neck. 'I think it's time we distributed these and made some noise about the orders,' he said, taking out an armful of parchments and handing them to Flavius. 'All units are to be disbanded. We'll keep the

Eburacum militia for the time being. Now send out the messengers.'

Riding back in the cool of dawn, Mannius, like everyone else in the column, felt exhausted after so long without sleep. Seeing men sail out bravely and then having to watch them butchered had been horrific. Even though he'd been preoccupied with his own crew's survival he'd swallowed back foul-tasting vomit that welled up instinctively when the small ship had been overwhelmed: they had been so close to safety yet he had been powerless to help them. He wondered if he would be strong enough to send men into battle against the huge and powerful Saxon army. He wished he had the hearty resolve of Coel, who hummed as he rode next to him.

Ahead of them a small fort guarded the northern end of the paved road that led south across the moors. Only three squadrons of cavalry acted as its garrison, patrolling and scouting the area, providing a means of warning of a Saxon advance. But it was the first, friendly marker of safety for them after their earlier perils.

Men and horses began to relax. Food was quickly prepared and everyone rested. Messengers were sent ahead to inform the camp at Derventio of the success of the attack. Mannius and Coel both knew that they needed a few small triumphs to boost the morale of their army.

With less than two hours of sleep the column moved south over the moors. Overhead, dark clouds created a discouraging, depressing atmosphere and for the first time Mannius appreciated the plateau's bleakness. Seas of purple and pink heather swayed in a cold wind that swept across rolling hills. Away from the paved road there were acres of bog and pools of stagnant water. He took comfort from the inhospitable landscape. The Saxons would have to bring their army down this route and he'd be waiting for them. But would they overwhelm him like the small fishing boat in this sea of swaying heather and bracken shoots?

Nearing the defences in the narrow valley, men working with spades and pickaxes stopped work and cheered them. Mannius heard an officer ask how many, then Coel's voice boomed, 'We caught them asleep – at least a hundred ships and twenty times that number of men, if not more – wouldn't you say Tribune?'

'Yes, at least,' he agreed. This was a victory and had to be enjoyed. Horses that had been ridden by those who had perished and weren't needed by one of the children had been left at the fort for the cavalry to bring back. No hint of casualties was permitted. Another cheer went up and the digging tools were waved in the air. All the way back to Derventio it was the same whenever they met a body of men.

Mannius and Coel rode side by side across the stone bridge that led to the growing settlement around Derventio. Between ancient oak trees that lined each side of the road, Votadini warriors stood in salute, holding back a cheering crowd. The column paraded up the hill towards the fort where Roman sentries hit the flats of their swords against wooden shields. In front of the gates Coel halted the column and theatrically threw down a round, battered Saxon shield he'd taken from a man who'd made it to shore. A roar went up, then the crowd was among the column, shaking them, patting them and hugging them.

Mannius leaned over to Coel, 'What are they chanting?'

'Coel Hen,' replied lord of the Brigantes. 'It means old Coel – on account of I'm the eldest to survive from my generation.'

'I feel old today: bone-tired and old,' replied Mannius.

'Nonsense, my friend. Today we are young and we celebrate.'

Mannius looked back to see that eight volunteers were bringing the children quietly and unnoticed over the bridge. Once he was certain that they were close to the Roman encampment he dismounted. Princess Caoimhe ran as fast as dignity allowed, hugged Coel and then Mannius, slipping an arm inside his.

'Did you really burn a hundred of their ships?' asked Caoimhe.

'We certainly let them know that they're in for a fight,' replied Mannius, and received a slap on the back from Coel. 'But I don't think we deserve a victory parade. You'd think we'd already beaten the Saxons the way this lot are carrying on.'


It seemed to Mannius that he'd only just got across the ditch and inside the wooden palisade of the temporary marching camp outside Derventio before he was being woken to receive a messenger from the fort. 'Begging pardon, sir. Centurion Prax, the prefect's guard commander, gives you his compliments and asks if you'd join him in his office.'

'What, now?'

'Sir, he said it's mighty urgent, needs your help in a hurry he does.'

The officer stood rigidly to attention behind his large, beech desk. Mannius slumped into a chair opposite. 'What is this urgent problem you have, Centurion?'

'Sir, it's the prefect.' Mannius waved the man to sit down. 'He came back from his tour of our coastal units, had lunch with some guests then fell ill. He's barely conscious now. Knowing how you're one of the best physicians in these parts, I'd appreciate you sparing the time –'

Mannius followed the centurion to the prefect's suite of rooms. Rugs were spread out across the floor and deadened their footsteps. A medical orderly met them in the outer room and led them into a darkened chamber. The prefect was propped up on an expensive cot. His eyes were closed and he moaned quietly.

'He complained that his fingers and toes felt numb, then he was dizzy and couldn't stand so we put him in his bed, sir,' said the orderly.

'I'd hoped to introduce myself properly,' said Mannius to the prefect, who grunted an acknowledgement. He felt his forehead and then put his fingers on the prefect's wrist in order to sense the pulse.

'Has the prefect been suffering from any ailments recently?'

'No, sir. Fighting fit is our prefect,' replied Centurion Prax.

Mannius leaned over the patient and pulled back the eyelids and saw the man's pupils had become small pinpricks. Then he caught a peculiar odour on the man's breath.

'Feel so cold,' whispered the prefect.

'Did he eat anything unusual or did something not taste or smell right?'

'I'll ask the slaves,' said Prax.

'The wine, the wine,' said the prefect in faint tones. 'Smelt a bit musty but thought that was because it was good quality.'

'Was the wine musty or mousy?' said Mannius slowly.

'Mousy, yes, yes, mousy.'

'Orderly, we need to make the prefect vomit, quickly,' ordered Mannius.

The medic ran into the outer chamber, rummaged through his bag and returned, mixing a powder into a cup full of water. 'Please try and drink this, sir,' said Mannius as the orderly held the cup to his lips. Prax raced out of the rooms and soon returned with a large pot. At the first sign of convulsions Mannius and the orderly rolled the prefect onto his side and let him empty his stomach into the pot. After several minutes of retching he lay still.

'Try to get him to drink as much water as possible before he falls asleep,' said Mannius to the medic.

In the prefect's office, Centurion Prax had placed a silver jug on the desk. 'This is the wine they drank, sir.'

Mannius bent to smell the wine and quickly recoiled on instinct. 'Hemlock, Centurion. Someone laced this with poison.'

'Sir, the prefect?'

'There isn't an antidote. That's why we made him get rid of as much as possible. Now it's a fight only he can have against the poison. Depends how much he's had.' Mannius had been troubled since he'd stepped into the prefect's chamber. He felt as though something was missing. Then it hit him. A man such as the prefect usually had his family at his bedside willing him to recover. Often it seemed a better tonic than any medicine he could prescribe.

'Centurion, where is the prefect's wife?'

Prax cleared his throat, clearly buying time to think of his reply, unusual for an experienced centurion. 'Guest of the senator, sir.'

Mannius could tell there was more. 'Go on.'

'A week or so before you arrived he sent his men and insisted that she and her son join him in Eburacum. Said it would be safer.'

'Safer. For whom?' wondered Mannius.

'I'll round up the slaves and check the sentries' duty roster and start quizzing them to find out who put this in, sir.'

Mannius tried to find a reason for the prefect to be the target of a poison. 'What about his guests? You said that he had guests for lunch. Who were they?'

'Sir, a gentleman, the new governor.'

'Flavius!'

'And there was Lady Felicita and Princess Caoimhe, they was with them, sir.'

'Check on Lady Felicita,' ordered Mannius as he fled from the room, jumped onto his horse and galloped as though Aelred's warriors were chasing him to the Votadini encampment. Outside the royal tent he pulled hard on the reins and almost fell off. Bemused sentries half-tried to stop him.

'Princess Caoimhe!' he called out.

Another guard blocked his path. Behind him Mo looked on, checking the disturbance. 'You can't see her at the moment, she's taking an afternoon nap.'

'Mo, tell this man to get out of my way. The princess – she's been poisoned.'

The big, royal bodyguard nodded and Mannius was admitted to the princess' tent.

'What is all the commotion when I'm trying to sleep,' shouted Caoimhe. 'Oh, no one told me – where's my maid?' said the princess pushing her hair into place. 'Was the parade not to your liking?'

'Princess,' said Mannius, 'did you drink any of the wine when you had lunch with the prefect and his guest?'

'No, it makes me too sleepy if I drink wine at lunch.' A smile spread over the princess' face. 'Is this a ruse to get to see me?'

'Please, Princess, it's serious.'

'Never mind,' she sighed. 'Heaven knows that nasty, pinch-nosed little man wanted me to. Kept saying what a fine wine it was. "Why not try a little," he said. I left them to it. Why do you ask?'

'The prefect was poisoned with hemlock in the wine. I've just come from his bedside. I'm not sure if he'll live.'

* * *

Mannius walked with Caoimhe, through the wooden gate of the temporary marching camp to his tent. Reassuring smells of frying eggs and bacon, coupled with the ever-present hammering felt homely and made him relax. Eithne smiled at him, trying to ignore the princess.

'Please can we have two mugs of your wonderful mint,' asked Mannius, sitting down heavily on a camp chair. With hands shaking from fatigue he pulled at the straps holding his armour in place. Caoimhe knelt beside him and started to free the leather buckles and knots. Eithne returned with a tray on which two mugs steamed.

'Begging your pardon, ma'am, but please don't be getting dirty on my account. It don't seem right you doing my job,' said Eithne, taking the initiative and finishing the job that Caoimhe had begun. The two ladies swapped jobs and exchanged cold stares.

Outside the tent Mannius heard the murmur of a confused conversation with the sentries. 'Let them in,' shouted Mannius.

The commander of volunteers, who'd missed the victory parade, appeared, followed by the children. Their faces were dirty and expressionless. Tunics that looked as though they had once been expensive were torn and caked in mud. Exhaustion had long since taken each of the youngsters. None of them spoke, though a few shuffled listlessly.

'Sit down now,' said Mannius waving to the children, who collapsed gratefully onto the rugs at their feet. 'Double rations for you and your men. And make sure your lads keep this to themselves.'

Mannius waited for the man to leave then he turned to Eithne. 'Please can you find some clean Saxon clothes for the children. Take them to Leofric's camp, let them sleep then make sure they are properly washed and fed.' His servant seemed to need more encouragement. 'I want you to keep this from everyone. Believe me, Eithne, if I'm right they could be as important as us burning the Saxon ships. I'll brief Leofric as soon as I've had some rest.'

'Of course, sir,' said Eithne, beckoning to the children to follow her.

'I think something has changed in you,' said Caoimhe when the last of the children had left the tent. 'You set off an honest soldier to fight the Saxons and you've come back more, er, statesmanlike, with devious plans in your head.'

'Do you like the change?' A yawn almost followed his words.

'Oh I like everything.' The princess stood in front of him and he caught a scent of flowers. 'You know that Eithne protects you, stops people like me seeing you?'

'Of course, that's her job.'

'But she's not here now so she can't stop me this time.' Caoimhe put her arms around his neck, pulled herself towards him and kissed him hard on the lips, lingering in the embrace. Then she freed herself and skipped towards the door.

No sooner had she left than she returned. The look on her face said that she hadn't decided to carry on from where she'd left off. Behind her was Coel and Centurions Curtius and Laurentius. Mannius' heart sank. Another delegation.

Curtius waved a parchment and Laurentius looked as though he would explode with rage. 'The governor's disbanded us,' he exclaimed, hardly disguising his contempt.

'It's true enough,' said the older centurion. 'We're no longer authorised in the name of Rome to be officers and command men under arms in the province. What's more there'll be no more pay either.'

'It's a cheap trick to get us to flee,' said Laurentius. 'If

285

officers report to Londinium within the week they'll be reassigned and retain their status and privileges.'

Mannius could see a confused look on Curtius' face. The man had long service with the legions and would be looking forward to a good pension in a few years' time. Coel and Caoimhe had worried expressions. If the Roman officers left, their men would probably vanish and the grand army, such as it was, would be catastrophically weakened. They'd never be able to give battle to Aelred's men.

'The governor has unleashed his best weapon,' said Mannius, playing for time. 'He's trying to split our alliance and destroy our army. I'm not for going and I'll tell any of our men the same.' He was warming to his task and felt a surge of anger driving him. 'If we run now we let down our friends in this province. Some even have families here. For crying out loud: this is our home now! Anyone who wants to go can, but I want their wages paid back – they've all got two weeks' pay in advance.'

'On whose authority do we now fight, though?' asked Curtius.

Coel cleared his throat. 'This is rather humbling but the Brigantes regard me as their leader, well, king actually. If Rome no longer wants an army here then I'd be happy to give you formal status, starting with you, General Mannius.'

'King Coel, I accept your commission and so will most of my men.'

'We'll have to put it to them. New oaths, sir,' said Curtius.

'Don't tell them until after,' suggested Laurentius.

'No, it's not fair,' said Mannius. 'A man has a right to know who he's fighting for. Tell the men and let me know how many want to leave.'

Mannius fell into his cot, exhausted. He wondered how

much had been a dream. Had the princess really kissed him? Was he now working and fighting for Coel? When he reflected a little he'd probably always been fighting for Coel and the Votadini – well, Princess Caoimhe anyway.

# Chapter XLIII

Mannius felt that no sooner had he fallen asleep than Eithne was waking him, another mug of minted water in her hand. Outside a commotion was taking place, getting louder and heading his way. He got up and Eithne helped him into a fresh tunic.

'The children?' It was his first thought.

'General Leofric has seven girls looking after them and has them well guarded.'

She always gave Leofric the title of general, presumably to elevate his status above the other, Roman, officers. With recent events he probably deserved the title. The commotion finally exploded into his tent.

A sentry entered, tried to make introductions but had no time before a senior Votadini officer followed with an injured man held up by another. Mannius recognised the officer but didn't know him by name. 'Captain?'

'Ros, sir. Sir, it's the princess.'

Mannius felt his heart sink. He looked at the injured man with Ros.

'He's one of the guards Princess Caoimhe took with her.'

'When?'

'About three, four hours ago, sir.'

Mannius looked at the setting sun casting shadows on his tent and realised he'd been asleep too long.

'They were ambushed, sir.'

Mannius lowered himself into his chair, taking in the dried blood on the man's face, his dirty tunic and distant gaze. 'Give him a chair,' he ordered. 'Can you help us?'

'Sir, they caught us cold.'

'Who did?'

'About twenty riders and some on foot. Dressed ordinary, not in uniform but good fighters, sir.' The man's voice faded and Mannius passed him minted water. 'There was too many of them, sir. We tried. Mo killed five or six before they got him.'

'Did they take the princess?'

'Yes, sir. Dragged her horse away with them.'

'Where was this and which way did they go?' Mannius wanted to get answers faster than the man could speak.

'I don't rightly know, sir. I got hit a couple of times. North – I think.' The man shifted uncomfortably in the chair and blood started to pour from his thigh. Mannius cut the man's trouser and exposed an embedded arrowhead. He looked at the man's bloodshot eyes and saw that one pupil was larger than the other.

'Get a medic in here,' he ordered. 'Where did they attack?'

'We was just over a wooden bridge, near the farm lane that leads to the place where Lord Taran was took, sir.'

'Soon as he's patched up he can lead us to the spot, sir,' said Ros.

'No time for that,' said Mannius. 'He'd bleed to death if we took him and anyway he won't be able to ride with concussion.'

Galloping west up and out of the valley Mannius found himself, albeit unintentionally, once more in an allied group. In addition to the two squads of Roman cavalry, Leofric supplied four trackers, Ros brought ten men and Coel insisted that he take eight of the most sour-looking men he had ever seen. He'd promised him that they were extremely competent fighters. Taking in their lean, wolflike appearance and the assortment of scars they carried Mannius hoped they would remember whose side they were on when fighting started. And he was determined to fight. His blood boiled and he wanted revenge on those who would dare to take his allies. If he was honest to himself, he knew it was more, that he cared for the princess. Last time he'd seen her ... but that was a world away from the violence he now contemplated.

Lost in a black mood of dark thoughts he realised they'd turned off the road and were nearing the likely ambush site. With his mind better focused he slowed the column and let the trackers go on ahead. Looking around the neatly tended fields he realised that they were close to the villa where Taran had been taken. Had they tracked the princess from Derventio or laid in wait here, which seemed more likely? But how did they know to wait here? If they knew where Taran was then surely he would have been taken as well, he'd only had six guards, far less than the princess.

A whistle brought him back. One of the trackers waved for them to follow. The hooves of their horses thudded and echoed on the wooden beams of a bridge. At the other side, almost sitting against the top of the ditch that protected the road from the stream, eleven men lay in a neat row. Mannius reined in his horse and waved some of the other men past to take up defensive positions in and around the forest of beech trees that threatened to engulf the track.

'Sir, these men attacked them,' said one of Leofric's trackers.

'Saxon?' asked Mannius.

'Mercenaries, sir. Not our lot, recent arrivals I'd say.'

'Where are the Votadini?'

'Looks like they were taken away down a track ahead, sir.'

'Why?'

'So that they could be attended to properly as befits a Votadini warrior,' shouted a voice from a dark recess of the wood. 'And two wounded men are in the farmhouse. You need pay them no attention, they will not die from the wounds they received.'

Branches moved and bushes reluctantly gave way near the edge of the forest. Taran stood before them.

'You look well,' said Mannius.

'Maybe it is my constitution or maybe a good physician attended to me, though if he'd been better I might have healed more quickly and this wouldn't have happened.'

'I will pass on your gratitude to my colleague. Now where did they take the princess?'

'I would appreciate you sending some of your men to retrieve my horse. Then maybe they could find us something to eat and we can talk.'

'There is no time to talk. We are chasing.'

'My dear Tribune, you are chasing shadows with blown horses. Your horses need rest and we need time to think. For too long we have been reacting to our enemies' actions. Now we need to take the initiative.'

Mannius looked at the sweat on his horse and knew the old man was right. He dismounted and walked with Taran. 'You have a smug look on your face like you know something that I should but don't.'

'The wisest words I have heard from a Roman,' agreed Taran. 'Now tell me what you see.'

'Saxons.'

'Exactly! And the group with the princess headed north towards the gathering Saxon army.'

'So we must make haste to catch up with them before they get to Aelred.'

'No! You wouldn't treat a patient with such a cursory investigation.' Taran looked around him, seemingly exasperated. 'All the time I tell men to see the world as it is not as they think it is. These men were sent by Romans to make it look like Saxons.' Mannius was confused. 'In addition to a few pieces of silver and bronze, all the men had four gold coins each – Roman coins. Come here,' said Taran, taking the tribune's arm and pulling him to the edge of the forest. 'One of their horses broke a leg and died there.' Taran pulled back a hawthorn. 'It carries the brand of a legion. It is a Roman horse.'

'Maybe the men ambushed some travellers and took the gold and horses.' Mannius knew it was unlikely that such men would still have coins so evenly divided among themselves.

'No, they were given them this morning.'

'How can you be certain?'

'Because one of the attackers had the misfortune to be alive when I found him.' An evil grin spread across the old man's face. 'Couldn't stop him talking so I killed him. The raiding party was organised by Flavius.'

'Flavius!'

'You see, the name is familiar to you. Then we now have the advantage.'

'How so? They have the princess.'

'Flavius obviously wanted to pretend that Saxons had kidnapped Princess Caoimhe or at least get himself some time to prepare for his next move – maybe see what you would do. But we already know it was him and we can put pressure on him now.'

'But where have they taken her?'

'Two of my guards watched them from that hilltop,' said Taran, pointing along the track. 'About four miles north of here they turned west then south – they've gone to Eburacum or I'm not a druid. And that is exactly where we should go tomorrow.'

292

# Chapter XLIV

Roman scouts on the edge of the marshlands first spotted Saxon scouts fanning out. They waited and ambushed two groups before deciding to retreat in the face of growing enemy numbers. Their retreat west was cut off by another large group of Saxons so they headed north only to encounter Picts and more Saxons. Afraid they were surrounded the men waited until nightfall and swam with their horses across two shallow lakes. When they were certain that there were no more of the enemy around them they galloped to raise the alarm that the Saxon army was on the move.

King Aelred kicked his horse to follow the men of his escort. At the top of a large grassy hill he looked excitedly down onto the plain below. Small villages sat in the midst of neat fields that gave out onto pastures and woodland. This would soon be his to divide among his loyal captains. Slaves from the villages would tend his soon to be acquired animals and work in the fields. To the west, plains stretched away for miles to distant hills. But left and right the fields and woods seemed limitless. No wonder the Romans had guarded this land so well. Even when he'd heard of its wealth he dared not believe it. Now it was his.

A few miles distant he could see the scar of one of the famous, paved roads that traversed north-south. From on high it was also possible to see small tracks that curved this way and that around and between obstacles that appeared tiny from his viewpoint.

Banners and dust rose from an army marching south. No one could stop them now. Once those forces joined with his they would sweep any resistance away in a breath. He started his horse down the hill, past woods and through meadows, galloping towards the paved road and the forces of his son, Prince Wybert.


Under the stars, Aelred held court. Reclining on bearskin rugs he drank a strong wine to wash down a plate of beef. On his right sat Wybert, silent, brooding and reliable as always. Also around the large campfire, on their own rugs, were the Pictish leaders and Ceretic. His allies took the opportunity to gorge themselves on Aelred's offerings. Their own supplies had dwindled and recent, bitter experience taught them that the Romans had left nothing of use in the villages they abandoned. Worse, regular ambushes on roads back to their homelands deprived them of much needed supplies. Aelred's own men were eating the last fresh meat they would be allowed until new supplies could be found. The king ordered some supplies to be kept back for himself and senior officers but he wanted his men to be like hungry wolves, hunting down their enemies in order to properly fill their bellies.

'Tell me, Ceretic,' said Aelred. 'Have you fought many Romans yet?'

'We've had a few minor skirmishes with some of their auxiliaries and taken casualties but inflicted grievous losses on them.'

'So have we,' chimed in the Picts almost as one. 'We've faced regular legionaries with cavalry. Fortunately we were too strong for them and they retreated quickly after we killed twenty or thirty.'

'It is good to hear our allies have such an appetite for fighting and clearing this land of Roman scum and their lackeys, eh Wybert?'

'Very heartening, my lord.'

'Tell us of your battles, Wybert,' prompted Aelred.

'My Lord, there is little to tell as yet. We fought some stout warriors near one of their principal towns, a place called Din Eidyn. They fought and died bravely to give their children and womenfolk time to flee.' The matter of fact manner in which Wybert delivered his summary barely masked the confidence of the quietly spoken man. Everyone left a respectful pause. 'But so far the Romans have chosen to avoid battle.'

'Do you think many Romans will fight, King Aelred?' asked Ceretic.

'A few maybe. Those with money invested, crops planted or men who've sown their oats here,' answered Aelred, laughing at his own joke. 'But not many. My sources tell me that the governor has signed orders to disband the remaining units so they'll all stand down in the next few days. All we have to do is avoid them for that time and they won't even trouble us. Easy!' Aelred saw that the only one not drinking a toast to that line was Wybert.

After the meal Aelred took Wybert to one side. 'Are they really as cowardly and self-centred as they seem?'

'They will fight, my lord, if pushed. But don't expect any heroics or brilliance on the battlefield. Their enemies do not flee in dread.'

'I heard that the Picts fled when some Roman officer deployed a handful of cavalry and dressed a few locals as legionaries. And that Ceretic had cartfuls of silver stolen from him.'

'The stories are true, my lord. And they are both keen to take the silver mine about which they have heard rumours.'

'Then we'll let them.'

'But surely it's a trap?'

'Of course it is. A rumour designed to lure us to a battlefield of our enemy's choosing.'

'So why do we let them spring it, my lord?'

'Because our enemies will have to concentrate all their forces on the battle and that gives us the opportunity to smash them at once instead of spending months chasing them round this country that they know better than us. Second we need a route to Eburacum that avoids too much contact with the soon to be disbanded Roman legionaries. And finally we'll cheat the trap by snaring them!'

'Are you certain of their plan, my lord?'

'I even sent a decoy of my less useful men to make it appear we were trying to outflank them. My spies tell me that the men have been killed and that our enemies are moving their forces into the valley trap.' Aelred clapped his hands together. 'Soon, all this will be ours.'

Wybert superstitiously touched the iron of his sword to avert evil. 'And if there really is a silver mine?'

'Then we'll share it out with our new friends and let them go home. At least we won't have to worry about our northern border for a while that way.'

'It seems too easy, my lord.'

'That's because it is, Wybert. This land of sheep-shaggers has become soft, ready for plundering by real men. Good luck to you, lad.'

# Chapter XLV

Mannius and his column of men followed Taran to Eburacum. Before nightfall they were safely camped within sight of the outer walls of the town. Taran excused himself, took four guards and disappeared into the night. Mannius hoped that the druid's claim to have agents in the town was genuine – he knew they'd need every bit of help they could find.

Inside the governor's walled villa Galerius and his men were being treated to a party. Even Una, the servant girl, had been invited. The general nodded to Senator Antonius. Obviously the man had come to oversee the conclusion of the transaction personally. Better than leave it to the wimp Flavius, who only seemed to make war on women. Surely he didn't care about the children and the gold they'd received was hardly much for a wealthy man like Antonius. There must be something else.

'General Galerius, Flavius informs me of preparations for war being made by a young tribune, Mannius, I believe, together with an odd assortment of allies.'

'I have heard the same, sir.'

'Tell me, how long do you think this force will last? How long before King Aelred controls these lands?'

'Now that Aelred's on the move, they'll break and run in less than a day. Then Mannius'll be crawling back to the empire with his tail between his legs. He's nothing more than a quack doctor,' interjected Flavius.

'A quack who seems to have given you a good run for your money, Flavius. Even spoilt your poisoning plot – though I hear you got the wrong person,' retorted the senator testily. 'Now, General.'

'Very difficult to say, Senator. I never underestimate any man I meet in battle so the physician may have a few surprises and put in one good fight. Even so, Flavius may be right. The only thing that's for certain is that, if they stand, it'll be bloody, sir.'

'It'd be good if a few Romans go down fighting gloriously against the Saxon invaders. We must write him up as a hero; make the natives think we care enough about them to shed our blood,' said Antonius. 'Flavius, you ought to get Prefect Leonius to march out with some men just to make things look good. Like they're shadowing the Saxons, that sort of thing.'

'But the troops have been disbanded,' objected Flavius, slurring his words.

'A few coppers and they'll put on a parade for you,' said Antonius with a tone that concluded the matter.

Flavius had already drunk himself senseless. He'd tried to get close to Una but she'd unceremoniously pushed him away and he'd fallen over a low table. Galerius narrowed his eyes threateningly when he met his gaze, just after he'd rescued himself. Coward that the man was, he'd sloped off looking for easier pickings among the house slaves.

Little was said but even the senator was in a light mood, drinking with the rest of them. Finally the evening had concluded with a toast from Senator Antonius to Rome and its empire. Galerius felt a little flat. He'd been beaten. The men who'd sent him on his mission were celebrating but he couldn't. He drained another goblet of wine to ease the pain and saw that Una had hardly touched her drink.

'Not drinking tonight?' he asked. 'This is a fine, old wine.'

'General, I ain't used to drinking such fine wines and in this company. Besides I have to check on the young ones before I go to my own cot, which I think'll be soon, sir.'

'I think you're right,' said Galerius getting to his feet.

'Please don't leave on account of me, General.'

'I have had my fill of wine for one night.' He leant close to Una. 'And the company.' He rolled his eyes in the direction of the senator.

Una dozed on her cot, waiting for the last noises of the night to cease. Finally, the villa seemed to be silent, save for sentries occasionally patrolling the corridors. They would be easy to handle: as far as they were concerned she'd be attending to one of the children. She pulled on a light tunic and checked again. Only distant murmurs from the overcrowded town came through her window. Barefoot she stole along the corridor, and down to the floor below, where the important guests were housed. She knew the room.

From under the door came a weak, yellow light. She tapped gently and quickly slipped inside when it opened. The room was smaller than she'd anticipated but well furnished. A large bed, draped with silk sheets, dominated the room. A highly polished beechwood table held a half-written parchment, a jug of wine, several silver goblets and an oil lamp.

'The world is full of surprises,' said Galerius.

'I no longer need to worry about the children, they are asleep.'

'Their loss is my gain I hope.'

'And you looked so sad at the governor's party tonight,' she said, slowly unfastening her tunic.

299

'Among the hostages was my brother's youngest son. I would have taken the mission as I had been ordered but Antonius forced my brother to send him so that he had additional leverage on me. I have started a letter to apologise for my failure.'

She let her tunic fall. Naked before him, she pushed her body close to his and felt its muscularity beneath his thin tunic. 'Now I will have a drink with you.'

Galerius poured wine for both of them and handed her a goblet. Not backing off for a moment, she pushed him towards the bed and watched him nearly choke the cup down. When she'd undressed him she poured wine over him and made him wait as she licked it away. She knew his appetites and played to them, each time filling their goblets. Unlike the last time, the general fell asleep first. Fitfully he rested, watched over by Una. When he retched she was there with a pot. She mopped his brow and helped him back into his bed. Only in the grey, dawn light, when she was happy that he was in a natural sleep, did she tear up the letter to his brother and leave.

# Chapter XLVI

The young, gangly optio in charge of early morning traffic through the gate worked part-time on half pay – an economy measure introduced by Flavius. With a trumpet call at the barracks having signalled the start of the day's business he gave the order to pull out the huge, locking oak beam and open the double gates. Half asleep he did a double-take and then looked back into the town. For the last few weeks there had been hundreds of people queuing to get in and dozens waiting to leave. This morning there was no one.

'Where the hell is everyone?' he asked no one in particular.

'Bollocksed if I know, sir,' replied the squad leader.

'Riders!' came a shout from the lookout above the gate. 'Fifty plus.'

'Shit, maybe the Saxons got here faster than we thought,' said the optio. Suddenly he winced at the thought that he might be the one responsible for letting the enemy succeed with a surprise attack. 'Sound the alarm, call for the centurion and shut the bloody gates!'

The lookout smashed an iron bar against a triangle of metal suspended in front of him. Immediately the alarm was taken up by others along the wall. More triangles, bells and trumpets sounded across the town. Uniformed men spilled out of their barracks, still chewing what breakfast they'd been able to stuff into their mouths.

\*   \*   \*

'You said subtlety wasn't an option. That we couldn't sneak in and get her because she was too well guarded,' said Mannius, heading the column of horsemen followed by a cart. 'It seems that everyone will be out to greet us. I hope your people have got it right.'

'Excellent!' replied Taran. 'We need our men up and ready. The noise ought to get them out of the drinking houses. And I have every faith in Borgach, I trained her.'

The gate slowly opened and a perplexed centurion stood in the centre. 'Sir, you, er, startled our lookouts. Things seem a little different today.'

'Centurion Germanicus, isn't it?'

'Yes, Tribune.'

Taran looked at the man with a blank expression. 'Wife Aurelia and three kids living in the town.'

'How the devil?' started the centurion, who was joined by his young optio.

'Ah, Optio Paulus, yes?' said Mannius. The young officer nodded. Taran had chosen the gate well.

'Hopes to marry a local girl by the name of Mor,' added Taran. Both gate officers looked at the new arrivals, shocked and uncertain how to proceed.

'I am Tribune Mannius and I need men willing to fight for this land and their families,' said Mannius in a voice loud enough to be heard at the other side of the stone wall. 'Saxons have landed in force to the north and will come this way soon. I intend to intercept them with a grand army of legionaries, Brigantes, Votadini and Parisi.' Mannius could hear murmurs and saw more helmeted heads appear at the parapet. 'If we beat them you will have peace, if not then we will have given your families time to get to safety.'

'We need someone to kick the Saxons out,' came a lone shout from the wall.

'Give it to 'em, Tribune,' came an anonymous reply.

'The governor has stolen two things that I need before I can face the Saxons.' The gates had fully opened and Mannius saw more men listening to his words. 'Firstly, Princess Caoimhe of the Votadini was kidnapped and brought here. It is only fair that she is released to lead her people into the biggest battle they have ever faced.' Mannius saw that nods now accompanied the murmurs. He still wasn't sure that Senator Antonius had ordered Caoimhe's kidnap but he thought it likely as Flavius seemed too cowardly to do something like that on his own. 'And secondly,' he said, theatrically holding up two fingers to emphasise the count. 'The governor has stolen the taxes we have collected. Gold and silver that should have been used to pay our soldiers.' This time men around the gate grounded shields repeatedly on stone walkways and banged their short swords against the stonework.

Through the rising din Centurion Germanicus approached Mannius and saluted. 'Sir, it's right good to hear that someone's willing to put up a fight.'

'Then give me a fifty as an escort to the governor's villa and tell your men to pass the word.'

Mannius followed his infantry escort through crowded streets, accompanied by the odour of desperation: the fug of unwashed bodies mixed with stench from over-flowing drains. Frightened eyes tracked their progress, more in hope than expectation. To the rear of the column of riders he noticed another body of men, armed with bows and swords. Taran had smuggled in Votadini warriors. Feeling more confident he approached the villa and gave orders to create a cordon around the walled mansion.

While men got into position he walked his horse to Taran, who had dismounted and was deep in conversation with a woman in a hooded, black cape. 'This is Borgach,' announced Taran.

'And you must be the famous, healing tribune,' said the woman in a surprisingly powerful voice.

'Pleased to meet you, ma'am.'

'You will be when you see what they can do,' replied Borgach, waving her arm at two large pottery urns that stood next to the villa's gates. The woman nodded to three men. One of them casually walked close to the villa's high walls and emptied a bucket of oily pitch onto the urns that spilled onto the ground, then he retreated. The other two followed, pushing heavy cartwheels, with iron plates on one side, that they propped against the urns.

Taran nodded to Mannius, who walked his horse to the gate. 'You sentries there!' he shouted at heads that bobbed on the parapet at either side of the wooden gates. 'Open the gates!'

'Sorry, sir. We're not allowed on governor's orders,' came a polite reply.

'We wish you no harm but we will open the gates, so tell your men to stand back.' With that Mannius retreated, dismounted and gave his horse to a legionary. Taran had insisted that all the horses should be held down the road. 'I hope this works,' hissed Mannius as he crouched down with Taran in clear sight of the gates over a hundred paces away.

'Tribune, this is my most powerful magic. When I visited Londinium, a man from lands far to the east gave me the recipe in exchange for all the gold I possessed.' Taran nodded at an archer who had a fire arrow ready. 'Now you may decide if the trade was a fair one.'

The arrow flew into the oil and immediately flames leapt up onto the urns. A hissing sound followed, then a lot of smoke, and finally the urns exploded almost simultaneously. Eburacum was silent. Dust and smoke surrounded the gateway. A loud crash sounded nearby and Mannius saw one of the cartwheels land hard on the cobbled street. The smoke gradually disappeared on a gentle breeze. The timbers of the gate were gone. Small flames clung to huge, charred posts. Beyond the gates Mannius could see stunned-looking men. Some helped comrades who hadn't heeded the warning.

'Knock, knock,' said Taran. Grizzled warriors next to him simply whistled in amazement.

'Druid,' said Mannius, getting to his feet, 'that was real magic.' His horse was brought and he led thirty men into the courtyard.

Inside the villa, Senator Antonius was trying to ignore the new day. He'd heard the alarm earlier, then the trumpet informing soldiers to stand down from the alert. After that he'd drifted off until his personal slave had woken him to inform him that a column of Romans was approaching. Romans could wait so he'd turned over, feeling a little nauseous. Perhaps he'd overdone the celebrations last night. Suddenly there was a deafening roar and his bed shook. He heard men and women screaming, guards shouting orders and their nailed sandals ringing out on the stone corridors. A surge of adrenaline helped him to rise, pull on a tunic and go to the balcony overlooking the main courtyard.

In front of the senator were twenty of his guards, some of them covered in dust. To his left five men were being attended by medics. Beyond them, in a fog of smoke that was slowly thinning were Roman cavalry. He felt light-headed and steadied himself on the stone wall. Below, General Galerius was in uniform and had his two officers with him, swords drawn. Then Flavius appeared on his right and promptly puked on the tiled floor.

'Senator, you may have trouble seeing so I'll introduce

myself,' shouted the man leading the column of cavalry. 'I am Tribune Mannius.'

'Mannius, isn't he the one leading the army against the Saxons?' asked Antonius quietly.

'Yes, Senator,' replied Flavius, looking as though he might puke again at any moment.

'He's a hard man to ignore,' said Antonius, 'but I'm sure it's worth the fucking effort.'

'Gentlemen, I have something that you have misplaced.' The cavalry parted to reveal a cart with seven children on it. 'These children are Romans and were latterly held as hostages by the Saxon king, Aelred. I propose a trade – these seven for Princess Caoimhe as well as the wife and son of Prefect Artorius, who you hold here against their wills.'

'If Galerius had done his job properly he wouldn't have anything to bargain with,' moaned Antonius. He put his full weight against a stone column and steadied himself on a rail.

'Do you want him killed, Senator?' asked Flavius.

'Who?'

'General Galerius.'

'Of course not! If that happened who'd kill that bloody tribune? Flavius you've tried and failed. Look at you: a pup, puking for the empire.'

Dignity had long since left Flavius. He was on all fours, surrounded by vomit. 'Give them the tart and kill the tribune, he's the one at the centre of their army.'

'Bring them out,' ordered Antonius. 'General Galerius will supervise the exchange.' The effort had been too much for him. He knew he could not stand while he waited for the princess and the other sharp-tongued woman to be dragged from their rooms to Galerius. He fell into a chair, felt his stomach burn and hoped that the princess wouldn't keep them waiting. Must be losing track of time, he thought to himself. Galerius was holding the princess and Titus held the arm of Artorius' wife. Both men looked for approval to continue.

Antonius had a sudden surge of adrenaline. 'Wait!' he commanded. 'There will be no trade. General hold them, let the tribune slaughter the children if he wishes. Romans do not mind making sacrifices.'

Mannius let his horse wheel around. 'Senator Antonius, it is not surprising that Rome struggles to fight its enemies when it is so disrespectful to its allies, never mind its own children.' Behind him a wail went up from some of the children who had got off the cart. 'I now realise that the empire has been thoroughly corrupted by men like you. You may play dangerous games with your children but we will not. General, your servant may collect them,' he said, nodding towards Una.

Una skipped passed the double ranks of guards towards the youngsters and began to usher them into the villa's courtyard.

'Seize him!' yelled the governor. His men shuffled forward, javelins at the ready. But they soon slowed when dozens of archers and spearmen appeared behind the tribune.

Mannius turned his horse. 'Governor, you are not feeling yourself. Your mouth is probably tingling and your stomach has started to burn. Soon, if you can't already, you will not be able to do so much as lace your sandals.' The soldiers had halted their advance. 'Last night you all drank wine, laced with essence of monkshood. It is deadly if not treated with the antidote, which is very difficult to prepare correctly. Fortunately, I have a supply of the antidote, just outside the walls of the town. Do I have your attention?'

'Go on,' said the senator in a resigned, fading tone.

'I will leave with these prisoners and my men. We will not be molested on our departure. You may send General

307

Galerius and his servant to collect the antidote and I will give them instructions on how to administer it. Gentlemen, without it you will die painfully during the course of the afternoon.'

Antonius slumped back in his chair. He already felt terrible and, if he had to wait several more hours before death relieved him of his suffering, he wanted none of it. Bollocks to sacrifices – this was one he wouldn't make. Feebly he waved for Galerius to release the prisoners. Caoimhe ran past the soldiers and jumped onto the back of Mannius' horse.

Slaves brought two horses from the stables at the rear for Galerius and Una.

'Shall I have you executed as an agent?' he whispered to Una.

'An agent to some, a nurse to others but a lover only to one.'

'Hah, I wish I could believe it.'

'The first time you paid and I went with you because my master told me to. Last night was on account of I *wanted* to. Anyway, when did you guess?'

'I knew when I found my letter torn this morning that you were leaving me a message, though I had my suspicions from the start.'

'There is still hope. From the look on your face, your nephew wasn't among the children Mannius brought. But don't give up: we're still fighting and if your nephew's alive we'll find him.'

'That's what I guessed, and I admit there were certain compensations in having you around. Anyway you were good with the children.' Galerius kicked the flanks of his horse and set off to follow Mannius' column. 'The trick with the exploding gates was impressive.'

'It's his best and most powerful magic.'

'Ah, druid?'

'So he claims but he's just a wise old wizard, I think,' explained Una. Galerius chuckled. 'What's so funny?'

'My dear, it is the irony. Four centuries ago, when we Romans first arrived in this land we rid it of druids who were deemed to be an intolerable nuisance. It seems that they are alive and are kicking us out right at the end.'

'End?'

'Last night, while you were busy poisoning everyone, I heard that the governor has signed papers disbanding all Roman military forces based in Britannia with immediate effect. It seems that for the time being at least, Rome will not be the power in this land.'

Galerius kicked his horse into a trot and caught up with Mannius. Coel's men scraped swords out but Mannius waved them down. 'Well played Tribune, you showed true courage back there.'

'Thank you, General. It was a little nerve-racking, I don't mind admitting that.'

'I presume that Una gave me the antidote last night?'

'She did, against the wishes of Taran, I have to say. But we have to bend a little to accommodate our best people sometimes, don't we?'

'I am indebted to you for returning the children and I will give you this as part payment.' The general lowered his voice to a barely audible whisper. 'You have been betrayed, Tribune. The plans I took from one of your officers were safe with me. I didn't give them to Aelred but when I met him he knew that you have two thousand seven hundred Votadini, one thousand legionaries, three thousand Brigantes and that the silver mine is a ruse. He used the phrase that they'll have to go and take a *Trojan Horse*.'

'Thank you, General.'

Now Mannius was reeling, struggling to stay on his horse. Betrayed! He felt as though he'd been hit by a powerful drug. The antidote that Taran was carrying was made from deadly nightshade and was a poison in its own right. He felt like taking it.

'It wasn't me,' he heard Caoimhe whisper gently in his ear. 'And thank you for coming to rescue me.' He'd forgotten she was snuggled tight behind him. He leaned his head back and felt her cheek on his neck. No he'd find the traitor, give them the poison and watch them suffer as he'd had to suffer the torture of command over the last weeks.

'I know,' he replied. The Votadini wanted their own lands back and the princess knew that the Saxons had to be defeated first. Likewise, Coel and the Brigantes might not like Romans but they weren't about to settle old scores by ridding themselves of the only chance of protection from the Saxons – and hadn't Coel even tried to stop him going on the fireship raid in order to keep him alive and the alliance together? Thus, someone in his own camp, a Roman, had betrayed him.

Outside the town walls Mannius handed over the antidote. 'Do you want to come with us now?' he asked Una. She looked at Galerius and shook her head. 'Will she be safe?'

'I am the only one who knows what she really is. There's no fight between us now that my mission is finished. I'll see that no harm comes to her, you have my word on that.' Galerius offered his hand and Mannius took his wrist in a legionary grip before he turned his horse and headed off to find the traitor.

# Chapter XLVII

In his tent outside Derventio Mannius sat at a rickety camp desk, his head buried in his hands. Eithne quietly entered with a goblet of steaming water, infused with mint. They exchanged smiles. She knew when to talk and when to leave him alone. He needed to think, and quickly.

A guard could have overheard one snippet of information and passed it on. But Aelred seemed to have a much more comprehensive picture of the allies, from different sources, and of course there was the matter of Princess Caoimhe's ambush. Only a few people had access to all that knowledge – his senior officers. But the hardest thing to understand was that whoever was feeding information to his enemies was giving it to the Saxons *and* Flavius. Maybe there was more than one person.

What possible reason could Flavius and the senator have for wanting to kidnap Caoimhe? She was the recognised leader of an ally. They had made no apology and had hardly tried to disguise their involvement, which suggested a degree of recklessness. That meant they were either desperate or didn't care. Mannius lost himself in tortured ideas regarding motives, forgetting his warm drink. Each time he came back to the same conclusion: Flavius and the senator wanted to wreck the allied effort against the Saxons.

Galerius had had direct dealings with Aelred to secure the release of Roman children, and Una had told Taran that there was a dispute over gold owed by the Saxons. But surely the Romans should have been paying gold to release the hostages. Try as he might it made no sense.

All he could see was that some sort of deal had been done between the senator and Aelred's Saxons. Probably the general was merely a convenient conduit to see their transaction through. He had too many questions and not enough time to answer them all. His only conclusion was that he had to be careful.

Sentries outside snapped to attention. Eithne dashed in, looking flustered. 'Sir!'

'Please, don't make a fuss.' A confident, powerful voice followed her. 'This is simply a visit I couldn't put off.' Prefect Artorius strode into the tent followed by his wife and son. Mannius stood and offered them chairs. Eithne hovered in the doorway, uncertain what to do. 'I think we'll take a small glass of wine with you, Tribune, by way of celebration.'

'I'm glad to see that you've made a good recovery,' said Mannius.

'My strength is yet to fully return and I have a certain numbness in my toes but I'm grateful to be in this world. All down to your prompt actions and that's the first of our celebrations.' Eithne returned with jugs of water and wine. 'But most of all I shall be ever in your debt for the rescue of my wife and son.'

Artorius' wife rose from her seat, pulled out a circle of oak leaves and passed it to Mannius. 'Recognition of courage and valour above and beyond that to be expected. My only regret is that I wasn't there to witness the humiliation of those scheming shits myself.'

'Sir, my dear lady, this is very humbling and I think any right-minded officer would have done the same.'

'Take it and enjoy – you've earned it.'

In a respectful silence, Mannius handled the oak leaves as though they might fall apart. The corona civica was one of the highest honours for bravery and rarely awarded. His mind was so full of ideas and theories of betrayal that for a moment he wondered if this was another scheme to build him up into a hero so that he wouldn't leave. Then he looked at the prefect's moist eyes and tears running down the cheeks of his wife. Their thanks and the honour were genuine.

'Now, Tribune, we have some business to discuss.' His wife and son immediately rose to leave the tent. When they had gone the prefect moved close to Mannius. 'Flavius came to see me a couple of months ago because my men weren't collecting enough taxes. Truth be told we weren't because they weren't there to be had.'

A familiar laugh came singing its way into Mannius' tent. 'I thought there was a party on here,' said Coel, spying the jug of wine.

'This is the other reason Flavius visited me.' Artorius waved at Coel. 'The governor wanted me to arrest some of his people for standing up for others who couldn't afford to pay taxes. He said that this command wouldn't last much longer so I told him to piss off. Then the governor's men got my wife and son to go to Eburacum and kept them as *guests*. Rather than wait here to be told what to do I spent most of my time away from the fort. When Lord Coel came back from Ireland, his followers went west to join him and it seemed safe for me to return here. I admit I had heart failure when you turned up and started to dig in around the village but Lord Coel told me of your meeting with Flavius and he said you were a proper Roman officer.'

'Thank you for the reference,' said Mannius to Coel, who seemed to be the only one drinking wine.

'A word of warning,' said Artorius. 'When I wouldn't support him, Flavius tried to bribe and bully some of my officers into spying for him. I expect he'll try the same on you.'

The prefect's words sent a chill through Mannius. That was his problem exactly.

# Chapter XLVIII

Borgach's arrest was swift and unexpected. Sitting by the gate, talking with Centurion Germanicus, she watched the governor's personal guards march up to her. Without warning they kicked her several times. Three Votadini warriors drew swords and moved to help her, killing one of her assailants. But they were quickly overpowered and cut down where they stood. Her hands were bound and a rope tied round her neck that was used to drag her to the governor's villa. She was sure two of her ribs were cracked but it was impossible for her to check the injury.

When they reached the villa she was taken to a rear entrance and unceremoniously pushed down a flight of stone stairs. At the bottom she was picked up and then thrown into a tiny, windowless room. The rope was taken from her neck and her wrists fitted into rusting manacles that weighed her arms down. She watched blood ooze from her wrists, then heard the door slam shut. An iron bolt scraped across stone and she was trapped in darkness. Taran had warned her that this might happen but she had not believed him. She had felt strong, especially when she'd got the poison to Una. That had shown that she could beat the governor. Now, though, he had her. She realised that the soldiers hadn't even asked her anything, not even her name, and that frightened her.

The poison had left Antonius weak. Propped up in bed he felt as though his life force had gone, tumbling out of him like a waterfall in flood. Only now was it slowly beginning to return and warm his heart. Flavius sat at the senator's bedside.

'I want that man dead, you hear me, Flavius?' The old man's voice sounded odd, even to himself, coming in short rasps. 'The lot of them. If you can't bring them back for execution just kill the traitors where they stand. Can you do that for me?'

'Yes, sir,' replied the young man eagerly. 'I've put money up for information about the tribune's spies in town. So far two different informants have identified an old woman, who seems to have been at the centre of things. It will not be long before she starts to talk.'

'Good lad, you're learning at last. Make sure you flog all the slaves until they talk or die. One of them must know who put the wretched stuff into our wine.'

'I will, sir. I'll get the spies and their accomplices.'

'Let our men here track down spies in the city. You must chase that tribune. Hound the bastard, Flavius, *hound* him. He mustn't stand in our way any longer.'

'I understand, sir.'

'I hope you do, Flavius. I hope you do. There isn't much time left and I need to recover my strength. Now leave me.'


Una overheard some guards talking of Borgach's capture. They said that Flavius was bragging to anyone and everyone about the capture of one of Mannius' spies and that he was anxious to begin torturing her. To add drama, the number of sentries on duty was increased in case an attempt was made to free the woman. Una knew she had to move fast for Borgach and for herself.

She ran to Galerius' room. 'I need your help. A short time ago the governor's men arrested a woman. Soon

315

they will torture her and find out that she supplied the poison that found its way into their wine. Then they will come for me.'

'What would you have me do?'

'I need to get to Borgach.'

'I will not help you get to her. If I, or my men, try to release her there will be a fight and innocent Romans will die in order to release a spy. No, it is not possible.'

'I'm not asking to go free, General. All I want is for Borgach and me to die decently and not suffer the humiliation of torture. If I can get to her, I can help her on her way.'

'How?'

'This,' said Una, holding a small, stoppered bottle. 'It is enough to help her along life's cycle.'

'And you?'

'I'm done for and I'll not have you involved, you're a general after all. I've only got enough poison for one – it's what Borgach gave me in case I was caught.' Una gave a resigned laugh. 'I'd appreciate you finishing me clean like. That way you'll be in the clear, catching someone as is trying to help a spy. Please, General.'

'I won't hear of it.'

'I'm dead anyway. Soon as Flavius gets my name he'll be after me and you won't be able to stop him.'

'Run now, child, while there's a chance.'

'Can't, sir. Flavius has been round getting out more guards to stop everyone coming or going.'

Galerius grabbed Una and pulled her from his room. Soon he had found Titus and Primus and briefed them in low tones. Both men looked solemnly at Una as they heard the general's plan. But when their mission was outlined, they grinned and walked purposefully away.

'We'll go this way.' Una felt the general's powerful arms steering her away from his two centurions. 'When you hear a commotion, that will be your chance. Titus and Primus are good at picking fights and it'll take a while to subdue them. I'll give you a minute or so then I'll be along to break the fight up and arrest you.'

Una shook her head and smiled. 'Don't try to arrest me, General. They won't let you keep me. They'll feed me to the dogs if I'm lucky. The best thing you can do is send me on right after Borgach.' She flung her arms round his neck and kissed him hard on the lips. 'Thank you.'

The makeshift dungeon was at the side of the villa, under the stables. Una hid in an empty stable, shaking with fear. For the few moments that she waited time seemed to slow. The hay was fresh and reminded her of the first time Galerius found her, sleeping under a tree. She became aware of individual strands of straw being disturbed by small, grey mice. Their tiny claws grated on the stone flags as though they wore nailed sandals. Heavy footsteps pounded across the cobbles at the other side of the yard and brought her back to the present. Fear came seeping back into her as though it poured through her skin. Her fine tunic felt damp with perspiration and her heart pounded more than she thought possible.

Titus and Primus staggered into the yard. 'You three look pretty little sentries,' shouted Primus.

'Yeah,' added Titus, 'Pretty fucking ugly!'

'Piss off, yer drunk bums,' retorted one of the sentries.

'Ooh, look Titus, that faggot can talk as well as look pretty ugly.' Both men laughed.

'Bet none of 'em's ever been in a real fight.'

'Course they ain't been in a real fight, Titus. They're too pretty to have been in a fight.'

'Come 'ere an' I'll show you who's been in a fight, ye Jovian poofs,' said the sentry closest to them.

'What yer call me, boy?' said Titus, moving quickly into

the face of the speaking sentry. Before the man could reply Titus hit him with a hard uppercut that lifted him off his feet and knocked him unconscious. The other two guards dropped their spears and jumped at Titus and Primus, who each wrestled their opponent away from the door to the stable cellar.

Una took a deep breath and ran to the door, stepping over the prostrate sentry. Releasing the bolt on the door seemed to take too long. Her hands trembled and refused to grab the rusted metal. With both hands she freed it and pulled the door open. Ancient hinges squeaked in protest. A flight of stone steps was lit by five oil lanterns, each in its own recess in the wall. Una grabbed a lamp and set off down a low-ceilinged corridor.

'Borgach!' she called out as she went. No answer. Tears came streaming down her face as she feared that the woman who had looked after her as though she was her own mother had been moved. Then she heard chains clanking.

'In here, child.'

Una steadied herself and paused at a heavy door. A lock secured the retaining bolt. But set in the top of the door was a small observation window that opened outwards. 'Borgach, it's me, Una.'

'I know, and what are you doing here? They'll get you too if you're not careful. Now get out of here and save yourself. Do you hear?' Borgach's words reminded her of the times she'd scolded Una as a wayward child and brought more tears.

'Borgach, I'm so sorry. I can't get you out. We're both done for. I brought you this to help you,' she said, holding up the small bottle and lantern. 'It's the hemlock you gave me.'

'So you didn't think I could hold out under torture?'

'I couldn't.'

'My dear, you're smart and I love you for it. But what about you? What'll you do?'

'I can't get out. No one can. General Galerius has agreed to kill me clean and quick. It's best all round I reckon.'

'I think you're right, dear. At least we'll have the satisfaction of beating that governor and his lackeys one last time – eh?'

'That we will.' Tears and laughter mixed. Una gently handed the bottle to Borgach then held her hand and felt the old woman's lips kiss her fingers.

'Thank you, Una. Be strong. Now go to your general.'

Una ran up the stairs. Her lungs seemed unable to take air in but still she climbed out into the daylight. The unconscious sentry had woken and was pulling himself upright with the aid of the door jamb. Beyond him Una could see the general with his sword drawn. Then a thin, weaselly voice came to her – Flavius.

The sentry turned towards her and blocked her path to the general. She saw Galerius turn and answer the voice. His lips moved but she didn't hear anything. Panic gripped her. There was no escape. Only torture and death lay ahead. She lunged for the sentry's dagger only to be caught and rolled onto the stone steps, winded. Breathless she looked up to see what her fate would be.

'Hold her, you oafish fool!' bellowed Flavius to the sentry. 'You men help him and tie her hands, you idiots.' Flavius had six men with him. Three held her as though she had monstrous power. She felt her arms go numb where they gripped her.

Una pleaded with her eyes for Galerius to lunge at her with his sword and send her to the next world. Instead of the quick, burning sensation she wanted there was an emptiness of disappointment. Galerius bowed his head and quietly sheathed his sword. She knew it was impossible

319

for him and gave him a reassuring smile. Behind her, from the depths of the dungeon, came a piercing, frightening cackle.

'You men with me, quickly!' Flavius was giving orders, wanting to find out what had happened to his prisoner. She heard the men's nailed sandals crash down into the cellar. 'No! No! No!' yelled Flavius at the top of his voice. There was real pain in his tone and it brought a smile to Una's face.

The young man was crimson when he re-emerged. 'So once again the poisoner strikes. This time though we have her and even General Galerius can't protect you now, *spy*.' Flavius moved close enough to Una that she could see the veins in his eyes turning red as blood pumped in rage round his body. She spat at him and received a sharp slap in reply.

'I believe summary execution is in order for a spy, Flavius,' said Galerius. Una felt it was a gallant attempt to help her. She could expect nothing more.

Wild-eyed, Flavius looked at Gallerius but just managed to hold his bloodlust in check. 'Not so quick, General, please. This woman is my prisoner and she'd probably welcome such an end. In fact.' A wicked glint flashed in the young man's reddened eyes. 'As she's your servant then you are responsible for her actions.'

'As you say, not so quick.' Galerius' voice was unwavering and confident. Una imagined him commanding a lion to stop and it skidding to a dead halt. 'I brought her in as a prisoner, who helped look after the children. It was the senator who ordered us to take her out to look after the second lot of children. So she is the senator's responsibility. Perhaps you would like to take it up with him?'

Flavius' eyes narrowed. His body seemed to shake and when he spoke his anger made his voice tremble. 'The senator has nothing to do with this as you well know.

The only unfortunate thing is that the old woman is dead. She was their main link and would, no doubt, have yielded useful information. This little witch,' he said, pulling a handful of Una's hair that made her neck twist painfully. 'Is at the end of the line. A nothing. And as she's been with you for so long she'll have very little of use to tell us beyond what the old woman told her. But I might find a use for her yet.'

# Chapter XLIX

Mannius was developing a sixth sense for aggravation coming his way. His afternoon had started well. After a fine lunch with Coel they received a report on the army's current strength. Men had heard that the combined, allied army intended to make a stand against the Saxons and were volunteering to fight the invaders in surprising numbers. A familiar building of noise went from vague murmurs to shouts, then sentries snapped into action and finally Eithne as usual bustled out to see what the commotion was. Yes, something was coming his way. Instinctively, he stopped listening to Coel, thinking about the logistics of moving the army into the prepared defences and braced himself. On cue, Eithne appeared, concern etched on her face. Before she could say anything a young centurion begged leave to enter.

'Centurion Fabius, there seems to be some excitement outside. Have the Saxons arrived ahead of schedule?'

Coel contributed a brief laugh that helped ease the tension.

'Sir, we've got some legionaries wanting to see you. They're some of Flavius' men, say they ran off.'

'Now why would they run away from such a nice man?' Again Mannius' words were accompanied by a few rolls of laughter.

With his full armour on, watched by Coel, Mannius inspected eight men standing to attention in front of him. Fabius had already removed the men's weapons as a precaution. Silently he took in their clean-shaven looks.

They all looked in good physical condition. Their clothes and equipment were likewise in a very respectable state. Mannius moved behind the men, a trick he'd learnt when he was an optio under Curtius. The men didn't know which of them he was focusing on so each man had to assume it was him, adding to the stress of parading in front of a senior officer.

'Which one of you is the spokesman? Quickly now,' said Mannius.

'I, er, suppose that'll be me, sir,' said a big, tough-looking brute at the right-hand end of the line. The man barked his replies out, keeping his eyes facing forward.

'Centurion Fabius tells me that you have come to join us. Why?'

'Sir, we're Christians and want to stop them pagan Saxons taking over like.'

'Oh, so the Bishop of Rome sent you, did he?' Mannius concentrated on keeping his voice even. 'What makes you think that we need any more legionaries here?' Deliberately Mannius walked up and down the line, studying each man's body language.

'Sir, we've heard that the Saxons have a huge army that's ready to massacre everyone. That's why none of the prefects or the governor want to go out and fight them. You're the only one that's brave enough, sir.'

'So you want to come and fight with us and get massacred. Doesn't seem very smart to me.' Mannius saw one of the men in the middle of the line twitch.

'Sir, but –'

'Don't *sir but* me.' Mannius drew his sword and rested it on the shoulder of the man he'd seen twitch. This time the legionary seemed to shrink and beads of sweat formed on his neck. 'What makes you better informed than your officers as to where you should be placed to face the enemy? I think you're deserters. So you better have a damn good reason for disturbing my afternoon.' Off to one side he could see that Coel was enjoying the interrogation.

'Sir, it's Governor Flavius,' said the spokesman. 'The senator's told him to get the gold that he's hidden safe like and bring it to Eburacum ready to take it to Rome.'

'What gold are you talking about?'

'Sir, the taxes and such like. The collections that should've been paid to the army over the last months and haven't.'

There was a ring of truth in the man's tale. An ordinary legionary wouldn't be able to dream up a story as preposterous as a gold hoard. He'd expect to be laughed at as though he'd just told a fairytale. 'What's it to you what happens to the money?'

'Sir, it ain't right. It's money as should be used to defend us against the Saxons.'

'Very noble and generous sentiments. When and where is Governor Flavius expected to collect this hoard?'

'Sir, he's going tonight with only ten men to an old villa a half a mile north of the Eburacum-Derventio road, near Dunford. When he's got the gold I heard him say he's going to torch the village.'

'Thank you for the information, most enlightening. Centurion Fabius, ensure that these men are fed as a mark of our gratitude once they are securely manacled in the stockade, we don't want them wandering off again.' Mannius noticed that none of them objected – they expected such treatment. 'Except this one.' Mannius laid his sword on the twitching man. 'Take him to the druid.' The man shot an anxious look along the line and briefly at Mannius. He was the one who'd crack first.

Coel watched the men file out. 'I know Dunford. It's a small village but it's a trap.'

'Of course it's a trap. The men are all strong, fit and too well presented to be deserters. The gold story's nearly true but would you hide it in a village, away from your soldiers?' Coel's laugh started. 'At least we only said there was an old silver mine. The bugger's using our own story on us!' Mannius had to smile once Coel started his laugh. 'He was too exact with the number of men – he wouldn't know that, Flavius probably doesn't know even now.'

Coel brought his laugh under control. 'So he can go shove his gold in a dark place, eh?'

'There is a problem. A sinister threat to torch the village. We, or maybe just I, have to offer ourselves to Flavius or he'll kill the inhabitants – your people.'

'Right, I'm going to get some men and kick his shitty little arse.'

'Easy,' said Mannius raising a hand. 'Let's try and spring his trap for him.'

# Chapter L

King Aelred was becoming more and more frustrated at the ponderous progress of his army. Since leaving the marshes they seemed to have barely travelled any significant distance south. Every day brought more problems and supplies were running low – virtually exhausted if he was honest. The sooner they were in battle the better. Aelred's captains put the blame for the current day's lack of progress on the Picts. He needed to vent his anger and the Pictish brothers were a legitimate target for his diplomacy.

'We were both very disappointed at the lack of progress today,' said Drostan.

'Disappointed?' fumed Aelred. 'I was fucking appalled. Why weren't your carts moving faster?'

Drostan shrugged his shoulders. 'No horses. Without horses the carts can't be moved.'

'Your men ate the bloody horses, your men can pull the carts.'

'Picts don't pull carts,' said Drostan.

'Yes, Picts are warriors not beasts of burden,' agreed his brother.

'Perhaps you'd like to ask the Romans if they'd be so good as to lend you a few oxen, maybe? In case you hadn't realised, we haven't even got enough horses for the scouts so you'll have to get your men to pull the fucking carts. The faster they pull them the sooner we kill some Britons and take their horses. Understand?'

'That is not fair on our warriors; we demand more slaves,' protested Drostan.

'Fair?' spat Aelred, failing to control his temper. 'Of course it isn't bloody fair and it won't be fair when I shove my axe up some bugger's arse but I'll damn well do it if those carts don't get a move on.' He wished he'd brought his axe with him and he'd have happily used it on the two useless Picts in front of him. With no weapon to hand he stormed back to his tent.

'My lord,' started Hengis.

'I know, I know, food is running low and the men are starting to go hungry. Damn these Romans. When I catch the man responsible I'll banish my hunger by eating his heart.'

'My lord, Ceretic's supplies are getting through more regularly now. Not much, I believe, but enough for you and your senior captains.'

'Then tell him to share it around. After all it's Saxon blood that's helped secure his carts.'

'I have suggested such a course of action for the reasons you wisely outlined. But he is still reluctant to part with much.'

'That bloody, self-centred toad! From what I hear, I doubt he'll even fight. He's only here to make sure he gets his cut from the deal. Tell him to share the food out or I'll think about sharing his kingdom out.'

'Very good, my lord.'

# Chapter LI

Dark clouds and a strengthening breeze towards the end of the afternoon brought rain that became heavier. Light faded quickly and night seemed to be descending early. Mannius and a century of mounted infantry hurried to the village of Dunford from the east. A wind that had become a gale whistled into their faces. The tribune was anxious to use the last light of the day to survey the area. Hidden by a bushy hawthorn tree at the edge of a field of grazing sheep, in fading gloom, he could see why Flavius had chosen the villa. Situated on a small mound it overlooked the surrounding flat lands. At least the foul weather would help to conceal their approach.

Mannius sent a squad of cavalry to the north preventing any escape via the meadows and another squad covered the main track to the paved road. The infantry had dismounted and were with him in a hedgerow close to the villa. Only a few fields and a copse of horse chestnut trees separated them from their target. All they could do was wait for the signal from Coel.

Coel took a hundred of his warriors to the south of the road and into the round, thatched buildings of the village. His men were welcomed by the locals. Families squashed them into their homes. All shared the available food, which was mostly vegetable soup, thinned to accommodate unexpected guests, and ladled into the soldiers' own leather mugs. Coel talked with village elders and learned that Flavius had been through in the afternoon with over a hundred men. Those men were now somewhere between Coel and Mannius.

The villagers recognised Coel as a rightful lord of the Brigantes and were willing collaborators. Not that they needed any encouragement. There was a general, low regard for the governor in his failing to meet the Saxon threat. Worse though, due to the village's proximity to Eburacum it could not ignore the ever harsher demands for taxes, which had crippled Dunford and its neighbours. So without hesitation the villagers volunteered to guide Coel and his men close to the villa.

Ten young men from the village, armed with old axes, daggers and scythes, led Coel's men. Soon after leaving the animal pens of the village they split into two groups. Everyone stayed low, behind bushes and hedges. Closing on the villa, the guides dropped out of sight and Coel followed them into deep drainage ditches. Rain had filled them to the height of a man's knee and their banks comprised a sticky, black mud.

At first Coel resented his feet and legs getting wet. But he knew his men were getting closer and in safety. Soon he got used to the dampness and became aware of an unpleasant smell of decay. He was wondering how long they would have to splash through the muck when suddenly the villagers went still, then slowly they pulled themselves out of the water and lay flat against the mud bank of the ditch. Forgetting the dampness of the ditch Coel slithered up the bank and saw two men looking down the track to the road, with their backs to him.

He signalled to some of the men around him. Silently they rose from the ditch, clubbed the men and dragged them back. One of the men was unconscious but the other shook with fear. 'Find out where the rest of the guards are and send a man to let the tribune know that we're in position.'

*　*　*

Inside the villa Flavius was becoming edgy. None of his men had reported movement along the road. How long would he have to stay in the cold, deserted villa? The initial excitement of baiting the trap had worn away. He started to notice little things and they annoyed him. Like the smell of damp, flaking plaster.

Sitting on an old wooden box in a first-floor room he comforted himself that he was reasonably secure. The only downside was a constant draught round his legs and water running down the walls. Below him waited thirty Gaulish mercenaries that he and the senator had brought with them. Outside he had placed a century of men around the cobbled yard to hold Mannius when he arrived. Then cavalry in the stables would cut him off and men hidden in a copse of trees close by would crush him in the trap.

At least he had a warm riding cloak to pull round him that kept out the worst of the cold. His prisoner had no such luxury. At the other side of the large room, bound hand and foot, sat the young Votadini witch. He didn't trust the men below him not to be distracted or beguiled by her vicious tongue. So she sat and shivered in the room with him. He'd noticed the witch staring at him, trying to unsettle him. Well he'd shown her. Now she had a hood over her head.

The excitement and suspense had got to his bladder. Flavius walked over to the witch and relieved himself down the back of her tunic.

'Bastard!' spat Una. Then she recovered herself. 'Bottle gone has it, Flavius?'

'Don't worry, witch. Just like to piss on my enemies.'

'Did you only bring me here to use as a latrine?'

'You're my insurance, in case things get out of hand. Tribune Mannius might want his druid spy back, so it gives me another advantage over him.'

'You'll regret everything you've done in this world or the next.'

'Shut it, witch. You're dead in this world and they don't let druids into the next – so tough.'

'What makes you so sure that Tribune Mannius will bother coming here at all?' asked Una after a pause.

'He's greedy,' Flavius said with contempt oozing through his voice. 'He stayed in this province, holding himself out to be a physician, taking as much money and slaves as he could from simple people.'

'You judge him by your own miserable standards. You don't know your enemy at all do you?'

'Don't try my patience any further, witch.'

A long time passed with only the sound of the wind and rain breaking the silence. 'You can still surrender and I guarantee you fair treatment,' said Una, changing her tone to patient and sympathetic. 'Why not leave now while you can?'

'You are in no position to bargain so don't waste time talking about what you don't even know.' Flavius gave the woman a kick in her ribs and was satisfied by a grunt as a worthy acknowledgement of his efforts.

Mannius nodded to the messenger and ordered his men forward. Along the line men tested their swords and checked that their armour was silenced by strips of cloth tied on. Then they rose and moved into the driving rain.

'Sir, a lantern,' said a legionary tapping him on the shoulder and whispering. 'In the trees ahead.'

'Bit sloppy,' replied Mannius. Quickly he gave orders for the men to move in three units, himself leading the central body. Closing on the copse of trees he could see two men either side of a lantern. Fifty paces and still the men made no movement. Mannius drew his sword. At twenty paces he charged at the men. He saw their arms go up in surrender and held his sword at the neck of a young man.

'Begging pardon, sir,' the other man spoke. 'It's Centurion Germanicus – officer in charge of the East Gate Militia.' The man removed his helmet. 'I got my men covering me from that bush back there.'

'And they're being covered by my men either side of them.'

'Like I said to Governor Flavius, sir. We're good but we're no match for your lads and by the way we surrender to you.'

Mannius was still suspicious. 'The lantern was a little slack, Centurion.'

'Sir, what we wanted was to get you here before you ran into the trap set by Governor Flavius.'

'Why switch sides?'

'Sir, we ain't never been on his side. He's no intention of fighting Saxons. Had Paulus, my optio here, flogged and broken to the ranks on account of he was talking with the old Votadini woman he had arrested. Sir, we'd rather die fighting Saxons than Romans and that's the fact of it. We're one of the only centuries that stayed on after the governor disbanded the militia yesterday. When we heard that Flavius was marching to meet you we volunteered so as we could get to see you, sir. None of us is sharp in the head like you, sir. We couldn't pull your army together. But we've got the wit to see someone as could. And we'd be mighty happy to follow you, sir.'

Mannius sheathed his sword. The man's tone was genuine and he'd rather not start a fight in the woods if it could be avoided. 'If it comes to talking the Saxons to death I know who to call on, Centurion. Paulus, you are hereby reinstated as optio.'

'Yes, sir!' agreed Paulus.

'What other soldiers has he brought here?'

'There's another century at the back but they're like us, sir,' replied the centurion. 'If you give them the word they'll come over to us. Inside he's got thirty or so men – mercenaries from his own guard, all tough lads and they'll probably fight. In the stables there's a squad of cavalry ready to spring the trap.'

'OK, let's get to the other century before our friends on the other side of the field do and send some men to barricade the cavalry in the stables.'


'Flavius!' bellowed Mannius, standing in the cobbled yard, behind a double line of shields spread out in a semicircle. 'Time to come out and give yourself up.' Doors opened and several legionaries, swords drawn and shields raised, rushed out. More looked out through open windows. 'Hold your positions, men. Easy now.'

Torches flared in the yard. Taken by the wind they cast shadows this way and that. There was no attempt to disguise their presence. Mannius wanted the guards to see the overwhelming odds they faced. Behind a double line of shields men stood ready with javelins. 'Every doorway is blocked and your cavalry troopers are unable to help. Lay down your weapons and your lives will be spared. You may choose to return to Eburacum or follow us to fight Saxons. Don't give your lives away needlessly.'

Flavius appeared on a balcony, sheltered from the rain. 'Get him! Kill them! I said attack them, you scum!' He prowled behind the stone balustrade like a caged animal. 'What are you cowards waiting for?'

'They are waiting to find a good reason as to why they should die,' shouted back Mannius. 'And you, the traitor that you are, are not it. You are a coward.'

'You're the traitor round here. You even let natives arm themselves.'

'To defend themselves and help our armies.'

'You're not a true Roman. You've been bewitched by that druid. Kill him before he kills us all.'

No one moved. Silence gripped both sets of men. Only the rain carried on, hammering a tattoo on metal armour and wooden shields. Sweat broke out on Mannius' back. He felt the beads form into rivulets. His heart seemed ready to burst through his armour. Either that or it would force its way up and out of his throat. Suddenly there was a high-pitched laugh of a woman. Flavius tore himself away from the balcony, momentarily, and returned with a woman. He pulled off the hood and held Una out in front of him as though she were a shield.

'Tell your men to back away or I'll kill her,' shouted Flavius.

'If you, or any of your men, harm her then I promise that the death of those responsible will be prolonged and horrific. Surrender now and I guarantee that you will receive our best treatment.'

Another tense pause gripped those in the yard. Javelins twitched on both sides. Mannius' mouth was parched. A clang of metal sounded as an officer in the guards threw down his sword. Another clanged onto the cobbles. Then several were thrown down at once. Shields fell and the men facing Mannius gradually knelt down, hands on their heads.

Flavius pushed Una away and fled into the room behind. Immediately, Centurion Germanicus pushed his way through the guards, taking twenty men with him into the villa. Soon he returned with Flavius, his wrists bound, followed by Una.

# Chapter LII

'My dear King Aelred,' said Ceretic in his most confident and sickly tone. 'I'm so glad that you saw my ruse and sent your guards for me. It saved me having to find an excuse.'

'Excuse?' growled Aelred, looking at the pathetic man in front of him. His guards had kept Ceretic outside, waiting in the rain for twenty minutes until the downpour passed. Now the confident voice was clothed in wet rags and his long hair was plastered onto his face. That gave Aelred some satisfaction.

'Those disgusting Pict brothers are watching me; they don't trust me.'

'I'm not surprised, I don't trust you either,' grumbled Aelred. 'Why won't you share food with your allies?'

'As I said, keeping the supplies was a ruse to get to see you.' Ceretic wiped away rainwater that dripped down his face and was forming into a tiny river on his nose. 'And you will trust me when I tell you what those Picts are up to.'

'So go ahead, impress me.'

'Since before we joined up with you they've been plotting to cut you out of your fair share of land we're about to conquer. They're going to keep their men back, let yours do all the fighting and dying then they'll move in and steal it all from you.'

Aelred offered wine to his guest. 'And how do you know all this?'

'They told me so. Wanted me to join them, figured

they couldn't take you on by themselves, probably because they're cowards. They might even have a few more men on their way down to help.'

'When is this betrayal to take place?'

'Soon as you've wiped out the Romans that are set to fight us. They don't like them and their fighting ways.'

'I thank you for this information and the offer to share your food with my men. Goodnight to you, Ceretic.'

# Chapter LIII

Mannius' body craved rest: every muscle ached and he couldn't focus his thoughts. Eithne helped him out of his wet clothes and gave him a goblet of warm wine. Just as he was thinking of collapsing into his cot, Taran – unannounced as usual – entered the tent, almost running. Rain dripped off the druid's beard but there was a power burning in his eyes.

'I've found it, Tribune.'

'Yes?'

'The duty rosters that match with the delivery made by Coel's men – the men who drove the carts for Flavius.'

A sinking feeling gripped Mannius. There had always been more urgent demands on his time that prevented him from looking for the traitor in their midst. Distractions, unwelcome as they were, had always been better than the sordid prospect of hunting a traitor. He'd put Taran onto it and all too quickly the man seemed to have got a lead.

'When Coel's men passed through the Wall they weren't logged,' went on Taran.

Mannius knew that Roman military practice necessitated everything to be recorded and reported. 'Who was on duty?'

'Laurentius was the centurion in command. He appears to have let them through and not recorded their presence.'

Mannius sat down. He should have guessed Laurentius. The man was from a well-to-do family and had no ties in the province. He'd be ideal material for Flavius. If he didn't cooperate he'd no doubt ensure that his family suffered. Maybe Laurentius volunteered for the job to inform.

'How sure are you?'

'Too much of a coincidence. A group of six men escorting two carts – contents described as *trading items* – were recorded going into Coria that same day. The following day the same party, same names, were recorded going through Vindomora and Longovicium. Then they went through Vinovia and Morbium. After that the messengers I sent to look at the Legion's records can find no more sightings of them – and the next fort on their route would have been Cataractonium.'

'I dread to ask but from the look on your face I guess there's more?'

'Flavius was in Cataractonium for a few days around the men's time in the area – with twenty of his Gaulish mercenaries.'

'So you think someone, probably Flavius, wanted to keep quiet the source of the *trading items*.'

'Yes,' agreed Taran, hopping around the tent in his excitement. 'Then, to make sure, he had the men who knew where the carts had come from killed to stop them talking.'

'It's circumstantial – we can't be certain without some concrete evidence or a witness.'

'Actually, I had a little help. Knew where to look so to speak.' The druid shifted, uncomfortably. 'You were busy so I talked to some of the prisoners who wandered in here and pretended to be deserters. Two of them, independently, gave the same story – even gave similar descriptions of the men they helped kill. Said it wasn't them, of course, but they were there, and so was Flavius.'

'What of the prisoners you interrogated?'

'Oh they're both dead. Thought it best, otherwise Lord Coel would ask for a public execution and it would take time, effort, and would look bad killing Romans, even though they're mercenaries.'

'Very thoughtful. Did you tell the other prisoners how they died?'

'Said it was food poisoning – lot of it about recently.'

'We need to check the names on the list with Lord Coel.'

'Already have and they're his missing men.'

Mannius gave a deep sigh. The only objection was that Laurentius didn't have access to the exact troop numbers that had been given to Aelred. They were kept in the secure chest for which only he and Curtius had keys. He had a thought that left him cold: sometimes he gave Eithne the key to retrieve or store items. Had she given the information to Laurentius? Of course, she'd been jealous of Princess Caoimhe – maybe she'd been involved in her kidnap. He'd seen Laurentius give her a purse of coins – was that payment for information or was it the centurion's own bribe money he was getting her to store?

'Taran, this news troubles me and I need to think it through with a clear head. We will deal with the people involved first thing tomorrow.'

Drifting off to sleep, doubts started to form in Mannius' mind about Laurentius, then about his own judgement of Eithne. Finally his negative thoughts began to eat away at his confidence for dealing with everything and anything, including Saxons. How much had he missed? He wasn't a soldier, much less a senior officer. Maybe he should give in, run to southern Gaul and join his father. He could ask Caoimhe to go with him but she might see him as a coward. If he stayed, how could he hope to defeat a numerically superior enemy he knew nothing of? What was morale like in Aelred's army, its state of readiness, skill and number of seasoned warriors, as opposed to unwilling farmers or fishermen drafted in to swell numbers?

*   *   *

339

After a fitful night's sleep, Mannius woke to the sound of heavy rain on the roof of his tent. Eithne was already awake and immediately brought him minted water. His tunic and armour had been cleaned and were set out for him. He ate a breakfast of porridge, cheese and bread with Artorius, while a steady stream of officers brought in reports. Most of them concerned the number of men and amount of equipment that had been moved to the intended battle site and its state of preparedness. But near the end a cavalry officer entered and Mannius hung on every detail the man supplied. Saxon scouts had moved to within three days' march of the battle site. Some had moved east along the main unpaved track that skirted the moors to the north while others had ventured south using an ancient drovers' route on the western edge of the peat bogs. The bulk of the Saxon army had reached the north-west corner and had started to follow the scouts, but it was too early to tell which way the main force was going to move. Without any prompting Artorius volunteered to take a large patrol of his mounted infantry across the moors to investigate.

Inside the fort, Centurion Germanicus and Taran stood either side of the tribune. Coel had supplied a senior officer and four of his best warriors to provide security as Mannius realised he didn't know how far he could trust his own men.

Laurentius was ushered into the room and relieved of his weapons by a sentry. Mannius noted the bemused look on the man's face. Stood at the other side of the large, oak table the cocky, confidence that he usually had was absent – good. Always better to have men disorientated, that way it didn't give them time to think any lies through: sooner or later a fiction would break down.

'Centurion Laurentius, you are not under arrest but this is an inquiry into a serious matter and I need to put to you some difficult questions. Do you understand?'

Laurentius tried to speak and had to clear his throat. 'Yes, sir,' he replied, having recovered.

Mannius started with some innocuous questions regarding his recent duties, then went to the heart of the matter. 'Have you given details of our present troop numbers or plans to anyone outside our own cohort?'

'No, sir.' The man held Mannius' gaze and didn't flinch when he gave the answer.

'Have you any relationship with Governor Flavius?'

'No, sir. Can't stand the odious man, sir.'

'Have you any idea how information about our plans and number of men have reached King Aelred?'

'No, sir. Except –' Mannius felt his heart skip. Maybe the man was about to give a vital clue. 'We wanted him to find out about the silver mine so that he'd go there. Beyond that I haven't got a clue, unless he got my satchel of papers, sir. The one that was stolen from me.'

'No, those papers were recovered.' A feeling of disappointment mixed with a tinge of relief swept over Mannius. He'd have to keep going but the man looked and sounded innocent. Maybe Galerius was wrong. 'When you were duty officer on the morning of twenty-fifth April, did you allow a group of six men, escorting two carts to pass through the Wall without recording them?'

Laurentius frowned and for the first time let his gaze wander. 'Sir, is that the duty roster?' He pointed at a parchment on the table in front of Mannius. 'If I might borrow it, I might be able to refresh my mind a little.'

Mannius nodded and Taran pushed a parchment across the table, holding a finger near the date. Laurentius closed his eyes. 'I can remember,' a triumphant smile spread across his face. 'Only because it was when Macro got himself flogged for fighting. Centurion Curtius switched the duties round at the last minute. Said that he had to be in Coria for urgent business in the afternoon. Yes, I'm sure of it. And this writing looks like his optio's.'

'Thank you, Centurion. You may wait outside,' said Mannius. A sentry led him through a different door and, after a nod from Mannius, handed his weapons back to him. An urgent call went out for Curtius and his optio. Meanwhile the questions continued with Eithne.

The servant girl entered the room nervously and stood before a sentry who towered over her. 'He wants to know if you're armed, it's normal procedure,' said Mannius.

'What would I want to be armed for, sir, with all you big men here to look after me? Them Saxons don't stand a chance.'

Mannius could see the woman was nervous. 'Eithne, some secrets of ours have been passed to the Saxons. Do you know anything about that?'

'Some of our secrets, about you and me, sir?'

Mannius saw two of the guards bite their cheeks to stop a smirk. 'The number of soldiers we have and our plans have been passed to King Aelred. They were stored in the secure chest. Have you passed those plans to anyone or let anyone else look in the chest?'

'No, sir!' Eithne was at her indignant best when accused. Mannius had the feeling that she might explode and he'd need the guards to calm her down. 'Never let anyone into that chest, sir. More than my own life's worth. You told me, never lend the key to no one, so, I don't. Not even Centurion Curtius when he's forgotten his key. Should know better. Instead of yelling and bawling at all and sundry he should attend to important things, I say.'

Now Mannius found himself having to bite his cheek. The nervous, fast-talking woman was putting the gravity of the hearing in jeopardy. But there was an honesty and truth behind her words. Again he had mixed emotions: relief that she wasn't involved and regret at having suspected her.

'Do you know anything of Princess Caoimhe's kidnap? Did anyone you know inform her enemies that she was leaving the camp?'

'Sir, I don't know about that. I know she's soft on you, sir, and I don't think she's right for a grand man such as yourself. But I'd never do anything to harm her, sir. She's a bit too independent-minded, sir. I think you can do better than her, sir.'

Mannius was sure that one of the guards was shaking, trying to hold back a snigger. If Coel had been in the room he would have shaken it with his deep, laugh. 'Thank you, Eithne you may go now.'

'Thank you, sir. Will you be wanting lunch?'

The last semblance of decorum evaporated. Mannius too had to laugh at the absurdity of thinking Eithne would ever do anything to harm him. She would be one of the last to leave his side – even if the Saxons broke the rest of his army. He ordered a short break to compose himself.

'Optio, on twenty-fifth April, the day when Macro was flogged for fighting, did you allow through the Wall a group of six men, escorting two carts, without recording them?' asked Mannius.

'No, sir. Everyone was properly logged while I was on duty. But I do recall the fight, sir. I went to stop it.'

'So you weren't at the Wall the whole time?'

'Mostly, except for that time, sir.'

'And how long was that?'

'No more than half an hour or so, sir.'

'And who took over at the Wall during your absence?'

'Centurion Curtius, sir.'

343

Mannius waved the officer out and Taran whispered an observation. Circumstances were pointing towards the senior centurion. But he'd been sure about Laurentius. Most likely Galerius was wrong.

'I'll ask this to you straight, Centurion Curtius: have you passed information to the enemy?'

Curtius stood to attention, his eyes fixed on a point above and to the side of Mannius. 'No, sir,' he replied in the definite and business-like manner soldiers use to address superior officers when being questioned.

'Very well, did you pass information either directly or indirectly to Governor Flavius or Senator Antonius about our preparations to face the Saxons?'

'Sir, I only follow orders.'

'Did someone give you orders that included passing information? I'd rather not play games.'

'Yes, sir.'

'Who gave you those orders?'

'Praefectus Legionis Agens in Vice Legati Leonius, sir.'

Mannius noted the way Curtius gave the man his full title, perhaps out of military deference or in an attempt to intimidate him. As the most senior soldier in the province, Leonius should have been leading the resistance; he should have been in Mannius' place. But the former governor hadn't trusted Leonius. A hint of order suggested itself amid the chaos. He could forgive the man for keeping an eye on him, but who had passed the information to Aelred?

'Did you arrange for a fight to divert your optio and allow a group of six men, escorting two carts, to pass through the Wall without recording them?'

'Yes, sir.'

'The prefect's orders?'

344

'Yes, sir.'

So the prefect helped Flavius. That was why the extra troops, from his slightly junior colleague reported to Mannius directly: their commander didn't trust the other prefect not to intercept them.

'Did you intend or know that sensitive information about us and our allies would be passed to King Aelred?'

'Not as such, sir.' Briefly Curtius looked directly at Mannius and for the first time he saw cracks in the hard military façade of the older man. 'Prefect Leonius said it was important that he knew everything about our plans, sir. At first I thought he was just keeping a watchful eye on us.'

'But you had your doubts?'

'Sir, carts often get through the Wall unrecorded with a bribe so I thought nothing much of it. But when we met up with Lord Coel at his villa and Prefect Leonius wanted him arrested, I found out that the men had been murdered.'

'So why didn't you alert me to this?'

'Prefect Leonius came to me soon as he was in our camp and told me not to tell anyone. Said he and the governor were acting in the interest of the empire and if I wanted to keep a senior post and my pension then I'd have to play along. I'm sorry, sir.'

'You've let us down on this, Centurion. You may have put the lives of men who look up to you for reassurance and guidance at risk. I'm recommending that you be placed under arrest and sentence will be decided by King Coel, who is now the legitimate authority in this land. Take him away guards.'

Guards escorted Curtius out of the room and left Mannius with Taran. 'I was wondering why Prefect Leonius' men hadn't attacked or at least harried Aelred and now we know: he and Flavius seem to be on the side of the

Saxons. But I don't understand how that can be in the empire's interest.'

'Someone's playing games with us, Tribune,' said Taran. 'At least we know who our enemies are now.'

'Maybe not enemies, but they're certainly not friends,' concluded Mannius. 'At least with Flavius as our guest he might be able to help us get a better understanding.'

# Chapter LIV

Through driving wind and rain, Artorius forced his men across the moors. At first they followed established tracks that shepherds used to move their flocks onto high ground. Gradually the paths narrowed until only vague lines wound between small lakes. Seasoned scouts alone knew the way and all the men stayed close. Visibility on the tops was poor. Low clouds scuttled across, thick as fog. Losing the way would mean a long time searching for the route or worse. If men rode the wrong way, they and their horses could be sucked down into peaty, bottomless bogs.

Flat, featureless mud as it was, Artorius began to recognise the area. They were close to the old drovers' track that ran north-south down the western side of the moors. He knew that he and his men could safely move parallel to the track, sometimes barely a hundred paces away. Saxons, especially heavily armed men, couldn't hope to cross the boggy fields that stretched left and right of his position. Even if they did, any chase would be difficult as the route only allowed men and horses to move in a single file.

On sighting the track Artorius followed the scouts north, leaving a long gap to the rest of his men. They heard Saxons before they saw them. The Romans took their horses as close to the bogs as they dared and watched warriors marching three abreast. A westerly wind carried their guttural-sounding conversations and unwashed smells across the moor.

Artorius took his men further away from the track, risking losing some of them to the bogs. He needed to go north and see more of the convoy. Men drove javelins into the soft ground and tied pieces of cloth to them as markers for the return journey. Over an hour's careful detour brought them to a slight rise that overlooked a bend in the drovers' track.

More men marched with shields tied to their backs, swords and axes pushed into wide belts. Several carts followed, pulled by oxen and some by men. The heavy rain and hundreds of infantry ahead had turned the drovers' track into a muddy mire. Men strained to help the carts as they skidded and slithered along. In front of the carts men marched with banners and were followed by several finely armoured warriors on horseback. One of them appeared to snap orders and the others responded by galloping up and down the column. Artorius couldn't be certain but the man seemed to fit the description he'd heard of Aelred.

With a westerly wind in their faces, the range was too great for them to trouble the Saxons with their arrows. Artorius signalled to withdraw and sent a messenger back to Derventio. The rest of the Romans eased themselves away from their viewpoint and retraced their earlier route. Artorius had a particular place in mind where they might ambush the column. Even with their detours around dangerous pools, his men were well ahead of Aelred and his baggage train. They ate bread and dried beef while they waited.

The rain stopped and the clouds lifted a little. At last Artorius could see Saxons all along the track. Some carts appeared, rolling slowly towards them. The Romans made ready. Bow strings, kept dry inside tunics, were fitted and arrows held ready. Aelred came on, little more than a hundred paces away, albeit into the wind. Artorius held his sword high. 'Loose arrows!' he bellowed as he lowered his sword.

Fifty arrows arced towards Aelred. Taken by surprise, the Saxons had no time to deploy shields. Metal points bit into flesh. Yells of pain came across the moor. Two arrows hit Aelred's horse, which reared up in pain and threw the king onto the muddy track. A rider next to the king took an arrow in his chest and fell backwards. Arrows hit the other horses. Two of them bolted in panic-stricken pain towards the Romans. They were soon floundering in a boggy lake, though their heavily armed riders toppled from their saddles and disappeared first.

Another three volleys of arrows hit the infantry running to help their king. Men went down but enough managed to arrange a wall of shields in front of Aelred. Artorius ordered his men to switch targets. They moved along the convoy and sent several volleys towards the carts. Again men and animals went down. Carts crashed off the track and into the bog. Several lost wheels or had them broken under the strain of animals, in panic, pulling too hard across the vehicles. Men tried to restore order and were cut down.

Artorius saw the king encouraging men to wade into the lake to chase the Romans. A few held their shields in front as they stepped into the peaty mud. They were all quickly stuck and became targets for the Roman archers. Saxon shields began to face them in a more orderly line and Artorius called off the attack. Their stock of arrows was running low in any case.

Aelred fumed as he walked through the track's thick mud. Three men at either side held shields in case of another Roman attack. 'I want Hengis flogged. It was his fault the archers weren't spotted.'

'My lord, Hengis is dead. He took an arrow in his chest when he threw himself in front of you.'

349

'Good! At least we don't have to waste any energy on killing him ourselves. How far must I squelch through this bloody mud?'

'My lord, it is barely five miles to a section of firm ground. It is well protected from archers.'

'Five miles! And not a horse to be had for any man. This is a shambles. Tell me, what did we lose?'

'My lord, twenty-seven men dead, over forty wounded.'

'Yes, yes, but what of importance?'

'Eight horses, two oxen and three carts: two with provisions and the other with your tent, my lord.'

'My tent! Damn Hengis. This is a fucking disaster! Make sure another one is found for tonight.'

# Chapter LV

'General Galerius.' A thin, feeble voice came from the large bed. 'It seems that the idiotic pup, Flavius, has managed to get himself captured.'

'Trying to trap someone as clever as the tribune was always going to be dangerous, Senator.' Well done Mannius! Galerius felt the arrogant aristo deserved everything he got. He only hoped that Una had been saved in the operation.

'If Flavius hasn't had the decency to die then it won't take long for Mannius to find out our plans. He might even go after the gold. You will bring the gold here.'

'Once Aelred engages Mannius' forces it should be safe enough to move it, Senator.'

'Indeed it should. I also wish for you to meet with Aelred and insist that he hands over the final payment.'

'And releases the last of the hostages, Senator?'

A slave mopped Antonius' brow with a damp cloth. 'Yes, yes. The hostages as well. But make no mistake, General, the gold is vital; the hostages are only vanity. The gold will give us power to restore the fortunes of the empire.'

'I understand, Senator.' Galerius answered in the manner expected of career soldiers. He had never liked Antonius. Now in his lust for money and power he was prepared to sacrifice the lives of Roman children – his brother's son among them. Any respect he had left for the old man's determination evaporated. 'I will do my best.'

'See that it is good enough or I'll have the hides off

you and your men.' The old man relaxed back on the pillows. 'Then we can leave this wretched province and return to civilisation.'


Flavius had been in one of the dark, stone cells of Derventio fort for nearly a day. Chained, unwashed and hungry he would be getting desperate. Mannius was his first visitor and could see panic in the man's eyes.

'You said I would be treated fairly.'

'And as a murderer you have been fairly imprisoned and will be fairly punished.'

'Punished?'

'King Coel believes that you had several of his men murdered after they brought two carts from north of the Wall for you.'

'That was Senator Antonius. He told me to kill anyone who might know where the cargo was taken or who might suspect it was gold.'

'We will find out about that and everything else in due course, I am sure.' Mannius stood to one side of the door. 'Let me introduce you to two people who would like to talk with you.'

Flavius instantly recognised the woman. 'Not that witch-whore. Mannius, you promised me fair treatment.'

'No, I promised you our *best* treatment and these two are our best. In fact Taran here has been itching to introduce himself to you.' Mannius had no need to turn to see the hatred on the old druid's face – Flavius' reaction was sufficient. 'You see, it was his companion you imprisoned, mistreated and who died in your custody.'

Flavius' eyes went wide with fright. 'I didn't kill her!' he protested.

'Of course, I realise that but I don't think you'll have a lot of success convincing Taran of it. I'll leave you three to get acquainted shall I?' With that Mannius walked out of the cell and watched Taran and Una go to work.

'Strip him!'

'With pleasure,' said Una, stepping up to Flavius. She stopped in front of the shaking man and swung a fist at his face. Blood instantly oozed from a split lip. Then she pulled a dagger from inside her tunic and waved it, menacingly, in front of the prisoner. 'Hold him!' she ordered two guards. Once he had been sufficiently restrained she started to cut away at Flavius' fine tunic. Tugging at the fabric he was soon naked, save for a loincloth. 'We'll have to watch this one,' she said to Taran absently as she worked. 'He likes to piss on people.'

'Then we shall suspend him upside-down while we skin him, that way if he decides to relieve himself he'll be the first to taste it.'

Una smiled and put her sharp knife between his legs. 'Then it'll be safe to get rid of this,' she said, bringing the knife up to cut through the ties of the cloth.

'Mannius! Mannius! Get in here quick – I beg you! Don't leave me with these people. I'll tell you what you want to know. Just get them away from me.'

Mannius pulled a chair into the cell and sat opposite the shaking figure of Flavius, huddled under an old horse-blanket. A slave brought a tray with a plate of bread and two mugs of hot wine. Flavius grabbed at the food greedily.

'Best start at the beginning,' suggested Mannius.

Between cramming bread into his mouth and gulping wine, Flavius readily unloaded his story. 'Senator Antonius sold Britannia to Aelred in exchange for gold and a promise for his tribe and those of his brothers not to attack Rome's frontier along the Rhine for three years.'

'But he can't sell a whole province. It's not his to sell. He's not even the bloody emperor, for crying out loud!'

'He and the other powerful families, the *nobilitas*, see

themselves...' Flavius looked down at his feet. '*We* see ourselves as custodians of Rome. Even emperors only exist to make the empire work for the *nobilitas*. And if the *nobilitas* choose to sell a province then they can.' Flavius altered his tone, almost appealing to be understood. 'We are losing the war against Saxons on the Rhine – even parts of Gaul.'

'And Antonius wanted to take pressure off Rome's forces there, give them some time to regroup?'

'Exactly. The Rhine forces have been doubly depleted because the emperor has used them to fight Constantine's army as well as the Saxons.'

'But what of the forces here in this province?'

'Since Constantine declared himself emperor and stripped the best units from here to fight his cause against the justly appointed man there has been no effective army here. In fact the senator was surprised that the land hasn't already been invaded.'

'So the senator wants revenge as well?'

'No. He's too calculating for that. But he does want Eburacum to fall. That was where Constantine was declared emperor. If that falls to invaders then it will cause loss of face and hasten his demise.'

'The children?'

'The children were given as hostages to show the good faith in which Senator Antonius acted. They were all from the *nobilitas*, Rome's richest and most powerful families.'

'Good faith? What faith has the man got? Why betray us, here?' asked Mannius.

Flavius took a breath. 'Reality of money and politics. The province has become too expensive to control: Rome gets less tax than the funds it devotes to its defence. Politically cut off from the rest of the empire, it can't be controlled effectively. Hence, men like Constantine are able to set themselves up as rulers.'

Mannius contemplated what he'd heard. The logic was powerful and convincing – too much for a desperate man to fabricate. 'What of the gold?'

'There's gold from the Saxons and money raised through taxes, some of which should have been paid to the army here. There's more due from Aelred but I doubt we'll see that.'

'And whose money is it?'

'The senator says it's to pay for our army so that we can regroup and re-invade but I also know that he's lost at least two large estates in Gaul to Constantine and feels he's owed compensation from those responsible.'

'The people of Britannia who helped Constantine.'

'I'm afraid so.' Flavius looked into the flames of one of the torches fixed to the wall. 'I'm sure a lot of it will be put in the imperial coffers to pay for an army to invade in a few years' time. When the Rhine frontier has been secured Antonius believes it will be easy to re-invade Britannia. He thinks its people will welcome the Romans back after suffering at Saxon hands.'

'He's got it thought out and stitched up.'

'Almost, except for one thing. He didn't expect resistance to be organised against the Saxons as effectively as it seems to have been. Certainly, he didn't foresee your alliance.'

'From the lack of activity at our Cataractonium garrison to engage or ambush the enemy I presume Prefect Leonius is part of this conspiracy?'

'He's looking after the gold for the senator.'

'But why didn't he order units away from me at the start?'

'Part of Antonius' plan. He wanted some Roman units to put up a glorious defence. That way it would be politically easier to convince other Romans to support a re-invasion and the locals wouldn't think that Rome had abandoned them without a fight. Didn't think you'd get much support – suppose he was wrong there.' Flavius sighed, looking old and drawn. 'Like I said, he never thought you'd be successful. Still doesn't, actually.'

'So have we upset his deal with Aelred?'

'Not really. He expected to have to fight someone for the province. Our deal was to let him land unopposed and disband the regular units. With you forming an alliance and making a stand you've given him the chance to wipe out all those who oppose him at one stroke.'

'And he won't be squeamish about losing a few men – that way he won't have to share the spoils with so many.'

'What about General Galerius? What was his role in all this?'

'His orders were to create diversions on the coast to help the Saxons land their fleet, then to collect the hostages.'

'Seems odd for an old soldier to be helping an enemy.'

'He had no choice. Senator Antonius made sure that one of the hostages was related to him – his brother's youngest son.' Flavius spread his hands out, trying to pull Mannius into his trust. 'Look, Mannius, I can help you get the gold. You can have it all – use it to pay your men.'

The man had no honour. He was disgusting to Mannius. At every opportunity he would switch sides for his own benefit and protection.

# Chapter LVI

Artorius bounced into the tribune's tent towards early evening, eager to tell his news. Mannius, Coel and Princess Caoimhe stood round a table, poring over maps. Coel dutifully unleashed his deep, rumbling laugh and the other two smiled politely. There was an unusual tension in the air.

'I bring you humiliation of the opposing king and all I get are faces so glum I think you might be pheasants having been told that game pie is on the menu tonight.'

'The Tribune thinks that King Aelred is going to try to do to us what we did to Flavius,' said Coel by way of explanation.

'He's going to spring the trap on us. With his forces split he can bottle us up in the valley,' added Mannius.

'I thought that you said we foiled an attempt to outflank us by smashing the invasion that took place,' objected Coel.

'It was a ruse,' said Mannius. 'Plain and simple. With us feeling secure in the south we'd move our forces into the valley. It's too dangerous to be in the valley – he'll block us in, grind us down and squeeze us like a pimple. And there's no way out for an army.'

'I saw Aelred today and he was marching through mud with his army on the drovers' road in the west,' said Artorius.

'So it seems likely the flanking force is the main strength.'

'All right, so the Saxons aren't going to play our game,' said Coel. 'But you knew they wouldn't, didn't you?'

357

Coel's usual charm had vanished; even Caoimhe looked shocked.

'Not at first, not until I thought about our victory against the few hundred Saxons the other day. You and I would have landed a bigger force, with better soldiers. The ones we faced were poorly trained, badly equipped and there was nothing in the way of leadership.' Mannius sighed, weary of trying to hold the alliance together; weary of guessing what Aelred was going to do next; weary of looking over his shoulder for traitors. 'Even without Taran's skills, my men found out that beyond landing and making a nuisance of themselves they had no real orders.'

'You mean they were sacrificed by Aelred,' said Caoimhe, shock on her face. 'Just to make us think we'd stopped his manoeuvre?'

'Exactly,' replied Mannius. 'I figure Aelred to be a vicious thug but I doubt he's a fool. He knows how to make war well enough.'

'You don't seem too surprised at Aelred's plan,' said Coel, in an accusatory tone. 'He outflanks our army, meanwhile, our trusted tribune outmanoeuvres us by getting our men working on defences that he never intended to use.' There was no disguising bitterness in his voice. 'You've had us on a fool's errand, digging trenches, building walls and practising drills, knowing that we'd never put them to use.'

Mannius held up his hand. 'The plan has gathered us all here with a common purpose. I admit that I had my doubts when I arrived and I've always suspected that Derventio would be his target come what may.'

'And how did you divine that? Did Taran look into a pile of ashes?' asked Coel.

'Practical necessity. It's the regional centre – well connected with coastal villages as well as Eburacum,' answered Mannius. 'It would give him a way to get reinforcements and, of course, its granaries are well stocked. Leofric's men have been making a nuisance of themselves; setting ambushes for Aelred's scouts and foraging parties. His men are searching further and further for food: the prisoners we've taken tell us they're getting desperate. And anyway, he couldn't lay siege to Eburacum without securing this place first for fear of us striking at him.'

'Why didn't you tell us this before?' asked Caoimhe, trying to keep an even tone.

'Because there are too many spies in the camp. Aelred already knows too much about us. Please,' said Mannius holding up his hands. 'I trust you all but somehow word would have got out.'

Artorius was the only one who smiled. Finally he moved to assist. 'So now we have the initiative over our enemy. He thinks that we're going to deploy our men into the trap and let him squash us. This'll unsettle him, make him think again; alter his schedule. His men will go without food for an extra day or so. And our men have been occupied, working together. Couldn't have done better myself – well done, Tribune.'

'I'm sorry. I tried my best; it was all I could think of,' said Mannius apologetically. 'I know you and your men have worked hard on the defences but we can't fight them in the valley on both fronts.'

'Of course we can't,' agreed Artorius. 'He'd trap us there while his main force marched on Derventio.' His voice carried authority but also enthusiasm for the task at hand. 'Have any of our senior officers had experience of fighting Saxon armies rather than raiders?'

Mannius knew the answer. 'The only one is my senior centurion but we arrested him this morning for giving away our secrets to Flavius, who passed them on to Aelred.'

'But he didn't give information to the enemy himself,' said Artorius. 'He really only followed orders.'

'No, but he had a hand in letting Flavius know where and when Princess Caoimhe was riding so that she could be kidnapped.'

'Princess,' said Artorius in a serious tone, 'Do you want this centurion to be punished for your kidnap?'

'I know where you're going with this,' said Caoimhe, turning away. She spun round to face them. 'No I don't. Like you said, he passed information to other Roman army units. It is their commander who should be punished.' She threw her head back: red curls bounced across her face and down her shoulders giving her an air of sensuous energy. Her face brightened and she laughed, 'And it was fun seeing them retching with the poison.'

'Are you willing to have the man back under your command, Mannius?' went on Artorius.

'Put like that there's no option,' replied Mannius.


Curtius was brought before the leaders, his wrists in manacles. 'Please remove those chains,' said Mannius to the accompanying guard. 'It seems that we may be able to do a deal. You passed information of a sensitive nature to other Roman army units that may be harmful to us. In any event it led to the kidnap of Princess Caoimhe. However, given the situation we find ourselves in, the princess has generously offered to forgive your part in her unfortunate experience. You will be free to resume your duties with no mark on your record if you are able to guarantee your wholehearted support to this army. Have we a deal, Centurion?'

'Sorry for being a nuisance, sir. Won't happen again. I'd like to help the lads best I can fight the Saxons and such if I'm allowed. Thank you, sir – Princess.'

'Good! Now, can you find Centurion Curtius' sword please,' finished Artorius, once again injecting optimism into the gathering. 'You've fought Saxons before, Centurion. How do you think they'll fight?'

Curtius paused, collecting his thoughts. 'Yes sir, campaigning in the Rhineland. Their strength is usually twofold: a strong shield wall and some of their best fighters in the middle was always the foundation of their attack. They'll try to break through our lines at the centre and open a way up for their very best warriors to get behind our men.'

'No flanking cavalry?'

'Not usually, sir.'

'Especially in this case,' added Mannius. 'It'll have been hard for them to get men here never mind horses.'

'And they don't usually have many archers, sir,' went on Curtius. 'They just rely on the skill of their warriors in a mêlée – their double war-axes are formidable weapons if they get the chance to swing them. If our men break formation they'll be massacred.'

'So bottling Aelred and his men up in a tight valley might even play into their hands.'

'It certainly would, sir, if we lose the initiative. Once formations break and there's no chance of cavalry pushing their men into tight units that can be targeted by our missile attacks.'

'How would you fight them, Centurion?' asked Coel.

'Break their shield wall on our own terms so that we can take their formations apart before they have a chance to use their mêlée skills.'

'But we can't fight them on the open plain – they outnumber us by, perhaps, five to one. They'd simply outflank and surround us,' said Coel.

'True, so we need a battlefield that gives us the best of both worlds,' answered Curtius.

'You have something in mind?'

Curtius smiled. 'They are poor at sieges but it's too

late to build new walls. We could strengthen these marching camps, put ballistae in them and dig one directly in front of the bridge. Put archers and our least skilful men in the camps and use them like forts. When the Saxons attack, their shield wall will be broken naturally and we could use our heavy infantry between the forts without risk of getting flanked.'

'Of course!' mumbled Mannius. 'Cannae.'

His outburst was met with blank looks. He cleared his throat and started to clarify his musings. It's part of our history – the battle of Cannae: Hannibal deceived a massed Roman army, far more powerful than his Carthaginians, to press forward into a trap. The camps will trap the Saxons, preventing them from making best use of their greater numbers – it'll be our Cannae.'

'Do you know, Centurion,' said Artorius. 'Not only have you won your freedom tonight but you may have got yourself promoted to general!'

# Chapter LVII

Mannius waited, respectfully while the slave announced his presence before he entered the private quarters. Silk drapes, Persian rugs, expensive furniture and intoxicating scents indicated that his aunt had settled into her *frugal* quarters.

'My dear Mannius. This is simply wretched of you. Why didn't you tell me that you were coming to visit? I am so ill-prepared.' Felicita waved to her slave to bring wine and checked her hair. 'And it is doubly wretched of you not to come and see me sooner, leaving me all alone with these terribly dull people.'

'Your safety is my prime concern, Aunt Felicita.'

'Always so prim and proper. I'm flattered anyway. Now, you must tell me what's happening – there's just no one to talk with here. I'm simply starved of news.' Felicita perched herself on a high chair with her back straight and hands clasped on her lap. Her large, dark eyes, emphasised with careful make-up, locked on to him as though she were a little girl about to receive a lecture.

'The army is about to move to its forward positions, in a valley on the plateau to block Aelred's progress. It's our best option but I'm afraid it's also desperate. It'll leave the town poorly defended so I think it best if you and your slaves go to Eburacum. Senator Antonius is still there with some of his own guards, I'm sure you'll be safe with him.'

'And Governor Flavius, what has become of him?' Felicita seemed to almost sing her words. She had a dangerous voice: it could soothe and enthuse a man. No doubt, thought Mannius, it could kill a man by breaking his heart. 'I heard he had become your prisoner.'

'True, but he is unwell, too weak to travel.'

'Oh, my dear,' said Felicita, worry on her face. 'You haven't tortured the poor soul have you?'

Mannius wondered how much of this was genuine concern and how much for show. 'Since we captured him his health has waned for no discernible reason. Now he refuses food. He seems to have lost the will to live – in fact his gaolers are convinced he's gone mad: talking to pieces of furniture in his room like they're people.'

'Such a shame for a young man,' said Felicita, looking comforted that he had gone mad of his own accord rather than being pushed by common gaolers. 'Still, there's no telling what the stresses of leadership do to a man. But look at you. I do believe you have grown taller since I last saw you, much more distinguished. Your uncle would be proud of you.' A glint shone in Felicita's eyes as though a shooting star had crossed her face. For an instant Mannius thought he saw anger and readied himself. But the moment passed faster than it had come. 'I can't possibly leave you. My place should be with you, Mannius.'

'I accepted your challenge to protect you and, reluctantly, I must now pass that on to a luckier man than I.'

'I feel flushed,' said Felicita, feeling her face with her palms to stress the point. 'Flushed by your flattery. Must I really leave?'

'I'm afraid I have to insist for your own good. Some of the senator's men are here as our prisoners. I have arranged for their release so that they can act as your escort.'

Felicita jumped up and took Mannius in tight embrace, forcing her lips hard onto his. Her perfume wrapped itself around him and her firm body, tight against his, reminded him of sensual pleasures he had not had time to sample in recent days.

'Come with me, Mannius,' implored Felicita with moist eyes. 'This isn't your fight.'

Mannius wondered whether the anger was at the prospect of their imminent parting. 'It is now. I am part of these people.'


'So the whelp is going to make a stand?' said Senator Antonius to his latest house guest.

'I tried to talk him out of it but his mind is set,' replied Felicita, reclining naked on the senator's bed and playing with a silver wine goblet.

Dressed in a modest white tunic the senator worked at a small rosewood desk. 'Glad you didn't. Would have made Aelred's campaign much longer. That would have upset our plans some.' Antonius scratched at a series of parchments. 'My final orders for this province, then I'm free of this place.' He put down his quill, squared it off parallel to the desk side, then did likewise with other writing equipment that was laid out. He stood back to survey his efforts. After making two small alterations he slowly left the desk, happy with its appearance. Only then did he retrieve his own goblet and gulp at the warm and reassuringly expensive wine. He called a slave to refill their goblets and take his written orders.

'You always reminded me of that statue of Aphrodite done by one of those fancy Greek sculptors: so beautiful yet so aloof.'

'That didn't stop you from getting close though did it, Antonius?'

'And it won't stop me this time either,' replied the senator, removing his tunic, carefully folding it and placing it on a chair. 'I seem to have found an urge to enjoy my freedom.'

Three riders were escorted past sentries on picket duty and through the Saxon camp to King Aelred. 'You have some neck, coming here, General.'

'I have given my word and I am duty bound.'

'Even if it means giving your life away?' asked Aelred.

'Dying in battle is a soldier's privilege.'

'It is good to find men who still follow their word. Too many men alter their allegiance according to the way the wind blows.'

'I have never hidden from a gale.'

'I can believe your words and, therefore, I trust them. You are not like the other cowards in this country who hide themselves away, afraid of battle, while me and my men march all over it.'

'I have no knowledge of their plans.'

'Very well,' said Aelred in a weary tone. 'What is it you want?'

'The remaining hostages and payment as agreed.'

Aelred laughed. 'You are in luck: the rain that is so attracted to this miserable land, has ceased and I find myself in good heart. Today I was attacked by Roman archers, lost my tent, made to trudge miles through mud after they killed my horse and I face an army in order to get what I want. And you ask for payment.'

'The army you face is not Roman, it is men who live here fighting for their land.'

'I understand and respect them for that. But they are nothing. I know everything about them and that even now they are moving their army into a valley where it will perish.'

'Your spies are better informed than mine,' said Galerius, looking to flatter the ego in front of him.

'General, like you, I am a man of my word. I will give the gold and hostages to you *after* I have defeated this army and my men control Eburacum. Not before!'

# Chapter LVIII

Around Derventio soldiers, slaves, men and women worked at a feverish pace. Under the guidance of engineers, forts with earth walls and wooden palisades were being constructed around the village. An arc of four forts, each a thousand feet from the other, ran from a river in the north to a paved road leading west. Inside the arc, another fort was sited to support the village's weak east wall.

Officers ensured that artillery and archers in the strongholds and main fort were able to cover gaps between the recently strengthened defensive positions. If the enemy could be lured into the killing zones the defenders would have a chance.

Wooden stakes that had been readied for the ambush near the old mine were brought to Derventio and hammered into position. Trenches were dug to break up the movement and momentum of men, pits were sunk for oil and deep traps with sharpened stakes in their depths were fashioned around the outer forts. Within each fort, platforms were erected to take artillery pieces and stockpiles were made of arrows, javelins, spare weapons, food and water.

Mannius and Coel inspected the defences, checking angles and killing areas. From their vantage point on one of the towers of the outer fort they could see the swollen river that ran in a wide semicircle around lands that surrounded the town. Water still poured in great torrents off the peaty plateau. 'We could slow them down, kill a few at the bridge if we barricaded it,' suggested Coel. 'It'd slow them up maybe half a day or so.'

'Make them even hungrier?' asked Mannius. 'It'd be risky for the troops concerned,' he objected pleasantly. He wanted Coel to take charge of part of the defence and reassert his authority. It would get him back into the spirit of the alliance again. 'Anyone on the bridge could be surrounded then slaughtered.'

'That river's as high as I've ever known and will take some crossing if we make it difficult. They've got to use the old stone bridge for the bulk of their men and baggage.'

'We can't ask any of our men to perform suicidal missions.'

'Why not?' protested Coel. 'It's going to be damn near suicidal staying here. All that happens is those on the bridge die a little earlier. Anyway, the marsh ground at either side of the bridge will stop any flanking move being swift. If Saxons want to wade through mud they'll make good targets for archers.'

'If we split our forces into small units that can't support each other then we'll die. I've no doubt of that.' Coel went quiet as though in a sulk. Mannius didn't want to lose him at this difficult time. 'However, if those men had a reasonable chance of getting back, then it might be different – eh?'

'Artorius' horse-mounted infantry, Votadini archers who can ride and a few cavalry to cover the flanks?'


Mannius walked with Caoimhe along the outer perimeter of the new forts and stopped at a point overlooking a makeshift altar, tended by a priest. Men and women stood in an orderly queue waiting to speak with the holy man.

A few final rays of red sunlight filtered through dark rain clouds. 'It'll rain soon – during the night,' pronounced the princess.

369

'It'll make fighting hard in the mud,' answered Mannius as he tried to gauge how the enemy would view the defences.

'You think they'll attack soon, don't you?' Caoimhe pulled her cloak tight around her neck, still looking at the priest giving out blessings.

'Yes, Leofric's been tracking Aelred and his army's close. Besides they're starving and can't afford to wait any longer.'

'Whatever happens tomorrow, I want you to know that I'm very grateful to you,' said Caoimhe.

'For what – organising everyone's massacre?'

'Don't say things like that,' chided Caoimhe. 'No, for giving us all hope. When I was in Eburacum I saw hundreds of people crowding into churches and temples, looking for salvation. They'd given up on this world: they had no hope.'

'People go to pray here,' said Mannius gesturing at the altar.

'Yes, but only respectfully. They don't wail from dawn until dusk as if they're not going to wake up the next day. We're closer to the danger here but people are more alive: they haven't given up and it's because of you.'

Mannius turned away from the priest, humbled. He knew he'd changed in the last few weeks but had no idea how far or what he'd become.

'I feel so cold,' said Caoimhe, turning to face the hills to the north but staying close to Mannius.

'It's been unseasonably bad weather for spring. Not really the sort of weather you want to remember the place by when you skip into the next world.'

'Don't say that!'

'Sorry,' said Mannius, turning to the princess. Tears ran down her marble-smooth cheeks. He tried to smile. 'It's a difficult time for all of us.'

'Hardest for you: you're the one we all trust to get us through this. You're the one giving us all hope. But I've got another, selfish hope.' She looked away, into the gathering darkness of the moors. 'That you'll be safe. I've lost too many family and friends already.' At last she could contain her emotions no longer and quietly sobbed.

Mannius put his arm round her tiny waist and pulled her close. 'I've felt cold since I started out to see your father. But now, with you, I can begin to feel warm again.'

Caoimhe turned to him, pushed herself into his arms and kissed him hard. As their lips parted, sobs returned. 'If you die in the battle, then so will I.'

He wanted to stay with her; feel her breath on his face; taste her scent. But that was a luxury he had to deny himself – especially as there seemed to be a lot of activity around the western defences. 'I don't want to have the death of a royal on my hands so I'd better look after myself, I suppose.'


Out of the darkening shadows of the west, just before the day's light finally faded, General Galerius entered the fortifications at the head of a column of five hundred men. At first their approach had startled nervous guards and men stood ready to face an assault. As danger faded, the laughs of men vented their pent-up tension.

'General Galerius!' shouted Mannius in greeting. 'Is this a pleasant surprise or have you come to arrest us?'

'I hear that you are now a general yourself, congratulations. I've brought some volunteers for your army. These men want to fight Saxons – against the wishes of Prefect Leonius and Senator Antonius, I might add.'

'Families around here?'

'Yes. They were preparing to leave to defend their homes but I persuaded them that it would be best to make a stand with your army rather than wait for invaders to come and pick them off one by one.'

'They are most welcome, as is their leader. We could do with your expertise.'

Mannius and Coel rode alongside Galerius towards the main fort. 'Tell me one thing,' said Galerius, turning in his saddle to face Mannius. 'Was Una with Flavius when you captured him?'

'Oh yes, she's safe and sound. In fact she even helped loosen his tongue – the prospect of talking with her seemed not to appeal to him.'

Galerius laughed. It lifted a tension that he seemed to have been carrying. His tone lightened at the news. 'With Flavius as your guest I suppose you've learnt the nature of Senator Antonius' mission here?'

'We have, as well as how he has applied pressure on you to serve him.'

'That is why I am here: to find my brother's son. But I will help in any way I can.'

Mannius outlined his strategy and received approval from Galerius. 'With the men you have brought, General, you may have solved two of our problems. Prefect Artorius will lead the cavalry, I have placed myself and most of the legionaries on the right, Princess Caoimhe and Lord Coel are to be based in the fort and hold the bridge to the village from the east.'

'So you need someone to look after the heavy infantry on the left?'

'If you wouldn't mind, sir?'

'Hah! There's no need to ask or call me *sir* any more.' Galerius swivelled in his saddle and admired the preparations. 'The longer you hold Aelred the better – his men are starving. You've already weakened them without fighting. I'll also give you an insight into the enemy you face: he's mad with you at your scorched earth policy and impatient to do battle. Either element could force a mistake from him but together I think he'll blunder. Well done, General.'

# Chapter LIX

'My lord, scouts report that the enemy has barricaded the bridge ahead,' said Horsa.

'How many men?' asked Aelred. The campaign was not going as he'd planned. Rain had slowed his advance by making tracks turn to mud after the first few units had passed over them. In order to negotiate mile after mile of quagmires, the men and carts following had to slow. Worse still, every stream seemed to have been swollen into a raging torrent by incessant rain, necessitating numerous detours. And adding to Saxon misery was a chronic lack of food left by the retreating enemy. Foraging parties repeatedly came back empty. Those that ventured further afield often failed to return or came back with men missing after being ambushed. At least the rain had stopped, though the ground was still sodden.

'They estimate no more than five hundred, my lord.'

'Well go and bloody well find out for sure. If it isn't some sort of trap we'll smash through their barricades first thing tomorrow.'

'Would it not be prudent to go round to the north and ford the river higher up, my lord? We could even bypass the village altogether.'

'It would take another day, maybe two or even three for the whole army to ford the river. They've played us for fools too long, sending us up that valley for nothing. Time is no longer on our side. My men are hungry and need supplies that our enemies have at Derventio.'

'Supplies, my lord?'

373

'That village is the place where Romans collect corn taxes from the area. There are huge buildings full of wheat and oats – enough to feed our army and their families for a year or two. It's stored there until it's taken to Eburacum.'

'Ah, so we must be careful not to fire the fort.'

'Exactly, and I can't afford to leave an army behind me as we march towards Eburacum. If we have to lay siege to the town I don't want my arse exposed. Too long these people have run from us – we need to fight them. We attack tomorrow. Now go.'

Even Aelred was beginning to feel the same hunger as his men. He knew their food supplies were exhausted. Men who'd joined them from villages around the coast barely brought more than they needed for themselves. Tomorrow there was a chance of a feast and the thought warmed him. He would tell his men about that and they'd be like hungry wolves tearing at anyone who stood in their way.

Mannius toured the forts, trailed by four bodyguards. An uneasy silence reigned – suddenly he realised there was no hammering. Only the sound of metal edges being sharpened could be heard over subdued murmurs. Veterans of earlier battles ate as much as they could and told tales of their heroism – real and imagined. Most men simply stared into the flames of fires, watched the stars or looked for signs of panic on the faces of those around them. Occasionally a nervous laugh rose up and was quickly joined by others from men wanting a release for their own tension.

Priests, mostly Christian, walked round offering words of encouragement. Best of all was Taran, the druid. Mannius had listened and been impressed by his confidence.

Even the Christian priests nodded a quiet approval from the shadows. He'd start by going over old ground: outlining how Aelred and his allies had come as unwelcome invaders; then he'd tell the men to place their faith in their god before reassuring them that if they fell their bodies would start a new circle of life, broken down to feed the plants and animals that would one day be part of another man. Meanwhile their souls would be taken to the next world, where their ancestors would greet them as heroes.

'May I join you?' Princess Caoimhe, wrapped in a long white palla trimmed with gold thread, walked out of the darkness into the light from a campfire. Her hair reflected the flames and made it appear as though an aura was around her. Her smooth skin with the thin features of her face and the brilliance of the white fabric gave her an almost unnatural, goddess-like quality. Men grovelled at her feet and begged to touch the cloth that she wore, hoping that some of her supernatural power would be passed to them.

Mannius watched the goddess glide towards him. Dewy grass hardly bent under her slight weight. 'Of course, Princess. I was talking with some of the men and listening to Taran.'

'He knows how to talk,' laughed Caoimhe. And the princess knew how to laugh. It carried a light melody that made those it touched smile.

'I think he has a voice that gives confidence and determination to men. I now know why we Romans feared the druids so much. Fighting against an army whipped up by men like Taran must have been truly formidable.'

Trailed by bodyguards the two leaders walked towards another of the hastily erected forts. 'What do you say to the men?'

'I praise their preparations, whether it is a finely honed sword or a polished shield. But each time they all want to hear the answer to the same question: will we win tomorrow?'

'What do you tell them – that we will win?'

'Of course.'

Caoimhe lowered her voice to a whisper. 'And what do you think – really?'

'That it will be a hard day for both sides and that many will die. If we are strong, resolute and very, very lucky we stand a chance.'

'Even though there are thousands more of them?'

'Numbers are important. They may wear us down through constant attacks but they will pay a heavy price, I am sure of that.'

'Ah, the battle of Cannae?' prompted Caoimhe.

'Yes, if they throw themselves at us in impetuous charges and squeeze men between the forts, we may win.'

'How so?' she asked, clearly interested.

'Because only men on the edge of their formation will be able to fight. There the numbers will be even – and our missiles will take a heavy toll.' Mannius looked to the ground, ashamed of the deaths he was planning. 'Win or lose it will be a miserable day.'

The couple walked across grass that was becoming sodden with dew. 'What will you do afterwards, when we have defeated Aelred and his thugs? Will you go from this country to Rome?'

'I used to think that I would join my father on his estate and practise medicine with him in the safety and luxury of fine houses in great cities. But now that seems far away.'

'My dreams are closer.' Caoimhe stopped and turned to look into her companion's eyes. 'If we win tomorrow this land needs people like you to make it strong again.'

'People or person?'

'Maybe both,' she said smiling. Quickly she turned and continued walking.

'I think it would be best if you left for Eburacum before dawn.'

Caoimhe stopped sharply and squared up to Mannius, an angry glint in her eye. 'I think not!' She prodded him hard on his shoulder to emphasise her point. 'I shall not abandon my brave warriors to their fate: I will share it with them and with you.'

'But you are the leader of your nation, the last of your family. You must survive for the sake of your people.'

'Do you care more for my nation or for me?'

'Er, both, I . . .'

'I will not run away to hear of defeat or glory second-hand. I will do my part tomorrow.'

He felt her grip his right arm tightly and when he gently placed his left hand onto hers she did not resist. Instead she pulled herself close. A powerful scent of lavender came to him. 'Just keep yourself safe. While you live, men will have hope,' she whispered.

'I will.' Mannius felt the princess squeeze his arm again and put her head against his shoulder.

'What's that?' he asked, pointing to a small bottle tied round her neck with a leather thong.

'If all else fails, Una gave me it as my last hope. I will not be taken prisoner.'

# Chapter LX

Before dawn Mannius left Eithne after a tearful hug and rode north, to the barricaded bridge. Half a mile from the crossing, pickets challenged him and he congratulated them on their alertness. Moving closer, still in darkness, he could make out figures.

'Taran! What on earth are you doing here?'

'Just preparing a few surprises for our Saxon friends.'

'I knew I should have given you a proper job to keep you occupied.' A deep, rumbling laugh came from shadows on the bridge. 'Not you as well.'

'General Galerius is here and Prefect Artorius also paid a visit earlier,' replied Coel.

'Nothing like exposing all our leaders to the same danger of attack at once,' moaned Mannius. 'Don't tell me Princess Caoimhe's dancing on the bridge.'

'No, she's with Una, putting poison on all her arrows,' replied Taran.

'It's always good to get up close to eyeball your enemy, get a feel for him and his weaknesses,' said Galerius, undistracted. 'And what brings you out here, General Mannius?'

'Good morning to you too, General. I just wanted to check on the enemy, like you say, make sure Aelred didn't want to surrender.' The laugh started again.

Across the bridge and beyond the barricade's heavy wooden stakes, twinkling lights danced across dew-drenched fields and meadows. With darkness melting in the first grey light of dawn Mannius could see that they were remnants of fires.

The facing hillside seemed to be alive; like a giant warrior flexing his muscles its surface rippled. Mannius realised that the movement was dimly-lit men – thousands of them.

With the first rays of sunshine a rainbow appeared. Ponderously, the Saxons roused themselves and started to get into formation. Light flashed off countless spears and polished helmets. As one the ground seemed to rise up.

Mannius watched Saxon officers ride along lines of men, waving their arms and, no doubt, extolling great deeds. A huge cheer went up, then a low beat of powerful drums rolled across the fields. Slowly, the hillside of twitching shapes flowed towards the woefully inadequate-looking wall of wooden stakes. Time seemed to slow and Mannius stared as dark shapes became men and finally snarling beasts intent on his destruction.

In front of him, archers slotted arrows into strings in anticipation. Mannius gripped a javelin and felt it slippery in his sweaty palms.

An officer ordered two old onagers to be loosed. Men at the side of the ancient and rotting wooden catapults released locking mechanisms. Large rocks, coated in flaming oil and pitch, rose into the air and crashed into massed ranks. Screams of men came across the fields. Birds close to the river rose and scattered, leaving the ground for men to kill each other.

The windlasses on the old weapons were pulled down until their ropes creaked taut. Another stone was loaded, lighted and launched. More screams, this time louder as the Saxons came closer. Archers made ready and their officers gave the order to shoot. Mannius saw Saxons at the front raise their shields. Those behind had little warning in the dimness of dawn and thin iron tips pierced armour and more men fell. More arrows flew. Gaps appeared in the massed ranks only to be filled as officers pushed men across to keep the line advancing.

The crew of a metal carroballista – a cart-mounted device capable of shooting rocks and iron bolts – stood ready on the bridge. Looking over the top of the barricade, the officer in charge identified those giving orders and his men targeted them. A bolt launched and Mannius watched it throw back a huge, axe-waving warrior as well as two men behind him. After reloading as fast as possible, the crew launched another bolt at a man on horseback. The iron projectile tore through the horse's neck and buried itself in the chest of a man standing at the other side. Both horse and man collapsed instantly, with the rider having his leg crushed by the animal's weight.

Despite the burning pitch and volleys of arrows the Saxons still came on. At eighty paces Mannius could see the faces of blond-bearded men twisted with hate. 'Fucking pagan scum,' a waiting legionary muttered. Demonising the anonymous enemy was the way most men coped with the horror of battle and the closer the Saxons came Mannius too began to think of them as monsters, not men, to be slain.

The centurion in charge of the defence calmly gave the order to hurl javelins. Barbs on the pyramidal, iron heads bit into flesh with agonising accuracy. Men fortunate enough to see the projectiles coming raised their shields only to find them rendered useless after the javelins pierced them and bent. Without protection they became targets for archers.

Saxons at the front drew swords and raised their oval shields. More volleys of javelins flew overhead. Slingers started to send stones hurtling at the enemy that rattled against shields and broke bones with more force than arrows. Still the Saxons braved the deadly rain. A few without shields picked up rocks and hurled them over the wooden stakes. Several spears skittered harmlessly across the cobbles of the bridge. Then a man turned towards Mannius, a spear through his upper leg. Blood spread across the cobbles.

Mannius threw his javelin and saw it go into a Saxon's shoulder. Automatically he drew his sword and raised his shield in time to bat away a small rock. In front of him he could hear Saxons screaming their war cry as they charged through the final ditch and up to the waiting legionaries. Metal clashed with metal, iron axes crashed into wooden shields and men screamed. At the front men used swords while behind them others lunged at enemy throats with long, heavy thrusting spears.

On the bridge, Mannius heard the splashes of men jumping into the water beneath. He looked down and saw Saxons trying to wade across, underneath the bridge. Too late they found the water deep and fast-flowing. Unable to release themselves from their armour a dozen drowned. Men at the edge of the bank turned in panic to push back others behind them. Archers on the opposite bank sent volley after volley at their exposed bodies.

An officer gave an order, inaudible to Mannius, but he saw archers light their arrows. Two volleys went up and flames leapt up twenty paces from the ditch in front of the palisade. Quickly, flames spread and men screamed in agony, tortured by heat and burns. Uncertainty gripped the frontmost attackers as they heard the frenzy behind them and the intensity that had driven the initial attack lessened. In the lull more javelins were thrown.

Saxon bodies lay strewn in front of the heavy wooden stakes. But behind the screen, the Romans had started to take casualties. Dead men were heaved aside while the injured limped or were carried to the rear. A centurion calmly ordered urns of water to be passed round.

One of the onagers launched a projectile that was

accompanied by a crack and the machine split. The carroballista was ordered back off the bridge to make room for wounded men and, Mannius suspected, a general retreat. Was the centurion giving him a hint that he felt his men couldn't hold much longer? Everyone knew it would be the senior officer's decision as to when they should pull back. He felt eyes looking towards him but instead of returning their gaze directly he concentrated on the dying flames of the fire trap.

Another round from the other onager and its timbers also snapped. Men poured oil over the wooden frames, ready to set them alight and use them as a screen for their retreat. In front of the ditch a shield wall had reformed and was advancing menacingly. Javelins and arrows flew once more. A shout went up, indicating the store of javelins was exhausted; the throwers drew their swords and joined their comrades, hacking at the attackers.

One of Mannius' bodyguards tapped his arm and pointed upstream. A little over half a mile away, where the river broadened and was shallower, hundreds of men were wading across and through marshes. Tall reeds bent as tell-tale signs of men moving over the boggy ground. The centurion looked towards Mannius, who nodded. Archers and slingers retreated first and joined other archers massed along the bank, covering the retreat of the legionaries. Rank by rank the heavy infantry disengaged themselves from the enemy, forming their own shield wall and steadily backing away.

The first few Saxons pulled themselves over the spikes of the palisade and were cut down by arrows. Slowly stepping backwards the centurion ordered the onagers torched and thick smoke quickly engulfed the bridge.

A man limped past Mannius, blood pouring down his leg. Instinctively, the officer gave the man his shoulder to lean on and helped him over the bridge. At the other side, sitting with his back against one of the stone pillars, was Taran. Light of the growing dawn showed his skin to be painted blue with black symbols, and his hair was spiked.

'Time to move back, my druid friend,' said Mannius.

'Please be my guest,' replied Taran, waving a lazy hand, encouraging him onwards.

'But –'

'I have a little present for Aelred and his men.' The old man smiled as though he were enjoying taking the early morning sun. 'A message from the druids, you might say, to welcome our new friends. Borgach helped me with it.'

'I think you should –'

'Rest assured I will.'

A testudo formed by the legionaries pushing their shields together with some held above slowly moved across the bridge. Mannius saw Taran nod to the centurion, who ordered two of his slingers to launch stones at several large urns on the bridge. Oil flowed out and over the cobbles. Still the old man sat and waited. Another Saxon shield wall was forming upstream and would start to move soon.

At last Taran rose, using a shield as cover, and joined the testudo, standing near to the centurion. The legionaries fanned out into a line but continued to walk backwards. Saxons came running across the bridge, screaming their war cries. Arrows flew and men fell. A few got across and lunged towards the Roman shields. Behind them men pressed onto the bridge, eager to join the expected slaughter of retreating soldiers. Taran waved an arm and several fire arrows flew onto the cobbles, igniting the oil. It was thin and men jumped over its weak flames towards the gathering fight.

Smoke suddenly billowed from three more urns on the

bridge. Mannius heard a loud hiss, clouds spewed out of the urns and Taran waved the legionaries down. Dutifully they formed a shield wall on their knees. Saxons slashed and hammered at the Roman shields, then an enormous explosion poured fire across the bridge. Men around the structure fell instantly. Metal nails and stones hummed through the air, killing and maiming. Helmets, shields and body parts landed around the bridge. The legionaries rose and finished off those around them who still stood. Using the confusion of the enemy as cover, the Romans backed off.

'What in Woden's name was that?' demanded Aelred as he looked at the dying flames on the bridge. When smoke cleared from the battleground he could see dozens of his men dead and dying. He had expected them to swarm over the bridge but the Romans had chosen their battleground carefully, forcing his men into a tight area and then unleashing a monstrous weapon on them. His body shook with rage.

'My lord, I have not seen the like before.'

'It seems that man enjoyed it,' said Prince Wybert, pointing towards a low mound that overlooked the bridge. 'Looks like some sort of wizard.' On its rounded summit an old man with a long beard, dressed in a tunic with antlers on his head and spikes of hair protruding from the sides, danced a jig, repeatedly pointing a long wooden staff towards the Saxons. After several minutes of dancing the man turned to the invaders, raised his tunic and bent over to display his naked buttocks to them.

'Bloody druid,' said Aelred.

'My lord, I thought the Romans killed them all centuries ago.'

'Evidently they didn't do a very thorough job. I'll have

that man and his fucking arse,' ranted Aelred. 'In fact I'll have his arse fucked good and proper. I'll show him where to stick his bloody antlers. Now, order the advance before we die of starvation standing here. And Wybert, go and make sure our friends remember when and where to attack.'

Mannius rode back to Derventio with Artorius' mounted infantry. Nearing the outermost fort he could hear cheering. Some of the faster riders must have relayed the tale of the battle at the bridge. Outside the fort, on a command from their centurion, the legionaries reined in their horses, drew their swords and lined either side of the road. Taran paraded through the middle, waving his staff high in the air. Mannius could feel the morale of his army surge as news of the small victory spread.

Galerius rode up to him. 'How many of the buggers did you get?'

'Difficult to say but the centurion's men laid into them well,' said Mannius. 'I'd reckon about four, maybe five hundred – though when Taran set off that explosion there could have been another hundred or so on the bridge that were killed.'

'Ah, the exploding gate trick. I have heard of similar things in lands far to the east but I have never seen such clever explosions made to order. He has a powerful weapon.'

'I hope he has some more because I'm sure we'll need it.'

385

# Chapter LXI

More and more men appeared in front of Derventio. Spilling onto low wet fields, three-quarters of a mile in front of the allies, Saxons gradually took up position opposite a double line of warriors. Horns sounded and drums started again. From the walls of the stone fort, shouts drew Mannius' attention to men advancing through the village on the other side of the river. Clearly they intended to cross the bridge into the heart of the village beneath the main fort. This was a flanking manoeuvre that had been expected. Facing the enemy were four centuries of men backed up by five hundred of Coel's warriors and other volunteers. In addition, five ballistae and four new onagers were greased, loaded and ready.

The Saxons paused. Mannius felt fear trickling through him. Had he missed something? Was Aelred waiting for more troops to arrive and surround them? Anxiously he looked across to Galerius and could see the experienced soldier casually looking around. Maybe this was all the Saxons had: brute force on two sides. But they had a lot of it.

A double line of warriors – Votadini on the left and Brigantes on the right – stretched in front of the forts. The Saxons jeered and waved weapons at the defenders, getting ever closer. More men trickled onto the battlefield and the throng facing the defenders grew, as did the noise. Over the river another line of attackers grew in number and formed a shield wall, preparing to storm the bridge's two protecting forts. Mannius knew the snare was set.

Instead of attacking immediately, discipline seemed to hold the Saxon line or was it – dare he hope – fear? Standing and waiting, men whipped themselves into a frenzied hate-lust. Mannius felt his nerves jangle again. His mouth was dry and adrenaline pumped through his trembling body. He wanted the fight to begin: the wait was jarring his nerves – exactly what Aelred had planned, no doubt. Skirmishers waited low in the grass and behind field hedges. Mannius pitied and envied them at the same time. Being so close to such a mass of enemy fighters must be unnerving. But they would be the first into the fight and their tension would be the soonest to evaporate.

Mannius let his mind wander and looked down on a skirmisher as though he were a raven flying overhead. He wheeled round, along the line of warriors facing the Saxons, then round the furthest fort and back over the centre of the village. Now he felt as one with the army around him. His nervousness lessened.

Saxon drums sounded once more and the frenzied monsters started a slow walk towards waiting lines of Votadini and Brigantes. Skirmishers, barely two hundred paces from the enemy, broke cover and started peppering arrows at Saxon leaders wherever possible. After several shots they began to retreat, chased by hotheads who could restrain themselves no longer. A few skirmishers turned to meet the threat and sent arrows into unprotected flesh. Flanking cavalry charged the Saxons and cut them down. A small victory but one for both sides to witness.

On the Saxon right a broad ridge rose gently out of the plain and allowed Aelred to watch the battle unfold on horseback. He saw some men break ranks, run at skirmishers and perish at the hands of Roman cavalry. Fools! Aelred nodded to an officer close by. A trumpet sounded a deep, trembling note, then war drums thudded the heartbeat of the attack.

Moments later an echoing drumbeat replied and lines of men came to life on both sides of the river, moving towards the enemy's defences. The Romans and their allies would have the life squeezed out of them. He would use this opportunity to crush resistance and send a message to any others who might think of defying his will. No one – man, woman or child – would be allowed to walk away from this.

A Roman trumpet sounded. Higher notes and a more urgent tone. Suddenly the shield wall facing his men disintegrated and they started to run. Wild whoops of joy rose, mixed with battle cries and a chase ensued. Saxons in the front lines ran at their retreating enemy, desperate to close the gap. But it was too great. The defenders disappeared behind ditches and earth banks, topped with thick wooden stakes.

Unnoticed at first, screams mingled with the noise of the attackers. Painted black to make them harder to see, heavy stones launched from unseen onagers crashed through the Saxon ranks. The third volley carried burning oil and cut murderous trails through hapless warriors.

Aelred quietly thanked his men that their bloodlust carried them on. Arrows filled the air. Men fell and the attack slowed. Shields were brought together to see off the menace. The Romans had taught them this lesson and now they would use it against them. Deliberately now, the king's men advanced. Only large rocks from powerful catapults or heavy iron bolts from the wicked ballistae punctured the lines.

Men in the centre of the massive shield wall had nearly reached the fort second from the left. Aelred willed them on and over the ditches. Against such a body of men the defences seemed puny. Soon they would sweep over the wooden stakes and the killing would begin. His men were close. Defenders appeared behind the stakes and javelins joined the battery of missiles.

In his mind's eye Aelred could only envisage victory: the obstacles his men faced seemed puny against the might of his army and the defenders looked desperate. Impatient to join his warriors and help with the killing, the Saxon king waved at another officer. The man rode off to give orders for the third assault to move into position. Aelred had calculated that by the time he got close to the small fort the javelins would have ceased and his men would have removed the stakes. Trailed by six of his trusted bodyguards, he kicked his horse into a gallop.

Ballistae mounted on small towers continued to spit bolts at his men. Soon, very soon, he'd have those artillery crews horribly murdered. An officer seemed to be directing the volleys of stones and bolts. He waved a spear, or was it a staff? Aelred pulled hard to rein in his horse, nearly falling over the animal's head. On the man's helmet were antlers – the druid! He'd have the druid as his prisoner. But something deep in his subconscious urged caution so he let his horse walk slowly forward.

Inside the second fort, surrounded by Votadini warriors, Taran organised the defence. Great catapults kicked as their spokes crashed into crosspieces and deadly stones were hurled from heavy leather slings. Infantry from the shield wall ran, as planned, into the fort and took up positions behind the heavy wooden stakes of the palisade. Archers made ready, then loosed arrows on his command.

War cries that had been a distant murmur quickly grew to fill the wooden fort. Men looked to Taran, many wide-eyed with terror. Calmly he directed the ballistae and encouraged the men working the onagers to increase their efforts. In front of him, he watched attackers fall to their knees in pain after stepping on one of the hundreds of small stakes that had been concealed in front of the shallow outer ditch. Ten men fell into a pit of stakes, and Taran imagined their cries and hummed a druid incantation to ensure their deaths. Breaks started to appear in the shield wall. Spears and arrows flew into the gaps, sending more men to the ground. The advance slowed as Saxon officers tried to pull their men into an orderly line.

On they came, over the shallow ditch, dodging round stakes angled at them. Pushed on by the press of men behind, the attackers threw themselves into the deeper inner ditch. This time Taran heard their pain as men were impaled on stakes driven into its base. Finally, warriors appeared over the rim and clambered towards the palisade. The Votadini defenders started to hack and lunge at the Saxons. Taran nodded to two archers next to him, who sent fire arrows into the outer ditch. Other archers along the wall did likewise. From a few small flames an inferno soon erupted along the trench. Hundreds of men screamed as they became horribly burned and Taran caught a smell as though meat were being cooked. Another small victory to cheer.

Saxons near the palisade turned to see the new threat. Too late they realised that they had become isolated. Without mercy Votadini soldiers cut down stranded men then waited for the wall of flames to die away and let another wave of attackers assault them. Behind them, missiles continued to fly out of the fort.

Waiting for the enemy gave Mannius time to check the opening exchanges. In front of all the forts the scene was the same: fires burned and killed; artillery kept launching lethal stone balls and iron bolts; clouds of arrows hummed towards the enemy; and slingers peppered the attackers with bone-crunching accuracy. And still the Saxons came on – too many to count.

To his left Mannius saw smoke billowing from the fire traps on the south-west side of the old fort. The outer fort was only held by a mixture of locals and a few volunteer veterans, not fit enough to fight in formation. He'd not expected the Saxons to get that far round in strength as any attack would face the high stone walls of the village and fort. Another body of men down there would tip the arithmetic in favour of the attackers – and threaten Princess Caoimhe.

There was no time to dwell on the issue. Saxons were once again advancing in front of him. This time he knew there were no more fire-traps to throw them back. Artillery and missiles could open great holes in the enemy's ranks and put fear into men's hearts but most Saxons would have to be killed face-to-face with swords and spears. The time for that job was close.

Taran watched as Saxons charged once more. Three lines of Votadini soldiers waited. Metal clashed with metal and the battle for survival started in earnest. From his position Taran could see deep lines of warriors being encouraged onwards. But there was an obstacle: his fort. Men started to push round either side of the fort and fighting rose up all around. Sounds of iron ringing against iron and men's screams engulfed him. He felt as though he was standing on a high rock watching a tidal sea come in, filling holes around him.

As General Mannius had predicted, a great many Saxons between his fort and the next were trapped, unable to join the fight at the front. They were effectively out of the struggle. The power of the attacker's greater numbers was being negated.

The mass pushed towards the fighting, trapping their own men on wooden stakes and preventing them killing the defenders. How long before they swamped his sanctuary? Surely sheer weight of numbers would see to that. He knew that engineers had dug trenches to break the enemy's momentum but such preparations seemed feeble against the horde that swarmed towards him.

Behind him, the supporting fort started to launch its artillery and arrows at the press of men. Taran watched in awe as first one then another polybolos started to hurl heavy iron bolts into the throng. After shooting, men frantically worked a cam that pulled the carriage backwards and another bolt was automatically forced up into position. Each machine was spitting out death at least four times faster than the one he stood next to.

From his vantage point he saw the rise and fall of rocks catapulted into the crowd and signalled javelins to be launched to take advantage of gaps in the shield wall. Below him attackers fell in great numbers. The Saxons were having to clamber over their own dead and wounded to launch their assaults. Maybe they could hold back the tide; the enemy dead were like silt in a harbour, making the channels narrower.

Inside the fort, Votadini warriors were also falling. Those mortally wounded fell down and were unceremoniously hauled aside as others took their place. Some men staggered away from the fight, seeking assistance with their injuries while others pulled out of the fight, took a gulp of water and used the time to regain their strength.

At the other side of the wall Saxons stood on fallen comrades. With their increased height they hacked down

on defenders with swords, axes and hammers. A fury
drove their screams and seemed to give them a terrible
strength. The smell of cooked meat had been replaced
by blood and opened guts. A burning torch landed at
Taran's feet and he threw it back at the Saxon horde.
Two arrows hit him in the chest, knocking him to the
wooden floor of the small tower. Quickly he was up and
drew out both arrows from the armour he wore under
his grey tunic. Holding the slender wooden missiles in
front of him he snapped them and threw them down.
Saxons who witnessed the act were visibly shocked to see
an old man pull arrows out of a plain tunic as though
they were merely bee stings. Warriors kissed metal rings
and others touched charms fastened round their necks to
avert the evil.

More torches hit the tower. Some embedded themselves
low down and flames started to take hold. Taran knew
that they would lose the tower. He pointed out three
targets to the ballista crew and made his way down to
see the captain in charge of the infantry. The officer
waved some of his soldiers down from the ramparts and,
with archers behind, made a shield wall across the fort.
Ballistae and onager crews severed the main ropes on
their war engines before they too joined the shield wall.
Flames leapt up from the tower and a great cheer went
up as stakes either side gave way and Saxons jumped into
the fort. The tide was on the flood.

Votadini warriors still on the ramparts made their way
to the defensive line. Those men able to keep their nerve
and slowly back away in disciplined groups mostly got to
safety. But those who turned and hurled themselves
recklessly away from the Saxon axes encountered only
death. Screams and cheers filled the fort with equal
measure. Taran put a torch to urns used to store the
lethal oil and pitch mixture. Flames erupted from one

side of the fort and smoke filled the rest. With officers screaming at their men to hold the line, the warriors backed away. Training with Mannius' legionaries was paying off: discipline held the men together. The first few charges from the Saxons were repulsed with ease. The gateway at the rear proved to be a bottleneck, testing men's patience as they waited for more attacks. Taran put a torch to two more large urns and ran back to the mass of escaping warriors, urging them to leap over the wooden stakes before the Saxons emerged through the thick smoke.

Outside the fort order was restored. Mannius waited with four centuries of legionaries. They let the Votadini pass through their ranks before they overlapped their shields and waited for the Saxons. Instead of the explosion that Taran had expected, only heat and smoke issued from the urns. His best magic had failed and he'd let the men down. He led them into the next fort, where most collapsed, glad to have a degree of safety about them. Instead of resting Taran climbed onto a tower and waved his staff in defiance. Then he saw Mannius looking at him and pointed towards the gathering body of attackers.

On foot, Mannius waited patiently. Lines of heavy infantry clad in red cloaks of varying hues stood either side of him. Some men wore segmented armour but most used chainmail for protection. He wished they'd had enough time to equip themselves in the same uniform, with the same armour and weapons: to go into battle as one smart, efficient unit. But Aelred had prevented that and he found himself loathing his enemy for denying such a trivial privilege.

Mannius saw Taran waving, came out of his reflections and ordered his formation forward. He hoped that he'd understood the druid correctly. Fog of war was all well and good but this was ridiculous. Ten paces into the smoke they encountered a few Saxons, choking for clean air. Their need was quickly ended with lethal sword thrusts. The formation climbed up the earth embankment, strewn with wooden stakes, and into the fort. After another twenty paces they started to emerge from the smoke and took the assembled Saxons by surprise. To the attackers facing the Roman infantry it seemed as though the druid had conjured them out of smoke.

The Romans blocked, stabbed and moved as one giant war engine. Resistance before them evaporated and soon they were over the other rampart and moving into the rear of the Saxons attacking the next fort. Legionaries took turns at the front, dropping to the rear for a rest.

Mannius wanted to lead by example: do more than his share of time at the battle's edge, cutting at surprised and startled warriors. But as the adrenaline subsided he felt stress, fatigue and lack of training take their toll. He had to drop back to rest.

Men ran before them, trying to push their way to safety. The only way they went was to their next world. Enemy soldiers on the ground were left by those at the front, trampled and finished by the rear ranks as they passed over.

Suddenly there were no more fighting Saxons. Thousands of once proud warriors waited for burial. A few threw down their weapons to surrender and were swiftly killed. Mannius turned and saw the fort protecting the weak east wall of the main fort, start to come under heavy attack. Immediately he turned the legionaries round, marched to the aid of the defenders and ordered reserves to join them.

# Chapter LXII

Caoimhe had wanted to be at Mannius' side but he had ordered her to command the main fort and she had obeyed, knowing that he didn't need her as a distraction. So, from an artillery tower, manned by three old men, Caoimhe watched the battle unfold.

Before fighting commenced she had been awed by the number of warriors gathered by both sides. Men were drawn up in neat rows and groups marched smartly together in close formation. At first the enemy lines moved harmlessly in step to distant drums and in the laziness of early morning she thought the Saxons might get bored and move on. The drumming grew louder: the air around her shook; she could feel their power; and felt as though the stone walls on which she stood would tumble if they got much closer.

Her concentration on the battle was broken by wailing and screams from inside the fort where women and children had sought refuge. Around her she could see men shuffle nervously at the noise. Soldiers were having their courage stripped from them by the very people they sought to protect. Hope was their greatest weapon and the shrill sound of fear could drain the fight from her warriors faster than the Saxons.

Drums and cheers went up across the battlefield and more wailing erupted. She knew what it was like to feel helpless while two armies fought. That was why she had chosen to fight. Caoimhe left the walls and strode across a parade ground. Seemingly from nowhere Una appeared at her side, dressed in a leather tunic and a short shirt of chainmail. Beneath the rim of an iron helmet her eyes burned with hatred and malevolence. A chill went through Caoimhe as she recognised the killer in the girl who had looked after her daughter. Unbidden she fell into step and accompanied the princess like a bodyguard.

Caoimhe stood on a platform but her voice was no match for the drums, cheers and sobs. She surveyed the crowd and noted the large number of knives carried. They would kill their children and themselves rather than fall into the hands of Saxons. Many of them had small vials tied round their necks.

'So you were busy last night, I see,' said Caoimhe touching her own vial.

'War pays, your highness,' smiled back Una. She actually seemed to be more animated, more alive than she had ever been.

The princess turned back to the crowd and reached out to a mother who dutifully passed her baby to her. Caoimhe kissed the infant and smiled at him. Soon others in the crowd were pressing forward to touch and be touched by the confidence coming from the young warrior princess. She walked through the crowd, letting those around her touch her arms as she passed. Now that the throng was distracted and quieted she told them, 'Pray for your husbands, sons and sweethearts. Be bold and give them strength.' Over and over she said the same words.

Outside the walls trumpets sounded and iron battered against iron. Some women fell to their knees and prayed but most held their nerve. The wailing had stopped.

She told Una to instruct the senior slaves to find work for the women. Soon they were separated into groups: some tore cloth into bandages, others made porridge in great pots and a number carried urns of water to the soldiers on the ramparts.

Back at the artillery post Caoimhe watched as fire and smoke rained down. The attackers were closer; they had become frenzied demons and a chill ran through her that made her touch the bottle of poison round her neck for reassurance.

She watched Taran lead his men out of the fort to safety and looked on in horror as Mannius had gone into the smoke towards a throng of Saxons. When she saw the plumes of his helmet emerge she breathed a sigh of relief.

A messenger arrived, 'Your highness, General Galerius asks that you prepare the west wall, ready to repel Saxons.'

Now the battle was coming to her. She spun away from the fight on the east side and ran towards the officer in charge of the west side. This was her chance to show the men that she could fight. Thus far the main fort had merely been the reception area for the wounded. Large, empty stables had been cleaned and dormitories created to tend the injured.

Legionaries hurried past her. 'The general's ordered them to reinforce the wall to the river,' shouted the officer she had been looking for. 'I'll go with them, you look after this lot.' There was no debate, no recognition of her rank as a princess. They thought she couldn't fight: she would show them.

Caoimhe nodded. The *wall* they were going to defend was a hastily dug trench overlooked by an earth embankment topped with a few sticks. Where she stood, the fort was stronger, with its original stonework still intact. Both walls needed to hold or the Saxons would be able to squeeze them as well as destroy the houses of ordinary people that lay within the extended walls.

# Chapter LXIII

Prince Wybert nodded to King Ceretic and the Pictish princes by way of signalling for them to start their advance. He'd seen the fire traps that had devastated several ranks of the advancing shield wall of the main offensive and ordered lighted torches to be thrown into every ditch they encountered. In a shallow trench in front of the main ditch, flames erupted. When they were in range of men behind a makeshift palisade he ordered his men to stay low behind their shields and endure an onslaught of missiles. Ceretic's men and the Picts did likewise.

Once the flames died away his men advanced again, unhurried and deliberate. Even so, missiles took a heavy toll. Around him men fell, crushed by heavy stones, impaled on javelins, skewered by iron bolts or pierced by arrows. Then the death rattle of slingshots started to hit his men's shields but still they pressed on. A few burned to death, caught in flammable liquid that was smeared around rocks hurled by unseen catapults. He vowed that the Romans and their allies would pay dearly for this carnage.

Dropping into a wide ditch he saw more death. Men had died in twisted agony on sharpened stakes. He stood on a pile of bodies in order to reach the lip of the death chasm and pull himself out. Urging his men on, he scaled the embankment. After blocking a weak sword lunge with his shield he brought his axe down on his attacker's helmet and satisfyingly saw the man's head split open. More defenders came and hacked down on him. He used both his arms to hold his shield above his head. Saxons joined him, several died, but there were soon enough to push at the wooden stakes. Heavy rain the previous night had weakened the foundations in which the obstacles had been embedded. In an instant he was tumbling down the other side of the embankment: the stakes had given way. Looking around he saw that his men were with him, swinging swords and axes at the retreating defenders.

There was no break to the killing. After enduring the rain of missiles the attackers had no mercy. Men were hunted and killed. Suddenly they were through the fort. Its walls now had huge gaps. Then a line of Roman legionaries appeared and Wybert's men, unable to halt their frenzy of killing, suddenly became victims to stabbing swords that darted out from behind massed shields.

Wybert gathered his men, readying them to attack the thin line of red-cloaked soldiers. Another storm of missiles hit them. Ballistae and onagers in the main fort were laying waste to his warriors. Then legionaries hit them with javelins. Soon the rat-a-tat-tat of stones and small pieces of shield-penetrating lead hurled by slingers started. He felt the collective consciousness of his men tremble with dread. They had to move or they would be whittled to nothing. Reluctantly he waved them back towards the shelter of the fort they had just taken.

Sitting among the smell of death he saw Ceretic and the Picts. Their men were just out of range of the Roman catapults. Wybert fumed. If only they'd joined the attack with the same enthusiasm as his men he knew they'd have overwhelmed the thin line. Now they'd have to advance over the killing ground once more.

Ceretic saw Wybert marching towards them and smiled as an iron bolt slapped into the ground near him.

Unfortunately the ricochet off a stone missed him as well. Pity.

'We've been taking the brunt of the fighting ever since we attacked King Cathal,' said Drostan.

'Those buggers hugged the coast so as not to have to fight the Votadini and those bloody auxiliaries,' moaned his brother. 'And they never went short on rations, like us.'

'I think,' said Ceretic, disguising his conspiratorial tone with a smile. 'That we are about to be given a choice by Prince Wybert. Either take on the red-cloaked slice and dice machine on the left or throw ourselves at the wall in front. Quite frankly neither appeals right now.'

'Too fucking right they don't,' agreed Fidach.

Wybert stood over them, axe in hand. 'What are you doing sat here when there's fighting to be done?'

'Our men have been on half-rations for weeks and are exhausted after taking the fort,' said Drostan, with mutterings of agreement from his brother. 'We lost a lot of good men when we stormed their palisade.'

'I lost nearly half my men killed and wounded fighting around that fort and then against the redcloaks. I don't see any of your men lying on the ground.'

'We've taken them to the rear.'

'If you'd put the same effort into fighting we'd have won this battle by now.' Wybert looked animated. Ceretic felt drops of blood flick onto his face as the powerful Saxon swung his axe this way and that.

'Prince Wybert is right,' said Ceretic, getting to his feet. They had to move or they'd probably all get the axe. 'We'll bring our men over to yours and together we'll be able to take the wall.'

Wybert grunted acknowledgement. 'We will take the wall of the fort itself. That will end their fight.' With that he turned and marched away. Ceretic followed at the double with his men and the Picts alongside.

'What the?' asked Drostan, jogging alongside Ceretic.
'Wait and see.' An evil grin spread across his face.


From the ramparts Caoimhe could see that the newly-made fort in front of the wall had been abandoned and a trail of bodies led to the north-west gate of the old fort. Galerius had taken his men and intercepted the main attack, giving the survivors a chance to get to the safety of the stone walls.

A tall Saxon warrior ran from the cover of the stronghold's embankments to a body of men a few hundred paces away. She watched an iron bolt hit the ground near his feet and cursed its miss. Men who had been out of range started moving with him, nearer the fort. Now they were within range. Caoimhe turned to shout at the officer in charge of four onagers but it was unnecessary: he had already given the order to release. Four flaming stones flew at the men and buried themselves among the crowd. Each seemed to cut down four or five enemy soldiers. Then ballistae started and more men fell. Archers made ready.

'Begging pardon, your highness,' said a grubby man with a spear and a toothless grin standing next to her. 'Are we winning?'

The man could see as much as she could. Judging by the ancient state of his armour, he'd probably been in far, far more battles than she had. Yet he wanted her opinion. What was it Mannius had said Taran was good at? Comfort. 'Of course. They've lost thousands of men on both sides of our fort. I think they'll run out of warriors to send at us soon.'

'Thank ye, highness,' said the man, smiling. It was the right answer. When he thought she wasn't looking he flashed a sign to a group of men and she heard mutters of approval that turned into a low cheer.

402

When the Saxons broke cover and ran at the walls, screaming their war cries, the defenders were ready. Arrows flew in thick waves. Ballistae opened men's chests with fearsome power, then javelins and slingshots made the advance stutter. Coming closer, Caoimhe realised that the men with the Saxons were Picts. Then she recognised Ceretic and watched him keep his body behind a large shield. A man close to him carried a Roman bow, took aim at the tall Saxon, barely thirty paces away, and sent an arrow through his neck. Instantly Ceretic was beside the Saxon, pointing up to the walls. Caoimhe unslung her bow and put an arrow against the string.

# Chapter LXIV

On the opposite river bank, Coel's men had inflicted terrible casualties on the attackers. In the narrow streets the Saxons were unable to use their extra numbers to outflank. Instead men pressed themselves into alleyways and yards to become targets for missiles. Bodies lay strewn throughout the twisting streets and tracks of the village. Leading from the front Coel had used his infantry and archers to goad the Saxons into impetuous charges. A group of several hundred had taken shelter in low, round, thatched houses with wattle and daub walls. The wooden lattice stopped arrows but provided no protection against fire. On Coel's orders torches and fire arrows were hurled at the buildings and many men died in the ensuing panic. Smoke still rose from the ashes of the houses but the fight had moved on through the village.

With locals on their side, Coel's men had ambushed the attackers before they fell back to another carefully prepared site. Despite the heavy toll his men were inflicting on their enemy more Saxons appeared and threatened to swamp the defences. Eventually Coel pulled his men back over the bridge, behind a secure stone barricade and waited.

'Will you let us attack them, my lord?' asked one of Coel's trusted captains.

Coel smiled. They'd already been through the worst fighting he'd ever had to endure yet his men still had courage enough to take the fight to the enemy. 'We haven't got enough warriors to make an assault on the village.

They'd get round us too easily, cut us off then cut us up,' answered Coel, concentrating on a group of Saxons assembling in front. 'We'll be able to hold the bridge – I'm confident of that. And remember our job is to stop them getting into the village. We might not be able to win the battle but if we get it wrong we could lose it.' Then as an afterthought, quietly to himself he added, 'If they persist with the same tactic.'

An officer tapped his armoured shoulder and he followed the line of the man's arm downstream. Due to heavy rains the water was too deep to ford and men couldn't swim it in armour. But hundreds of Saxons were removing chainmail, breastplates and other protective equipment as well as piling shields on the riverbank.

'Do you want me to strengthen the south side of the fort, my lord?'

Before Coel had chance to reply another officer shouted above the growing noise of Saxon battle cries.

'Sir! There's more, upstream now.'

Coel spun round and saw more men preparing to enter the water. The Saxons had realised that it was easier to bypass the stronghold by swimming. That would put them into the old town, which was guarded by makeshift walls and the allies' least able fighters. The soldiers with Princess Caoimhe appeared to have their hands full with an assault on the west wall so there were no more warriors to help.

'Get our archers spread out along the banks as fast as possible and tell someone to turn those catapults on the swimmers,' said Coel, waving at the onagers. The man sprinted off and Coel called another officer over.

Suddenly the bridge was alive with men frantically running to new positions. Coel watched and wondered if they'd secure the banks in time. There was some activity to his front and he realised that the Saxons were coordinating their efforts.

405

Coel ran along the grassy bank, downstream. The defenders seemed fewer at that side. Archers ahead of him grabbed bundles of arrows from a pile. Passing the stock of weapons, Coel took four javelins.

The river appeared to be a seething mass of men wading and swimming through the dark brown water. To Coel there seemed to be enough bodies for anyone else to merely use them as a bridge.

Archers began sending arrows down on the swimmers and clouds of blood drifted downstream. Dead bodies joined a slow procession on the current. Here and there Saxons held onto their dead comrades and used them as shields. A few men climbed up the stonework of the retaining wall at the water's edge and were met by a small force of infantry. The defenders were old and slow but managed to kill a large number of Saxons before they were cut down.

Coel got to the archers and started to organise infantry into a shield wall in front of them. With the veterans finished the Saxons charged, desperate to stop Coel's men becoming organised. Coel hurled a javelin and saw it plunge deep into a man's chest. The next two he threw in quick succession. One man fell and another stopped when a gash, the length of his arm, opened after he tried to fend off the projectile. Suddenly Coel realised that he and his men were hopelessly outnumbered – probably six to one. They had to kill the Saxons as they clambered onto the bank. If their enemy gained enough ground to organise themselves then they would surely perish.

The shield wall took three paces back because the swimmers were landing over a wider area. Coel found himself on the front row. He thrust his remaining spear into the chest of an axe-wielding man and drew his sword. All around him metal clashed with metal and wooden shields. Time and again he thrust his sword into flesh, twisted and pulled. Men screamed and fell but Coel was oblivious to the noise, focusing only on the next man in front of him. The shield wall turned and Coel realised that no more Saxons could get ashore over the bodies that lay strewn around them. Blood, spilling out of corpses, gathered in pools and made the grass slippy underfoot.

Maybe the general was right: the Saxons might not have the energy to swim and fight because of lack of food. Best of all, they had no armour and that made them easy targets. Bodies piled up as the slaughter continued. Coel saw men in the water deliberately floating farther downstream to the other side of the defensive ditch. That was fine. They might win this yet. He felt strong and started to feel confident.

A burning sensation bit into his side and he heard a crack of wood. Coel looked down and saw a spear had been pushed through the side of his armour that must have come loose. The man in front of him was wide-eyed with fear. Coel thrust the tip of his sword into the man's throat and then felt his strength drain away. Men helped him onto a shield and carried him to the rear of the fight. On the way up the hill to the main fort he passed out.

# Chapter LXV

Caoimhe released the arrow and watched it fly towards Ceretic. The missile pierced his armour and bit deep into his shoulder. She chided herself for being inaccurate and sent another arrow at the vile king. This one took him in the thigh and he squealed like a stuck pig. Then his men put their shields in front of him and carried him out of range. Caoimhe had other distractions: a determined assault on the wall in front of her was under way.

Some Saxons had crude wooden ladders that they pushed against the fort wall. Others carried thick poles with holds cut into them or cross-pieces drilled through. The attackers would be on the parapet soon. Caoimhe's mind went numb with fear. She looked at the men around her and saw terror on their faces also. She thought of the poison she carried, and of that on her arrow tips. Ceretic would die in agony, and with that thought she felt calmer. Without conscious thought an arrow found its way onto her bowstring, she let it fly and watched a man on a ladder die.

She screamed at her men to fight and continued sending arrows at the Saxons. Men hurled rocks, thrust at the attackers with spears and hacked at the ladders with axes. To her right, she saw Seneca leading a cavalry charge. Men and horses were so close that they bounced off each other as they thundered at the enemy. Below her, Saxons either ran back or jumped into the ditch and risked the stakes. A clear gap was created between the two forces attacking the wall. Following the ditch line, Galerius led his men in an orderly advance and cleared away the Saxons, taking the opportunity to break their ladders. Ceretic's men and the Picts had mostly retreated past the outer fort, hounded by Seneca's men. Then the cavalry wheeled round and joined the attack on the Saxons by now fleeing downhill to the riverbank. Many tried to surrender and were cut down. Others turned to fight but there seemed no resolve and they quickly perished. Realising that the fight on the wall was over, Caoimhe ran to a horse and galloped through the old village to the other wall.

Behind a makeshift wall protecting the old village, bare-chested men glistened with sweat as they hauled on ropes and carried great rocks. Giant catapults sent an almost continuous hail of rocks towards the enemy. Reaching the wooden stakes that marked the palisade, Caoimhe saw men fighting everywhere. Axes swung in great circles, knots of red-cloaked Romans appeared, then smoke drifted over and a wall of shields appeared. She spotted Mannius for a fleeting moment, then he was snatched from view as the line charged. His men were at an angle to the defensive ditch in front of her. Surely there were too few to hold the shield wall? Caoimhe prayed.

A trumpet sounded and more warriors charged into battle. Leofric led his men at speed into the rear of the Saxon horde. The allies had a mass of Saxons surrounded but their grip was thin.

# Chapter LXVI

'My lord,' said Horsa, 'now is the time to attack the main fort. The men in front have moved.'

'They'll only have moved to a better place to fight,' replied Aelred. 'Down there, by the river. That's where we should go and finish the job. If that's where the Romans want to be slaughtered, then so be it.'

'But, my lord, there are no troops between us and the stone fort.'

'No buts! I decide where we fight.' Aelred thought about attacking the fort but guessed that they'd have to overcome more fire trenches and other hidden traps. He preferred his less able infantry to go into such places first. Every time something had looked like an obvious attacking point, it had been a trap.

A messenger whipped his horse towards the king's party, pulled hard on his reins and fell to his knees in front of his leader. 'My lord, bad news.'

'Speak, man!'

'Prince Wybert has fallen. A Roman arrow took him.'

Aelred's heart turned black. Wybert was his eldest son and most trusted officer. 'The wretched luck of battle! Why of everyone did it have to be him?' The king was silent for a moment. No one dared speak. 'What of his men?'

'My lord, they were attacking the west wall, near to the river with the Picts, when he was killed. Roman cavalry chased the Picts away, then infantry swept them from the walls.'

'Those cowardly Picts! If they'd kept going we'd have been inside those bloody walls.'

'Sire, King Ceretic has also been hit and is in great pain.'

'It's those Picts – Ceretic warned me – those bloody Picts. I'll have them skewered so I will.'

Aelred felt anger pulsing through him. He would deal with his cowardly allies later. For now he wanted to avenge his son's death. Smoke that had hung over the battlefield cleared on a strengthening breeze. 'There's that bloody, dancing druid. I want him and his men – now! Look,' he said waving an arm at the fight between the outer stronghold and the east wall. 'Those Romans are trapped. Time to squeeze the life out of them. Advance the guard.'

The battle had not gone according to plan. Mannius had expected the strongholds to hold out for a little longer. That way his legionaries would have been able to use their skill and discipline to manoeuvre between the obstacles, trap and slaughter the enemy a few hundred at a time. It had worked at first. The Saxons seemed to fall in numbers too great to guess. But after the first stronghold was overwhelmed they appeared everywhere. The only positive was that the allies hadn't been outflanked – yet.

Desperately Mannius tried to think his way over the battlefield. Where were the dangers? How was the stronghold by the river faring? He had started with nearly seven hundred legionaries supported by over two hundred Votadini spearmen – he had no idea how many were left. Instead of taking charge of strategy, he was fighting for his own survival; fighting on the front row, blocking, stabbing, twisting and pulling. Then he moved to the third rank at the rear, gasping for air, as men who had rested moved forward. His men were holding but for how long could they endure this level of effort?

Two dead Saxons lay at his feet. Using a legionary's shoulder to steady himself he stood on the bodies and rose above the line of fighting. Enemy soldiers were pressed into a small area between his men and the stronghold Taran occupied. Their huge number was working against them. Most of the attackers were trapped in the middle of the crowd, unable to fight. Onagers from all sides still sent heavy rocks into the throng. That was a good sign. He motioned to a trumpeter to signal Leofric to bring his men round.

Soon, too soon for his tired, aching arms, he was back on the front line. The press of men seemed even worse this time: the grass was slick with pools of blood and dead men remained upright, unable to fall. Mannius blocked, lunged and slipped. His opponent whooped for joy and brought his sword down. Urgently, Mannius brought his sword up to block the blow. Metal hit metal. His own sword smashed into his face but the blow had been lessened. He thrust upwards at the man's groin and heard a spine-tingling scream, then a spear from the rear rank was pushed into the man's throat, finishing him.

Again Mannius used fallen enemies to elevate himself. Leofric's men had started to cut into the horde and a ripple of pressure seemed to compress the Saxons even more. But his men were taking casualties: the shield wall had become desperately thin. To his right, on the makeshift wall, he could see archers and some of Coel's spearmen standing ready.

'Centurion!' shouted Mannius to the officer next to him. 'When I give the signal, have the men near the river pull back and form an extra line behind us.' The man nodded his understanding and sent a messenger to relay the message to other officers down the line. Mannius waved, a trumpet sounded and the line of legionaries wheeled away.

'Hah! Look at the red cloaks crumble!' shouted Aelred as his guard charged down on the left wing of Leofric's men.

'My lord, cavalry behind us!' shouted an officer.

'Tell –' Aelred started to order the man then gave up as the officer was knocked from his horse by an iron bolt that took most of his head off. The king waved his axe in a circle, trying to get his guard to turn and face the new threat. Some of his men, unaware of the danger, were already falling to cavalry spear thrusts. Others turned and tried to fight but they had no order. There was no time to form a strong line. The cavalry were well coordinated and Aelred wished he'd got a force like it. They attacked in waves, passing through the broken ranks of his proud guard. Then they wheeled round and charged again. His best and bravest perished, waving their axes, taking down a few of the terrible horsemen, but not enough. Soon Aelred's men were running for cover only to be cut down by spears and swords in their backs.

The druid appeared, next to a ballista, on top of a tower. He could see that the man held a staff and shield in one hand and a spear in the other. Aelred charged, determined to lead the remnants of his guard to help his men assaulting the embankment.

# Chapter LXVII

Taran had awed his enemies and he knew it. Word had spread about the druid and his magic. Brave Saxon warriors would rather face the swords of redcloaks than mysterious, wizardly magic. Not that Taran complained. The fort around him held – just. Militia men from Eburacum were proving to be disciplined and surprisingly tough. Even though the wooden palisade had mostly disintegrated, the soldiers fought on, filling gaps with double ranks of their men and holding the enemy at bay. Behind the lines of infantry, archers and artillery kept sending missiles into the horde on his direction. This was a battle to enjoy: so close to death and mayhem, yet he was able to bring an order that held it at bay.

The old wizard watched in horror as Mannius' men retreated. It looked as though the infantry had finally collapsed. Without them there would be no crushing force on the enemy: no hammer to smash them on his anvil. Finally, his entrance to the next world seemed close. He uttered a druid's curse on his enemies and told Borgach to be ready to receive him. He watched Saxons pouring through the gap, down the hill towards the river. He breathed a sigh of relief. The move had been planned. Archers on the wall launched volley after volley of arrows at men happy to be free of the squeeze. Desperate to rid themselves of the torture of battle, Saxons started to throw themselves into the river in a bid to escape to the other shore.

Leofric's men were cutting into the Saxons with murderous efficiency and the flow of men seeking refuge by the river increased. Mannius' men surged forward and cut off more of the enemy, leaving two pockets that they set about eliminating.

Taran spotted Aelred riding towards his position; then the king stopped and turned as Artorius' cavalry charged. The druid urged the ballista crew next to him to target the Saxon leader. A bolt flew at him but his horse moved and Taran watched in frustration as a man's head exploded near to the Saxon king.

Aelred turned and rallied his troops to face Artorius. Saxon infantry close enough to see their king turn away from them at last gave up – hungry and exhausted. Men backed away as best they could. Swords and spears started to be thrown down. Then the allies backed away. Only on the stronghold's embankment did the fighting continue until cheers made the Saxons turn and see that the horde behind them had quieted. In the pocket by the river more warriors gave up. A few fell on their own swords rather than face the ignominy of surrender. The roar of battle was replaced by quiet murmurs.

To the north of the battlefield Aelred fought on. A body of his warriors, no doubt his very best, had formed a line strong enough to repel Artorius' cavalry. But they too were moving away to the west.


Aelred ordered men into a line, ready to beat off the Roman cavalry with long, thrusting spears. He had less than twenty horsemen with him; most were tired and between them they carried an assortment of wounds. The red-cloaked men looked exhausted, their horses blew great jets of steam and their lungs heaved. Without infantry support any attack would be beaten off. Stalemate.

The Saxon king looked to the press of men he had been heading towards. At first he couldn't understand what was happening. His grand army of warriors was throwing down its weapons – surrender. Men able to get to his position were running as fast as they could across the battlefield. To his right Ceretic's men and the Picts stood out of artillery range and did nothing – cowards. On the other side of the river the fighting had been desperate. Smoke rose from burning buildings but his men had failed to get across the river and into the old village to push the Romans out. He needed to move his men so that any survivors could join them. With the Picts they might be able to launch an attack to free the men surrendering. Wearily the infantry moved west towards the river, picking up survivors wherever possible.

Passing close to the Romans and their allies inside their strongholds he heard cheers turn to jeers, goading his warriors to attack and die on their spears. Returning the compliment, some of his men taunted those inside the fortified positions, challenging them to come out. Such bravery was heartening.

Mannius watched the slow retreat of Aelred. There was nothing he or his men could do to hinder the Saxons. Both sides were exhausted. He looked down the thin red line of cloaks that he had fought alongside and saw tired, drawn faces. Every man was covered in blood and many carried injuries.

The mass of Saxons in front of them looked like cowed animals. The snarling herd had been tamed, whipped into submission and was waiting to learn its fate.

Mannius knew he had to act quickly. Before he could stand his men down for a much-needed rest they had to secure their prisoners and prepare themselves against further attacks from Aelred. Two strongholds were cleared of useful implements and wooden stakes were replaced on the embankments where they had been pulled out. Then the prisoners were marched in, searched and guarded. Any men identified as officers were taken to the main fort, away from men they might lead against their captors.

A force of around four hundred men with two squadrons of cavalry was stationed between the forts in case the prisoners rioted or escaped. The threat was clear: rebellion would result in death. Meanwhile Artorius gathered another six hundred men to support his horsemen and placed them between the stone fort and Aelred's force.

Carts from the main fort emerged to take weapons and wounded inside. Mannius looked around. Though bodies lay everywhere, many men lay in lines, where the fighting had been at its most intense. With combatants leaving the scene like a retreating tide it was as though a great storm at sea had washed up flotsam and debris. Stillness settled on the battlefield and the only sounds breaking the silence were the low moans of men struggling with mortal wounds, clinging to the last vestiges of life. Some bodies twitched like stranded fish.

One of Galerius' officers galloped up to him. 'Sir! Sir!' he shouted. 'It's the general. He'd like you fast as possible please.' Mannius commandeered the horse of a cavalryman and followed.


By the side of a track that led north and west from the main fort, up a broad ridge, a group of Roman infantry had formed a square around some Saxon carts. Inside the square a few children sat in shock. Mannius realised that Galerius had captured the Saxons' baggage train. He looked for the old soldier and saw him propped against a cart, armour removed and blood coming from his side. Next to him Centurion Primus scribbled on a parchment.

'I am sorry for what you have had to go through,' said

Galerius, biting back pain. 'Don't worry about examining the wound. It goes deep. She caught me unaware – I thought she was one of the hostages and she skewered me as I helped her down.'

Mannius looked to where the general nodded and saw a bloody heap of rags with slender limbs attached. His men had taken a swift and bloody revenge. 'Rest easy, General, I needed the exercise anyway.'

'Hah! I'll soon be able to get enough rest, but first I must do my last work. I need your promise that you'll see the children safe.'

'You have it. I will make sure that they have a proper escort back to Rome.'

'I am the highest-ranking Roman official left in the north of this province.'

'What of the governor and Antonius?'

Galerius gave a weak laugh and held up a hand. 'I will get to them soon. As I was saying. Being the official in charge I will sign that document that Primus is dithering over.' The general gritted his teeth, determined to finish his message. 'The emperor knew of the scheme Antonius dreamt up and wasn't a supporter, but he couldn't do much about it since he's got his hands full. So after he met Coel he was impressed enough with the man to have his spies check out his support and gave me this document as an insurance policy. If Antonius failed then he figured Coel could unite the Brigantes to fight the Saxons. He'd rather have strong friends fighting a common enemy than give his enemy a new base.' Pain went through Galerius, making his body spasm. 'None of them thought that a Roman would be at the centre of the resistance. With my signature added, it makes the bearer officially *Dux Britanniarum.*'

The Duke of Britain was the highest authority in the province, in charge of all land forces. It was an honour

418

Mannius desperately wanted to avoid. Peace and a chance to practise medicine was all he wanted – not second-guessing the machinations of scheming politicians or fighting bloody battles. He was neither born to it nor sought such fame.

'Don't look so worried, Tribune. I know it's the last thing you want – especially when you head off with your princess. It's for Coel. He's got the support of the emperor, not to mention the Brigantes and some Irish. And what's more, he hates Saxons so he's got my vote as well.'

Primus handed a stylus to the general, whose ashen face looked old. With difficulty the document was signed. 'Now you witness this and keep it safe, do you hear?'

'Yes, General.'

'You've got to finish these Saxons off and get the senator before he leaves, and he's greedy, petty and vicious so he won't go until he's got as much gold as he can carry. If you leave him alive he'll get to your father and anyone else round here – maybe even send assassins after you. Now go, and take Primus with you,' the general coughed. 'He just needs a good kick to make him work hard. You stop gawping, Titus, and make me a fire. I'm feeling in need of some warmth.' Galerius, his job done, relaxed. 'By the way, Una knows –' But before he could finish his last sentence he smiled, then died.

# Chapter LXVIII

Mannius rode in search of Coel. Surrounded by guards, in a room above the quadrangle of the main fort, he lay motionless on a cot. Mannius cleared the room, except for his wife, Lady Fianna, and personal physician. Even with tears streaming down her high cheekbones Fianna had a beauty that brought light to the darkest corners of the room.

'He has a broken spearhead deep in his side, probably ruptured his appendix,' whispered the physician. 'Such a wound is always fatal. I have told Lady Fianna that he will die.'

'Of course he'll die,' replied Mannius. 'But not today, if I have anything to do with it.' With that he set about organising boiled instruments, drugs and bandages. Lady Fianna sat by her husband and reassured him with a gentle dignity. Coel drifted in and out of consciousness, sometimes trying to mouth replies to his wife. Mannius went to work, opening the wound, removing Coel's appendix and with it the shattered iron head. Then he cleaned the wound, bandaged it to heal naturally and left some medicine to help the fever that would engulf him.

Aelred stood face to face with the two Pictish brothers. Fatigue was replaced with a deep anger. 'Why did you not support Prince Wybert's attack on the wall?'

'Roman horsemen charged down the hill at us. We had no time to form a shield wall to hold them.'

'You could have followed Wybert's men into the ditch

and gone onto the walls. Cavalry aren't that good in stake-filled ditches.'

'Our men were tired after the fight for the stronghold outside the fort.'

'But not so tired that they couldn't run like hares when saving their own miserable skins. They don't even look like they've done much fighting. I can't see any blood on them.'

'Are you calling us cowards?'

'No, I think we all know what you are already. You have betrayed me and Prince Wybert.' Aelred turned to face his men, hefted his axe and spun at Fidach. The edge of the axe ripped open the prince's throat, nearly removing his head. For a moment there was silence. The Pict stood motionless then collapsed in a bloody heap. Swords, axes and spears clashed in a disorganised mêlée that officers on both sides tried to control.

Men from both sides were drained by the stress of battle, tired after weeks sleeping in the open and weak from lack of food. At first the Picts, aided by Ceretic's men, had the best of the fight. They occupied higher ground and had done less fighting during the main battle. But the Saxons were seasoned warriors and slowly the balance of fighting swung in their favour as the Pict shield wall collapsed in the centre. Aelred's men poured through the gap, swinging axes and mighty war-hammers that took a terrible toll.

Drostan fought hard but found himself pushed back with his men. He nearly tripped over a shield that was being used as a stretcher for Ceretic. 'This is what your grand alliance brings!' he shouted angrily at the prone king. 'Failure and betrayal.' With that he thrust his sword down into Ceretic's throat and was himself cut down by three of the king's guards.

\* \* \*

Hunks of bread and cheese had been brought out of the fort and were being passed round. Artorius stopped munching and mounted his horse in order to get a better view of the confused fight taking place in front of him. When the Saxons smashed through the Pictish shield wall he ordered his men forward. Both protagonists in front of him carried on their own battle, ignoring his men as they marched closer.

Behind three lines of legionaries archers stood with arrows on strings. Artorius waited until the Picts and Ceretic's men looked done for, then gave the order to loose arrows. Cloud after cloud of wooden shafts bit into the Saxons. Steadily his men advanced towards the rear of Aelred's force. A few turned and tried to alert their comrades to the new danger. Their king ignored them: he had no time for anything other than sating his bloodlust on his new enemies, who had betrayed his son.

Slingers started to whirl stones at the Saxons. Too late, their officers began to turn them to face the new threat. The first of five javelin volleys hit them. The legionaries increased their pace and crashed into the confusion. Exhausted men fell easily. Many tried to surrender but that was no longer an option. The Picts broke and ran, chased by Roman cavalry. More cavalry fell on the exposed Saxon flanks and the slaughter continued.

Leaderless, exhausted and full of fear, those who escaped could wait a few hours to die. Aelred's body was brought before Artorius. His men turned over the dead king to display the weapon that had delivered the fatal blow: a Pictish dagger was wedged tight between his shoulder blades.

With the help of Leofric, Artorius organised a force to hunt down those who'd escaped. Leofric led his men and Artorius' mounted infantry around the enemy to block their retreat, while infantry with Artorius squeezed them in the trap.

# Chapter LXIX

The next day, before dawn, Mannius was woken by Eithne. He was bone-tired. Surfacing from his slumber he could hear raised voices: another problem coming his way.

Eithne passed him a tunic before retreating from the room. Normally she stayed.

A guard swung the door open and Felicita burst in, only to throw herself at Mannius' feet. She wrapped her arms around his right leg and sobbed.

'I gave you the chance to leave, to go with Senator Antonius.'

'I know.'

'It was more than you deserved.'

'How did you know?'

'Curtius had to have help and you saw to it that some of the Parisi gave him that help to get messages out of here. You corrupted and blackmailed them. Taran got the truth out of them soon enough.'

'And you still let me leave? You are a noble man for sure.'

'If there was one scrap of evidence linking you to my uncle's death you wouldn't have been so lucky.'

'Antonius used me, like he used this province. And I swear that I had nothing to do with my husband's death. We'd become separated but I couldn't bear to leave him: being close to a man who has absolute power; a man who decided who lived and died in the province was like a drug. So I endured my time with him.'

'So who murdered him?'

423

'Flavius – on the orders of Antonius. That little worm hadn't the gumption to do so much as wipe his arse without asking for Antonius' permission,' spat Felicita.

'You stayed silent; you even tried to get me to attack Coel and his people for murdering the governor.'

'I only found out afterwards and by then Antonius had promised me so much that I couldn't refuse.'

'You could have joined us instead of working against us.'

'But – I'm sorry – no one expected you to win. So I spied on you for Antonius. I'm sorry, truly I am.'

'You are the most manipulative person I know. How can I be sure that you're not trying to turn me even now? Why return?'

'Because when I was no longer of use to Antonius he left me. Said I'd broken off an affair we'd had years ago. He likes to be the one in charge. Doesn't like it when someone alters his plans.'

'You've been played at your own game: manipulated, deceived and abandoned. You've no one left, so you turn to me for charity.'

'No, no. I only want a swift end for myself. He abandoned the children he'd used as hostages. He wanted people to think that he was still in Eburacum so he left them with orders that they should be killed tomorrow. I'd had enough so I bribed some guards and brought them here. I know you'll look after them properly. I trust you.' Felicita raised her head and looked into Mannius' eyes for the first time. 'I beg one last kindness of you, one I don't deserve: please make my end swift.'

'As far as the children are concerned I have given my word to help them all I can.' Mannius bent down and dragged Felicita to her feet. 'My problem is that you are too good at manipulating men's minds. Even now I am uncertain as to whether there are other motives behind your actions.' Mannius stepped back and surveyed his aunt. She still carried herself with dignity and style; she had beauty and her mind was sharp enough to be dangerous. 'There has already been too much killing. There will be no more if I can help it. But you have to be punished.' He saw tears in her expectant eyes.

Taran, still painted, bloodied and unwashed from battle, stood in the doorway, a scorched parchment in his hand. 'You need to see this, General.'

Mannius pronounced sentence. 'If I make you a slave, you will send messages to your friends and have your freedom bought. If I imprison you, it won't take long before you twist the minds of your gaolers.' Mannius rubbed his chin, deep in thought. 'I will place you in the custody of someone cleverer than yourself; someone who will spot your schemes for what they are. Taran has lost his companion and housekeeper. You will serve him – and faithfully – or you will face execution.'

Felicita turned to face the druid and her mouth twisted in horror. 'Don't fret so,' said Taran, thrusting his thighs at Felicita. 'There's still plenty of magic left in my wand for a woman as good-looking as you.'

Felicita fainted and Mannius left the guards to lift her onto his bed. 'What must I see?'

'It seems,' said Taran, waving the parchment, 'that Antonius had to write orders for everyone still under his command, whether he could get the messages to them or not. Maybe it was a superstition or some weakness. Well, he sent orders to Flavius that a slave decided to lose in a fire, only my new wife found them and brought them to us.'

'What are the orders?'

'That he should report to the villa.'

'Doesn't help much, except ... I wonder ... where's Una?'

# Chapter LXX

Mannius led a column of mounted troops guided by Una. Caoimhe was with him. He'd tried to make her stay and take charge of operations around Derventio, but she would hear none of it. Artorius had returned around dawn at the head of a column of prisoners but with a leg wound. He knew how to organise prisoners better than she so he stayed and she accompanied the expedition. Also with them, manacled and quietly muttering to himself, in a world of his own, was Flavius.

The column moved fast. At first they travelled along a paved road, then turned off and followed well-used tracks. Towards late morning, Una called a halt. Ahead of them fields rolled gently down to another paved road and a large villa.

'This is the one,' proclaimed Una. 'The one we stayed at with the children.'

'Certain?' said Mannius and got a nod in reply.

Scouts moved ahead. After quickly examining the buildings and surrounding area they whipped their horses back to the column in order to report.

'Looks like a century of men, sir,' reported the officer in charge of the scouts. 'Well drilled, marching like, and accompanying three heavy carts.'

'How long since?'

'About half a day, I'd say, sir.'

Mannius calculated his options. 'For safety, give them a little more time. Even with heavy carts they'd be able to get to Eburacum.'

'The river, that's where they'll go,' pronounced Caoimhe triumphantly. 'The senator's left Eburacum. He's sent his troops to collect his booty and he'll have a boat waiting to collect it. We can go faster than the carts and go across country to cut them off.'

'Great,' said Mannius, a hint of sarcasm in his voice. 'If Artorius had been with us he might have known likely spots where they've hidden their boats or places we might be able to ambush them.'

Before anyone could dwell on their predicament further, Flavius shouted, 'The willows!' kicked his horse and headed south. A guard went to chase the prisoner. 'Leave him,' commanded Caoimhe. 'We might as well follow him.'

'Truly the world has changed,' pronounced Mannius. 'A fool's errand, led by a madman.'


A few times Flavius pulled on his reins and slowed his horse; mostly though he just kept going. Since his earlier pronouncement he had remained silent, in his own world. Somehow he had enough wit left to know his location and destination. Wherever possible he kept to paved roads but for over an hour they had used tracks that led into meadows that gave out onto flat, wetland marshes. Still he rode on, taking them deeper into a land of slow-moving creeks, small lakes and abandoned fish traps.

Mannius judged they must be roughly halfway between Eburacum and the silted-up harbour of Petuaria, an old fort that guarded a fording point across the mud banked estuary of the Abus Flavia. Flavius had at last stopped and seemed to be searching for something in the tall grass. Then he made his way slowly along a narrow path that wound between reeds and yellow blossomed gorse bushes towards a copse of willow trees on a rise. At its centre, towering over the willows, were the gnarled branches of a long-dead oak. Was it a marker to Flavius? Fearful of an ambush, Mannius tested his sword, as did his men.

Flavius dismounted and walked through the gorse, accompanied by two guards. Mannius, Caoimhe, Una and a few officers followed carefully. Around them, legionaries fanned out. Barely a hundred paces through the trees, they could see four transport ships beached on a mud bank at the edge of a narrow, tidal river. It was a tributary from the north that fed the main navigable route from the Oceanus Germanicus to Eburacum. Scouts quickly confirmed that the main river was less than half a mile further.

Mannius' men had little difficulty in boarding the transports and subduing the crews. The captains of the grain ships were clearly loyal to Antonius and protested long and hard that seizing their ships was piracy, until Mannius informed them that he was investigating allegations that the grain in their holds had been stolen. Turning their gaze to the decks of their ships the men shuffled uncomfortably and fell silent.

'Africa!' pronounced Caoimhe. 'They're bound for North Africa.' She brandished an armful of charts and parchments.

'So Antonius wasn't ever intending to return the children to their families or help the empire with the gold, silver and supplies they've plundered,' said Mannius. 'It's been one big excuse for him to fill his own purse.' Without thinking he'd drawn his sword and was waving it at the captains. The men appeared pale – their sullen looks having been replaced by sickness. 'This is nothing more than common thievery! You'd better bloody well impress me, or you'll be wishing for a merciful end.' The men nodded their acquiescence.

*   *   *

After the chase they had to wait what seemed an eternity as the tide came in and floated the boats off the mud bank. Mannius ordered the captains to sail to the main river and turn a little way upstream until he found what he needed: a narrow bend where it was difficult to manoeuvre.

Again they waited. One ship jutting out into the tidal stream was held fast by ropes. At the prow, Flavius stood, keeping his gaze upstream.

Scouts reported two ships coming downstream and Mannius checked that his men were ready.

'We could trade,' suggested Caoimhe quietly. 'No need to fight again.'

'If my guess is right he won't bargain.' Mannius looked expectantly upriver. 'And I was warned not to let him go. Besides he's taking a lot of gold and silver that he's plundered with him. With the slaves we've already taken and that treasure there'll be enough to rebuild your kingdom and pay for the defence of the Brigantes.'

Caoimhe fell silent. She could see that Mannius was intent on attacking. There was no deflecting his purpose.

Hidden by trees and hawthorn bushes, the first Caoimhe saw of the approaching vessels was two masts, like bare trees, gliding across the fields. Flavius stood still but pushed his manacled hands inside his cloak.

The captain of the first ship gave the order to back oars in order to slow his vessel's momentum. Gently the ship glided up to the transport.

'Flavius! How good to see you,' shouted an old man in an expensive-looking tunic. As the ship drew closer she recognised him as Prefect Leonius, the man who had kept his forces behind the Wall instead of helping her father. Hidden from view, she silently put an arrow on her bowstring and tested its tension.

She saw Flavius smile in acknowledgement. Then he

raised his arms and his cloak fell away to reveal the manacles. A look of uncertainty came over the prefect and he turned to the captain. But it was too late. Mannius led a boarding party onto the vessel. Arrows flew from the bank and Caoimhe let fly with her own arrow.

# Chapter LXXI

Mannius hurled a javelin at a man barely five paces from him. Then he drew his sword and leapt onto the ship, screaming at the defenders. He felt the ship move as more men followed him. Fleetingly he remembered he hated boats and abhorred the prospect of fighting on them. Arrows flew at the soldiers on board, quickly making the deck slippery with blood.

Leonius' expression turned from uncertainty to shock. When the prefect saw Mannius he drew his sword but it was too late. He let out a howl of pain as an arrow stuck in his thigh. Another took him in his shoulder and his sword skittered across the deck. The defenders quickly threw down their weapons and knelt in submission. Legionaries with Mannius sheathed their swords and took up wooden clubs. Leonius' eyes were wide with fright. He knew that taking him alive would mean a trial or at least a horrible death. 'Mannius, please. Let me leave honourably.'

Mannius nodded. Trembling, the prefect drew his dagger, turned it on himself, and lunged.

Caoimhe watched the second ship turn slightly away from the line of the first. Its captain was waving frantically and shouting orders. Arrows flew from the bank and she let three fly towards the vessel before her aim was obscured by the first ship.

In front of her the second ship hit Leonius' with a

431

crunch. Then oars interlocked and timbers snapped in the ensuing panic. But the turmoil on the vessels was nothing to the terror that gripped Caoimhe when she saw Mannius jump onto the deck of the other ship. She ran along the bank to get a better view.

Resting below deck, on the second ship, Senator Antonius heard a commotion and went to investigate. He saw Flavius standing on the prow of one of the transport ships and felt a wave of relief sweep over him. He'd feared the young pup had been killed and was wondering how to break the news to the boy's family. Now he needn't trouble himself with such a detail.

Like the captain next to him, he was struck with horror when Flavius held up his arms to show the manacles that bound him. An officer appeared and threw a javelin into a man's chest. Then arrows flew from the bank and men were falling.

'Go round them, man!' urged the senator. 'Round them!' He emphasised his intention by waving his arms.

'But Senator,' protested the captain. 'We may run aground. The tide is only halfway in and the channel is narrow.'

'Get round them if you want to live,' replied the senator, unsheathing his sword and pointing it menacingly at the captain.

In front of them, Gaulish mercenaries had formed a line of shields to protect themselves from the rain of arrows that started to hit the vessel. Even so, missiles skewered flesh, men fell and blood started to form in pools on the wooden deck.

A shout went up from the bow of the ship. 'Ships ahead!'

No explanation from the captain was necessary. They were in imminent danger of being trapped and boarded.

'Back oars!' bellowed the captain.

Slaves in the depths of the galley pushed the long timber arms against the direction of the ship's momentum and it started to slow. Finally the ship came to a halt and started to move, slowly – too slowly for Antonius – upstream, gradually gathering speed. Missiles from the transports hit them and took more men. The deck in front of him appeared to be awash with blood.

As they retraced their route more arrows came from the bank. A sailor on the steering oar gave out a high-pitched yell and fell to the deck, blood pumping from his neck. The captain jumped to replace the man but he too took an arrow in his side then, as he twisted in pain, another two hit his back and he slumped on the oar. Antonius crouched down under the protection of the deck sides, away from the murderous onslaught.

There was a sickening crunch of splintering wood as the ship collided with Leonius'. Men tried to push the vessels apart but were cut down. Below decks slaves – shackled to their benches - started to scream in fear of the ship sinking. Oars snapped. Boarders jumped onto the ship and swords clashed in front of the senator.

With enemy soldiers aboard, the rain of arrows from the bank subsided. Antonius pushed the captain off the steering oar and heaved it across to make the vessel turn away. An officer in charge of the slaves appeared on deck.

'Get the slaves into action, man!' shouted the senator. 'Pull us away from them.'

Antonius heard whips cracking and felt a reassuring acceleration. A gap started to open between them and the other ships. In front of him, his mercenaries were exchanging blows with the small boarding party that had mercifully been cut off from reinforcements. The senator's men seemed to be getting the better of the fight. He dared to hope that they would win through. He cast a

433

look to the other ship and saw Flavius still standing in the prow and smiling at him. There was a sudden jolt on the steering oar that knocked the old man across the deck. They were no longer moving, but caught on mud at the edge of the channel.

With Leonius dead and prisoners being shepherded off the ship, Mannius turned his attention to the other vessel. It was retreating in the face of a barrage of missiles from the other transport ships. He saw Antonius with the captain and a sailor by the steering oar.

Men close to him threw ropes with grappling irons across to the other ship in an attempt to lock the vessels together. He looked back to the senator who appeared to be the only one at the helm. He braced himself and felt the collision of the ships, heard the screams of slaves below decks. Without hesitating he gestured for men to form up and follow him across.

Fighting was desperate. Instead of a coordinated body of men marching forward they fought individually: as soon as they jumped across they punched their shields at an opponent and stabbed. In the chaos men screamed and fell. The wood of the decks was slick with blood and still they fought.

Mannius felt the ship move and looked back to see some of his men waving to him. Ropes connecting the vessels came taut. Suddenly, the ship shuddered to a dead stop and he lost his footing.

Like most on board Mannius careered across the deck. He rose to his knees and felt his arm explode with pain as a huge brute of a man kicked out. His arm went numb and he could only watch his sword clatter to the ground. Surprise was equal for both sides but the enemy had greater numbers and quickly overwhelmed the boarding party. The attackers who lived were forced to kneel in a line by Mannius, hands behind their heads.

Senator Antonius beckoned for two men to join him before he moved along the deck, protected from arrows by their shields. 'I thought I spotted a loser,' said the senator, looking down on Mannius.

'I recognised your foul odour the moment your ship rounded the bend,' replied Mannius.

'Tribune, you are fighting odds you cannot even begin to calculate.' Antonius nodded to an officer who stepped forward and removed Mannius' helmet. At another order the officer hit him on the jaw. 'A little more respect please, Tribune. I am a senator of Rome, the highest ranking official in this miserable province and as such I have absolute authority.'

'It's General now,' gasped Mannius. 'I'm no longer a tribune. You disbanded the Roman units – your orders. Now I'm a general acting for King Coel, *Dux Britanniarum* – appointed by the authority of the emperor himself.'

'Don't be so absurd, you little shit.'

'Absurd or not, you are now our guests and this is our ship.'

'You have delusions of grandeur. Remove his armour.' The officer cut at the thongs holding Mannius' armour in place. Hauled to his feet, he felt naked. 'Throughout my time in this wretched province you have been a constant irritant. You even made my stomach burn with poison. Now I can make your guts burn.' Antonius flashed a gladius at him: a short sword used by the legions of old. It was an anachronism of an earlier fighting age but no less deadly, judging by its finely-honed point.

'I am taking charge of this ship and arresting everyone on it,' said Mannius, for want of a better reply.

'You have no right as you well know. And you have no

435

power with which to bargain – except, you may be of use in a deal. Bind his hands.'

Mannius was pushed across the deck toward the vessel where Flavius still stood impassively. Around him the detritus of battle lay: blood, gore and broken swords.

From the bank Caoimhe watched in horror as Mannius was stripped of his armour. He was lifted to his feet by two Gaulish mercenaries and pushed along the deck. Instinctively she slotted an arrow onto her bowstring.

'If you want this traitor back then give me the half-wit, Flavius, in return,' shouted Antonius.

The tide was filling the channel faster than before. Soon the senator's vessel would be out of the mud; lifted free by the tide he could continue upstream. Then he'd use horses to make his escape.

Without thought, Caoimhe pulled the arrow back and held the tension. Flavius still stood at the prow of the boat, smiling as the distance closed between the vessels. The only time he became animated was when the two ships bumped together and the jolt made him adjust his stance. Otherwise he remained impassive.

The senator seemed to be in control of the tide as well as events: his ship lifted free of the mud and the galley slaves had enough water in which to row. 'Step this way, Flavius,' ordered the old man.

Flavius clambered over the side. After his stoic pose he seemed ungainly in his movements between the vessels. Landing awkwardly on the planks of the senator's ship he fell to the deck. After a moment he rose, smoothed down his cloak and moved forward, hands beneath his cloak and composure restored.

Caoimhe saw the look of contempt on Mannius' face as Flavius drew near to him. She knew that her general would rather die than let the traitorous madman go free. But she was glad of the trade and watched it with hope.

When Flavius was barely three paces from Mannius he pulled his hands out of his cloak. A smile of contentment came across his face. In horror, Caoimhe saw a blade. He was too close to Mannius and moving too quickly for her to chance an arrow. All she could do was watch the grim faces of the Gaulish mercenaries. A few men, close to Flavius, had seen him produce the blade – a discarded dagger from the earlier skirmish – and grinned in anticipation of it being embedded in Mannius. Flavius pulled back his arms and made to thrust.

Too late, Mannius saw a blade and recognised the danger. There was little time to react and his hands were bound behind his back. Instinctively he moved away and saw the blade go beyond him. There was a commotion and Mannius ran for the edge of the ship, intending to jump to the other vessel. With the deck slippery his launch foot skidded and he sailed, head-first into the timbers of the deck. Then everything went black.

Flavius was still calm: his face betrayed no emotion. As he passed Mannius he pulled his manacled arms back and quickened his pace. Five steps beyond Mannius stood the senator: the perpetrator of the mission, his personal torturer. He had not wanted to follow the old man out of Rome. His father had been compelled to order him as the family owed large debts to Antonius. All along he'd been treated like an imbecile: too stupid to do anything of his own volition. Well this time things had changed. He'd planned this himself, ever since he'd been

437

put on a horse at Derventio. If the chance came he'd take it and to his surprise it had presented itself.

The dagger was sharp – he'd tested its point under his cloak and drawn blood. Now he would use it to draw more blood and lance a boil festering on the good name of the empire. He lunged at his target.


Caoimhe saw Mannius slip, crack his head on the gunwale of the senator's ship and flip over the side. She knew he was injured: there was only a splash as he entered the water then nothing, no movement.

Flavius launched his arm at the senator. He stabbed once before two guards instinctively cut him down. Horror-stricken and pale, Antonius fell back, clutching his chest. His scarlet cloak betrayed a dark stain. In front of him Flavius, his assistant and murderer, lay dead.

# Chapter LXXII

Mannius woke and wished he hadn't. His head throbbed and screamed with pain. He felt sick, his right arm ached and he had a soreness that he couldn't as yet localise. He gave up trying to diagnose his problems and sighed.

A warm hand brushed against his cheek. He opened his eyes and tried to focus. Light triggered pain in his head and he closed his eyes for a moment, steeling himself for greater efforts. He caught a scent of lavender.

'Eithne?' he whispered.

'No,' came an equally gentle reply. 'She's looking after one of Leofric's captains, I'm glad to say.'

He felt soft lips caress his forehead and some of the pain melted away. 'Caoimhe, what happened?'

'Don't worry so. Other men can fight as well as you.' She took his good arm in her hands. 'Stupid thing it was to crack your head like that then go swimming. You were lucky you weren't wearing your armour – though King Coel says you should keep your helmet on next time. It looked like a dozen men jumped in after you and fished you out. Then Una tended your injuries so that we could bring you here. And she did a good job, according to the chief surgeon.'

'Where is here?' said Mannius, pushing himself up on what felt like silk pillows.

'The governor's villa at Eburacum.'

Mannius surveyed the bedroom and spotted a large chair with a pillow and blanket. She'd been with him, nursing him. 'How long?'

439

'Two days, and I was getting worried, I don't mind telling you,' she said in mock-scolding tones. 'Long enough for Coel to get back his laugh and Leofric to round up the last of Aelred's men. You've not to move until your head's better.' It was a lecture he was in no mood to hear though he couldn't argue. He closed his eyes and drifted back to sleep.

Mannius was brought round by the smell of mint. 'Eithne?'

'No sir, it's Una. Checking on you, like, while Princess Caoimhe's running round telling everyone you're awake. Don't know which way to turn she doesn't. Master Taran looked you over and said you've got an imbalance caused by that crack on your head. It'd have killed most folks as would the drowning. Now lie still and I'll get you something to eat.'

'Thanks – thanks for treating me.'

'Thanks nothing, sir. You'd have done same for me. And we all owe you as it is.' The girl hummed as she stirred a bowl of soup. 'Everything's happening just as it should. King Coel's getting better and General Leofric's rounded up them that got away. Now there's nothing for you to worry over so go back to sleep. Let the others worry for a change.'

'What about?' Mannius didn't bother to finish. There were dozens of people he wanted to know about. Una, though, clearly wasn't going to let him start a debate. He'd had enough of fighting and killing. It seemed that he was too tired to help people live when all he had energy for was killing. The thought made him despise himself. It took him a moment to remember.

'Una, I'm sorry about General Galerius. He was fond of you and you of him, I know.'

'Thank you, sir. But there's a lot of people as what

440

have lost lives and loved ones so it seems selfish to dwell on it.'

'The children, the hostages?'

'The little ones are all fine, sir. Checked them myself, I did.'

'I need someone I can trust to take them back to their families, I promised the general as much. Will you go with Curtius and some of his men to Rome? I'll make sure you have enough money and letters of introduction.'

'Sir, I'm right flattered that you'd trust me with them. And it'd be grand seeing Rome.' She looked at him thoughtfully. 'I'll accept your commission on one condition.'

'Yes?'

'That you'll see Princess Caoimhe and talk to her serious, like, about you two. She needs to know. She's desperate to see you well an' all.'

'She wants me to help her.'

'Course she does, sir. But it's more than that. Taran keeps telling her that you're a leader that men will follow and fight for and that the Votadini need you.'

'What does the princess say?'

'She says that's all well and good but she won't trick you into helping. She wants you frantic like, but for her own reasons – not as a fighter. Only thing is she's the last of the royal family and Taran keeps telling her that she can't betray her people by just going off with you, much as she'd like. It's like she's getting squashed, sir. Doesn't know which way to turn.'

'You win.'


Caoimhe sat on the edge of his bed, cradling his left arm in both of hers. Tears moistened her reddened eyes. Thin, silk drapes thankfully filtered the harsh brightness of the late spring sun. In the softer, diffused light the princess' face was even more beautiful than he remembered.

'Had a rough time?'

Caoimhe nodded. 'Taran said that bump could easily have killed you. But he said he didn't think you had sense enough to die from it.'

'Thanks, I think.'

'King Coel wants you to be his general-in-chief and conquer lands together.' The princess bit her cheek and looked away. 'Eithne tells me that you've told her to pack. Are you going to join your father in Gaul?'

'I've been tempted these last few days. It seems an easy way of life compared to this. But I thought I'd go to a land of farms, rivers and endless pine forests, where the only sounds on warm, summer afternoons are gurgling streams and trout jumping for insects. That is, if there's still an opening for a king north of the Wall.'

Particles of dust, stirred into action by a gentle breeze, danced in a shaft of light. Tears streamed down Caoimhe's dimpled cheeks and Mannius felt as though his heart had come to a thudding stop. The only sound was a lark's chirping melody that came through an open door to the balcony outside his room. A huge smile spread across the princess' face. She flung her arms round his neck and pressed her lips onto his.